I0523898

Edward H. Dixon

Back-Bone

Edward H. Dixon

Back-Bone

ISBN/EAN: 9783337085421

Printed in Europe, USA, Canada, Australia, Japan

Cover: Foto ©Andreas Hilbeck / pixelio.de

More available books at **www.hansebooks.com**

BACK-BONE;

PHOTOGRAPHED FROM "THE SCALPEL."

BY

EDWARD H. DIXON, M. D.

Society—" Light and darkness, majesty and mud : nectar and poison, in one goblet."—HARO.

NEW YORK :
ROBERT M. DE WITT, PUBLISHER,
13 FRANKFORT STREET.

Entered according to Act of Congress, in the year 1866, by
ROBERT M. DE WITT,
In the Clerk's Office of the District Court of the United States, for the
Southern District of New York.

TO

HORACE GREELEY AND PETER COOPER,

FRIENDS OF

THEIR COUNTRY AND MANKIND,

THIS BOOK IS OFFERED

BY

THE AUTHOR.

PREFACE.

THE first volume of selections from the *Scalpel*, entitled "Scenes in the Practice of a New York Surgeon," was published ten years since, and was received by the public in a manner very gratifying to the feelings of the editor. The present volume is of a widely different character, and far more illustrative of the scope and object of that journal : whether it will be equally acceptable, remains to be seen.

If the photographer would secure a faithful picture, he knows that his lens must be accurately ground and adjusted, that the rays of light may not be distorted, and the image be truthfully conveyed to the sensitive surface, prepared to receive it ; and even then, if the subsequent chemical manipulations be not carefully done, the pure sunlight will only serve to show more darkly the spots made apparent by his want of skill. It is quite possible the editor has been writing as Leigh Hunt said to some friends who asked him how he got home in one of those miserable foggy nights so common in London—he went home by mud-light. If so, he can only say, he fears a great portion of the human family have reached their long homes, and a great multitude are still traveling thitherward by medical mud-light.

Our professional friends (?) will be surprised to learn that the title was furnished by a President of the New York Academy of Medicine! In a conversation with one of those aspiring young gentlemen whom we have elsewhere classified as the literary *Lumbrici* of the profession, and who was at the time editing one of those ephemeral and albuminous monthlies devoted to the interest of the great medical Trades Union, he felicitated himself, on the issue of our second number, that the *Scalpel* would soon expire. Our distinguished preceptor, (the late Dr. Valentine Mott,) who was then President of "the Academy," and who always most emphatically condemned the journal, and its object, replied, "There's too much *back-bone* in it, my dear doctor, to admit the hope."

Society has been said to be a joint-stock partnership, opposed to the manhood of any one of its members who may chance to show a little more strength in his spinal column than his brethren. We trust our own will prove able to support us, for some time to come, against the medical anthropophagi. Our professional pursuits will not admit of the regular issue of our journal, but we shall carry out the original prospectus, *i. e.*, "publish it when we please, put in it what we please, and trust we shall have sense enough to stop it when we have nothing more to say."

EDWARD H. DIXON.

42 Fifth Avenue.

CONTENTS.

INTRODUCTORY.

A RIDE ON THE PHYSIOLOGICAL BUFFALO—THE HUMAN TEMPERAMENTS—CHIPS
FROM THE PHRENOLOGICAL LOG—WHAT IS THE LIFE LINE? 13

THE FACULTY AND THE SCALPEL.

POSITION OF THE FACULTY AND THE SCALPEL—CONSERVATIVE ANTIQUARIES—
FOSSILIZED MORALISTS—PROFESSIONAL TURNERS AND THEIR TURNING LATHES
—EDITORIAL ECCENTRICITY—DIPLOMAS AND THEORIES—CRIBS, TEA-KETTLES,
AND CORN-BASKETS 17

SCENES IN WESTERN PRACTICE.

FROST FOLIAGE PAINTED BY MOONLIGHT—THE MERCY ANGELS—CHILD MESSEN-
GER—THE WEDDING-RING FEE—A MIDNIGHT RIDE—ARE THEY HUNGRY IN
HEAVEN?—THE DAUGHTER OF A CITY MERCHANT—THE FIRE KING—THE GOL-
DEN AND THE SILVER RULE—ADVERSITY AND LABOR THE SOUL ELEVATORS—
DEATH THE GREAT PURIFIER—THE CLERICAL SPECULATOR—MORALITY AND
MAMMON—CITY AND COUNTRY CORRUPTION—GRAIN SPECULATION ; AWFUL
CONSEQUENCES ON MORALS—THE MIDNIGHT VISIT OF THE ANGELS TO THE
GREAT CITY—ITS CONDITION—THE CHILD THIEF—THE ANGEL'S BLESSING--
DEATH OF THE MERCHANT'S DAUGHTER 26

SCENES IN CITY PRACTICE.

LEAVES FROM THE LOG OF AN UNFLEDGED ÆSCULAPIAN : FISHING FOR PRAC-
TICE IN A FASHIONABLE NEIGHBORHOOD—MASTER TIP TAPE AND HIS NOSE—
IRISH PRACTICE—A SCENE IN HIGH LIFE—THE MANIAC 47

VILLAGE PRACTICE.

SKETCHES OF VILLAGE PRACTICE—SABBATH IN THE COUNTRY—MY FIRST CASE
—A MALADY OF MIND AND BODY 59

INFIDELITY OF MEDICAL MEN.

INSTINCTIVE IDEAS OF CREATIVE POWER—THE RED GLOBULES OF THE BLOOD
—WHEN AND HOW FORMED—EARLY SUBSTITUTE FOR LUNGS IN THE CHICK—
USES OF THE RED AND WHITE GLOBULES—WHAT IS THE LIFE CELL? .   69

AN UNDELIVERED AND UN-ORTHODOX ADDRESS.

THE THIRD ANNIVERSARY ORATION FOR THE NEW YORK ACADEMY OF MEDICINE
WHICH WAS NOT DELIVERED BEFORE THAT REMARKABLE BODY, BUT OUGHT
TO HAVE BEEN, AT THEIR ANNUAL MEETING, HELD IN THE CHAPEL OF THE
UNIVERSITY, NOVEMBER 14TH, 1849, BY THE PHYSICIAN WHO WAS NOT
ELECTED FOR THAT OCCASION. (PUBLISHED WITHOUT THE KNOWLEDGE OR
CONSENT OF THE ACADEMY)   81

AN ARTIST'S REVERIE.

THE ARTIST IN HIS WORK-CHAMBER—WEBSTER—THE CHILD—THE UNCOVERED
BUST—THE BUILDING OF THE EARTH—THE GARDEN—ADAM AND EVE—THE
FIRST SIN ; ITS FRUIT 102

TARTAR EMETIC.

AN EXCELLENT SWEATING, NAUSEATING, AND VOMITING ARTICLE FOR—THE PRO-
FESSION 112

SCENES IN A MEDICAL STUDENT'S LIFE.

A FLYING LEAP WITH THE DEAD—A MUD-BATH AT MIDNIGHT—OLD JEMMY'S
CURSE—BLUE BLAZES—A RACE FOR OLD RUTGERS—SAFE AT LAST . . . 125

A GONE FOX.

THE LAST WORDS OF AN OLD MEDICAL FOX, CAUGHT IN THE HOSPITAL TRAP, TO
HIS YOUNG BRETHREN OUTSIDE—THE OLD TURKEY ROOST—YOUNG FOXES
MUSTN'T EAT TURKEY 137

ABORTIONISM.

DIABOLICAL WICKEDNESS OF ABORTIONISM—WOMAN'S GENTLENESS AND BEAUTY
ATTRACTIVE TO CHILDREN—DESIRE FOR OFFSPRING AN ESSENTIAL PART OF
HER EXISTENCE 144

ICHTHYO-JECORO-PLASTY.

AN ASTONISHING DISCOVERY—HOW TO MAKE GENUINE COD LIVER OIL—OUR
SIGNATURE IS OVER THE CORK 158

GREAT PHILANTHROPIC ENTERPRISE.

THE GENUINE BEAR'S GREASE—OUR MR. SWIZZLE-EM 161

SCENES IN EARLY PRACTICE.

THE OLD EAST WING OF BELLEVUE; ITS TRANSFORMATION—SCENES IN THE CHOLERA OF 1832—POWER OF ART 163

SKETCHES OF THE PEOPLE.

WATCHING YOUR DIGNITY 174

LIFE SKETCHES OF EMINENT NEW YORK PHYSICIANS.

THE OLD COLLEGE IN DUANE STREET—THE PROFESSORS—THE URSA MAJOR (DR. FRANCIS)—AN EXAMINATION—THE PHENOMENON, JUST ARRIVED FROM PARIS —A LUDICROUS SCENE—DR. BUSH 178

AN ARTIST'S REVERIE.—NO. II.

MIDNIGHT—THE RISING STORM—THE DEATH OF ABEL—THE MARK ON THE MURDERER'S BROW—HIS PRAYER 190

A VISION OF THE DAMNED.

WHAT BECOMES OF THE DOCTORS AND APOTHECARIES WHEN THEY DIE? . . 195

TOBACCO.

ITS INFLUENCE ON THE MIND AND BODY OF AMERICAN MEN 200

HUMANITARY SKETCHES FROM THE HIGHWAYS.

THE RATTLE-SNAKE ANATOMIST—THE LAST FEE—RELIGIOUS PREJUDICE—DEAR SUE, DO I RESEMBLE YOU? 208

SMALL POX.

INOCULATION—VACCINATION—WHAT ARE THEY?—IS VACCINATION A PREVENTIVE OF SMALL-POX OR NOT? 221

AN ARTIST'S REVERIE.—NO. III.

PAGANINI—MEMORIES OF ITALY—RAPHAEL—MICHAEL ANGELO—EDOM THE SOLITARY—THE SPHINX—CLEOPATRA—MARY STUART 228

SCENES FROM CITY PRACTICE.

A TRIAL FOR CHILD-MURDER—THE VALUE OF EVIDENCE—CRIMINAL LAW HELPLESS WITHOUT PHYSIOLOGICAL EVIDENCE 238

BEAR-BAITING IN THE STAR-CHAMBER.

THE "ARMIGEROS" OF THE NEW YORK ACADEMY—THE SIMIA IN GRAND COUNCIL—THE GRIZZLY BEAR OF THE WEST—A TERRIBLE SCENE—THE ACADEMICIAN FROM "AULD REEKIE"—DR. GODMAN 249

SCENES IN CITY PRACTICE.

DIFFERENT WAYS OF PREPARATION FOR DEATH—THE MISER—THE OLD MUSIC
TEACHER—CHEATING THE UNDERTAKER—THE PHILOSOPHICAL GAMBLER . 260

DISCOURSE ON MORALS.

THE GREAT SURGICAL GOOSE-PEN—THE OLD FOX—HE ESCAPES FROM THE TRAP
—MEDICAL CANNIBALS—VISIT FROM A HEAD-CHEESE—A BUTCHER SURGEON 270

EARLY TREATMENT OF CHILDREN.

AIR, BATHS AND EXERCISE—ABSURDITY OF BANDAGES—TEMPERATURE AND
EFFECTS OF BATHS . '. 280

NATURE AS PHYSICIAN.

NATURAL POWERS OF THE BODY—IMPERTINENCE OF DRUG-GIVING—UNCERTAIN-
TY OF REMEDIES—SUPERSTITIOUS NATURE OF MANKIND 286

MEDICAL SHEEP-SHEARING.

GREAT CRY AND LITTLE WOOL—THE MADMAN OF SEVILLE—A DESPERATE EN-
COUNTER WITH FOUR BUCKRAM ROBBERS—A BONA FIDE ENCOUNTER—A MYSTE-
RIOUS BODY FOUND IN TURTLE BAY—THE CORONER'S VERDICT—THE AWFUL
CLASP-KNIFE—A MEDICAL AND PSYCHOLOGICAL PHENOMENON 297

A BOY'S THEOLOGICAL EXPERIENCE.

FAMILY ANTECEDENTS—PARENTAL AUTHORITY IN THE LAST GENERATION—COR-
POREAL PUNISHMENT AND ITS EFFECTS—READING HABITS—A "SERIOUS LI-
BRARY"—TWO BOOKS AND THEIR CONTENTS—ETERNAL PUNISHMENT—FAN-
CIES ABOUT HELL—ILLUSTRATION OF THE IDEA OF ETERNITY—OVERPOWER-
ING DREAD OF BOTH, AND OF DEATH—IDEAS ABOUT DROWNING—IMAGINED
LOCALITIES OF HELL—OF PEOPLE IN IT—THE DAY OF JUDGMENT 307

AN ARTIST'S REVERIE.—NO. IV.

AN HOUR AFTER MIDNIGHT—UNEARTHLY SHAPES—THE DELUGE—THE HUMAN
VOICE—THE THRONE OF MAN—THE TROPHIES OF HELL—DUALITY IN ALL
THINGS 318

CRUCIFIXION OF CHILDREN.

CRUCIFIXION OF CHILDREN BY THE ROUTINE SYSTEM OF EDUCATION—THE
NATURAL CAPACITY CAN ONLY BE KNOWN BY THE STUDY OF THE TEMPERA-
MENT—EVIL EFFECT OF CRUSHING THE WILL—THE SENTIMENT OF OMNIPO-
TENCE—WILL MAKES THE MAN 327

FASHIONABLE DRESS.

ITS INFLUENCE ON THE HEALTH AND DIGNITY OF WOMAN 339

WORK WHILE 'TIS DAY.

LINES DEDICATED TO THE EDITOR, ON READING THE SIXTH VOLUME . . 342

HOTEL PRACTICE IN NEW YORK.

AN INFERNAL ABUSE 343

MEDICAL EXPERIENCES.

BRANDY AND TOBACCO, COFFEE, OPIUM AND TEA—WHY HAS NATURE PRODUCED THESE ARTICLES?—ARE THEIR INFLUENCES WHOLLY EVIL?—DO THEY SERVE SOME PURPOSE IN NATURE? 346

SHOTS FROM THE CAVE OF A RECLUSE.

THE MEDICAL CRUSOE—HOW TO GRIND YOUR OWN AXE 352

PERCENTAGE ON MEDICAL PRESCRIPTIONS.

THE DEVICE OF A MEDICAL VAMPIRE 355

ADVICE TO COUNTRY PEOPLE SEEKING MEDICAL AID IN THE CITY.

SHUT YOUR MOUTH AND OPEN YOUR EARS 359

THE LIFE-FORCE.

DISEASES OF DEFECTIVE NUTRITION IN THE YOUNG GIRL—CAN MEDICINE CURE SCROFULA OR PULMONARY CONSUMPTION?—HAS IT ANY INFLUENCE ON SPINAL DISEASE OR DISEASES OF THE JOINTS?—WHAT SHOULD BE DONE FOR THEM? 364

CAUSES OF THE WAR.

GOD IS NOT A LIAR—LIBERTY IS THE ORGANIC LAW 372

THE CONSUMPTION CURER.

THE MEDICAL VULTURE—THE PRICE OF A COFFIN AND A SHROUD 374

PRINCE MURAT'S DEFENCE.

VALUE OF SIX KICKS—A POWERFUL APPEAL—THE REPLY 376

THE SYMPATHETIC NATURE OF DISEASE.

DISEASES OF THE RECTUM, BLADDER AND UTERUS—THEIR POWER TO SIMULATE
DISEASE IN OTHER PARTS OF THE BODY—CONCEALED ABSCESS OF THE RECTUM
OFTEN PRODUCTIVE OF FISTULA; VARICOCELE AND STRICTURE 379

CURING DISEASE.

CAN IT BE DONE?—THE DUTY OF A CONSCIENTIOUS MEDICAL MAN 389

AN ALLEGORY.

SOCIETY—ITS REQUIREMENTS—THE OLD CEDAR 390

WORMS IN PORK AND MUTTON.

WORMS IN THE ORGANS AND MUSCLES OF VARIOUS ANIMALS—DEATH IN GER-
MANY FROM TRICHINÆ—CASES IN THIS COUNTRY—THE FILARIA OR THREAD
WORM IN THE EYE OF A HORSE 392

A REMARKABLE QUACK.

MOVEMENTS OF DISTINGUISHED PERSONAGES 395

INTRODUCTORY.

WHAT ARE THE TEMPERAMENTS?

It has for so many centuries been the custom to look to certain gentlemen in spectacles, whose manners are somewhat formal, and whose conversation not very intelligible, for the purchase of a very useful commodity called health, (an article without which we are not able to make a very useful or graceful addition to society, and the non-possession of which, like too little money, is particularly inconvenient) that such wares as we offer have not met with many very dignified and conservative admirers. Now and then, however, we receive some gratifying assurances that Japonicadom begins to feel there is something rotten within, that makes her petals turn pale and the leaves fall off. She discovers that the hot-house and the ball-room do not make a very durable bloom in her darlings, and begins to suspect there may be some defect in the cutting or the seed ; something too is now and then suspected to be wrong in the process of inarching or grafting, that accounts for the early death of so many of the darlings of the second generation ; the juices which nourish the blossoms are poisoned in some way, and the doctor's skill is unsatisfactory ; rosewood,

satin, and silver nails, are often required in their place ;
but black is very interesting, and then Dr. Creamcheese
is so very consolatory in his attentions ; the "mysterious
providence of God" is so incomprehensible, and we
should submit "with becoming resignation."

Suppose, now, my lovely and fashionable reader, you
lay aside your crochet-needles, and your box of bon-bons
that Augustus has brought you, and endeavor to make
the discovery whether the brain of that "charming young
gentleman" is probably as like in its structure and functions to a starved cauliflower, as the anterior portion of
its envelope is to the oblong segment of a goose-egg ;
you will then have some wholesome exercise of your own,
when you reflect upon the propriety of selecting him as
your guide and counsellor through life, and the father of
your children, in preference to "that horrid creature"
whose head resembles, about as much as anything, the
hump of a buffalo. We select our classical comparisons
according to our existing humor ; at present you may
consider yourself mounting a physiological buffalo ; make
yourself perfectly comfortable, dearest ; all you need
do is to sit quietly behind the hump and hold on to us ;
we have neither dined to-day on wolf, wild-cat, or rattle-
snake ; it is true we are going, as we often do, to tell
you some disagreeable truths, as we have lately told our
male friends about their tobacco and some other vile
habits ; but we presume it will not annoy you, and you
will soon forget the disagreeable exercise and resume
your rocking-chair, bon-bons, and plumcake. Sweet
Frederick Augustus will console you.

Forgive us, darling, for such naughty talk, and let us
have the felicity to assist you to mount ; don't be afraid
—what a charming little foot ; there, my love, you are
safely seated ; let us you assure the "horrid animal" will

be perfectly gentle with such a freight ; we control the creature perfectly ; he is very gentle to the sex.

What do we mean by "the temperaments?" They are the visible measure of a man's life-force and bodily and mental capacity, and may be just as well understood, if you will take the trouble to learn, as the speed and bottom of a horse.

Mere vegetative life is the sum total of the powers that resist decay. We call its degree, the constitution ; and each man has his own, in common with other animals. A man has strong or weak vital force ; he breathes powerfully or feebly ; he feeds to advantage or disadvantage ; if he have strong vital force, he is usually fond of animal food, and is very active and energetic in his movements ; if he be weak in his vital force, or lymphatic in temperament, he is more sluggish in his movements and is satisfied with food that yields less fibrine and red globules to his blood ; these make muscles. Vegetarians are generally cold-blooded and phlegmatic ; hence we deduce the temperaments : sanguine, sanguine-bilious, and lymphatic, (popularly called phlegmatic,) of the old standard physiologists. The temperament means nothing more than the physical condition of the man, that gives him his position as an active or passive agent amongst his fellows.

A man of fine physical conformation, and plenty of red blood flowing through his face, with clear bright blue or gray eyes, capacious lungs, broad shoulders, and wavy brown hair and beard, is of the highest sanguine temperament ; he has high vital force ; and if he have a well-balanced brain and a good early education, he is susceptible to the best influences ; if not, and he be so unfortunate as to marry a mean and soul-less woman, he will go to the devil.

A man with a full and well-rounded person, and a much paler face, and light straight hair and beard, with shorter limbs and fingers, and built like a fat woman, is slower in his movements and passions, and colder in temperature ; he is lymphatic (phlegmatic) in temperament, and whoever marries him will be obliged to take great care of him ; his blood circulates too slowly to admit of generosity ; she must have his slippers, and tea, and toast, ready betimes, or he will let her know that she has committed a sin not easily forgotten ; he will count every cent of her pin-money.

Such people usually join societies and churches, for they cannot stand firm without some one's aid to sustain them ; they are acute at a bargain, and are generally called "exemplary members of society ;" but they are often cursed by the widow and orphan after the settlement of their estates, to which occupation they have a great proclivity ; and neither the little children nor the poor negroes greet them with a smile as they pass them on the road.

A lean man with well-defined and hard muscles, big nose, no fat, tall and long-limbed, with brown hair and beard, and gray eyes, and very active and energetic in his movements, has the highest degree of executive and vital force combined ; he is sanguine-bilious ; the bile hides the red blood in his face, and makes him darker.

If he be an educated man and fond of domestic life, a woman of soul and delicacy of sentiment, if she be in some degree his opposite in temperament, may control him to any extent compatible with his honor ; but we advise all wire-pullers and designing or cunning men to give him a wide berth, he will prove a most impracticable creature "to operate on."

We occasionally observe marked examples of the mixed

temperament, especially the nervous and sanguine, and nervous and bilious; these are characterized by the peculiarities of their respective types, with the addition of a greatly increased quickness of movement and speech; when the nervous element predominates, the individual is sometimes said to be of that distinctive temperament; but this is in our opinion wrong, as it is impossible to class the degree of mobility as a temperament, when it is never uncombined with the far more distinctive characteristicts of bile and blood.

These are the old and well-defined temperaments of the books, with which every person of ordinary attainment should be acquainted. Many persons are no common judges of character and temperament, who know no arbitrary distinctions, but give evidence by their conversation and the tact they show in their communication with their fellows, that they possess great powers of observation and sagacity in their conclusions.

It will be observed by the medical reader, that we have left out the melancholic temperament; we do so because we consider it impossible to mark such a one distinctively, any more than the nervous temperament. Constitutional melancholy is inherited; and although it doubtless depends upon physical organization, its victims only become marked by it, when grief has done its work on the organism. Dr. Powell calls the melancholic the "Encephalic" temperament; it is, according to him, denoted by an unusual development of the anterior brain; we consider the term happily expressive; whether it be synonymous with the melancholic temperament or not, it is certainly not indicative of vital force. According to our own observation, a child who has a great predominance of the anterior brain, and especially of the forehead (popular) is about as unfortunate in his sus-

ceptibility to early disease and death, as he will undoubtedly prove in after-life should he survive, in tenacity of
purpose and effective pursuit of the practical business of
life ; if he possess both the anterior and posterior portions equally balanced, he will be a comprehensive and
philosophical man : if the posterior be still larger than a
large anterior, he may be a Webster ; but if he have a
little round head, say a third of a circle of seven inches,
he will be a selfish man, who uses the smallest means to
attain his objects ; and whatever caution he may have
used to preserve the semblance of integrity in early life,
if he reach seventy, it will inevitably leave him, and
vanity and selfishness will assert their full power.

With good perceptive faculties, indicated by a large
brow and moderate forehead, but with a high brain behind, a man even with a very limited education, if fond of
domestic life and happily married, will speedily show his
superiority in all the practical business of life where perseverance and firmness are requsite ; but if his posterior
brain slopes suddenly downwards, he will be looking out
early for a gold-headed cane and a rocking-chair ; he
must be somebody's ditto or second somebody's resolution ; for he cannot get up the necessary brain-force to
form an opinion of his own ; such men must be sustained
by others ; and if we were so unfortunate as to possess
such children, we would purchase annuities for them at
once, for we know they never could help themselves.

But we did not set out to write an essay on phrenology,
for which we have neither the credulity nor the ability ;
commercial phrenology, like commercial physic and surgery, we heartily despise. Can the life-force be cultivated by regularity of life and intellectual pursuits ? We
answer that it can, and think it can be proved. We
propose to attempt it in the following pages.

BACK-BONE.

"We shall never fail to crack the satiric thong wherever it is deserved, either by ignorance or impudence."—*Prospectus*, 1849.

POSITION OF THE FACULTY AND THE SCALPEL—CONSERVATIVE ANTIQUARIES—FOSSILIZED MORALISTS—PROFESSIONAL TURNERS AND THEIR TURNING LATHES—EDITORIAL ECCENTRICITY—DIPLOMAS AND THEORIES—CRIBS, TEA-KETTLES, AND CORN-BASKETS.—*Scalpel*, 1856.

"In enterprises of great pith and moment, it is better that a man be somewhat absurd than over formal."—BACON.

SIXTEEN years have been added to the great volume of the past since we launched our little shallop upon the ocean of experiment, without a doubt of its success if industry or energy would secure it, but with deep-felt misgivings of our ability to meet the intellectual requirements of that class of readers for whose approbation alone we felt willing to labor. In commencing our twelfth volume, we are so far assured of the success of the enterprise, that we feel we may draw upon the good nature of our readers whilst we attempt to give an account of those early impressions and experiences which first originated the idea. In several past numbers of our journal, we have gone somewhat into detail on the subject, but, hon-

est as our occasional expositions have been, either the
manner or assertions in most of them have drawn upon
us the wrath of a portion of our professional brethren,
and made some proselytes for the complaining party
amongst the more conservative class of the people. It
is true that our professional opponents, by reason of the
extreme delicacy of their position, have been somewhat
numerous, and their assistants in the foray rather formidable, so far as wealth and modern piety went; but the
intellectual battery they have brought to bear upon our
little craft, has not been calculated to disturb our equan-
imity. Both parties are evidently members of the great
conservative and commercial society of medical and religious antiquaries; their animal heat has been so long
chilled by inflating their medical and religious stocks,
that it fairly admits of a doubt if they have not produced a new or white-blooded species of humanity.
Indeed, we have long suspected many of them to be
partially fossilized by the ancient learning and morality
with which their leaders have so long saturated them.
Their remains will doubtless some day be found, like
the fossil tortoises and other reptiles of the genus, imbed-
ded in the earthy debris of an effete morality. Whilst
our friends are engaged in selling the small wares of
humanity to their awe-stricken admirers, let us be content to assist in clearing the forest and letting in the
light of nature upon those outside barbarians, who believe
that there is some truth and dignity in the heart's
impulse and in nature's laws. In short, we wish to
address our long-suffering and indulgent readers.

But badinage apart; we started to make some confes-
sions to the reader, not because we desire to obtrude
ourselves upon him in an increased dose, but simply to
explain the charge of eccentricity which is chalked up

against us by every medical teetotem, diplomaed and turned out by the professorial turners, at their college turning shops, like tops for the children's bazaars ; to be whipped round and round in the great civic nursery of commercial snobdom by doting mammas, and then kicked into a corner for some freshly imported apothecary, or ci-devant gentleman's valet, who has either bought or stolen his master's coat and diploma, and rushed to the great American Alsatia to try for a rich wife, or to earn a cropped head, a striped jacket, and a degree at Uncle Sam's great college on the banks of the Hudson—honors which are richly merited by a vast number of foreign medical adventurers who carry themselves with high heads in our good-natured metropolis.

It was not, however, in consequence of the venality of colleges in selling their diplomas to the incompetent, nor yet the national predilection for foreign quacks and vaga- bonds, that originated this journal. It is true such circumstances were rather depressing to an aspiring youth, depending solely upon a profession, and about to offer his abilities in his native city, where, with three preceding generations, he could claim two hundred years of nativity. "A prophet has no honor in his own coun- try," but we never offered to prophesy ; had we really done so, from the now humiliating extent of superstition, we would have anticipated the public taste and gained money by frightening their souls, if our fellow-citizens would not allow us to cure their bodies. For this, how- ever, we never had a penchant. Standing upon the shore of time, with the same brittle thread of life, and with all the affections common to our fellow-creatures, our per- haps stolid moral conformation, shared none of those exciting fancies of looking into the future. We were content to believe it simply unreasonable to suppose we

should enjoy a happy future, if we prepared our appre-
ciative nature by the practice of dishonesty during our
present existence. With such sentiments, as we have
somewhere before told our reader, we lettered "our shin-
gle" with our own hand, and stuck it up in the front
window of a "very respectable house" in Bleecker street,
some twenty-three years ago.

We have chosen to present some of the events that
constituted our professional experience during the past
thirty years, under various guises, in our pages—sometimes quaintly, sometimes seriously, as we felt in the
mood. On one occasion, we perceive we chose to appear
as an entrapped fox, listening to our youthful brethren
outside, whilst we were awaiting the morning and our
captors. This, and much other nonsense we have been
obliged to commit, in order to entrap the reader into an
interest in the more didactic part of our pages. At present, we feel in a philosophical mood, and inclined to
speculate upon the extraordinary apathy, and the still
more extraordinary method chosen by our people, in
selecting their medical attendants—we were about to say
advisers, but the term is simply ridiculous, as claimed by
our brethren ; our countrymen never take *advice ;* they
"hire," or "employ" a "medical attendant," and too
often treat him with the same degree of respect they do
their hired waiter or their barber. We had, during our
pupilage, very extraordinary opportunities of observing
the estimate and importance of manner and temperament
upon those who seek medical and surgical advice. Dr.
F——s was an example of great benevolence, and immense excitability, and love of literary admiration,
combined with a keen sense of the ridiculous. Dr.
B——e was bold, brilliant, and horribly overbearing and
insolent ; and Dr. M——t had but one ruling passion, the

love of money, and a heart-felt conviction of the supreme-ly glorious position of surgery, and the unapproachable glories of tying the iliac and innominata ; for him, the human body was an arterial machine, created to have its arteries tied and its legs cut off. We will give the reader a few illustrations of each as we proceed with our sketches in future numbers.

Amongst the students who flocked to the office of the two former gentlemen, there was every variety of the genus, from the childish and good-natured young gosling, whose highest ambition was to be perfect in the scientific nomenclature of the Materia Medica, to the distressed investigator of the holes and processes of the sphenoid bone ; some were lean and some fat ; we had spongers, borrowers and loafers, musicians, litterateurs, dunder-heads, and rascals. Dr. B——e used to say that he never saw a more unclassifiable assemblage even in that city of contradictions in humanity—Dublin itself. Feeling the responsibility of my chosen profession, (for I was then in quite active obstetrical practice amongst that trying peo-ple the low Irish,) I used to speculate sagely upon the possibility of this or that student ever being able to secure confidence, and get his bread from the community. There was such an ocean of difference between some of them, and between all of them and myself, that I used sagely to conclude that, if the most wonderful of them succeeded, I was sure to starve ; and I often contemplated the probability of my testing practically the great physio-logical problem of the minimum amount of nutriment that would maintain vitality in my body. Dr. F——s used to speculate upon me awfully over his gold specta-cles, although he took to our formal evening examinations very much as I suppose the chafed buffalo draws up and presents his front to the hunters ; he could not make me

out, I know ; I was certain that, if he had "discovered
my stops," he would never have attempted to instruct me
in the Materia Medica.   I always thought a drug-shop
the most preposterously ludicrous thing on earth, and
wondered how it was possible for a doctor to sit down
and write a recipe without laughing in his patient's face.
I got on, however, without disgrace even in that ludicrous department, and bestowed most of my time on
Anatomy.   I felt that if I ever could practice my profession it must be surgery alone, for I never could have the
face to give people physic to cure their diseases, when
they were either destitute of proper shelter and food, or
oppressed with gluttony and lived in unventilated
houses.

Most of my time was devoted to the study of my preceptors and the students.   There was one pupil who gave
me a new insight into the human character.   He was
both intellectually and physically of a very low order of
the genus ; bearing in his face unmistakable evidence of
his devotion to sensual pleasures, in the loss of the bridge
of his nose, and evincing by his desire to trade his newly
acquired talents for quarters, or even sixpences, his
intellectual beginnings at home.   Low and base as he
was, it was only a phase of the same spirit that actuates
a large proportion of our college graduates ; so I see no
reason why he should not be made the medium for the
exposition of the infernal results of the wretched system
of diploma huckstering ; he had the same right to sell
what he had dishonestly obtained, as his examiners had
to sell him their diploma, and the sin must lie at their
door of all the murders he committed.   ·

Our specimen had filled the position of a Yankee schoolmaster, and much as he was despised, he occasionally
made it appear to some inferior student, that he was by

no means inclined to admit his intellectual inferiority in argument. He made hay of the English language, and he used to get wofully befogged with his anatomy. Finding it rather too expensive to meddle with the demonstrative part of that science, I was occasionally honored by his presence at an anatomical demonstration in my room, where he would try, as his nose obliged him to express it, "to pick up a little sutthick"—meaning something in the way of a knowledge of anatomical structure. I used to endure his presence as well as I could, and swallowed the annoyance with tolerable submission, unless he began to ask questions through that nose of his, when I could stand it no longer, and would rush out convulsively, and lock the door, pretending a suddenly remembered engagement.

I knew nothing of his mode of subsistence till one day, on occasion of a sudden illness, he sent for me to see him at his boarding house, when the riddle was solved, and for the first time I was made to understand the full extent of the trading propensity on a low intellect. Observing a number of articles of a character rather incongruous to a medical student's lodging room, I forbore to make any impertinent inquiries, though I was really curious to know what use he could put them to. A copper tea-kettle, a child's crib, and three new market baskets! The latter articles at length overcame my good breeding, and with a little astonishment I took up one of the baskets and inquired, possibly with some slight expletive, what use he could put them to. My question evidently annoyed him, and upon its repetition he got so far nettled as to let out upon me for what he was pleased to call "my infernal pride," assuring me, by way of a flattering apology, I suppose, that "talent was not all a man required, to get a living by the profession," and that he

could teach me a thing or two that would do me good as
long as I lived. I apologized immediately, as I saw it
would be the most likely way to attain a knowledge of the
sources of the heterodox articles in question, and assured
him that I was very far from under-estimating his business tact and capacity for "getting along ;" he was
evidently pleased, and became quite talkative. He assured
me that he thought a certain knowledge of anatomy and
chemistry well enough for those who had time and
money to acquire it, but that he was convinced of the
superior value of "the practice." "No longer ago than
last week," said he triumphantly, "I bled a man three
times for rheumatism, and relieved him so that his hidden disease declared itself in the form of a legitimate
fever and ague." I expressed my astonishment at the
decision of the practice, and innocently inquired where
the patient lived? The reply was sufficiently indicative
of the extent of his knowledge of physiology, and the
depth of his therapeia. He said his patient, a poor negro
basket maker, lived in a cellar kitchen! He had bled the
poor creature into an attack of ague, and received the
three corn baskets for the exploit. The child's crib was
obtained of a cabinet maker in the more excusable manner of an obstetric fee. On the tea-kettle I could get no
light ; he always fought me shy on that ; probably it was
the hoarded household souvenir of some poor woman,
and my fellow-student had some very distant misgivings
of the unmanliness of receiving it.   ·

This trading student was an extreme case, I admit ;
but he served an excellent purpose in my mental alembic
as a comparison. In what respect did he differ from the
man who visits day after day some unfortunate creature
of the wealthier rank of society, smitten with selfishness
and indolence, with every sensitive function warped and

turned aside by gluttony or hysterics? Which of the
two fills the most dignified position? Nay, which is the
most honest? he who robs the negro of his thin and
watery blood, and drives him into an ague for three corn
baskets, or he who continues day after day to administer
his wretched potions when nature demands wholesome
food, vitalizing exercise, and the consequent expansion of
the lungs and the affections into a wholesome and manly
forgetfulness of self? Who can strike the line of respect-
ability between the two? One sells diplomas, and absurd
and antiquated theories to an idle and roguish schoolmaster ; and the other trades his roguery and ignorance
for cribs, tea-kettles, and corn baskets!

SCENES IN WESTERN PRACTICE.

FROST FOLIAGE PAINTED BY MOONLIGHT—THE MERCY ANGELS—CHILD MESSEN-
GER—THE WEDDING-RING FEE—A MIDNIGHT RIDE—ARE THEY HUNGRY IN
HEAVEN?—THE DAUGHTER OF A CITY MERCHANT—THE FIRE KING—THE
GOLDEN AND THE SILVER RULE—ADVERSITY AND LABOR THE SOUL-ELEVATORS
—DEATH THE GREAT PURIFIER—THE CLERICAL SPECULATOR—MORALITY AND
MAMMON—CITY AND COUNTRY CORRUPTION—GRAIN SPECULATION; AWFUL
CONSEQUENCES ON MORALS—THE MIDNIGHT VISIT OF THE ANGELS TO THE
GREAT CITY—ITS CONDITION—THE CHILD THIEF—THE ANGEL'S BLESSING—
DEATH OF THE MERCHANT'S DAUGHTER.

Strange—" that virtue and work should be so cheap,
And bread should be so dear."

THE bright frost-sparks were on the trees in the forest,
and when the moon, with her mild torch, lighted them
up, they glittered like so many fairy diamonds ; they
glowed with light and lustre, changing from sparks of
light to blue and green gems; and all the air flickered
with these specks of frost, painted into diadems by the
rich, soft moonlight.   There is nothing so beautiful in
all nature as one of these evenings; the air is so still that
if the soul listens, it cannot shut out the 'angels' whispers
that come to us mingled with music that cannot be
printed.   Angels never speak when the sun shines,
nor when the white robe of winter has folded all
nature into its pure mantle; no, they only come when
the moon shines in late autumn, when the nights are

clear and the air keen, and the frost sparkles with cold. Then all earnest souls can hear them. They do not address the ear ; they speak to the spirit, and fill it with love and harmony, with mercy and blessings.

Spring, with its flowers and birds, had passed, and scattered its smiling glances on all the works of God. Summer had succeeded, and ripened the fruit, and dressed up the year with a full-lapped bounty; and then had come one of the frost-nights, mingled with moon-fire—the nights on which the mercy-angels are abroad on errands of goodness.

I had sat a long time in my window, watching the white fleecy clouds that floated over the deep-blue sky. They were brilliant with reflected light, and as gaudy as the royal diamond-spangled robe of some Eastern queen. I went to the window, and returned to my library, and then went again, with uncovered head, into the boundless sea of mystic cold and light, and listened to the seraph voices, (I listen with my spirit,) and then returned again to my warm room, to enjoy the delightful contrast between bathing my body in dead heat, and plunging my living spirit into the fathomless sea of glittering light.

Why I could not sleep I know not; but I could not. I was too happy; I felt a serenity that spoke of mercy, of some good to be done; some suffering spirit, that needed the hush of a last blessing, was speaking to me, and seemed to say: "Can you not watch one short hour, when I have not slept for two long nights, and shall never sleep again till I awake into everlasting life? Know you not that Love darts her message into the human heart through space, over seas, mountains and plains? and when sorrow pleads for mercy the spirit hears it—it hears it just as a merciful God hears our prayers and listens to our wants?"

My soul was so full of thought and blessings, that I was in a sea of thankfulness and joy, when I was roused by the patter of two little feet on the door-stone. I knew it was a child's step, it was so soft, and yet so confident ; a child's step has no fear in it—the innocent have no fear. A faint rap fell on the door ; it was a soft rap, for her little hand was covered with a mitten to keep the frost-diamonds from biting it. The frost has no feeling for little hands ; it only loves to shine and sparkle, and sparkle and shine, before the warm sun shall come and spoil its beauty and power to harm. I opened the door, and in stepped little Julia, muffled in a shawl, and mittens, and hood ; and her shoes were stiff with cold, and they creaked on the floor, and her face was all covered with love, and looked very bright, and the still tear stood in her eye, and she could not speak.

"Oh, Julia !" said I, "are you not cold, child ? and why is my darling out alone ?"

"It is so light, sir, that I could come easily without being lost."

"I know it is light, but it is very cold ; you came alone, did you not ?"

"Oh yes, sir, Mr. Doctor, I came alone, but I was not afraid, nor cold any ;" and her bright-red lip trembled, and she could not speak ; and on her cheek the frost had painted a full, red blush, and the skin was white as the snow-flake. She looked very beautiful, and her heart was full, too full to tell me more.

"And you were not afraid, you said, and you are only nine years old, I think, and have come three miles, in the night, too, all alone—did you come to see me, Miss Julia ?"

" Yes, Mr. Doctor ; my mother is very sick, and I came
to get you to cure her, and she said God protected all
good children, and then she seemed to be with me all the
way, and I was not afraid ;" and here the dear child
burst into tears.

I was very busy warming the child, for I was enchanted
and bewildered by the fidelity and confidence of the
charming little girl ; I had often seen her light form
tripping along the highway to school, her blue eyes as
mild as a summer dew-drop ; now she lifted toward me
something that glittered, and said, in her sweet, low
voice, " Please will you go and see my mother, to-night,
Mr. Doctor ? She sent you this gold ring—she had no
money—and she cried when she gave it to me, and said
it was one my dear papa gave her when they were married in New York city, and she wanted to keep it for me,
but she will give it to you, sir, if you will come and see
her to-night ; she is afraid she will die before to-morrow,
and then she cannot tell you what she wants to ; and she
is all alone, too, only a little girl, Katy Wharton, came
over to stay with her while I came after you ; so please
do go and see my dear mother to-night, good Mr.
Doctor."

The fervent love and artless simplicity of the child had
so overcome me, that I had prepared myself to start,
unconsciously. My wife had risen from her slumber, and
was listening to the story of the child, and when I
returned to the gate with my robes and cutter, I found
little Julia and my good wife waiting to accompany me.
Folding them closely in my thick, warm robes, I drove
rapidly over the ground ; a slight snow had fallen, and
covered the dark-brown earth. My residence was near a
close wood, and my track to the dwelling of the sick woman led me through a thickly settled part of the large

and flourishing village of A——. The house was small, and forbidding in its exterior, and when we reached the gate, little Julia bounded from the sleigh with the elastic step of a young fawn, glided across the yard, and entered the house in advance of us, and, rushing to the bedside, she held up the ring and cried for joy, as her tiny arm clasped her sick mother's neck, while she covered her pale cheek with fervent kisses. "Dear mother," she said, in a soft, low voice, "don't cry now, nor cough any more, for the good doctor has come now, and the lady has come too, to help me take care of you ;" and she ran to the table to bring some drink for which her mother had motioned.

Myself and companion stood by the bedside of a sick and dying woman, who had been nursed in the halls of luxury and pride, and whose parents had taught her to love self and forget all else in the world beside.

Come into the apartment, gentle reader, and see where the daughter of the rich and proud sometimes ends her days. A small room, with scanty furniture, some poor, and a part of it very rich, the broken fragments of a splendid outfit, given her by her father when she left New York for her home in the West.

The whole scene was really comfortless, although the hand of taste and pride had evidently tried in vain to hide the real facts by great tact in arrangement, and perfect neatness throughout the room. The address of the lady at once marked her as one who had been bred in a far higher circle of life than she now occupied, for she saluted us with that dignified simplicity that always characterizes the woman of good breeding. Our first duty was to provide for her comfort, and then receive her bequests, for she was rapidly drawing toward the close of her weary pilgrimage.

My wife had arranged her couch anew ; her cough had been quieted by a soothing draught, and she lay resting her failing body, gathering strength for this last conflict with her fate, when little Julia rushed up to the bedside and asked, in a very earnest tone, "Dear mother, do Isaiah, and David, and Joseph have to go to a public soup-house in heaven to get something to eat? or do they have bread enough in heaven, mother?" "My strange child," said the dying mother, "why do you ask me that?" "Oh, you know the other day, when we were so hungry, you made me read to you in the Bible that 'God hears the ravens cry,' and then you sent me down to the store for a little flour, and when he sent me back because I had no money, and you cried so, I kept thinking about the famine in Samaria, and how Joseph's brethren went down into Egypt to buy corn, and Joseph wept when he saw them, and gave them something to eat ; and I knew, because you said so, that even some good people now could not get bread to eat because it costs so much, and you said they had to go to soup-houses to be fed, and beautiful fine ladies had to go there in the great city of New York last year, and I wondered if people were ever hungry in heaven." The poor child relieved herself of all this with great earnestness.

A deep crimson flush overspread the face of the poor mother, and her eye glanced wildly at the face of my wife, as she said to the child ; "No, my dear, children are not hungry there ; but you must not talk so strangely."

Great God! what thoughts rushed across my soul at this strange scene! Have we become a race of demons, thought I, and do *children begin to doubt the justice* of God?

A sudden silence seized the group, and through my
2*

soul rushed whole years of anguish. Children starving in a land of bread!—mothers, nursed in pride and luxury, brought to feel the bony finger of Want, and grapple, on a dying-bed, with pale Famine's icy touch! What, thought I, shall I hear next? Surely something heart-breaking has preceded such a train of thought in the mind of this child. And who can this sick lady be, inquires the reader, and where did she come from, and whose daughter was she, and had she any mother alive ; or was she some poor outcast—one of those whom God almost forgets to comfort? She was none of these.

Mary E—— was the daughter of a rich merchant in New York city. About twenty years before I was called to see her, she was seated in a gorgeous parlor, surrounded by splendid mirrors, playing on her piano, and courted by rich suitors, and flattered by a poet's love. The world may not know it, but the Western physician does, that among the surging tide of wealth and home-hunting life that swells across the great lakes, and spreads across the prairies of the West, even to the shores of the Pacific, there are a smaller number of emigrants that swarm out from the houses of the merchant princes of our great commercial metropolis. The place is too strait for them, and luxury, vice, and indolence have enervated them too much to enable them to buffet the rude breakers of Western life. These sons, from the euchre tables, and drinking saloons, and club houses of that refined and Christian city, are married to the highest bidder who has cash to give with his daughter ; and the young pair are shipped west with bales of goods and boxes of merchandise, to become the aristocracy of the villages and cities of the West. While the West is thus peopled with these ribbon men and women from the commercial capital, the hardy sons of toil and exertion flow back from the farm and places of toil, to fill the places of clerks in the great city's trading-houses, and become the future merchants of that vast Babel of trade.

Among these adventurers, in the year '34, was a young merchant of much promise, who ranked much higher than the average of this class of men. He had become the husband of the accomplished Miss E——. The doting parents had dismissed them with their blessing and a stock of goods, and they had taken up their residence in the village of F——, where a year or more of prosperity had placed them at the head of the village aristocracy.

But Fortune has her changes, and rolls her mad waves over the hopeful and the stout-hearted. One of those tempests of fire, that a just God rains on cities, as he did on Sodom for her sins, came upon New York; and on a cold night in December, the red tongue of the fire-tempest lapped up the heart of the city, and scattered her proud merchants as beggars in the streets.

The man of millions, in a single night, found himself without the means of a breakfast; the family that dwelt in a palace, were houseless and naked; the mothers who who toiled for their daily bread, were rich as the richest.

I shall never forget the strange scene that was presented in the capital, for the whole state suffered; so wide-spread was the desolation, that none could measure it; but every heart was touched with pity for the homeless and the breadless.

The night was intensely cold; the water froze in the hydrants, and the devouring element rioted unrebuked on the labors and the hopes of men. The sun rose in the east on a sea of smouldering ruins; all night had mothers mourned and wept, and when daylight came, fathers of stony hearts, that never prayed before, prayed then, "Give us this day our daily bread."

So wide was the desolation, that no one could see its shore, and thinking men rushed up to the capital, to ask the loan of a million of dollars, to blunt for a little time the sea of suffering that none could really fathom. I saw the whole struggle, and heard the prayers of the sufferers, and the proud buffetings of those who held the purse-strings.

Men implored for the love of God, and the tears of suffering and helpless women and children, that aid which the State alone could give. They repeated the *golden rule*, and wept hot tears of suffering, for the fire had painted with red flame a soft spot for once in the heart of the gold princes. They knew that men could suffer ; they had seen their own wives and daughters clinging to them in despair, asking where they should sleep and eat. And the pitiless politician now spoke with a tongue of fire, and repeated those golden words, "Do unto others as you would that others should do unto you," and wept for aid ; but those words sounded as strangely as the song of a seraph chanted in the halls of Bedlam. "Now," said the wily wire-worker, "is the time to punish New York. She has refused us all succor at the West, she has no heart ; when the flame has died from her ruins, a heart of ice will again beat in her bosom ; show her no mercy, for she deserves none. Give her the *silver rule*—she repeats the *golden one*, but will never live by it."

Such was actually the language that fell from the lips of Christian men, stung by the demon of a golden selfishness. Said one, "I will vote to relieve this cry for mercy, but the words stick in my throat—so much selfishness deserves no pity." The boon was granted, and the tried and suffering city drew one long breath of love and gratitude to the bounty of the State. Reader, we must now return to the bedside of our sick patient, prepared to understand who she was and the cause of her condition. She was the daughter of a wealthy merchant, who lost his last dollar in the huge fire of '35 ; he saw the labor of a long life swept from him in an hour, and the hope of his family went down in that whirlpool of fire.

His son-in-law had a few thousands in his Western home, but an inexorable necessity compelled him to recall the whole. Beggary stared him in the face, and he informed his daughter of his fate and asked for aid, and with the noble impulse that ever guides the great-hearted, full-souled woman, she resolved to send her father all to save him from want. Their business had been prosperous, and they lived in the first sunshine of a gay prosperity. Her husband responded with as full a heart, and in a week his splendid stock of goods had disappeared under the hammer, and the cash was forwarded to the parents in New York ; and then came the new life, in which the heart grows amid the rushing of wild tempests, and we feel that life has a dignity in it, because we have humanity in our hearts, and can weep with those that weep, and rejoice with those that rejoice.

Our patient had the form of a queen, and her face bore the impress of nobleness and love. Her manners would have graced the hall of a Hapsburgh princess—no daughter of the Tyrol was ever more lovely. Her husband was a man, and only needed the rod and the scourge to make him shine. He sought a position as a clerk, their servants were dismissed, and she resolved to learn the art of managing her own house. She could play her piano, but could not make bread for her husband and her child. She knew not how to wash and iron her own garments. She had been taught that to do so was vulgar ; but now it was to contribute to her father's comfort, and send joy to her aged mother's heart, it became a pleasure and a joy.

George had returned one morning from the store, and found his wife weeping. He spoke words of comfort to her, and asked her the cause. She responded, in a tone of firmness, that she was ashamed of her education, and had resolved to learn to work : "I will know how to make bread for my husband in less than a week." George smiled at his wife's resolution, and a shade of sadness passed over his face. Their life's morning had opened bright and cloudless as the rays of the early dawn. One year of life had been all sunshine; now they were without means, his store closed, his fine house relinquished; their parents were aged and helpless in a city where the wheels of fate revolved so fast and so rudely, that the stoutest were often crushed in its wild whirl. Their infant smiled in its wicker cradle. Mary said to her husband, "We cannot keep servants, and you and our darling may starve, for aught that I can do for you—what a poor creature am I! why, I cannot make bread!" When the husband had left for his daily business, meditating on the change in their condition, Mary started for the minister's house, and frankly told her friend her resolution, for all knew by this time their necessities.

They both started for the residence of Dr. P——, and it was soon arranged that the ladies would alternate in their visits, and aid the resolute wife in acquiring a knowledge of arranging her house, setting her table, and cooking her food. In a few weeks she had acquired considerable knowledge of the duties of a useful wife. She now knew the joy of contributing to her own and her husband's

wants, and no ·bread was ever so sweet to her as that
which Mary set before her husband—made with her own
hands. But a year passed, and her parents sunk under
the heavy stroke of disaster ; the current was too deep ;
it bore them to the grave. Now more than ever Mary
felt the blessedness of her good deeds to her parents,
and learned that to be useful was to be happy, to be good
was to be like the angels.

George struggled on in his new position in life. Pride
rose up and mocked him, but he looked it steadily in the
face, till his manhood outgrew his early training and he
learned the real power of self-dependence. But woe betide
us when all the winds blow calamities to our hearthstones !
George was seized with a typhoid inflammation of the
lungs, a disease that sweeps hundreds of stalwart men in
miasmatic districts to a sudden grave ; and in a week the
noble Mary was a widow and Julia an orphan.

She thought her cup was full before, but now it ran over
with bitter sorrow, and she bowed her head before the blast
and said in the deep faith of a smitten spirit, "Thy will
be done, O God !" The black hearse came, the pall covered the form of her husband. With Julia and a few
humble friends she followed their stay and support to the
grave ; the last hymn broke on the silent air ; the
coffin was lowered; the earth fell heavily on the lid ;
fainter and fainter grew the sound, and a long earth-
mound covered the body of the noble young father.

It is natural and seems appropriate for the young and
the old to die ; but when the thread is cut in full life,
and hope, home, wife, child, are all made desolate by the
blow, it looks as though the law of life was reversed in its
enactment, and a great wrong was done. Our friend now
missed the hand on which she had leaned, and turned
herself to find some ray of light beaming on her destiny ;

she saw no star beyond her on the sky-verge of her coming days, but she committed her all to the hands of that
great and loving One who stills the young raven's
cry, and looked up with cheerful hope.

What now was to be done? The fire had devoured her
father's wicked gains, gathered up by speculation in bread,
and the tears and heart-burnings of hungry children, and
heart-broken mothers ; her father, mother and husband
were dead, and naught was left to her but poverty and her
little feeble Julia. She had learned how to work, could
cook her own food, and she resolved to know more of honest, inspiring toil. In less than a month she had command
of her needle, as a tailoress and dress-maker, and with her
superior genius, she soon found employment among the
best of her sex; for the truly noble among them, who
had known her as the gay and beautiful wife, now beheld her with admiration for her courage and her vigorous struggles with the reiterated blows of a mysterious
Providence.

She felt a deeper joy for the blessings of her humble
table, because procured with her own hands, and Julia
was delighted with all the little gifts that the heart of a
mother so joyfully brings to the being it loves. In the
fierce fires of suffering, Mary had learned that other hearts
could suffer, and to the poor she became a messenger of
mercy, wherever suffering human hearts could be found.

She made the widow's heart to sing for joy, and the
orphan, at the sight of her loving face, smiled through its
tears. She found that "to give is more blessed than to
receive.' She was known by all the poor as the "good
Mary," who came to make them happy, and if she had
nothing to bestow, she smiled on the sufferer, and his pain
grew lighter under its sunny power. Through long years

the loving Mary had supported herself and child by the toil of her own hands. Unfortunately she had removed from the scene of her trials to the village where I found her for better prospects, where at last her powers sank under accumulated labors, and a severe fever had brought her far away from her humble friends, on that cold night. I found her on her last bed of rest, neglected and forgotten by the busy world, attended by two little children, adorned with most saintly meekness and full of the most joyful expectations of a bright and immortal future. As the night was far advanced, and my duties for the next day very arduous, I left my excellent wife, whose heart was ever open to the child of want, to watch the balance of the hours before day, and made my way homewards. I slept little till towards morning. I had heard too much for sleep—a thousand unvailing thoughts rushed through my brain.

I have often been startled by the revelations of the grain traffic, and the fearful inroad that the spirit of speculation has made upon public morals. It converts our Western farmers into heartless and griping Shylocks ; they take the pound of flesh at hazard of the blood and life of their victims. The moment they are offered fair prices for their products, they stand for more. When wheat brings two dollars, the vision of three instantly rises in their heads, and they harden their hearts more rapidly than did Pharaoh. Nay, they seem to desire a famine, that the grim horror of stalking death may force the people to disgorge the last bit of gold to obtain needful food ; its consequences engulf both the people and the clergy. "One morning, on my trip West," said a grain speculator to me, "I staid over Sabbath in the city of Buffalo, and regretted that time hurried me away. The Rev. Mr. T——, of the Baptist church, invited me to his house.

Speculation in the city was at its height ; he had himself just made sale of city lots that left the sum of one hundred thousand dollars in his pocket ; he is a devout and exemplary man, and yet I could not reconcile his two pursuits. He told me that he was startled by the revelations of crime constantly occurring in the city. It was filled, he said, with thousands of young men, who had come there to make their fortune, and he assured me that more than three thousand dissolute girls swarmed through all the city ; two thousand of them, at least, were known by the police to be strangers from the Southern and Eastern towns and villages, who had just arrived, and he feared, he said, their object was evil ; for why should young women work and sew, when young men got rich by speculation ? Money indeed, he said, seemed to have usurped the soul of all things—honesty, religion, virtue, were dead. In passing with him over the city on Monday, to view some lots, he urged me to buy, and spoke enthusiastically of the certainty of a rapid increase. The city, he said, had never been so prosperous.

The banks swarmed with men eager to draw the last dollar to invest in wheat and beef. The storehouses from Buffalo to New York were crowded with vast stores of wheat, while common Ohio horse-tooth corn, worth in dull times twenty-five cents, had risen to a dollar, and the laboring classes all over the rich Genesee valley were eating potatoes and this coarse kind of corn. There were vast fields of wheat in that region, that waved their golden riches in their sight ; but they could not taste it ; no poor man could eat wheat at twenty shillings a bushel. The large farmers had caught the spirit, and they held on to the last bushel ; they would not sell it, said they, for it will surely be four dollars by the next spring.

"Such enormous prices," said I, "for bread and beef

must take away all the money from the cities, and what
then will become of the poor?"

"I know it," said my opponent, "but how to avoid it, I
do not know. I have invested fifty thousand in wheat,
and what shall I do? I must realize a profit. Elder T.
told his people that bread was getting so high in B——,
that he feared half the sewing women in the city would
be tempted to sell their virtue for bread for their children." And here he quoted Hood's lines :

> "Oh, that *virtue* and *work* should be so cheap,
> And bread should be so dear."

The parson shuddered when he told us that a multitude
of girls had disappeared from families as servants, and
sewing girls were more scarce, as the prices for labor
were made lower, because it cost so much to live.

"We know too well," said the minister, "where they have
gone. They may be seen here, fluttering in silks and
satins. Daily fathers visit the city in a state of horror,
hunting for lost daughters. This is horrible."

" But, doctor, we know that such facts are not strange ;
they follow from a law of things ; for speculation, especially in bread, is the highest species of gambling ; and a
nation never yet engaged in it without stabbing to the
heart all public virtue. As the males grow reckless in
the great cities, the centres of social life, the poison
spreads to every domestic circle, and into the country,
infecting all classes with a spirit of reckless gain-getting,
and during the period marked by this dreadful mania,
not less than twenty thousand girls fled from the country
to the northern cities for purposes of rapid gain ; and as
many more in the cities went down into the polluted
whirlpool of pride and fashion.

" During one period of speculation in France, the whole

nation was given over to idleness and lust. Fine ladies
collected in saloons, drank to excess, broke glasses, and
used the language of men ; great numbers engaged in
playing with *pantins*, little bits of pasteboard, marked
with spots, and attached to a string, with which the little
figure was set in motion. Nobles, high-born ladies, and
princes of the blood played with these paper pantins, or
were engaged in gay drawing-rooms, resplendent with
satin and lace hangings, and rosewood furniture, in
making ribbon knots, or cooling their burning lusts in
debauchery and sin. Your city education in New York
is a play with *pantins ;* idleness eats out the soul, and
many die a moral death, before the body decays from
dissipation.

"Industry, my dear doctor, is the law of the universe;
and the nation that neglects sober, honest industry, for
a life of speculation and rapid gain, is sure to lose its
higher life and sink into corruption. God worked, and
man should work ; not one class, but all classes ; that class
that live by turning the thumb-screws of trade, to wring
high profits from the price of bread, are moral lepers on
the fair fame of any Christian society. Why, my dear sir,
only last winter your great city was filled with starving wi-
dows ; proud daughters pawned their garments for bread,
and when the relief committees visited some parts of the
city, young American women hid themselves in closets ;
they had not garments to cover their poor bodies.

"Children have starved lying on the cold hearth-stone,
where the last embers had died—the fire of the hearth
and the soul of the child fled together. And this, too,
great God! when there was bread enough in the land ;
but it was hoarded in strong-barred houses, and guarded
by the mocking Shylocks, who had bought and bolted it
from the reach of the people."

I had but shortly before my visit to my poor dying patient had this conversation with the grain speculator, and when my patient told me that her own dead father had been engaged in the same cruel business, and that the red flames had lapped up his ill-gotten wealth, it filled my soul with intense thoughts. I had almost seen the angel of mercy in the frost-spangled air just before the dear little cherub came from the bed of its dying mother over the snow to bring me her sad message ; and now, my troubled brain again carried me in sleep to the Heavenly messenger ; I dreamed that I saw him ; but his face was sad. He walked through the city, and the sights of sin that he saw covered his flaming robe with spots of perfect blackness ; he found temples where loud prayers were offered ; pews, cushioned, and gilded pulpits, where pride, and lust, and Mammon engulphed the preacher and the worshippers ; prayers went up to proclaim in the ear of God that the people were thankful for all their Christian privileges. And the angel saw whole streets given up to debauchery, where tobacco and rum, mixed with music and the discordant yellings of the revellers, made night hideous ; the dagger, the slung-shot and the pistol were often found on the persons of young American men ; woe-stricken wretches were idle in the streets, or quivering with white lips at the door of the public *soup-houses.* Plenty of outward piety, and high-priced prayers—while lust and sin overflowed the whole city. Plenty of men and women with bodies richly dressed and with souls like ice ; law and the police leagued with robbery and crime, and the proud judge polluting his office by receiving bribes from harlots and thieves.

As the angel wiped the dust from his feet, and passed from the city, he said, " This outward wrong indicates a rot in the soul, and I see plainly that God will soon gather that city to the place where he keeps cinders and ashes." As he passed from the city, he met a female child, hastening along the street, with a little bag under its tiny arm. It had on no shoes, its head was bare and its thin face was pale. The messenger stopped to kiss it ; but the child said, " Please, beautiful stranger, don't stop me ; I must go home ; my mother is starving in a garret, and this meal in the shot bag is to feed her, and this bit of coal is to warm her. We had no fire, and I took it from the coal heap as I passed ; it is only a little piece, and mother was so cold! so please, beautiful stranger, don't send me to the watch-house, mother will die and freeze if you do."

The angel blessed the child, and told it to hasten to save its mother ; and as he passed from the city, he dropped a tear on the grass that burned to blackness ; and as he went on, he met two other angels, coming to curse the city where children stole to keep their mothers from dying.

I awoke in deep despair ; my soul was very sorrowful. What marvel, thought I, that the starving child, who walked alone over the cold earth by the frosty starlight to get a doctor for her dying mother, should ask if the good folks in heaven kept " public soup-houses " where all the poor could have enough to eat? The story of my patient had chilled me to the bone ; and I sat speechless for some time on the bedside.

The sun was shining cheerfully when I crossed the yard for my faithful pony, and I soon made the few calls my limited practice required, when I again sought the humble cottage of my patient. I had bought a few comforts at the country store, and found my angel wife—ever faithful, and now gone to her reward—at her post by the bedside. She had been weeping over the little Julia, who slumbered sweetly by her mother's side. She, too, slept.

Both awoke shortly after my entrance, and I took my wife's station at the bedside, while she went into the only other apartment of the little cottage, to prepare some tea and a little toast for the poor sufferer ; she closed the door, to render her as free from the annoyance of noise as possible, and to allow her to make what communications were necessary to me ; the child remained near her mother, from whom she would not allow herself to be separated scarcely a moment.

Gazing tenderly upon her little face, the mother closed her eyes and murmured a few words of prayer, and then addressed me as calmly as though in health. "Doctor, you know all of my history that is of consequence, except what relates to my dear child. I have penned a few directions for one of her aunts, who will doubtless discharge the trust I bequeath to her. Would to God I could lighten the pecuniary part of it, but that is impossible ; these few memorials of better days are all that are left to me. I beg you will appropriate what remains after this poor body shall be disposed of, to some use in your little home, and think kindly of the former possessor. This ring I would urge upon you had not your kindness already refused it, and reminded me that it will soon be the only sacred link between the dead parents and the living child. It was the gift of my dear husband on my bridal day ; my father put it on my finger as he gave me away. Other costly gems sparkled in my hair, but they were appropriated to a better use ; thank God! they were left to find comforts for my dear husband and bread for our child, before I had learned the sacred duty of labor. Your kindness has brought you here, as I learn it ever does at the summons of the wretched ; I shall need no medicine, the lamp is exhausted ; the flame even now flickers ; in a little while I shall go hence."

She had wearied herself by the exertion of speaking, and dozed ; I went into the little kitchen to consult with my wife upon our future efforts. I kept my eye occasionally on the face of my patient, and had withdrawn it but for a moment, when I saw her move convulsively ; I ran to her, and she asked distinctly for water ; she swallowed a little, and thanked me, even gracefully, so quiet was she ; she closed her eyes, and her pulse fell rapidly. Suddenly she drew her child to her breast, and calmly uttered, "To God and you I leave her!" My wife was instantly at her side. I turned my eyes towards her face ; it was placid as heaven ; the spirit of the good and beautiful had fled to the home of the immortals.

SCENES IN CITY PRACTICE.

AFTER the removal from my neighborhood of the lovely Mrs. Mackerel, and when Mr. Mackerel's check for $150 had been cashed, and the dear child had been enjoying the waters of Saratoga for more than a week, I relapsed into a very miserable condition. Mrs. Tip Tape, although she expressed herself most graciously on my surgical merits after the conclusion of my attendance on Master Tip Tape's bumped nose, was neither as amiable nor as beautiful as Mrs. Mackerel ; besides, she had an ugly hand and clubbed fingers, and used depilatory powder for them and her forehead, for she was an amateur phrenologist, and kept a bust regularly mapped out. I could not bear to feel her pulse, which she was very fond of requesting me to do ; she wore a number of diamond rings and very rich lace, in such profusion that I used to be obliged to hunt for her pulse like a chicken under its mother's wing, and I always felt the pin-feathers. Moreover, she ate onions or garlic, and had a horrid habit of applying her tongue to her teeth, and that used

3

to put me in a passion, which I had hard work to conceal. My feelings were rather tender when I thought of
dear Mrs. Mackerel, and I was rejoiced when the nose
resumed its natural dimensions, and Master Tip Tape
saluted me with a kick in return to my kind inquiry
touching its condition. He was a wretched little whelp,
and horribly spoiled by his dam ; the nose, at best, looked
like a piece of putty with a couple of key-holes in it ; and
it did me good to remark before a roguish young lady,
that the little pup was rather pug-nasi-ous. The mother
did not understand it, but the pun was subsequently
retailed to my loss, by the young lady. Mrs. Tip Tape
could never endure the sight of my old wind-dried gig,
and was particularly scandalized when I persisted in carrying home a beef-steak or a pair of chickens passing her
" splendid " residence, and giving her a profound saluta-
tion on purpose, as I had also done to plague the lovely
Mrs. Mackerel.

I had an instinctive feeling that the wealthier ranks of
my commercial neighbors would never tolerate my plain
habits and manners, nor my direct utterance. I was of
Quaker notions, and had offended the parson because I
could not conscientiously pay pew rent, neither could I
afford it ; I despised ornaments and black clothes ; my
horse was coarse and ugly, and my gig old ; I would
carry home my own marketing, because my two servants
were otherwise employed, as my wife was an invalid.
Some called me a murderer, because I was suspected of
practicing dissection, and had my office full of anatomical
preparations, and two grinning skeletons ; others said I
had bought them and kept them as a decoy. I snapped
my fingers at them all, and made myself as democratic as
possible among the vulgarians, and resolved to get my
living from them. But I soon found, however, that for-

mality of dress, and above all, the display of vulgar
jewelry on the person, and brass on the carriage and
harness, was the chief means by which these poor people
judged of medical attainment; the presumption with
them being a very natural one, that every man would
procure such evidences of wealth if he had the money,
and he would assuredly possess that, if the wealthy employed him. Moreover, I found that sympathy and
attention were lost upon most of them. If I showed
extra attention, it was imputed either to misgivings of
my ability to manage the case, or a desire to make higher
charges; and if I was kind and social, there was no use
in making any effort to collect my bills. Medicine was
cheap, and it was my duty as a philanthropist to attend
to the poor; but the great fault was, I attempted to
teach them how to avoid disease by regulating their
dress and selecting their food; I condemned tobacco and
liquor, and gave little medicine. I was fond of flowers,
and would gather them from the hedges when I rode out
of town. In short, they got the notion that my head was
full of crotchets, and that I was a very eccentric person.
This furnished my professional brethren with a capital
wet blanket with which to cover up my character behind
my back, and I am ashamed to say they were not slow
in using it. One, since distinguished for the cure of
cholera, and the receipt of imaginary silver pitchers, in
an especial manner distinguished himself; he got so far
in his slander, that I was fain to send a man of the law to
stop his mouth; he apologized in a most abject manner,
and for some time I heard no more of his villainy.

Thus matters went on for some years. My friends
called on me whenever they wanted a dinner, or some
one to bore with their dullness and selfishness; now and
then they honored me by asking advice; but I was too

wise for that ; where I could get no money, I was resolved not to be paid in slander. True, I was obliged to
listen to the praises of some tyro who had not yet shed
his surgical pin-feathers, and to hear my own want of
confidence (meaning my skill) and my modesty (meaning
my knowledge of their own meanness) deprecated by these
people ; but it was cheaper to give them meat, and bread
and butter, and to allow them to bore me, and abuse me
behind my back, than to incur their patronage and their
fidgets. Mean people are always excessively troublesome, and continually asking the surgeon they intend
to cheat, "If he had ever seen or heard such a case
before?" as if the phials of wrath had been opened on
their especial heads, and nature had created their organism especially to torment themselves and their surgeons.

There is evidently always on hand a large class of people, that were no doubt manufactured expressly to train
young physicians in patience, and to punish old ones for
their sins ; many of the former are such conceited fools,
and of the latter, some are such knowing old scamps, that
they would derange the best regulations of Old Nick, and
completely subvert his discipline ; they ought in justice
to him to receive their reward here.

I found the Irish women the most awful scourge ; to
please them was impossible ; and to cure them in their
filthy abodes next to impossible. The only way to get
your obstetric fee, was to take it in advance. The mercantile rule of " cash on delivery," would never answer.
The commodity delivered was worse than useless to the
surgeon, and Patrick could never get the cash out of his
pocket when the "ould woman was aisy." I have had
them come at midnight to my door-bell, and swear by all
the Saints they had not a penny, and no sooner had I
crawled into my bed, than they would be there, money

in hand, begging me to come for the love of the Holy Virgin.

About this time it was that I learned the method of making most enduring enemies out of my best professional friends. I had been indebted to a young physician for frequent friendly visits and offers of aid in my operations, and in my natural trustfulness received him as a friend. A violent case of illness existed at this time in my family ; it was of such a character as almost to preclude hope, and the despair attendant on it, and my natural disinclination for display, made me indifferent to professional formalities, and I was pleased and encouraged by his assurances of a recovery. I invited my friend to witness a surgical operation of some consequence to my reputation, and when I arrived at the house of the patient, whither several of my professional friends had preceded me, I proceeded to my duties in such an informal manner, and with such seeming indifference to all surgical custom, that I found my friend was greatly annoyed ; for he had assumed all the dignity of the consulting surgeon. I always had a spice of fun in me, and when I saw him imitating in every movement his eccentric preceptor, I gave a triplet to his double, in a very diverting manner, and, as I was subsequently told, greatly to his chagrin. On requesting him to tie an artery, I saw he was provided with his tools, and had probably calculated . to be invited to perform the operation, though I knew he had never attempted one ; he affected to be greatly shocked at my carelessness, and tried to frighten me and make me "lose my head," as surgeons say, but I laughed and joked at him so, that he was quite scandalized at the cheapness at which I held his dignity. Poor fellow! like Don Quixote watching his rusty armor all night on the cistern top in the inn-keeper's yard, he has been at the same occupation for twenty-five years, and a terrible hard time he's had on't ; it has now become so rusty that it scarcely serves the purpose of a scare-crow.

I had occasionally, however, some capital opportunities to study character amongst my magnificent friends. Mrs. Tip Tape still nodded distantly to me in the by-streets, and now and then I was sent for by other distingué personages. One morning, very early, a carriage drove rapidly to my door, and a liveried footman rang furiously my modest door-bell. I was summoned to visit instantly a lady whose fame had reached me as the possessor of boundless wealth and a dazzling establishment at a near village. My fame as a physician to one of the public charities had reached her, but it was deemed prudent by the liveried footman to check my aspirations by inform- ing me that "the family physician was out of town." I took my seat in the gaudy vehicle, and was whirled away without my breakfast at a furious rate. I tried to stiffen my cervical vertebræ like my ambitious brethren, and prayed to Heaven for a white stock and a black suit. I think if I had been thus adorned, I should have tried the professional plan for once in my life, for I began to be a little frightened at the showings up of my cash book, and I was really afraid my old gig would fall to pieces. I had consulted the carriage-maker about the . possibility of repairing it, but he cooled my hopes, by assuring me that he could do nothing more than put a hoop about it. I looked forth upon the lovely landscape, and wished for my little queen to enjoy it with me. I had no hope of a fee, for such aspirations are not wise in the young physician when sent for by his rich commer- cial neighbors in New York ; the honor of the call is deemed quite sufficient for a year's interest of the mon- ey, if not for the liquidation of the debt ; he usually receives the interest, however, in scandal, should his necessities compel him to send for the fee at the end of the year.

On my arrival, I was ushered into the gaudy parlor, where every color vied with each other for the mastery. Two china mandarins grinned at two stacks of artificial flowers on the mantel-shelf, and red and blue books were piled on the centre-table. I sat still, and shut my eyes to avoid amaurosis, for I began to think myself a piece of colored glass in a kaleidoscope, and her ladyship turning it round and staring at me through t'other end. Her shrieks now reached me from above stairs, and a message commanded my instant presence. I found her lying on a gorgeous-colored bed, with the richest kind of satin coverings, and every particle of the wood that sustained the huge load, was painted and carved and gilded most elaborately in white, blue and gold. She was enveloped in a mass of lace, and throat, ears, arms and fingers were resplendent with jewels of every hue, from the diamond to the ruby. The lady must have weighed at least a couple of hundred, and her features were individually of marked similarity ; every one of them would have made a very fair representative of the other, and their remarkably florid hue made them collectively like the setting sun in a dry August. My boots creaked, and gave timely notice as I commenced my ascent on the oaken stair-way ; her ladyship gave a shriek, and I distinctly heard the exclamation, "Oh! the Douglas, the Douglas!—to think that the blood of the Douglas should come to this—to this—to this." I knew that there were some wild sprigs of fashion in her family, and at once scented the whole affair. A forbidden matrimonial alliance, thought I : and who the devil is the Douglas? We shall see.

I approached the bedside with profound interest in

every lineament. I was most impressively professional ;
I gazed with studied interest upon the radiant countenance.   Heaven and earth! what a contrast to the divine
Mrs. Mackerel was now before me! and yet both were
gotten up in the most approved style of either end of the
upholsterer's scale for enticing the fashionable devotee to
commercial grandeur.   My patient had the good taste to
make everything harmonize with her person ; the *tout
ensemble* was unique.

The external arrangements, scenes, drapery, etc., were
all of admirable getting up ; but the pathology was not
so fine ; it did not work at all to advantage.   In the first
place, the choking was not well done ; it was nothing
more than a vulgar gulp ; it came so natural, however,
that I began to think that physiological and spiritual exercise had something to do with the attack, and that
some powerful internal aid had helped along the other
diagnostic, viz., the evidently studied exclamation, "Oh!
the Douglas, the Douglas!—to think that the blood of
the Douglas should come to this—to this—to this!" and
then a powerful gulp with a badly done convulsive shudder.   I was a mere chicken, to be sure—a gosling, if you
please ; but I was not to be gammoned by such a con-
trivance.   I saw the lady watching me, evidently enough,
through her trembling eye-lids ; I was used to that, and
looked as though the tears were about to start at her
distress ; but oh! my fond heart, such a contrast to the
lovely Mrs. Mackerel!   Alas! those silken fringes resting
on Parian marble—the drapery of the stars before the
windows of the soul, soothing the o'erburdened spirit ;
angels' wings, fanning the lovely creature to repose after
the disappointment of the new carriage! and shutting
out the hateful tobacco-chewing Mackerel ; and the lovely
and exquisitely jeweled hand, as it lay like a dear little

dead dove on the lace counterpane! Alas! alas! such a contrast! Do not think me unkind, dear reader ; but what do you think I did to confirm my diagnosis ? I am afraid to tell you, but truth and my professional character obligo me to say it ; though I confess to you I would not speak the word if I was in the way of attending hysterical ladies, from which, thank God, I have been excused, since I attained my hundred and fourth year. Well, then, if I must confess it, I must. I applied my nose near enough to catch her ladyship's breath, and to efface the odor of Patchouli, which was intended to deceive me. I became as strong as a giant in scientific diagnosis. I would have bearded Hippocrates or Dr. Francis. The lady was overcome with excitement from too highly charged—spirits! I sat down by the bedside, and most learnedly tried to feel the pulse ; it was concealed in fat like a squab pigeon. My temper was tried severely by the persistent silence of the patient, and I resolved to open her mouth by operating on the stomach. I pretended to give her a restorative, but slily put in four grains of tartar emetic. This I was confident would cool the memory of the Douglas, and bring my lady out of her tantrum, and let me go home. I fed her a tablespoonful every fifteen minutes, in rose-water, and talked soothingly occasionally about her to the nurse, who was a pretty black-eyed girl, and looked particulary *au fait* at the scene ; showing by her conduct that it was an old story. On the fourth dose, the deep began to be troubled, and I called for a basin. The surge began to heave ; a copious ejection of miscellaneous ingesta occurred ; "the blood of the Douglas" was silenced. I was no, coward, reader, but I thought it prudent to avoid the reaction of her ladyship's recovery. The carriage was in waiting, and I knew what I should get when she came

3*

to, so I took my leave, with the assurance to the nurse,
that all would now go on well, and was whirled home to
my Irish patients. I subsequently learned that the
" blood of the Douglas " was a Scotch peddler, of only one
remove from a " laird," and that the cause of her ladyship's attack was the marriage of her son to the daughter
of a cotton broker ; the old Douglas, having made up
his last pack, had gone to heaven.

Such ridiculous scenes are calculated to destroy, for
a time, our finer sensibilities ; but I bless God that I
never remember the time, when my heart was steeled to
that resistless pity the true physician should ever feel for
the innocent and defenceless. I know not the man in my
profession, and God forbid I should ever meet him, who
has lost his sympathy for the victim of disappointed love.
Oh ! how the heart will sometimes reply to some rapid
utterance of the poor maniac, when in one little sentence,
incoherently uttered, she tells the story of that grief that
has marked each sad hour on the dial-plate of memory,
and turned away the smile from her face and the light of
reason from its throne ! It was my sad chance once to
hear an expression I shall never forget, from a poor
young creature who had been deluded by a wretch into
the belief that he loved her ; she was the elder of two
daughters of a respectable professional man in this city,
and they were left, at his death, with a kind and affectionate mother and a handsome fortune ; this was the attraction to the villain. She married him, but on his discovery
that he could only realize her fortune on the attainment
of manhood by a young brother, he basely left her and
went to France : thither she pursued him, for she loved
him with all the passionate earnestness of a young heart.
She found him living in splendor with another wife,
whom he had won by the same power of persuasion that

made her his victim. By the aid of counsel she obtained a divorce which her wounded pride at the humiliating discovery of the second marriage made her covet; but her return alone to her native country overcame her reason, and we were soon obliged to place her in the Bloomingdale Asylum. On our way thither, accompanied by the kind friends to whom she was attached, a flash of lightning (it was in the month of May, and a thunder storm came up) revealed a beautiful peach tree in full bloom; some of the blossoms fell into the carriage as the driver hastily turned a corner and brushed against a projecting limb. The kind lady, on whose shoulder she had rested her head during the entire ride, asked her if she did not see the beautiful blossoms: "Yes, yes," she replied, "how beautiful! but they never bloom for me." After a few years she died, but not until her sister also had become hopelessly insane.

She may now be seen in a neighboring city, basket in hand, picking chips; she speaks rapidly but kindly to all who address her, and is allowed to wander about unguarded, for she is perfectly harmless and makes no attempt to injure herself. She often speaks of her sister, and always with the most exalted reverence, calling her a queen, and says she "sits on her throne up yonder," pointing to the clouds. Exaltation of fancy is, I believe, the usual accompaniment of the insanity of the wealthy. The humble occupation she has herself chosen, is her fancied duty as a punishment for her pride, for she had the religious element largely in action during her early youth.

Thus it was from day to day, that I was gaining the lesson that in every phase and position in life, there is some blight that obscures and puts out the young heart's impulse to love and honor our fellow-man; and when the stormy period comes, and we can look back upon an experience of more than half the life allotted to us, it will be well for us if pity remains, and contempt for the follies of our fellow-creatures does not usurp the control of our lives, and obscure all our finer sensibilities.

VILLAGE PRACTICE.

SKETCHES OF VILLAGE PRACTICE—SABBATH IN THE COUNTRY—MY FIRST CASE:
A MALADY OF MIND AND BODY.

> "It is not all of life to live,
> Nor all of death to die."

SABBATH in the country! The serene, peaceful Sabbath; the time of rest, God-given to man, for purification and prayer! In the city the day never seems so truly good, so infinitely holy as in the country. The sweet sound of distant village bells; the sight of cattle released from labor, browsing in contented herds in the quiet of green fields; the very chirp of the countless insects, and the innocent song of the myriad of birds, all breathe of a Sabbath morality, which in great cities is lost entirely. The noise of active life ceases; naught meets the ear but the lingering echoes of those calm church-bells, as they float on the unadulterated, healthful air, to the distant farm-houses.

"God made the country, man made the town." It is not unnatural to suppose that a greater blessing rests with the Divine work than with that of mere, however glorious, art.

I had been a resident of M—— some three or four weeks, but had been detained from attending church each

Sabbath by violent storms ; and, to confess the truth, I did not regret this as much as I should, from the fact that I dreaded my first meeting, as their sole and newly-established physician, with the wealthy and aristocratic inhabitants of that pretentious village. I shrank nervously from the unavoidable introductions, and the criticism which I knew must as inevitably follow. However, one morning I was bereft of my excuse of bad weather, and awakened betimes to find the day most obstinately clear. There was not a cloud in the heavens that I could reasonably persuade myself was the signal of coming rain ; therefore to church we went, my wife and I—she all aglow with expectation, and looking, as I thought, unusually charming in her pink ribbons, and I (I acknowledge it candidly) somewhat oppressed with an indefinable sense of doubt and dismay.

It was a small, fantastically designed building, of an antique style of architecture, that would have puzzled the wisest to determine ; yet it was striking, artistic, and displayed decided and refreshing originality. Ivy and other vines crept in thick masses over the roughly-hewn stone walls, and darkened, with their close embrace, the low, arched windows. Internally everything was plain and simple, as all houses of true worship are, yet there was not wanting a certain air of quiet elegance. The pulpit was strongly indicative of classical simplicity in its form, and had few adornments ; opposite it, at the other extremity of the church, was a small, veiled gallery, containing an organ and accommodations for a choir of singers.

We were early. I seated myself quietly, and having nothing to occupy my thoughts, half unconsciously I watched the entrance, one by one, of the villagers. Among them I saw a face, which, as I beheld it then, has

haunted me for years. It was that of a man in the prime
of his life, handsome, well bred, and intelligent, but so
inexpressibly sad, so indicative of evident stagnation and
despairing dissatisfaction, that I turned away in sorrow
that anything made by God should carry a countenance
like that.

The services began with slow, sonorous notes of prelude
from the mellow-toned organ. Throughout the aisles of
the little, antique church, up to the very rafters, floated
that rare, sobbing music, penetrating all hearts, sensitive
either to good or evil, with that delicate sorrow which
Longfellow says "is not akin to pain." It faded as the
burden changed from sadness to jubilant hope, and ended
in sudden *staccato* chords of triumphant joy. All eyes
were then turned towards the pulpit, and all heads
reverently bowed, as the minister, an aged man, arose
and uttered a brief and impressive prayer. It was one of
the most solemn appeals to which I ever listened. Its
beauty lay in its naturalness, undefiled, as it was, by the
arts of showy rhetoric. It seemed to pass from the venerable clergyman's lips up to heaven, as the sincerest language in which man could address and adore his Creator.
By contrast, the cold brilliancy of the sermon that followed
lost all effect ; it could not touch me like that simple,
honest supplication for Divine mercy. All the after services of the day were nothing to me ; I had poured out my
whole soul with that prayer, and had no further power
or desire to worship. I was satisfied.

I discerned no lack of eloquence or ministerial learning
in that aged divine's exhortation, and although, as we left
the church, I heard many speak of it with expressions of
lively pleasure, I felt assured that he himself was discontented with the discourse. It was like thin, fitful sunlight,
veiling a lowering December sky ; or, like snow, blinding

the eyes with glitter, yet in its actual self, very cold and
unsubstantial.   I perceived that there was that beneath
all this sparkle of words, which few present understood.
Was it private grief?   Was it some hidden agony warring
against unnatural restraint?   I recognized the evidences
of insincerity, but whether temporary or habitual, I could
not discover.   When he had ceased, I felt merely the
silence ; there was none of that strange sensation at the
conclusion of impassioned and earnest delivery which
I had experienced often before.

" Certainly," thought I, " that man is either very heartless or very miserable."

The congregation was passing quietly out, when, in
the usual organ voluntary, came an abrupt but slight
pause, followed by deep stillness.   Immediately a human voice, a full and rare man's voice, commenced
chanting that celebrated solo from Felix Mendels-
sohn Bartholdy's "Messiah" "I know that my Redeemer liveth."   Perfectly in time and tune, although,
with no further accompaniment than the few opening
chords, the voice issued from the choir, bearing to world-
weary listeners consolation and peace.   It was not the
noble words, nor yet the nobler music, it was the *expression* gathered by that fine voice from the two, uniting in
one glorious whole, till the very atmosphere seemed to
thrill with its wealth of melody.   On the last notes of the
solo, as it faded magnificently into silence, the organ's accompaniment recommenced, proving, by the purest unity
of the two sounds, the successful intonation of the unknown vocalist.   Many curious eyes were directed towards the gallery, but the curtains were tightly drawn,
and the mystery still remained mysterious.   Some casual
movement, however, momentarily displaced a portion of
the floating screen, and revealed to me a glimpse of the

dark, handsome face I had before noticed ; and it was no
less dark, handsome, or discontented, than when I beheld
it then.   I asked myself in wonder, if that soulful singing, and that morose, unhappy·countenance, belonged to
one and the same individual.

The close of this Sabbath day was destined to reveal to
me a strange fragment of the life-history of this very man.

The night fell, dewy and starry, but with an oppressive-
ness of atmosphere that was not, in that part of the country, an uncommon consequence of the long absence of rain.
The ground was almost destitute of moisture, and the
grass of that vivid green, so delightful to vision.   The
air was heavy and oppressive, the very stars seemed
to blink with the universal drowsiness.   We were just
seated at our plainly furnished tea-table, when there came
a startling peal from the little primitive knocker on the
hall door.

"A visitor," said my wife, settling her cap.

"A patient," said I, rushing from the room, just in time
to upset a black boy who ran violently against me.   Alternately rubbing his bruised sides, and grinning from ear
to ear at the adventure, he informed me that "massa was
took sick in a great hurry," and then scampered off, having·
first pointed out a large and conspicuous house, quite near
to my own, as the residence of the sick man.   I had often
before noticed it for the elaborate arrangement of its extensive gardens.

In a few moments I was in the chamber of the first patient to whom I had been called during my residence in
M——.   The room was large and brilliantly lighted ; bou-
quets of delicate flowers were scattered over it—evidently,
illness had been totally unlooked for by the master of the
dwelling.   As I entered, the face of my patient was hidden from me by the pillows in which it was buried.   The

wife, a young, slight thing, half sat, half reclined beside him, her head bowed on her bosom, her pale hands tightly locked one in the other. She raised her eyes as I entered, and on seeing me, a sudden gleam of something which, if it were not hope, had all its beauty, passed over her features.

"Doctor!" she cried wildly, advancing to meet me, "Doctor, save him—save him!"

Before I had time to answer, a voice from the other side of the bed uttered in a low, but self-possessed tone :

"It is too late!"

Glancing quickly that way, I saw the grey-haired minister. On his hands were great red spots of blood ; the pillows, the sheets were marked with it ; and on the white dress of the young wife glittered also fresh crimson stains.

"He is dying," said the old man, reverently kneeling at the bedside ; "human aid is of little consequence now. Again I say, it is too late. Abner, my son, my boy, do you hear me?—you are dying!"

I approached the bed, and as I did so, the sick man raised his head, and I saw before me the beautiful, despairing face of the morning. The eyes were closed, and deeply sunken in their sockets, while the heavy masses of hair and beard gave the ghastly complexion a still more unearthly hue. He had ruptured a bloodvessel. At a glance I saw that the case was hopeless, and that the little I could do, were almost as well undone. Life was ebbing fast—mortality verging into immortality. I caused his face to be bathed, and the clotted blood washed from his nostrils and beard—that was all.

Meanwhile the old man sat there on the bed's edge,

clasping one of those colorless hands in his own. He kissed the almost lifeless forehead, he bent over that dying man with the anxiety which none but a father could feel at such a moment.

"Abner, Abner," he whispered, "do you—can you hear me? If you can, for God's sake give me some signal!"

The eyes opened, assuming a dull, dreamy look, closed wearily, and opened again very slowly.

A low wail burst from the wife. The old clergyman turned upon her quickly, and said, with bitter imperiousness :

" Be still, I *must* speak with him." Then bending again over the bed :

" Abner, have you thought of DEATH ? Shall we pray —have you made peace with God?"

There appeared to be a sort of convulsive effort on the sick man's part to attain a sitting posture. For a moment he seemed possessed of perfect consciousness.

" God!" he echoed hoarsely ; " father, how *dare* you name him! God! You, who made me what I am ; you, who goaded me to sin, and all for money, money! Was it so precious to you that I must sell myself, body and soul, *marry* for it? Don't speak to *me* of God. There is none—no God—no God!"

He sank back on his pillows exhausted. Blood burst anew from his mouth. He tried to say more, but the words were drowned in the warm tide that bubbled over his chest. And she, the wife, stood there in marble calmness and heard that which was to blast the rest of her young life. Her hands were clasped again, her eyes fixed unflinchingly on the floor. She neither moved nor spoke. Looking at her, you would have felt your very

heart melt with compassion, so wild, so forlornly miserable was the expression of that sweet, girlish face.

"Abner, Abner, my son," was all the father spoke with
his blanched, quivering lips.

The momentary flush faded from the sick man's features. I stood by him and wiped the blood from his
mouth, and I knew that in a few moments all would be
over. There was no struggle, but there was that gathering
shadow on his forehead which is so terribly understanda-
ble. Seeing this, the intense despair on his wife's face
grew, and her hands locked themselves involuntarily
tighter, till blood stained the smooth palm that came
in contact with the finger-nails. Not a word was spoken, not a sound broke the deep stillness of the chamber, but the indistinct and oppressive breathing of the
dying man. I thought it grew fainter and slower, and I
bent down to place my finger on the wrist, and to listen
more intently ; but the old man waved me fiercely,
jealously away.

"Touch him not," he said, "for he is dead !"

And I thought, indeed, that it was so ; for even as he
spoke, the faint respiration suddenly ceased, and the
pallor of an everlasting unconsciousness crept slowly
over the still features. But in another moment, I saw
that life was not yet extinct. The eyes again partly
unclosed in the same powerless, dreamy way as before,
and an indescribable radiance for an instant lit up the
pale, handsome face—handsome even then, but with an
unearthly beauty.

"God !" the colorless lips muttered, "God—there is a
God !" and a smile, whose serenity I have never seen
equalled, flickered around the mouth. Then the shadow
deepened, and he expired. It seemed as though the
soul had been half freed, and, returning, gave evi-

dence of that eternity which it but partially had entered!

A woman's voice, sobbing, at last broke the dreary silence.

The old man rose, and approaching his dead son's wife, said feebly :

"Esther, be comforted ; God is over all."

She drew her hand from his clasp with a gesture of unequivocal abhorrence.

"Comfort!" she echoed, with a great defiant flash of her black eyes ; "comfort! *you* preach to me of comfort! Hypocrite !"—she hissed the word from between her closed lips with startling, indignant energy. "It is all clear to me now. Who was it plotted and schemed to bring us together? Who tempted him into marriage where 'there was no love on his side—none, none, oh my God—but for money? Answer me *that.*"

Her dark hair had become disentangled of its fastening, and now fell, in wild, confused grace, over her bare shoulders. Her white, upraised arms glittered in the bright light of the lamps, the scarlet ornaments floated from the sleeves, falling over them in vivid contrast. Never shall I forget the impression created by that indignant appeal, and the tragic, excited beauty of that injured woman. All this was many years ago, yet I never recall that Sabbath night without a shudder. Frequent as are terrible or touching scenes in the life of a physician, I remember none that own power so to unman me as the memory of that. And the sequel was no less sad. Within a year another grave was made for the poor, deceived wife. On the death of her husband, she sank into a stupor from which nothing could arouse her, and which terminated at last in rapid consumption. It is strange that I should recollect so well the day she died. It is as new in my mind as yesterday. White, freshly-fallen snow lay on the ground. It had come early that year, and many leaves were still hanging crimsoned on their boughs. The trees were loaded with light fleecy fragments of snow, among which these brilliantly-dyed leaves gleamed out in the sunshine like blood on a woman's fair face.

INFIDELITY OF MEDICAL MEN.

INSTINCTIVE IDEAS OF CREATIVE POWER—THE RED GLOBULES OF THE BLOOD
—WHEN AND HOW FORMED—EARLY SUBSTITUTE FOR LUNGS IN THE CHICK—
USES OF THE RED AND WHITE GLOBULES—WHAT IS THE LIFE CELL?

"Spirit of Love and Beauty, of Order, Justice and Truth—Great Law-giver and Soul of the Universe—God: grant me, I beseech thee, a knowledge of thy will."

WHILST the Persian bows his face in silent adoration towards the Sun, the Mohammedan reverently salutes the East as most acceptable to the Deity in his thank-offering, and the North American Indian addresses the same glorious Orb of light and life, as the signet of the Great Spirit who watches over the happy hunting-grounds of the departed, the Modern Theosophist, as he retails his small samples of sectarian selfishness, with a self-satisfied assurance of their superiority to those of his neighbors, and a pious upturning of the eyes and windy suspiration, gravely and self-complacently regrets the irreligion of the unfortunate disciples of Esculapius and Harvey, and whilst he hopes that "God, in his mysterious providence, will yet open the gates of Heaven to the wretched infidel," he fails not to make him the unwilling and distressed recipient of the thrice-told tale of his corporeal woes, and characteristic fear of death. Truly, the nations which we, in our vanity, call heathen, should put our quarrelsome Theologians to the blush for the sublime simplicity of their recognition of that great truth, which medical men acknowledge, not only from the same instinctive conviction, but by reason of the very nature of their pursuits.

We have again introduced our subject with a defence of our profession from the aspersions of that self-satisfied sanctity, that contents itself with a wretched formula of piety, and, like the Pharisee, in all its actions, thanks God that it is better than others. Think for one moment, reader, what feelings of indignant scorn must be excited within the breast of that man, perhaps a father— a father who has closed in death the eyes of a child—it may be an only child—a wife or mother, dear to him on earth as the hope of a reunion with them hereafter— think what feelings of contemptuous pity must be excited within his breast for the mental condition of the poor creature who asks him, as we have lately been asked by one of them,—" What have you to do with such things ? You know you don't believe a word of them." And is our moral worth and responsibility to be determined by men who cannot expand their intellectual vision beyond a pile of bricks and mortar, fifty by a hundred feet, who find their account in constant appeals to the superstitious fears of their votaries, and in quenching the earliest glimmer of intellect with the funeral pall of a benighted and sectarian theosophy ?

No man should attempt to teach the will of God, till he becomes familiar with the laws that govern, and the phenomena that accompany the earliest development of his body ; there it is written in letters of living light : obey the laws of the body and you obey the will of its Creator! Least of all, should he attempt to instruct a physician, who, by education and his daily pursuits, is brought into the closest relations with human structure and frailty, and whose aspirations for a better state, and admiration of the great leader, who has taught us how to attain it, ought not, one would think, to be diminished by the privilege of daily study of poor humanity in its multiplied afflictions; afflictions, be it noted—and we speak what all our profession know to be the truth—that none bear with less fortitude than the class we have attempted to portray through our questioner. Every man amongst us, whose moral nature is not debased in common with a bodily organism derived from ancestors who have studied no laws either mental or physical, accepts the law of Christ as the acknowledged guide to his duty on earth ; but he also reads a living volume whose first page was lighted up by that Sun that gave LIFE to the first living atom, millions on millions of years before the birth of the great law-giver, or the creature who requires his aid to enlighten him on the Divine will. But this will never answer ; we must not suffer feeling to lead us astray from instruction ; knowledge is the only remedy for bigotry and sectarianism.

Those great and unchanging principles, those ORGANIC everlasting laws, coeval with the first great mandate, "Let there be light"—must be understood by every man who would obey the law of God ; obey them and you obey the will of the CREATOR. Light and life for the body—light and life for the soul : they are written in letters of living truth upon every blade of grass, and every organism around you. The humblest mosses and their microscopic flowers of either sex, and the little violet in its grassy nest, shadow forth the first visible lessons of life in silent beauty and sweetness, from their many-colored leaves and lovely petals ; the pitcher-plants of our pastures and the African deserts, as they dispense their beneficent earth-

4

drawn draught to the little feathered wanderer of the air
and the thirsty traveler, the tiny humming-bird as he
sips the nectar from its lovely laboratory, both itself and
its contents secreted from the formless and tasteless
gases and salts of the earth, the wondrous and delicate
aphis, that elaborates from its vegetable nutriment the
honey dew for the bee and the ant, and carries, so subtle
is the life-force, three generations of the life germ within
its tiny body—all speak to thee with their "many tongues,
and open wide their pages for thy soul to read." All
speak the laws of life and love ; attraction—secretion—
elaboration—birth—change ; there *is* no death!

> "Life never dies ;—but verging at its ease,
> From sire to son through Nature's vast decrees.
> Its destiny to fill, the body falls."

The spark that animated it returns to the great source.
In letters engraved by Creative Power, as unchangea-
ble as the mighty source, we read—"The life-force of
every living creature is proportioned to its producers."
It will be quite useless to attempt to read this article un-
derstandingly, without a reference to the great nutritious
and formative material of the blood, ALBUMEN. This is the
great starting point, whether we are contemplating the
nourishment of our bodies by our daily food, the chick in
the egg of the bird, or reptile, the human germ of the
female, or the male—all start with albumen as their
basis. This substance, in connection with fat—which
the reader will remember, can never become a *living* part
of a tissue, but is only distributed throughout the body
to be absorbed and burnt in the lungs during starvation and sickness—forms every animal tissue, or membrane. Gum held in solution in the watery parts of the
sap, and thus circulating through the plant, is the basis

of all the soft vegetable tissues ; whilst LIGNIN, or woody
fibre, forms the wooden skeleton of the tree, as Phosphate
of Lime does our bones.   This albumen is held in solution, or rendered liquid and capable of absorption and
conveyance through the arteries and veins of the body to
its various parts, by the water or *serum* of the blood,
which, as we have said, constitutes full three-fourths of
the body.

Albumen, is the *first appearance* of the blood, without
its red particles ; of course it precedes the formation of
the bodily organs, as they are all formed from it.   The
egg of the bird is a perfect example of its use, in the
grand role of nature.

The first evidence of organic life in all animated beings,
as revealed by the microscope, consists of a single sac or
cell, precisely like a little vesicle, inclosed in the centre
of the egg ; this has the power of attracting to it the
albumen of the egg, which furnishes the material for the
formation of other cells growing from it, and assuming,
during gestation or incubation, such forms as were intended, when the Almighty first created the type of its
peculiar genus.

The first cell impressed by Creative Power, leaves the
organism of the male during the sexual union, and meets
the ovum that issues from the ovarium or egg-bed of the
female in the womb.   That mysterious agent, that spark
from the undiminished SOURCE OF LIFE—gives the life-
power to the ovum *before* it passes through its appropriate duct into the womb, or if the egg of the bird, into its
" oviduct," whence it is to issue from the body ; unitedly
the double germ acquires power to attract albumen from
the blood of the mother, or the egg, and thus to form the
living creature.   This is the starting point of animal
organization ; the cell growth of the physiologist.   The

minutest of the vegetable fungi, or the mosses, the butterfly, and the elephant, are alike indebted to it for their
growth.

The first visible evidence of life in the egg, occurs at
the twenty-seventh hour, when the outlines of the heart
are apparent ; it is thus early formed entirely of albumen or white blood, and it is sufficient in its power of
contraction for the circulation within the egg. As soon
as the fœtus, or chick, breathes the outer or atmospheric
air, the blood becomes far more stimulating : it is fibrin-
ized and imparts greater powers of contraction to the
heart, and all other muscles. The heart is extremely
simple in form, being a mere dilated bulbous blood-ves-
sel ; receiving the rudiments of its veins behind, and
sending off arteries on its front surface ; soon it appears
divided into three cavities ; the fourth one, intended to
fit it for propelling the blood through the lungs, is not
yet perfected, but it is reserved for a more advanced state
of the organism, viz., when the lungs are used. The
heart, during the earlier weeks, is like that of a fish or
oyster—the simplest form, and quite insufficient for a
breathing animal.

The central living and life-creating germ, attracts to
itself and appropriates to the formation of the intended
being, first the albumen of the yolk and its oil, gradually
approaching the yolk sac, and then the colorless albumen
that surrounds the egg, or what is commonly called the
white. In the egg of the bird, when this store of material is exhausted, the chick is complete ; in the human
ovum, the microscopic smallness of the quantity of albumen in the germ, proves the necessity of its speedy
connection by blood vessels with the womb. The mother's
blood is the material that forms the new creature. This
is effected by the life or blood-attracting membrane lining

that organ, and the corresponding rough envelope of the minute ovum ; they interlock their fibres, which soon become elongated, and assume the number of two arteries and a vein, between the uterus and the child. All these appendages are deciduous in all the mammalia, and are thrown off when the product assumes independent life. They form the placenta, or after-birth.

We will now speak of the red globules, or that part of the blood which causes the red color ; these globules serve an admirable purpose in tracing the formation of the blood vessels in the egg, and one much more intelligible to the learner, because of their color rendering them visible ; we must remember, however, that the heart is earliest formed by white blood, *i. e.* fibrine and albumen, and is quite visible before the red globules exist.

But how, says the reader, does the blood become red within the egg-shell? No such color is visible in the recently opened fresh egg ; nor is there ; because the life power, *i. e.* the *attractive* power, has not yet been lighted up ; warmth will soon show its power to fan the latent spark of life. Air is doubtless the cause of the redness ; we reason from its action on the purple blood of the veins going through the lungs in the adult animal ; air, it is proved, gives the blood its arterial red hue, so unlike that of the veins which bring no other than dark colored blood *to* the heart. The air undoubtedly passes through the pores of the egg-shell. Fortunately the origin of the red globules themselves, is partially known.

Remember now, we are still confining our observations to the earliest appearance of life, in the egg during incubation ; consequently we cannot refer to food as their origin, for the chick is not yet formed ; nor can it get any other food than the albumen, even when it has become so large as to be moving briskly within the egg ;

therefore the red globules are formed from that substance
alone, and air, for they are to be distinctly seen by the
third day ; and what will strike the general reader with
amazement is the fact alluded to in our last, that they
first appear in little patches having no visible connection
whatever with each other, nor yet with the little white
heart which is already distinctly formed by the fibrine
and albumen of the egg ; it is white because it has as yet
received no red blood.

These little red islands of living blood stretch out their
radiating vessels like the roots of a tree, towards the
heart, and towards each other ; and by the fifth day we
have before us, when we open the egg, a distinctly formed
and pulsating heart, with two large branches and a great
net-work of blood vessels, spreading around and com-
plely enveloping the yolk of the egg.

The first rudiments of the heart appear, as we have
already said, by the twenty-seventh hour. The reader
may possibly remember that the heart has been said to
be in its earliest form like that of a fish. This is true in a
degree ; before they breathe the air of the outer world,
both the chick and the human embryo have no occasion
for the two additional chambers necessary for the circulation of the blood through the lungs. These, as we shall
see hereafter, are more gradually developed and not fit
for their office until the chick or infant can receive the
air in the lungs.

The blood vessels are exceedingly simple in their
arrangement in this single heart ; this wonderful organ
is at first nothing more than a tube at the upper part of
the chest, receiving its veins behind, and sending forth
its arteries before ; there is but one large artery, which
subdivides into branches as it ascends to the neck and
descends to the body. This greater artery gradually

assumes the form of a posterior chamber, called an auricle, simply because it is thought to resemble an ear; this receives the blood returning from its circuit after it has performed its duties among the net-work of vessels enveloping the heart of the chick, or throughout the body of the infant. This auricle, or entrance chamber, communicates with the ventricle, (so-called from *ventriculus*, the stomach,) and from this proceeds the great single artery which, by its subdivision, conveys the blood to the membranes enveloping the chick, and to every part of its body. But now of these membranes, what are they? It has probably already occurred to the intelligent and thoughtful reader, that as the red part of the blood derives its vivid scarlet color in the arteries from the air, and has lost it by the time it gets into the veins in its return to the heart, after performing the duties of growth in the embryo, whether of the chick or human being, there ought to be within the shell of the egg some substitute for the lungs of the perfect bird ; and so there is ; we have reserved its description for fear of complicating the subject. Do not forget, however, that the mother breathes for her child before its birth, for it is part of herself ; not so with the egg of the bird ; we have said nothing as yet of the formation of the intestines and stomach ; now it becomes necessary to allude to them, because it is a prolongation of the intestine, as it were, that nature uses in this early stage of the development of the chick as the lungs. Nothing more is necessary to fulfill all the purpose of the lungs, than the conveyance of the venous blood where it can imbibe the external air through the delicate coats of the vessels, and the pores of the egg-shell.

The lungs, it will be remembered, we have several times compared to a bunch of grapes, with the pulp or

body of the grape, and the pith of each stalk, supposed to
be removed, leaving nothing but the skin of each grape
attached to its hollow stalk ; it will be readily seen that
by blowing air into the main stalk, all the lesser ones, as
well as the skin of each grape, would be inflated with air.
Now it is around the circumference and through the
walls of the delicate linings of the myriads of air cells of
the lungs as each communicates with its little tube, and
each tube in turn with one larger and larger till all the
branches from each lung end in the wind-pipe, where the
air rushes in, that the deadly carbonic acid of the used
blood is thrown off, and the life-giving oxygen of the air
imbibed.

But now let us describe the beautiful substitute for
lungs in the chick, and admire the wonderful economy
of means always visible in Nature's works. There is
found in the embryo of birds an exceedingly delicate
membranous structure connected with the intestines ;
of course all its blood vessels come from that membranous
tract ; this subsidiary and temporary membrane is produced by the intestine. It is a delicate membrane
passing from the intestine within the embryo bird, to
the outside of the yolk bag, and completely envelopes it.
It is situated directly under the shell of the egg, and
receives the oxygen of the air through the shell. Whoever in his childish curiosity has opened a hen's egg at
the latter period of incubation, cannot fail to have seen
the great branching blood vessels spreading all over just
under the shell upon the tough, membranous bag that
holds the chick. Often has our own heart beat rapidly
as we saw the first movements of the little creature beneath it, and a sigh escaped our breast when we thought
of our diminished family of little chicks, always so delightful to the fresh and joyous heart of boyhood.

Now the reader will please to remember that this substitute for the lungs is in full play, till the chick breathes the outer air by means of its own proper and then perfectly developed lungs inside its body. Enough of air could not enter its tiny beak, even if the complicated and half-developed lung inside were perfect at the first week of incubation ; it is a great extent of surface that is wanting ; because the air can but slowly penetrate the shell, and were it not for the great surface completely enveloping the chick and in contact with the shell, enough oxygen to vitalize the blood could not be absorbed, and the chick would not grow. Other and important offices are performed by an analogous structure in quadrupeds and the human being, which we shall allude to hereafter when speaking of the bladder, with which it is intimately connected.

Quitting now for a moment the consideration of the heart and lungs, (for we shall be obliged to make their uses the subject of a second paper,) we must endeavor to trace in what manner the seemingly independent red globules become inclosed within the blood vessels and connected with the heart ; for that is the living engine that is to compel each one of them to make the entire circuit of the body every few minutes as long as life lasts. We chose in our last the expressive selection of the wool, the spun yarn and the woven cloth, to show the uses of albumen, the fibrine, and the perfectly formed membrane. And it will be recollected also that all our preceding articles on the materials of the tissues were designed to prepare the reader for the mode of their formation and their diseases.

We may here anticipate what we have to say on their uses so much as to offer a highly probable idea, that each red globule is in all probability a cell of latent life. These,

4*

when arranged in lines, as seen in the egg on the third day of incubation, resembling to the eye a continuous blood vessel, either pointing towards the heart or towards another similar red line of globules, must attract to themselves the albumen of the egg, and, like the chrysalis, weave round themselves their own arterial tube! Here we have no power but that originally impressed by the Creator when he said, "Let there be light!" The wondrous power first derived from the undiminished Soul of nature, God, is continued through the mystic chain from the first atom that ever passed from its Almighty Source. Millions on millions of years it has continued its mission—millions on millions more will His glorious signet, the LIFE-giving Sun, continue to vitalize the elements and render them to their divine Originator, an offering fit to beautify this magnificent theatre of Almighty power.

What then is this life? who is this great moulder of the elements? The only answer yet permitted us, is amply sufficient to satisfy the mind of the true philosopher. If we rightly view the continuous chain of organic life as revealed by the zoologist, we shall unquestionably find that man occupies a position "midway from nothing to the Deity."

The sublime page of physiology teaches the calm and humane student of nature, that the first organic atom the imagination can conceive, even the humblest of the masses that ever opened its leaves to the atmosphere, or the minutest of the infusoria that ever moved in the waters, not only implied the necessity of every subsequent organic being up to the oak or to proud man, but it gives him equal assurance that he little knows in what more perfect state of existence, far, far beyond his finite view, he shall approximate even on this earth the Great Source whence he derived his being.

AN UNDELIVERED AND UNORTHODOX ADDRESS.

THE THIRD ANNIVERSARY ORATION FOR THE NEW YORK ACADEMY OF MEDICINE, WHICH WAS NOT DELIVERED BEFORE THAT REMARKABLE BODY, BUT OUGHT TO HAVE BEEN, AT THEIR ANNUAL MEETING, HELD IN THE CHAPEL OF THE UNIVERSITY, NOVEMBER 14TH, 1849, BY THE PHYSICIAN WHO WAS NOT ELECTED FOR THAT OCCASION. (PUBLISHED WITHOUT THE KNOWLEDGE OR CONSENT OF THE ACADEMY.*)

LADIES AND GENTLEMEN :—The occasion of our assembling together this evening, is one of deep interest and great importance. It is the annual opportunity afforded us of reminding you of our existence, and informing you of our value. The fact of our existence is demonstrated by our appearance, *in propriis personis, in numero, et extenso.* Excuse the occasional use of the learned languages, which I may feel it requisite to resort to in the course of my address ; for when I think of our persons, our numbers, and the extent of our acquirements and influence, I confess that I am at a loss for language in my vernacular tongue, and am obliged to draw upon the resources of the noble languages of Rome and Greece.

It being an admitted fact, or as that lively and ingenious people, the French, would say, *un fait accompli,* that

---

* To "the Fellows" of the New York Academy of Medicine, who advertised themselves alphabetically in the New York Directory, as the " Medical Profession Proper," this very inadequate appreciation of their worth, and imperfect exhibition of their merits, is gratuitously prescribed by the Editor,

we have an existence,—although it is doubted by skeptics, and denied by revilers—it is my pleasing task to detail to you the inestimable blessing which we are to this City in particular,—to the Community in general, and to the World at large,—and the indisputable claims which we therefore have, to the patronage of all who can pay for medical attendance—and to the possession of the medical officers of the State.

The French Academy has filled the world with its renown, and immortalized itself by the most splendid achievements in science and learning. The United States has now an Academy, and New York has given it birth. Whence arose the science and learning of France? From the Academy! Now that New York has an Academy, science and learning, of course, will flourish here. All that she needed was an Academy—and that she now has. *Vivat Academia Novi Eboraci!*

The sober and significant silence with which you received my last remarks, gives me full assurance of your appreciation of their merits. Indeed, the entire absence of discussion or observation, relating to our merits or value—with the exception of the scurrilous portion of the press, and a bastard—I beg pardon—an unorthodox medical journal, gives us the most comfortable assurance that we are fully *appreciated* as *far as we are known*, and that all we need to give us our *merited position* is publicity. What Isocrates said of the institution of the Mysteries, may, with greater truth, be said of our Academy. "It is *the thing* that New York most evidently needed."

What would our city be without our Academy? Its augmenting commerce, and increasing immigration, although the two great sources of our riches and our glory —but for our science and skill, would lead to our dissolu-

tion as a country, and our decimation as a people. Ship
fever, yellow fever, cholera, and a hundred other
diseases of most fearful character, would, during the last
three years, have spread over the land, but for our timely
interference. On this subject I claim your serious and
attentive consideration, and hope you will be as interested and absorbed in the subject, as Dido was in the
story of Eneas, who is described as "*Ore pendente
narrante*,"—suspending with breathless interest on the
narration.

The great question to be decided, in these cases, was,
whether they should be considered as contagious, or not.
Numerous and important interests were depending upon
our decision. If we pronounced that they *were* contagious, a fearful discouragement would be given to commerce, and many of our best paying citizens would
remove their families from the city, to the great loss of
our tradesmen and—ourselves. As we have always
regarded our interests and our principles as identical, we
could not, of course, come to such an unprofitable conclusion. If we pronounced against the theory of contagion, we should be obliged to account for every fresh
case,—by the condition of the air, the people, or the
streets ;—and although that might give us a great deal
of trouble, and put the city to a great expense, yet as we
should be pretty certain to profit by the trouble, and pay
little if any of the expense, we decided, on the whole, that
the diseases were not contagious—at least, for the
present.

There were persons who had the temerity to say, that
it was of no consequence what our decision might be, or
whether we came to one at all! for that the facts and
truths of the case could not be affected by our decision.
Such persons showed themselves utterly unacquainted

with the first principles of our Academy. Could it be supposed that we took the trouble consequent on such an Institution—and endured the expenses incident to it—for the mere purpose of gathering up such facts, and truths, as were apparent and evident to the ordinary community? Undoubtedly it was the province of the Academy to furnish both the facts and the truths. Had they done nothing more than collect and classify the occurrences of the day, they would simply have performed the work of the penny-a-liners of the press, without even obtaining their penny-a-line.

On the service which we rendered to this city and country, and especially to the profession, during the the prevalence of the late epidemic, I venture to stake the value of our corporate existence. I firmly believe, and unhesitatingly declare, that great numbers of cases of cholera, never would have been discovered, much less reported, had it not been for our untiring zeal and diligence.

Many cases of diarrhea, dysentery, drunkenness and even fever, would have been entirely omitted from the cholera reports, but for us. In order to bring the profession, and especially the Academy, before the public, in a sufficiently prominent manner, it was requisite to array a formidable amount of disease before them, in order to justify the number of the medical troops which they were called upon to sustain.

A Board of Health was established, a Sanitary Committee appointed, and the utmost diligence enjoined. Many cases were discovered which had never been suspected, either by the physician or the patient; and more had been so completely overlooked, as to have escaped any medical treatment at all. We rejoice to be able to say, that almost all these cases terminated favorably.

This, no doubt, is to be attributed to the benign influence upon these persons, arising from their implicit confidence in the wisdom of those to whom the health of the city was intrusted.

It is however to be admitted, that there were some persons who doubted the very existence of cholera, and many who doubted its prevalence. Never was the wisdom of Heaven and Earth more manifest, than in the established existence of our Academy at this critical conjuncture. Notwithstanding that there are two medical colleges in this city, each amply supplied with a corps of professors, fully capable of deciding any question of ordinary medical importance—yet on such a question as this, no body of the profession could be supposed capable of sitting in judgment, except the Academy. Indeed the Fellows of this learned institution seem to me to occupy, in our age, the place of the *Kritoi* of Athens, of whom Cicero says: "*legum morumque humanitatis exempla, hominibus, ac civitatibus data, esse dicuntur.*" That is, "They were given to man and the civilized world, to be examples of the laws and morals of humanity."

Doubtless, the question will occur to you, "what mode of treatment did you recommend in this disease?" We are ready to answer the question most explicitly. We recommended the most thorough orthodox treatment; Bleeding, where any blood could be obtained, in order to lessen its quantity—calomel in large doses, to change its quality—opium in powerful doses, to stupefy the senses—and external violent stimulating applications, to rouse the stupefied sensations. With proud exultation do we look back upon the science and learning which we displayed in our treatment of cholera, and challenge the world to furnish a mode of treatment comparable to it.

We have indeed sanctioned many other modes of treatment, as experimental, so that our sphere of observation has been most ample ; yet we have not found any mode so safe as the orthodox one. If any person suppose that the lives of those who were subjected to the various modes of treatment, were necessarily tampered with and placed in greater peril than those under orthodox treatment, we are happy to be able to relieve you from the fears which you might naturally entertain, by informing you that every mode of treatment was alike uncertain and unsuccessful. Do what we would, the real cases of cholera all seemed to die. *"Pallida Mors, æquo pede pulsat pauperum tabernas, regumque turres."*

> " Pale death, with equal step, for rich and poor,
> Knocks at the palace and the cottage door."

Considering the fact, that very few respectable persons died of the disease, we presume that your anxiety is very much diminished, and that you will, like us, content yourselves with submitting to the will of Providence, and thank God that, whoever it took, it did not take you. All that science could do, was done. Miracles are not to be expected, and we are conscious of our imperfection as physicians as well as men. Death, moreover, is a necessary part of this system. As our excellent-hearted and profoundly observant friend, Shallow, has remarked ; "Death, as the Psalmist saith,—is certain to all—all shall die !"

But let us not look on the gloomy side only of the picture. The death of the cholera patients has been the very life of the Academy. The Board of Health has been established, and in constant and successful operation for more than half the year. Some of our most needy and deserving members have been comfortably provided for, and helped into practice. Several have been appointed as ward physicians, who were hardly heard of before—and many have had their bills paid by the Corporation, (on the recommendation of the Board of Health,) who had scarcely experienced such an occurrence hitherto. Whatever the Board of Health, (the origin and supervision of which we claim,) may not have done, undoubtedly it has done great good for that portion of the profession who were members of the Academy.

We regret that a few medical gentlemen, for whom we entertain some respect, have not joined us ; because, not only is every dollar that we can obtain needed—but as our object, from the formation of the Academy, has been to impress the public with the belief that we represent the science and moral worth of the profession, every defection of able and honorable men is a great loss to us. Like the Augurs of Rome, we need every aid that can be obtained, to keep us in countenance.

It has not escaped our notice, that the surplice and gown of the clergy have had their use, and we seriously think of adopting a medical dress, which will vastly assist our dignity. In some countries which we have visited, the doctors wear a peculiar hat or cap, and black tight pantaloons, silk stockings, and pumps ; a great deal, however, will depend upon what sort of legs, on the whole, the Academy possesses ; and much will be left to the taste of the ladies, who—God bless them!—have always been our best patrons—especially the elder ones ! A committee will be appointed to confer with them on this very important subject.

It must not be supposed that we have overlooked the

apparently minor matters of beards, spectacles, neckcloths, and gloves. On the contrary, we have paid great
attention to all these matters. The practice of the clergy
in these things is our general rule ; and as their dress
and appearance have usually been taken from the habits
of monastic life, which were adopted for the purpose of
impressing the people with a firm belief in the learning
and sanctity of the monks, we cannot have a better
pattern to imitate. The rule, therefore, is thorough shaving, gold spectacles, white neckcloths, and black gloves.
If a ring be worn, it ought to be a massive one ; a mourning one is the best. It has the appearance of being the
gift of some deceased wealthy friend, relative or patient.

We have long had a most thorough conviction of the
importance of a carriage, and a pew at church. We
admire the newly adopted plan of a massive silver plate,
with the name on the pew door. It is undoubtedly a
very necessary part of our profession to show a respect
for religion—or at least for the clergy.

Our younger brethren will find it one of the most certain modes of obtaining notoriety, and gaining friends
and practice, to attend steadily at some respectable
church. We would principally recommend the Presbyterian or Episcopal Church, as they are most influential
and wealthy. Still, there are other respectable denom-
inations—and much depends on circumstances. " *Verbum sapientiæ sufficit.*"

I now approach the most important part of my discourse—the denouncement and anathematization of all
irregular practice and practitioners—a task which I feel
great pleasure and satisfaction in performing, as I, in
common with my brethren, have suffered exceedingly,
both in person and purse, from these vampires of the
profession. Our learned President has most zoologically

said, "all kinds of cattle are permitted to practice medicine in this State!" I take the liberty to add to that scientific sentiment, one of my own, " All sorts of reptiles, also." Why, we have Thompsonians—Reformed Practitioners—Eclectics—Hydropathists—and Homeopathists ; —besides Chrono-thermalism, and that greatest, of all innovations, the Throat Disease Treatment !

I shall spend as much of my time on each of these as my limits will enable me ; and I beg to assure you, if I do not succeed in annihilating these reptiles, it is not from want of intention, but solely from want of power and opportunity. To begin with the Thompsonians. Their practice consists in the use of lobelia—a substance so fearfully injurious, that I have carefully and conscientiously abstained from knowing anything about it I should as soon think of administering liquid fire to my patients. If any of you have unhappily fallen under the maltreatment of one of these reptiles, you can tell more than I can of their mode of treatment ; all that I know of them is, that they are exceedingly ignorant, vulgar, and dangerous persons. In the words of Hamlet to the players, I say, "Pray you, avoid them."

Of the Reformed Practitioners, something more is known—because one of them has published a book. It is true that I have not read it ; I should feel degraded if I had ; but I am informed by those who have heard much about it, that the principal value of the work consists in its piracies from our orthodox authors. It is affirmed, on good authority, that the author, or rather the compiler of this wretched production, sent a copy to every crowned head in Europe, and received from almost all of them autograph letters of thanks and commendations, as well as gold medals. If anything were needed to sicken me of monarchies, it is this silly affectation in monarchs to pretend to judge, as well as to patronize, medical systems. "*Ne sutor ultra crepidam!*" Happily for this country, few people care much for the "*ratio regum!*" Royal wisdom and judgment are at a very heavy discount!

Of the Eclectics, little is known, except that they select such principles and practices as may suit their purpose, from any and every system of medicine. They proceed upon the supposition that there is no true system, and that they are more capable of judging what is true or erroneous, good or evil, than the founders of our time-honored and authority-approved system of orthodox medicine. This is an individual assumption of wisdom, the possession of which can be possible only to corporate bodies. The value—nay, the very essence of the value of corporate bodies arises from their individual incapacity. There is not one of us that does not feel his personal incompetence, single and alone—yet there is not one of us that doubts our corporate and Academic capacity and competence.

The Hydropathists are a set of pretended physicians, who were spawned by that amphibious reptile, Priessnitz, one of the most illiterate of the Silesian peasantry. The science of this school consists in the abjuration of all orthodox medical knowledge whatever. No one is fit to become a practitioner of it, if he be acquainted with anatomy, physiology, chemistry, and pharmacy. So far from it being a help, to know the structure, composition, and laws of the body, it is a positive hindrance. The practice consists in administering and applying water to the body, inwardly and outwardly, in every conceivable unnatural and injurious manner. The rascally impostors take the patients into their houses, where they are fed on the worst of food, subjected to the most contemptuous and degrading treatment, and charged most enormous sums for being pumped and spouted on, *à la Graefenberg.*

It is awful to think of the infamous prostitution of our Croton water, to the vile purposes of these miserable dabblers in human health and happiness. I am happy to inform you, however, that whatever mischief may be perpetrated by them on the community, they have done us, the members of the Academy, very little harm, if any—their patients being generally of that number upon whom we had exhausted our science, and found quite incurable. If such choose to be hydropathed to death, instead of dying professionally or naturally, let them do so—who can help it?

The Homœopathists are a more formidable brood. I am grieved to be obliged to admit, that in this city and neighborhood, there are upward of fifty of them, who are not only sustaining themselves and their system—"Save the mark!" but are actually perverting young men who attend our colleges, for the purpose of enabling them to practice the profession of medicine, by instilling into them the trivialities, the nonentities, the absurdities and impossibilities, the inanities and insanities of the Hahnemannic imposture. *"O tempora! O mores!"*

We feel toward many of these as the hen feels toward some of her brood, when she sees them assume the cockatrice form, and devour their fellow nestlings. Perhaps, of all offensive characters, those of traitor and apostate are the most exasperating, while that of seducer is the most detested and abhorred. Only think of the pangs of mortification which some of our excellent professors experience, when their paternal—I might rather say maternal—feelings are lacerated by the discovery that they have been nourishing a young homeopathic viper in their bosoms, instead of an orthodox spaniel—who, on the first occasion that offers, will not hesitate to suck its parent's blood, or strangle him in the struggle for existence. Surely he might with just propriety employ that express-ive line of Euripides,

"I'm full of miseries—there's no room for more."

Indeed, their conduct can only be compared with that of the Ishmaelite who disgraces his profession by the publi-cation of the *Scalpel*.

I will first describe the homeopathic system of medical treatment. Its basis is this principle, if it ought to be so called, that the same thing which will cause a disease will cure it. Thus, bleeding from the nose, caused by project-ing that organ against a lamp post, would be checked by a succession of similiar projections! Delirium tremens from drinking brandy, would be cured by drinking more brandy! Cholera, produced by contact with an infected person, or exposure to mephitic gases, would of course be cured by a continued exposure to such causes! And indeed, death itself, from any cause—from that of the taking of arsenic or Prussic acid, to the cutting of your throat or blowing your brains out, may be averted, by simply repeating the injury! They do not teach in this manner, but they ought to, and should—had I the power to make them.

Their theory is, that not the same, but a similiar affec-tion being produced, cures the disease—and they give as examples of their principle, the well-known cases of mer-cury relieving diseases of the glands, especially of the throat—opium relieving the terrors of a brandy delirium —lead relieving colic—and copper assuaging dysentery. If they mean to claim the manifestation of these practical facts, we deny their claim, and put in our plea of prece-dence. These facts occurred in our practice and they happened to observe them—picked them up, and stole them, in order to make up their system! Permit me to give you an illustration of their honesty in this matter. You invite your friend to your house, and show him your library, containing books, of the contents of which, or even their language, you are entirely ignorant ; but your friend easily reads. He finds a valuable secret, and by means of it realizes income and fortune. Did not he, by means of his knowledge, steal from you, in consequence of your ignorance?

It is well known that in our zeal to find something which would relieve or cure the various diseases which the human body is subject to, we gave and used, without knowing why or wherefore, anything and everything in our way. This furnished a large field of observation, and the homeopathists stole from us the truth, that particular substances act upon particular parts in a particular manner, and cure particular diseases. Galileo, Kepler and Newton observed the laws of the spheres, and gave us our system of astronomy ; but pray, who furnished them with the worlds to observe? By how much superior the star maker is to the star gazer, by so much orthodoxy is superior to the homeopath!

Thus much for their honesty as professors of a science. Now for their honesty as practitioners of it. If by producing a certain affection of the body, or a part of it, we can remove disease, the sooner we produce that affection, the sooner will the benefit be produced. Now surely quantity and power hold some relation to each other. They do in the mechanical and chemical departments of nature : why should they not in the therapeutical department? No doubt you have all heard of the infinitesimal doses of medicine which these practitioners give! Is not the object of them apparent? Their patients are hardly ever

out of their fingers.   It is quite common to know of cases
of five, seven, and even ten years' attendance.   Much as
we regret the loss of good paying patients—we are more
sorry for the unhappy condition in which they are placed
under the care of these men—I should say reptiles.   I
apologize for letting my natural politeness get the better
of my temper.

Perhaps no part of the homeopathic system is so objec-
tionable as that of degrading the administration of medicine to a mere sweetmeat business.   Every medicine is administered in sugar, and much of it is kept prepared in form
of globules or comfits—so that it is common for the children of homeopathic patients to ask for medicine as a
treat, and not one of them is ever conscious of taking
anything unpleasant—much less nauseous.   I am not
aware that they ever give emetics or cathartics—but I
am of opinion that they do not.   Moreover their patients
are scarcely ever conscious of any painful, nauseous or
uncomfortable sensations from the medicines which they
take ; which is proof positive that what they take is of
no use.   Their pretended cures, I most positively believe, are effected by Nature—while their medicines, I
hesitate not to affirm, are mere placebos—that is, pleasant
trifles.   Indeed, the sight of one of their medicine cases
is enough to convince you that they are a petty, paltry
set of peddling pretenders.   "*Homunculi, non homines.*'
manikins, not men.

I suppose you are aware that they abjure bleeding,
cupping, leeching, scarifying, setoning, issuing, caus- ◆
ticing, blistering and every other kind of mechanical or
chemical lesion of the body ; and you may know by
this, if by nothing else, the utter uselessness of their
system.   Indeed it has nothing to recommend it ; it is
the imbecile offspring of the thirtieth dilution of a fanatic.

The homeopathists, as a body, are beneath our notice, and below contempt. As a system we may say of it, "*nihil sed nominis umbra.*" It is nothing but the shadow of a name. Euclid's definition of a point is the best description of it : " Without length, breadth or thickness." A mere nonenity.

Now let me give you a brief sketch of our system of medicine. We are men of substance ; what we give hath length, breadth and thickness. Our Materia Medica cannot be carried in our pockets. We give teacupsfuls of salts and senna—sometimes even to children—none of your contemptible fantastical comfits and globules! tablespoonfuls of castor oil—teaspoonfuls of jalap and calomel—tartar emetic and ipecacuanha in becoming quantities to vomit them—scammony, colocynth, aloes, gamboge, etc., in respectable doses to purge them. The effects of these things are felt and lasting. I assure you I have often known patients be a week or more ere they recovered from one of such doses. Compare that with your homeopathists' thirtieth trituration—and then answer the question—" Who are most entitled to the appellation of practitioners of medicine ?" I verily believe that I give more medicine in one week, than some of them give in a whole year! Why, if we were all homeopathists, the drug trade would be ruined, and the tariff seriously injured. I would enlist your political and patriotic feelings against such an atomic cachectic monstrosity.

Then for the mode of preparing and exhibiting their medicines. They have their everlasting powders and perpetual drops. "Toujours la même chose." See our variety! We have our powders, pills, boluses, suppositories, draughts, mixtures, lotions, liniments, ointments, plasters, injections, collyriums, troches, embrocations, fomentations, cataplasms, sinapisms, vesications, pustu-

5

lations and cauterizations! " *Non verba sola, sed substantia rerum.*" Real things, not merely names. These are *our* medicamenta, our Materia Medica.

Let me now call your attention to what we *do*, as well as what we *give*. We believe in bleeding, and practice it with a generous freedom. It is one of the essential features of our system. How could inflammations and inflammatory fevers be subdued without it? In many instances of inflammation of the lungs, liver, brain, and bowels, we are often obliged to bleed persons almost to death, in order to avert the terrible consequences of the rapid and fearful disease! What are we to think of the philosophy of a system of therapeutics which abjures bleeding? Many of our patients have a periodical instinctive sense of the necessity of the lancet—and if we were to decline to use it for them, they would certainly apply to less skillful and conscientious persons. Moreover, we should lose many fees, and those of the best kind—ready money. Many of us are entirely supplied with pocket money from this source, and from that of snipping tongue-tied children. It is well for us, that the homoeopathists do not profess to know much about the anatomy of the body, healthy or morbid, or they would convince the people that nine tongue-tied cases in ten do not need snipping.

Again, look at our superior advantages in the relief which we are able to offer by local blood-letting—by cupping, scarifying, and leeching. Some of our patients, even delicate women, have been cupped almost from head to foot. In many cases of apoplexy, paralysis, epilepsy, and spinal disease, the established mode of treatment is topical blood-letting. How, I ask, could we proceed, without these modes of effecting our purpose? Where the homoeopathists would give a millionth of a grain of calcareum, aconite, or veratrine, we extract six ounces of blood! Our system is physical, sensible, impressive, indelible! We leave the marks of science behind us, at every step! Their system is fantastical, metaphysical, mystical. They leave neither trail nor trace of their operations. Their patients are not conscious of any, inwardly or outwardly. The candy and comfit dealers might as well be accounted physicians, as the homeopathists! They are a sort of medical Brahmins or Fakirs.

I have scarcely time and opportunity to do justice to that part of our system, consisting of setons, issues, blisterings, sinapisms and pustulations. Of these things, so exceedingly effective in their mode of operation, and so admirably adaptive in their administration—the homeopathists know nothing. While we employ some hundreds of thousands of blisters annually, they do not use a single one. I am sure that I need not enlarge upon this subject, to so enlightened, so experienced, and I dare say I may add, so well blistered and pustuled an audience, as the present. How the homeopathists sleep in their beds, when they have cases of inflammation under their care, and they neither bleed, cup, nor blister, I know not ; except their consciences have been as much diluted by fanaticism, as their intellects have been triturated with mysticism.

For my part, never until I have abstracted the last ounce of blood by some one of our modes of depleting, and obtained the last drachm of serum by some form of vesication, do I feel at ease, in cases of inflammation. Oh, what a comfort to my soul it is, when I pay my last visit to my dying patients, that no congested blood in their veins can cry to Heaven against me for vengeance!

I now feel that the time is come to address a few words of exhortation to the clergy. Their sanction and countenance is of great importance, for good or for evil.

Can they, after hearing this calm, dispassionate, unpre-
judiced, philosophic, and theologic comparison of the two
systems of medical practice, consistently and conscientiously countenance the attenuated, mystical, superstitious, Brahminical, heretical, and antiscriptural system
of Hahnemann—so notorious a schismatic? They will
perceive, that the success of medicine, as well as theology, requires the shedding of blood, and purging.
Never, I hope, will they favor and foster a system of
medicine which threatens to pave the way for the return
of Arianism and Pelagianism, to sweep from the civilized
and Christianized world the orthodox physician, as well
as the successors of the Apostles, the Orthodox clergy—
and to undermine the very belief and understanding of
the Scriptures! " *Diis sacer est medicus, divumque sacer-
dos.*" Sacred to the gods, are both the orthodox physician and clergy.

I do not feel called upon to say anything respecting
the subject of chrono-thermalism, except this—that at
present only one case of infection has appeared in this
city—and it is currently reported that it does not pay.
Certain it is, that whereas it formerly went about in a
carriage, it now goes afoot, and they say it is paralytic.
It also abjures bleeding, but believes in poison, and
large doses.

We merely say to it, " *Noli me tangere!*" If it do,
most assuredly it will have cause to repent, whether it
do or not.

Concerning the throat disease treatment, there is much
to say, but our limits do not admit of more than a brief
notice of it. One of our present number ventured, without the sanction of the leading members of our profession,
to propose and practice a new mode of healing diseases
of the throat, by topical applications in the windpipe.

As the entrance of any substance into this part was known to be accompanied with fearful strangling, and convulsive cough, they considered the plan of treatment was impossible, and therefore denounced the proposal of it as an ignorant and impudent imposture, and the propounder as a quack.

We have, however, appointed a committee to select a few proper subjects from the poor at our new school for experimental surgery, at Bellevue, and to try the process of injecting the abscesses of such of them as are past all hope of life, and to report to our Academy the result. We anticipate no benefit, but have thought it due to science and humanity to test the absurdity in order to satisfy the public of our zeal. The subjects selected being unknown in society, it cannot affect us injuriously whatever the result may prove, and we shall, in the event of fatal issue, from our official position, be able to avoid the disgraceful scandal of a coroner's inquest.*

You will all perceive the danger of admitting discoveries. If we allow the existence of a new truth, we become liable to the charge of imperfections, ignorance, or error—which is fatal to our pretensions to orthodoxy —and that once doubted, our prestige and power are gone. A committee of the most prudent of our number will be appointed to deal with the phenomenon of a discovery. It is so rare a thing with ourselves, that we shall seldom, if ever, cause any trouble.

I feel confident that the clergy will approve of our course in this matter, for we have acted upon their principle, that of resisting every innovation, until it could no longer be resisted—and then incorporating it in the body

---

* It was done, and resulted in the death of two of the subjects, with fearful symptoms. See *Scalpel*, No. 28. We called on the district attorney publicly, to indict the parties concerned, but it was not done.

of the text. Ever since the clergy assumed the control, nay, the very existence of the church, they have undeviatingly resisted the introduction of any new truth, from whatever quarter, whether of learning or science— and reserved to themselves the right to introduce whatever may be necessary to the well-working of the system. It is upon this principle that all Ecclesiastical bodies have been founded—from the Roman Catholic Church down through the Greek and Armenian Churches, the Protestant Episcopal Churches of every country, the various forms of Presbyterian Churches, and the Methodist Episcopal Church of this country, as well as its Sister Church in the British Dominions, the large and now respectable Wesleyan Body, or rather Conference.

Every one is acquainted with the trouble which Galileo gave the church, by his introduction of unauthorized and unsanctioned discoveries—and the manifest necessity which required their suppression. In our own day, the geologists have given the church the same sort of trouble. A few of the leading men of each important denomination, have admitted and espoused the geological innovations—but the great proportion of the clergy, who have no time for the investigation, have very wisely refused to entertain the question at all, and steadily voted it down. It was very manifest to them, that if they admitted the discoveries of geology, they would not only affix their sign and seal to the document of their ignorance and error, but impose upon themselves the labor of learning that of which they felt themselves very incapable, and more unwilling to attempt. Their maxim has always been, " *obsta principiis !*"

If anything could shake our faith in republicanism, it is the traitorous conduct of our Legislature toward orthodox medicine. They have opened the door of liberty to quacks and pretenders, and every one now may poison that pleases. Although we are forbidden to curse our enemies, yet we are not only at liberty but are commanded to pray for them. In the language of prayer, we say—"May everlasting fire and brimstone rest upon the bodies and souls, the senses and limbs, of those, and their children also, to all generations, who despoiled us of our vested rights, and profitable monopoly. Let them perish forever! And let all the people—at least the orthodox people—say Amen, Amen!"

AN ARTIST'S REVERIE.

"Spirits are not finely touched, but to fine issues."

The artist rests in his work-chamber—a spacious room, with walls in middle tint and light direct from heaven. Statues stand about—that were shaped two thousand years ago by such as Phidias, and three hundred years ago by such as Angelo. Fragments are strewn around ;—here is Scott's death-face—there, a bas relief from the frieze of the Parthenon. In a folio, are skillfully cut engravings by Doo and Finden after Raphael and Titian, and Edwin Landseer after his brother. On a table lie softly penciled lithographs from France, and marvelously done daguerreotypes ; together with spirited drawings in pencil and crayon—a cast, in porcelain, of the Portland vase—illuminated books in vellum—casts from antique gems—bits of precious woods and marbles —tresses of hair, and an ebony-and-ivory cross and Jesus.

Then there are several easels, bearing works unfinished ; such as a statuette—a colossal bust of Webster, remarkable for its massiveness, ponderous forehead, bull-like throat, down-set mouth, sunken, fire-gleaming eyes, *set in areola*, and carelessly thrown hair—a half length of a cherub child, with its sinless, sunny countenance, un-broken, dimpled, glee-like laugh, (*the eyes laughing as well as the cherry-like mouth,*) large head, abundance of curly, dangling, wind-tossed locks, tiny neck, and funny little breasts. These works are covered for the time with damp cloths; but there remains one that is yet uncov-ered. It is the bust, of life size, of a very lovely woman, of slender though full form, *stag-like.*

She has an oval outline of face, eyes like the gazelle's, nose of the costliest Greek mould, delicate and sensitive ears and nostrils, and a mouth of noble curvature, yet amorous expression. The flower of her form has just opened its capital leaf; her forehead looks serene, and her whole countenance and bearing teem with both grace and guilelessness. Her hair is luxuriant and silky, and gathered up so as not to hide the lovely neck and low-falling shoulders. *Her bosom is yet undraped.* And at this work the artist, as he reclines in his chair, gazes spell-bound, as artists often will at their last-touched work, when the brain and hand are tired and droop.

To the modeler, the sitter seems now present, now dimly away. The effect of the work on the artist's frame flits up and off again. Professional jealousy and gener-osity wrestle. The labor of concluding the work is rehearsed—and then all care dies for the day and pleas-ure reigns. * * * *

The pipe drops unwittingly to the smoker, who reposes with a corpse-like stillness; not in simple sleep, but bodily trance and profound mental reverie. For a time he is loose from all earthly chains, and roams through ages after ages, o'er a theatre, with hell for its footstool and heaven for its crown, and *vice versa.* Where tragedy and farce, grief and joy, love and hate, lock together, and the lip of falsehood enriches the lip of truth; the tear at-

5*

tends to misery, and the chamber of death is but the portal to fresh life!

The rain-storm refreshes the faded grass, and the globe's revolutions balance its clouds, and Night and Morning bear the gentle twilight.

Sin calls for the Redeemer; a dark and slippery way raises the value of a covert under the grandest wing; what but the darkest ground of night can wear the richest set of stars?

Envy not the artist his brilliant pleasures, for he has to return to opposite things, that seem, by contrast, as the rack, and drop, and stifling inquisition cell! He has no even tenor to his way. His mind sweeps through hell as well as heaven. He has to study the Magdalen and Christ, imps and angels, plump youth and pleated age, mountain pinnacles and cavern floors, *all* the passions, strange comminglings of character and color, anatomy, history, mythology, costume—he has to search deformity to find beauty, turn over the hill to find the jewel!

Some live long like Domenechino, but almost all receive an early death like Raphael. Life is hurried through to get quickly at its finest essence. Remember Bulwer's "Warner," his young corpse sitting in a chair in a gallery of art at Rome; the fair hair, the while, playing about the insensate face and shoulders, by the sporting of the wind, like little ones, who whisper to, and kiss, and otherwise caress, but mother's clay. There are hundreds of such Warners; hundreds who enthusiastically love great art—so love it as to forget to sleep well, eat well, and follow the rule of heat and cold. So, covet not this one's lot, as he enjoys his momentary, though golden Vision. God is with him now, but even now the tempter is returning. The diamond sheds about itself a precious

and quite splendid glory, uniquely splendid, but its possession is often accompanied by an unhappy train. Its
ownership and guardianship are big with care, as well as
pride and beauty ; they continually do cry for things to
match. Paste is more plentiful and modest, and infinitely more unfluctuating. It remains safe when the
diamond is insidiously stolen off. The one has a serene
and unchanging climate ; the other a day in the garden
of Eden, a month in the mines of Siberia.

The vision that floats first is that of THE BUILDING OF
THE EARTH, and our reverist, in lounge so sloven, closed
eye, prostrate body, and with brain on fire, follows, by the
lamp of his soul, and with deep wonder and affection,
the hand of the divine Guide.

A black, opaque, dancing ball appears. It expands
and lightens up ; larger and larger it grows ; becomes
tremulous and full of creeping mites, and now assumes
ten thousand times ten thousand shapes, and all the
striped colors of the rainbow.

The earth's life has begun—centuries pass along ; and
millions of years ; the chaotic needle's point springs up
into a mass gigantic of matter, animate and inanimate.
The living things creep, or wind along on their bellies.
None of them stand erect ! A dusky light broods over all ;
a cold, heavy twilight. All colors look shadowy, sickly,
unbrilliant, and of insipid tinge . Generations after gen-
ations of the worm and lizard, are, at long intervals, the
mere focus of the Almighty's burning glass, and are em-
bedded into vast masses of granite and marble, and immense caverns of rock, sealed for the time with lava.
Vines, of humble shape, run wild and get entangled and
kept down, like pinned net-work, for final petrifaction by
the Supreme Chemist !

Billions of years flit by, and the needle's point has

expanded to a diameter of nearly eight thousand miles. The mighty ball grows more and more lit up, and richer and richer in colors, and monsters as well as mites people it. Mammoths tread it with a thundering footfall sound ; and colossal serpents carry lightning on their tongue-tips, and roll over the globe's form like ocean billows, and their breathings whistle like rushing winds, and sing as the Æolian harp ! Moisture increases, and beds of slime appear, embasking the great crocodile ; and centuries of living things are again frozen into stone, to consolidate the throne of coming Man, and give materials for his pleasure-look, and matters of utility. Layer on layer of the dead remains of by-gone time sleep in their graves—fragments of the dead—clay to mould the living.

The giant caverns, so still throughout the march of ages, now burst off their lava seals, shake the whole globe, stretch their walls angrily above the surface for miles, and then clap on their caps conical. Hecla, Etna, Vesuvius, and Cotopaxi! dread fellows those, to belch forth flames of fire, spit up balls, and slobber molten stone! Grand designers those for ice bridge, leaping cataract, and dizzy staircase! Mighty demons those, to fascinate, and smother, and embalm whole cities at a time, and build to them amusing monuments of sport and horror! Spirit so choice! ye buckle Naples city to the instep ; look down upon the clouds and wear them as a belt, and claim best lip-touch from our Lord of light! Starters of rockets! Mortars of war! Miserly collectors of the ancient statue, vase and wedding-ring ! Why sing ye like the thunder-claps and mutter like the field of Austerlitz?

Now, bowels, veins, and arteries appear, to fill themselves with mammoth, ibex, forest leaf and tree, to yield to after times beds of both coal and marble. Away, in the ocean's lonemost parts, rise countless piles of coral and stiff, crimped, spongy looking stone foliage, a thousand times larger than the pyramids of Egypt! Vast structures of the worm, rising step by step to be chief giant! Generous creatures! to strip your arms of your peculiar ornament, to please the little child, both civil and barbaric! Oracular voices! that join all cheerily with myriad others to declare that, "united we stand, divided we fall," and render it quite wonderless that the poor worm when winged becomes a symbol of the soul!

Now, a profusion of material exists, for man to show his cunning workmanship, and well supply his wants legitimate. Away with his winged servitors, to bring in the Earth's lamps—the golden sun, the silver moon, and the ever-dancing stars! Now start the messenger comets ; and hark to that strain of angel-sung music, and now the voice-play of heaven's grand artillery, while the unconscious shape of Adam is lifted from its bed of descending clouds, by a group of angels, and placed in the garden of Eden, to be breathed upon by the LORD GOD!

THE GARDEN.

A divine scene. Nature unbroken by Art. A climate most delicious ; and exquisitely beautiful and grand shapes, *infinitely varied.* The waters seem as magic mirrors, clasping to their bosom the sublimest revelations of the sky—the storm—the calm—the cloud-done battle pieces—clusters on clusters of glittering stars and planets, and the air-sailing-and-diving bird.

The lily and the stag are looking at themselves—and the simple daisy, too. There are no dim eyes abroad—no checked heart currents—no halt movements—not a stammering tongue. Ecstasy of feeling is regnant—all

shapes and colors harmonize, and every blade of grass is
bespangled with dew.   All nature is a harp in tune, and
every breath gives forth the note exultant.

The melody of the bird and bee, and the soft whisper-
ings of the breeze-swayed grass, chime in with the voices
of the streamlet, the tear-drops of the rock clefts, and the
never-tiring waterfalls that are hissing and dashing, curling and flashing, tumbling and sparkling, and casting up
their spray as incense toward the Divine halo.

Luscious fruits abound, and so do wonderfully inter-
woven arbors.   The ivy embraces and adorns the oak,
Handsomely curve the valley and the hill, and "distance
lends enchantment to the view!"   The elephant treads
in state—and bounds the colossal-headed lion—and darts
the basilisk and hare.   The elegant and lithe tiger well
displays his coat of ermine, springs o'er the long lawns,
and leaps tremendously amid the congregations of the
rocks ; and the peacock proudly flaunts its tail of satin,
emerald, and gold.   Forests stand like armies, yet mingle in sweet converse as the tenor with the bass.   They
catch and play in tune with the nightingale and eagle,
and welcome to their arms the serpent and the dove.
The fish sport noiselessly in school, or leap delightfully
along in single leap, or summerset thrown o'er their
looking-glass—or further still, as knights in tourney, have
sham battles done in gorgeous scaly armor eclipsing that
of supple Saladin.   Flowers throng the paths and water-
sides, and give away their perfume.   How fragrant is
the air and big with innocent intoxication!   All things
are chanting praises to heaven's centre—but such as we
may but feebly imagine and make note of the infinity,
majesty and highly divine impress, of the first home of
our own and Nero's chief forefather—whose one child
was an angel boy, whose other—a mere fratricide.

And over all this nobility of nature looks the monarch Adam—his figure erect, countenance serene and of soft smile, and whole shape and action significant of grace, intelligence, agility and strength. His skin is glossy, limbs round, chest spacious, and hair of fine thread, rich color and high polish, hanging in clusters about the ivory face, neck and shoulders.

Rather than a monarch, he seems himself a god! and at his Apollo-like presence, the lambs skipped for joy, and the grandest hills and caverns sharply clapped their hands.

He walks proudly over his domain—gazes with rapture at mountain, tree and bower—tastes of the most delicious fruits—closely scans the dazzling palace dome —inhales the faultless air, *and yet he murmurs.*

With perfect self-possession he openly complains that every creature but himself hath its mate, while his own life-harp lacks the sympathetic string, as all pleasure and glory chiefly consist of a sweet interchange of soul, and life's best enjoyment dies out at its first breath unless it lock with a responsive heart-beat.

The ever-listening God said "Sleep!" and Adam slept, to awake like the Sun with the moon by its side—the silver with the gold. By him lay the maiden Eve, at whom he gazed with perfect joy. And the noble and beautiful pair arose like the eyelids of morning, and throughout the eventful day they chatted, and ate, and drank, and reclined together ; and the pulses of their every glance and wish arose and fell in unison. At length they heard the electrifying voice of their Creator, saying in sonorous tones, "One fruit in this garden is mine, *exclusively* so ; eat not of it lest the spell of your present perfect happiness be broken, and you wed many a misery ; but when you closely approach this fruit you will meet with a last warning."

Then o'er the spirit of our lovers sat a shadow. They stood at first abstractedly, yet soon, with ear alert, to listen to philosophy and prophecy done by a passing serpent.

"I see," (it said,) "the mightiest magnet 'gainst the lightest needle—the finite 'gainst the infinite—who'll be the conquering hero? An apple changes like painter's pencil from grave to gay, from weal to woe, from bay to cypress and a crown of thorns! A ladder pointed to the sky, reels off its scalers into ruin, yet the fox climbs on toward Zeuxis' grapes, the bees will light on Plato's lips, the worm becomes an angel and the serpent a prime minister! Again, I see circuits on circuits of ages, and Sisera fighting the stars in their courses, and a courtesan of Thebes, building a pyramid with the forbidden fruit of her debaucheries, and now, a stolen child returns to the bosom of its mother at the hands of superior wisdom." The serpent's subtle tongue now stops, as the sun sets behind the faintly blue hills and lingers on the loftiest mountain peaks. Fish leave their watery attic, and birds take to their pedestals and fold the wing.

Soon the royal lovers were o'ertaken by the twilight with all its gentleness and witchery. Then they rested on a velvety knoll under a great and vine-embowered tree. Now they feel creeping over them a delicious languor, and lean together their ivorial shoulders and rose-entinted cheeks. Then Adam clasps Eve's beautiful form and ardently kisses and kisses her scarlet lips, looks with a thrilling delight over her pearly tracery of vein, passes his fingers through the masses of her cool and silky hair locks, clasps her wrists and ankles and admires their delicacy and faultlessness of chiselry ; and in every thought, glance and touch, meets with the sympathetic harp-string ; but lo! a serpent near them hissed, they start at the intrusive sound, the unnatural and rejected warning! while the serpent lies quite motionless, as around its open and illuminated mouth an ambitious and music-loving bird circles and circles, and then darts swiftly as the lightning into its living tomb!

The singular order of high heaven was disobeyed, but a mother's love was won. The globe trembled, but was it for grief or joy? Clouds distill and drop the dew.

The trumpet was made to bray—and the hill of hymen is a gateway to the mercy seat as well as sepulchre. The grandest passions and emotions need a world and not a garden. The Supreme power can comprehend the dust of the earth in a measure, weigh the mountains in scales, and measure the waters in the hollow of his hand ; but Lucretia, a child of disobedience, so loved virtue that without it life was impossible. Sin and penitence gave the Magdalen to Christ, and fashion spoils the waist to feed the grave-yard, and chisel youthful portraits on the costly tombs of church and cloister. The world peoples, and Galileos arise. The children of Eden may not guide Arcturus with his suns, or loose the bands of Orion, or bind the sweet influences of Pleiades, though they may draw down and harness up the lightning, defy the winds, and glide across the ocean! We'll roughly hew the precipice, not polish at a pebble. 'Tis true our path's not thornless, with its wooden Bible and its gilded priest— but they themselves enhance the beauty of our blind man's dog.

TARTAR EMETIC.

AN EXCELLENT SWEATING, NAUSEATING, AND VOMIT-
ING ARTICLE FOR——THE PROFESSION.

BY THE MEDICAL HERETIC.

THE original name for the substance which is the basis of this article, is "Antimonium Tartarizatum," which, being interpreted, means " Infernal Ejector." It was formerly imagined that the Devil endowed certain substances with malignant properties, for the express purpose of tormenting mankind, whom he hated, on account of an ancient quarrel which never had been adjusted to his satisfaction, and seemed never likely to be.

As his Satanship is generally emulous of acting upon a large scale—doing an extensive business—he has usually engaged and employed, on tolerably liberal terms, a nu-merous corps of assistants. Great warriors, emperors and kings have held very conspicuous and important com-misions from their great exemplar. Not only whole kingdoms, but whole continents have been assigned to them, to be tormented in the most systematic and thorough manner—and the work has generally been done to order, pretty effectually.

Another class of persons that has been largely engaged in the work of tormenting mankind, is the priesthood. Under Pagan, Jewish, Mohammedan and Christian, whether Papal or Protestant, priestly dominion, mankind have been well and sufficiently tormented. The poisons which they have prepared for the soul, and the tortures which they have invented for the body, sufficiently attest their ardor in the cause, and their success in its prosecution. Indeed, the clergy are usually considered to have proved themselves very much more capable of their business, and more ingenious and resultful in it than the laity. It is said, upon high authority, that Rome Papal has tormented the world a thousand times more than Rome Pagan.

The philosophers have undoubtedly been enlisted under the banner of the same leader, for from the most astute and possessed of masters of the art, to the most stolid and destitute teachers of it, all seem to have been engaged in the cause of tormenting men's minds, if not their bodies also. From the Grecian masters, Plato and Aristotle, down to the humble village schoolmaster, there is evidently the same disposition displayed, to torment their pupils. The incomprehensible axioms propounded by the great masters of instruction, and the inexplicable explications of them by the small teachers of it, sufficiently attest the truth of our position, that the Devil has pretty considerbly be-devilized our philosophy.

Although the lawyers, who received so remarkable a condemnation from their gentle but terrible Judge, the Saviour—as recounted in the Gospels—were not engaged in the study, teaching and practice of mere human law, but were the teachers and administrators of divine law; yet there can be little doubt but that the lawyers of all countries and ages have merited the charge brought against their Jewish prototypes and brethren, that they "bind heavy burdens, and grievous to be borne, and lay them on men's shoulders!" Indeed it has been well said, that " The object of modern law, and the practice of modern lawyers, would seem to a disinterested, upright and benevolent observer from another world, to be the obliteration of the demarkations of justice, the confounding of right and wrong, the mulcting of the innocent, and the clearing of the guilty from their deservings! "

However, though martial and political tyrants plague the estates and conditions of mankind—though priests harass their souls, and oftentimes their bodies—though philosophers distress their minds, and lawyers augment the misery of their disturbed relations and actions—the physicians have been granted the possession of men's corporal estate, in fee simple, for ages past, as a *corpus vile*, on which to experiment, after the manner in which Job of Uz was operated upon by Satan himself, and by the Chaldeans, and Sabeans, etc., who were employed by that distinguished firm aforementioned.

It would hardly be fair to quote Scripture to the lawyers, and not cite a little for our fraternity, the physicians. It appears that that ancient patriarch, Job, was acquainted with some in his day, a few specimens of whom have been found in every subsequent age, confirmatory of his observations upon them! They were described by him—but possibly he was in a bad humor—he had enough to make him so—as " physicians of no value."

It is possible that some ancient Chaldee MS. of the book of Job may throw a shadow of light upon this very obscure passage ; and, therefore, we quote more benevolently and justly from the New Testament, where, after having critically examined the Greek text, we find in the Gospel by Mark, a statement to the effect that a woman "had SUFFERED *many things of many physicians, and had spent all that she had, and was nothing better, but rather grew worse.*" Lest some justly sensitive persons, more intimately acquainted with prescriptions than with Scripture, doubt the authenticity of the quotation, we give chapter and verse :   Mark v. 26.

Our own experience would enable us to write a very instructive and illustrative commentary on this remarkable text. However, for the present, we will proceed to make. a few observations on the subject which we have chosen for our article.

When a person is exhausted, terrified, or dying, he is generally affected with profuse sweats—and ordinary persons might imagine that they were only alarming proofs of his debility.   Nothing can more manifestly prove the fallacy of non-medical logic.   In these cases, the " spasm of the extreme vessels " has been overcome and relaxed, and the " vis medicatrix naturæ,"* is resuming its power over the functions.   The learned Stahl observed that the breaking out of a sweat preceded the termination of a fever, as well as that of a man's recovery from a fainting fit, exhaustion, or terror.   The only reason why it did not resuscitate the dying man was, that it did not continue long enough ; continue the sweating, and the man would recover, or never die !

The salutary effects of sweating are very many, and very manifest.   In hot weather it cools us—in cold weather it warms us.   When a man is ready to burst his brain with anxiety or rage, a copious sweat relieves the vessels of a quantity of serum, and saves his medullary and cineritious Batter—y ! How many of our fellow-citizens, who have been suddenly afflicted with that distressing disease ycleped *Quandary*, might have died upon the spot, but for the salutary relief of a copious sweat.

---

* Wherever this term is used hereafter, the editor hopes the reader will remember it means " the curative power of nature."   It is the medicine he always prefers.

We opine that some of the medical readers of the *Scalpel* would increase the Inspector's weekly report of deaths from congestion, were they not saved by a timely perspiration. Indeed, we have constructed our present article entirely for their benefit, and we hope that by the time they have read thus far, the warm stage of the Scalpel Fever has come on. In this belief, we proceed to give the sweating dose.

Suppose a physician be called in to a case of fever or inflammation, and he has bled his patient *secundum artem, per scalpellum chirurgicum, scarificationes, et hirudines,* and purged him until he cannot stand ; has given him calomel until he cannot eat, drink, or sleep ; and has blistered him until he cannot lie down, and still the disease remains unsubdued, in spite of medical treatment enough to make a well man ill or even dead,—what can be done next ; We say, give him Tartar Emetic and sweat him.

It is well known that when we take anything into our stomachs which seems very unwilling to stay there, or let anything else, a copious sweating is produced, which is usually followed by an ejection of the offending substance. If the disease will not run off through open veins, nor by the inflamed, distended, and broken-down mucous lining of the bowels, nor be destroyed by "mercurial action," vulgarly called salivation, but by the doctors' "ptyalism," it is perfectly lawful, according to medical law, to sweat it out of the pores, if it will go that way, or even vomit it out of the stomach, if it is in.

Now the effects of Tartar Emetic on the body, are so close an imitation of disease, that some persons might imagine there was as real a Tartar Emetic disease as there is a calomel one. On taking a sufficient quantity, there is first a coldness, shivering, headache, and dullness felt ; then there is a nausea, and this is followed by sweating. It is said by some who profess to know some-thing about the matter, that this process is so exactly similar to fever, that it is impossible to distinguish the one from the other. There are, however, some very im-portant distinctions between the two, which we shall lay before the reader.

Common fever is caught you hardly ever know how; whether by infection, malaria, exposure to cold, fear, or exhaustion. Tartar Emetic fever is taken—by taking Tartar Emetic. Common fever, if let alone, will usually leave you in a few days. Tartar Emetic fever will, if well supplied with Tartar Emetic, last a few weeks. Common fever is caught cheap, even gratis. Tartar Emetic fever is pretty expensive if the physician who prescribes it, and the apothecary who prepares it, be paid.

There is a still further difference between the two. Common fever permits you to get well very rapidly, as soon as it has ceased. Tartar Emetic fever causes you to get well very slowly. In common fever, the blood has nothing in it which prevents its reorganization. In Tartar Emetic fever there is something in the blood, which, as long as it is there, effectually prevents its reorganization. Moreover, with regard to common fever, there is a commonness, a vulgarity about it. Emigrants, vagrants, paupers and prisoners can and do have it. Tartar Emetic fever is a scientific, respectable and genteel disease, which the upper class generally endure The educated and refined class of patients will, of course, prefer the Tartar Emetic fever!

We do not intend by any means to assert, nor even to insinuate, that emigrants, vagrants, paupers and prisoners and the patients of dispensaries and hospitals, do not enjoy the benefits of Tartar Emetic treatment. On the contrary, many of them owe their permission to depart this transitory life entirely to that substance, given *ad libitum*—that is, with professional freedom. The chief difference between the Tartar Emetic treatment of the rich and the poor is this, that the rich are nauseated and sudorized into a long and profitable sickness, while the poor are vomited and purged to death, *bene et celeriter*.

Next in importance to calomel in the profitable treatment of disease, Tartar Emetic is certainly entitled to take the lead. It is given in small quantity, has but little taste, does a great deal of mischief, and no one either knows it, believes it, or suspects it. So far from this, everybody supposes it to be either harmless or useful. Its effects are very lasting, and can easily be attributed to anything else in the world ; so that its good can be reported far and wide, and its evil kept quiet or silenced. Its power of doing harm, under so fair an outward garb, entitles it to its very expressive name, and renders it worthy of its paternity.

See what an admirable medicine it is for medical practice amongst children. An infant is ill, and the physician cannot tell what is the matter. He tries to look at its tongue, and feel its pulse—he does feel its skin, and inquires respecting a number of immaterial and trival matters—bibs, napkins, and diapers. He can come to but one conclusion. Whatever may be the matter—respecting which he is totally uncertain, and perhaps equally unconscious and unconcerned—Tartar Emetic is the remedy. The child must be put into warm water, and take a dose of Tartar Emetic. It will either make the case better or worse, or change the symptoms decidedly. The uncertainty or the child will be removed, and the case, of course, terminated.

In that domestic and popular climatic disease, the hives, the nature and symptoms of which, every woman thinks she knows thoroughly,* but of which the physician knows nothing more than—that it is an eruption—it is undoubtedly proper, that for an unascertained disease, an uninvestigated medicine should be given. Let sweating be proposed, and Tartar Emetic can be administered. If the hives are not very apparent, let it be given for the purpose of bringing them out. If they are out, let it be given to carry them away. If the fever be high, give it to lower it. If it be low, give it to raise it and sweat it off—but any how give it.

When a person has experienced a sudden chill, and the mere act of being wrapped up in a warm room, or of going into a warm bed, would relieve him, it is very advisable, if we mean to make anything of such a case, to give Tartar Emetic. Let the person put his feet into warm water, and take enough of the medicine to cause nausea, shivering, and headache. The chances are many that by such a course of treatment a tolerably long case of fever may be induced.—Try.

We are deeply indebted to some newspaper which we looked at a short time ago, for an excellent suggestion as to the use of Tartar Emetic. It was to this effect: "If a fish-bone stick in your throat, take a dose of Tartar Emetic to vomit you." Now, it will either drive the bone out, and perhaps tear the lining membrane of the throat, or drive it into the substance of the throat, so as in any case to clear the road.

This commended itself at once to our benevolence and commercial disposition, as an admirable way to make business. If the former of the two probable results happened there would be an opportunity for applying leeches, lotions

---

* The editor does not here mean the Croup, for which some people substitute the word Hives, but an eruptive complaint about the body, generally though not always, occurring in infants.

6

blisters, and ointments, externally, and using gargles, probings, caustic touchings, and so forth, internally, beside giving drops, if not mixtures, and troches, or powders to dissolve on the tongue. Very probably a moderate salivation might be prescribed for such a case.

If the latter probability occurred, the throat might require the operation of pharyngotomy, or in plain language, the cutting of the throat—and a long, troublesome, and expensive attendance would be requisite. We do not remember the name of the medical philanthropist who proposed this excellent mode of treatment, but we presume that some of our professional brethren have *profited* by his proposal.

With regard to rheumatism, concerning which more has been written than has been read, and more has been read than is worth reading, it is the opinion of the vulgar, that this disease is brought on by exposure of the body, while sweating, to cold, in some way—probably a draught of cold air. Ordinary and unscientific persons would therefore imagine, in their ignorance, that to stop the sweating, and to apply heat, would be beneficial.

They, of course, do not know anything, except what they learn by observation and experience; and those modes of knowledge having long been discarded in medical philosophy, the mere *common* sense of mankind is not to be regarded. One of two modes of treatment is open to you, that of calomel or tartar emetic. If you employ the former, the sweatings will be of the cold kind, and occur principally at night. They will be very distressing, and perhaps even dangerous—but as they will be put down to the disease, and not to the remedy—which is very true, there being no *remedy* employed—you may, if you think proper, try that mode of *treatment* for a week or two, but the tartar emetic *treatment* presents advantages superior to those of calomel.

The Tartar Emetic treatment enables you to operate in a most effective manner, on so many parts and functions of the body at the same time, without the knowledge or consent of the patient. In a pleasant mixture of tartaric acid, syrup of red poppies and water, you can put, undiscoverable by the patient, as much of Tartar Emetic as will render the stomach incapable of receiving or digesting any food—the brain unfit for thinking or feeling—the limbs as useless as those of infancy—the skin unable to retain its fluids—and the blood unfit for any of the purposes of life, except that of producing and preserving disease. How valuable such a medicine is to medical men, they only can tell. It is also very good for the druggist. An eight ounce mixture costs six-pence, and brings half a dollar ?

By combination of the advantages of the calomel and tartar emetic treatment the simplest and shortest case of rheumatism may be converted into one of inexplicable complexity and interminable continuance. A dose of calomel at night will sufficiently derange the blood to prevent any useful sleep, even though opium be combined with it, for the purpose of procuring some artificially. A few doses of tartar emetic during the day, will so far decompose the blood, as that neither pleasant sensation nor appetite can by possibility affect the patient. He is therefore entirely at your mercy,—just where he ought to be, or at least where you wish him to be. Indeed, whether you or desire it or not, there he is, and there we leave *him !* We proceed with *you.*

You doubtless have frequently experienced the salutary relief of a potent sudorific, when, in the course of your medical incursions on your patients, you have been re-

quested to state the nature of some disease, of which you
were entirely ignorant, and to explain what you were aim-
ing to accomplish—in order that they might have something to say to their friends, who were all, not only anxious, but anxiety itself, to know the probable fate of the
patient.   We give you an excellent specimen of a learned
and scientific mode of treating such a case.   We have
learned much from it ourselves, and hope you will learn
something :—

A lady of our acquaintance, deeply interested in the welfare of a friend, who was under "medical treatment," inquired anxiously of the attending physician what was her
friend's *complaint?*   The learned Esculapian replied with
admirable technical tact—"Oh! she has—hem, hah—
hydrothorax, and probably *hydrops pericardii.*"   The lady,
unconscious of the meaning of the great long words, gently inquired what it *arose from?*   "I believe," said he,
making an excellent deep, long *hem*, "she has had an attack of *pleuritis*, or *pericarditis.*"   The *lady* now began to
perspire, but with that perseverance which characterizes
a benevolent woman, she ventured another approach to
the medical luminary for a ray of light, and inquired
what might be the *cause* of her ailment?   The resources of
our medical brother were beginning to fail, and perspiration in *him* was beginning to appear ; when he recovered from his quandary, and replied with an admirably important deep guttural exclamation, vulgarly called a *grunt*,
"Why--ee--a--a--*General Anasarca.*"   As the patient
had been suspected of being *enceinte*, the announcement
of so distinguished a supposed military gentleman being
the cause of the ailment, was almost enough to throw our
friend into hysterics.   She, however, with her handkerchief in hand, ready to be applied to her face in case of
necessity, meekly inquired what the probable result might

be, when she received the consoling information, that probably the patient might become *anemious !* The lady was silenced.

[The editor takes the liberty to explain, that *hydrothorax* means dropsy of the chest. *Hydrops pericardii* means dropsy of the heart. That *pleuritis* means inflammation of the covering of the lungs. *Pericarditis*, inflammation of the covering of the heart. That *general anasarca* means common dropsy, and *anemious* signifies want of blood. He deems these explanations due to the dignity of the profession.]

We shall now treat of the valuable properties of tartar emetic, in cases of lung disease. We are at present attending a lady in the last stage of consumption, who might have sunk to her grave very comfortably, without requiring our aid, but for the administration of tartar emetic by some previous physician, who positively assured her, that two or three vomits with it would certainly cure her. She declined that mode of cure for a long time, but at last, overpersuaded, she took one, which caused a vessel to burst in her lungs, and made *us* a very interesting case ; for the lady dismissed the emetic doctor and sent for ourselves. Of course we are obliged to both doctor and patient, as we obtain a few fees, and acquire some valuable information—*heu mihi !*—and the means of filling up our article ! No one, without trying, can conceive the difficulty that is experienced in "getting up" an article like this. Were it not for the ignorance and error of our beloved brethren, we should not have anything to write about. As Touchstone says to Audrey, "Praised be the stars for ignorance !"

In the inflammation of the lungs, tartar emetic is a specific—that is, it exactly suits the case. In this disease, the substance of the lungs through which the blood has to pass, is disorganized, so that it cannot admit the blood through without much pain, or cannot admit it at all. In the exercise of sound medical logic, tartar emetic is required to disorganize the blood, in order to accommodate the condition of the blood to that of the solids. It has been most satisfactorily proved by the celebrated Louis, that fewer patients are killed by this mode of treatment than by being bled to death, and many of our ablest physicians are not only convinced of this truth, but converted to it. Before the discovery and announcement of this pathological myth, it would have been considered a murderous proceeding, to give half-drachm doses of tartar emetic to persons with any sort of lungs or stomachs! However, now, it is clear that we are unpardonable, if we let any die of inflammation of the lungs, since they can be killed so much more speedily and easily by tartar emetic.

But we recollect that this is entitled a diaphoretic for the profession, and as we desire their recovery, not their demise, we must be careful not to continue the diaphoresis beyond its therapeutic effect. We are convinced that *sweating* may be kept up too long and profusely, especially if the patient be a doctor, for he is usually of a very impressible nature ; we therefore propose to allow a considerable interval between our doses. This will give time for reflection on our next prescription, and the " vis medicatrix " to act. Wise doctors always prefer to keep that loving old mother as near by as possible, consistently with their own dignity.

SCENES IN A MEDICAL STUDENT'S LIFE.—RE-
SURRECTIONIZING.

"The sleeping and the dead
Are but as pictures : 'tis the eye of childhood
That fears a painted devil."

"THE body of man, decomposed by putrefaction, remains a light skeleton and a little earth, when the ground
and the winds have withdrawn all its juices." This
beautiful quotation of the physiologist will convey to the
reader an idea of the indifference to censure with which
we proceed to give some reminiscences of our student's
life ; and yet, as it has been our custom to appeal to the
judgment rather than the passions, pray tell me, reader,
if you can realize the fact that you are only human, and
may some day require the aid of the actual scalpel to
preserve your life, on which would you prefer the first
experiment to be made—the dead body, soon to be resolved into its elements and to mingle with the earth and
air, or on your wife or child, or your own precious person ? Over the broad extent of this favored land there
is an awful amount of accidents, originating in our
national carelessness and hurry, requiring the minutest
knowledge of anatomy. A hair's breadth often inter-
venes between a vein or artery and death. There is, we
will assure you, a vast diversity of talent in the surgeons
so heartlessly diploma'd by our shameless colleges. You
cannot always be in New York, and have an expert oper-

ator ; you may require instant surgical aid in the far
West, and be obliged to summon your farmer surgeon
from his log cabin. Would you have him more familiar
with the plough than the scalpel? The first operation
we ever performed was for strangulated rupture, at midnight, on a pauper woman, in a garret, with the light of
a single dip candle in a black bottle, held by a drunken
woman. We had made, when at college, most diligent
use of the shovel and the scalpel, and our poor brains
besides, but verily we found no surplus anatomy on this
trying occasion. You will perceive in our sketches, that
we never unearth gentle clay, and we were very careful
to restore to order all visible indications of our midnight
doings about the grave, and even in the pauper burial
places, precisely as we all do with our faces and our deportment after some wanton and wicked outrage against
our fellows ; such, for instance, as destroying a human
life for want of anatomical knowledge. Poh! away with
hypocrisy. ʼ We will tell our story as we please, reader ;
you know us, or we would not give much for your perception of character if you did not by this time.

In the year of 1831, when the feud between the old
Barclay Street College and the Rutgers Faculty, who had
seceded from that old medical Chelsea, where they now
humanely keep some of their professors for their antiquity
—when Hosack and Mott, Macneven, Francis, and the
glorious and lamented Godman had intrenched themselves in Duane Street—when the feud was at its highest,
among the amiable methods they contrived of annoying
each other and rendering their separate classes more fit
for the responsible duty of surgeons, was that of cutting
off the supply of _matériel_ for the dissecting room. Whoever bid highest to induce the keeper of Potter's field to
tie up his dogs, get drunk, and go quietly to bed, was

allowed to monopolize the pauper bodies, and so one or the other of the colleges was sure to be in the vocative, greatly to the injury of the unsuccessful one. It is true that such deprivation of college privileges was not very distressing to most of the students, who were traveling the scientific highway in silk stockings, and felt the intimate relation between a rich father's pocket and their sheep-skins proper and prospective ; but there were a few of us who looked to our profession only for advancement, yet who could not forget the charms of whiskey punches and choice Havanas, with an occasional theatre or opera ticket. This drew so deeply on the pocket, and our surgical anatomy was so imperative in its requisitions, that we resolved to turn resurrectionists for ourselves.

Our class consisted of four, but one was indolent and wealthy, and so three of us had to do the work. This, however, was just the number required ; one to take charge of the wagon and horse, one to look out, and one to dig, occasionally relieved by the sentry, who was usually posted behind a stone fence near the road ; by throwing small pebbles he gave notice to the digger when the approach of a pedestrian or horseman required the cautious handling of the shovel. Remember, reader, we always unearthed common clay, where there were no aristocratic monuments to skulk behind ; the slightest token of affection, the frailest memorial, would have protected the humblest remains from our touch, as though guarded with the flaming sword ; living affection would have hallowed the spot with either of us and rendered our steps sacrilege, for a noble heart was his who assisted me ; alas! he lies far away in a southern clime, a victim to science. That noble heart, that clear intellect, intent on ambition's most holy return—the knowledge of curing

6*

disease—has ceased to beat.* "Closed for aye is the speaking glance that dwelt on me so kindly." Yet, as I pen these boyish lines, I recall with a tear and a sigh that one so true should have been cut down on the very threshold of the temple, whose corner stone had been laid so securely on the foundation of anatomy.

Uncle Sam's men were in high repute with us as subjects, from their fine development of muscle ; and when the poor fellows would "slip their wind," after returning from a cruise, they were at that time planted in a very convenient place, in rows, on a certain side hill, somewhere in a place which it would at present be difficult to recognize. We will tell you a tale about that hill that will move your risibles a little. We took a flying leap there of some thirty feet or so, in company with a six-foot fellow we had bagged, that made the darkness of our intellectual regions for a few minutes a little more apparent than we thought either agreeable or wholesome ; but let us begin at the beginning.

One stormy day in December, when we felt very little like investigating the intricacies of the sphenoid bone or dissecting the semi-lunar plexus, we had dispatched our friend to our favorite ground to reconnoitre for the fresh spat of a shovel at the end of the row—for they put the poor fellows "in line," even when dead, and ground is dear where affection does not select the spot. We were talking very learnedly, no doubt, beneath the roof of old Rutgers College in Duane Street, when his clear voice was heard coming up stairs, and singing, "Oh! 'tis my delight of a stormy night, in the season of the year," interspersed with "And a hunting we will go—o—o—a

* Abel J. Starr, the editor's class-mate ; he died at Madeira, from phthisis, developed by a wound received in dissecting, and hastened by constitutional irritability, the result of excessive smoking and the injudicious use of mercury.

hunting we will go!" Then came the Scotch growl of
old Jemmy Henderson, the janitor, outside of our door,
"rousing and growling in his den," and muttering,
"And a braw time ye'll hae o't, ye deevil's babbies—hell
taak ye. I'll niver say to him nae should he come this
minute." Poor old Jem! If ye were judged on yer own
merits "down thar," ye know by this time a thing or
two about yer own comparison of the dissecting room
furnace to a certain place. Jemmy was only blessing us
in his amiable way, for doing him out of his perquisites
by the profits he made on the subjects that ought to have
been brought in by the employed resurrectionists of the
college, who were bribed by the Barclay Street professors
to cut us off. Cursing us in his throat, he bawled out to
our class-mate as he crossed the garret where the general
students were accommodated—we occupied our private
room—"Ye'll no find the dhure apen and ye bring all
Potter's field wi' ye ; and I dare say ye'll raise the divvel
some nicht and bring the haal police on us." Our friend
said nothing, for he knew Jemmy was only reminding us
how to open the door with a silver key ; he brought the
news that a body had been deposited that day, and we
adjourned immediately to prepare. Our rendezvous was
at the ferry house, at twelve o'clock ; one was to go for
the wagon, a couple of shovels, a sort of pry to get off the
lid, and a few bunches of straw to cover the suspicious
outline of a large salt sack, when on our return we had
bagged the game,

A man may cross the Atlantic a dozen times, and even
go over the New Haven Railroad, and not be killed, and
then step from his door-step and break his neck ; and so
it proved on the expedition we are going to relate. We
had been near a dozen times to our favorite ground, and
brought away as many good fellows ; but this time we

were destined to experience a most laughable combination of accidents. 'Twas dark as Erebus (we never
courted moon-light on such poetical occasions :) we rode
comfortably on, and had made nearly all the sinuosities
of the road, and our steed was so entirely acquainted with
his journey, that I am puzzled to this day to know what
evil spirit possessed him on this unfortunate night. We
had already arranged our plan of action as we neared
the ground. S—— and I were to dig and act sentinel
alternately, and H—— to drive up and down the road a
mile or so and return, till called by the sentinel, when
the body should be bagged and brought up to the stone
wall next the road ; we were jogging slowly on, when all
at once off the side of a high bank we pitched into an infernal mud-hole, where horses had been driven from the
road by the farmers, to wet their wagon wheels. We
were all pitched clear over the mud on the other side of
the pond, and arose bruised, but not seriously hurt ; our
steed lay on his side, head and nose under the mud, and
the shaft broken and under his side, most ominously
still ; we all started to our feet, and as we were pretty
cool characters, our first thought was for him. I raised
his head and placed it on my knee ; he soon breathed,
and snorted vociferously ; S—— had to hold him down
by the bridle, while H—— pitched into the mud knee-
deep to unbuckle the traces. He soon got loose the one
on the upper side, but was obliged to cut the other ; this
we were glad to do, for we greatly dreaded that the ends
of the broken shaft which we had heard snap off should
pierce his body. As soon as we got him on his legs we
examined his flank, and found all sound, to our great
relief, as he was a valuable animal. A passing couple of
countrymen hailed us, and offered assistance ; but we
thanked them, and played drunken dandy, " dem foine,"

just enough to disgust them, and they went on highly
amused at our disaster.   On hauling out the wagon, we
found the cut trace and the broken shaft were all the
damage it had sustained.   A piece of the rope which was
to be used to raise the body, answered well enough for a
trace ; but as we could spare no more of it, we found a
substitute where none but the sagacity of a surgeon
would look for it.   The shaft was fractured obliquely ;
we " set the bone and bandaged the limb."   We will give
you time to guess where we procured the bandages.
They were not exactly made of " snow-white seventeen
hunder linen," like poor Burns's cuttie sarks, but we certainly did all of us complain before we left the ground of
the unusual coolness of our extremities.   We had taken
off our over-coats, to be sure ; but that was not exactly
the reason, either.

I said that old Jemmy's curse would stick, and so it
did ; for surely the " deil had set his seal on this vara
nicht."   We were working about half-way up a hill whose
apex was full thirty feet above the level of the road where
we left our wagon.   The sentinel had repeated occasion
to warn the digger of the approach of wagons and pedes-
trians : several had stopped to listen whilst I was on
watch ; but two or three pebbles, timely thrown, stopped
the digger.   I "kept shady" under the wall, and they
went on apparently satisfied.   When the body was in
the sack, and the grave filled up, we consulted on the
propriety of summoning our wagoner when he should
next pass, and had concluded to carry the body down to
the wall immediately next the road, as usual, and have
all ready to lift it in ; but so many persons passed whilst
we were both skulking behind the wall, and we had kept
our place so unsullied by suspicion for two years, that we
concluded it would be better to carry our prize around

the apex of the hill to the stone wall on the other or
opposite side, where we knew there was also a road ; for
we had driven round the hill before, and H—— had several times done the same that night, whilst we were
digging, for I had observed him coming up from that
direction whilst on the watch.   Accordingly, S—— was
deputed to go up the road where H—— had last gone
with the wagon, and go round with him to meet me with
the body on the other road.   Off he went, and I having
taken a good pull at the bottle of port we always took
with us, shouldered our prize.   'Twas a dead lift in
good earnest, but I trudged on manfully, feeling the
importance of the trust.   I certainly had not got more
than forty rods, and began to think myself every inch a
man, when, presto! down went I, body and all, down,
down the precipitous hill-side, and found myself in the
middle of the road, with the dead body beside me.
Heaven and earth! how my ears did ring, and how the
fire did fly before my eyes! darkness was of no use to
me, and such light as I had rather worse.   I gathered
myself up and stood on my legs, to assure myself that
Jemmy's prayer was not really answered, and I on my
actual road to the place where he so often wished me ;
the coolness of the air gave me assurance ; I was still on
earth, and the fire had left my eyes.   I dragged the body
to the side of the road, and limped off to go round the
hill where I knew they would expect me.   They had cut
a street through the hill, and completely divided it, since
we were there the winter before.   This explained my
mishap, and afforded facilities to approach the body with
the wagon and my comrades.

I fortunately found my friends just as I had reached
the end of the newly cut road, going round to the other
side of the hill as agreed on when I left S—— to convey

the body there. S—— was inclined to blame our companion who drove the wagon, for not discovering the new cut; but I took his part roundly, for that was not suspected by any of us, and formed no part of the plan, as preconcerted and practiced on all previous occasions.

We had always entered and come out of the ground on one side, and that was agreed upon as usual. There happened to be more passing than usual on this night, and that caused the change in our plan. I soon laughed them into a good humor; and H—— went for the tools on foot, whilst we drove slowly on.

But the curse of old Jemmy pursued us. We got on well enough till we had driven on board the boat, and were half-way over, when our steed began to shiver and shake as though in an ague fit; he was frightened at some moving lights in a little shallop that passed us. H—— was capital at mimicking a drunkard, and he usually took the precaution upon crossing to lie down on the straw by the side of the body, with his cloak over both.

On this occasion a couple of fellows were unusually impertinent, and amused themselves with peering into the wagon and talking to him. My other companion was inclined to give them some idea of the hardness of his knuckles; but fortunately the boat reached the landing, and they ceased their impudence, before his wrath culminated to the striking point.

Now, at least, we thought our prize secure; but devil a bit; we were not yet done with old Jemmy's curse. It was four o'clock, and the lamps gave an uncomfortable view to the watchmen of our bedraggled steed and equipage. We dared not play drunk to break the suspicious silence, for then they would nab us for sure; and the thought of the station house and "his honor," a snub-

nosed, half-drunken justice, was very repulsive to Esculapian dignity ; and then the loss of such a tall fellow as
we had bagged! 'twas hard to contemplate. As we
neared the college we drove round a square extra, to give
time, and sent S—— to see if the door was open, as old
Jem had promised. We were to go down Duane Street
directly up to the college, and had turned the Broadway
corner when he appeared, and muttered *sotto voce*, " Go
round Manhattan Alley to the back gate ; the old rascal
has locked the door." I have never heard it remarked,
because there were few stirring at the hour, but I fancy
if any one had been looking at our wagon just as that
announcement was made, that they would have seen blue
flames on all sides of it ; and just at the same moment
old Jem must have felt his old Scotch blood get warmer
in his bunk ; had it been in our power we would have
given him over at once to Auld Clootie. We often talked
of Burking him, when subjects were scarce, but concluded
'twas no use ; for there was not a set of scalpels that his
hide would not have turned the edges of, in the college ;
indeed, it is very doubtful if fire has yet touched him,
and he be not this very minute at his old trade of sorting
over the " soojets," as he always called our subjects, in a
more uncomfortable place than even old Rutgers.

We drove round, and found the gate barred, of course ;
but there were no watchmen to plague us ; such wretches
as lived in that delectable and aromatic alley were not
worth watching. S—— climbed over the fence, and in a
few minutes we had our game safely in our own room.
Jemmy looked very mean next morning, because we had
not been captured by the watch, which he undoubtedly
intended, and muttered his Scotch curses as usual when
he saw us all enter the college hall at nine o'clock, as
though we had been safe in our beds all night. He did

not come "oot o' his rume" when we entered by the
over-the-fence way, and therefore did not know how successful we had been. We saw him peering through the
key-hole next day, but he pretended to be only sweeping ;
nor would he condescend to speak to us for several days.
The first distinct utterance of his amiable eloquence that
reached me was more than a week afterwards, after he
had received a blowing up for not attending to his duties,
by the professor of anatomy. " How can sich meeserable
wratches expect a mon to waat on 'em when thae young
deevils would go ayont h—l for a soojet, and taak the
vara bred oot a mon's mooth! I'll gie up the place, I
will."

And what think you, reader, of resurrectionizing ?
Who was hurt ? The poor clay lately "stretched in disease's shape abhorred," or trained to be " mown in battle
by the sword," "like grass beneath the scythe ?" The
heart that animated that frame was never " pregnant
with celestial fire," nor could those hands "have waked
to ecstasy the living lyre."   " No frail memorial implored
even the passing tribute of a sigh." The living were
glad to hide it from view, as a loathsome, worthless
thing. We have the pleasing consciousness, whenever
called on to use our anatomical knowledge to relieve human misery, that we made a use of the body far more
acceptable to God and our own conscience, than had it
been embalmed in the spices of Arabia, and entombed in
the most costly mausoleum of affection. One mother's
heart saved to beat a little longer whilst watching over a
helpless family, one pair of toil-worn hands yet animated
by life through the knowledge derived by the possession
of that poor body, is more comforting to our soul this
day than the applause of millions, had we led him to the
fight and freely let out his life's blood, to win for ourself

the praises of a thoughtless nation—a nation who have required a century to learn the awful importance of legalizing the science of anatomy! It was the wish of that dear friend who was our active companion on that occasion, that his body should be applied to the uses of the science that finally destroyed him. And the body of the glorious Godman, who taught anatomy in that college before the lamented Bushe, now fills a niche in the Philadelphia College, with this memorable inscription : " A teacher of anatomy in life, a willing tributary in death." We sympathize with the loving heart that lingers round the spot where rest the ashes of the loved one ; but when we reflect that all that live are but as nothing to those that have returned to dust, we are inclined to think that he who supposes we were wrongfully employed on that occasion is cultivating an emotion that will never expand into philanthropy or justice.

P. S.—Whilst these lines are passing through the press, we read in the papers the braying of a senseless idiot who holds a position as probate judge of Covington, Ky., that our beloved friend and correspondent, Dr. Byrd Powell of that city, is pronounced a madman because he had the generosity and dignity to leave his head to illustrate that science his eloquent pen could no longer illustrate. He was the pupil of Godman, and the illustrious discoverer of the law of physiological marriage.

A GONE FOX.

THE LAST WORDS OF AN OLD MEDICAL FOX, CAUGHT IN THE HOSPITAL TRAP, TO HIS YOUNG BRETHREN OUTSIDE.

My Dear Children :—It is natural for one so near the close of his career, to feel the affection of a parent for the little band of young brothers, who have so affectionately stood by him for the past six years of an eventful life, and I hope that the words of advice and caution I may deliver to you, will be duly appreciated. There can be no doubt, that when the heartless wretches come to seek the result of their infernal trap, I shall behold you for the last time ; indeed, I would advise you, however your hearts may bleed, to take leave of me before that hour ; for your solicitude can do me no good, and you may wear out all your precious young teeth in gnawing upon this accursed old trap, and not rid me of a single fetter. I, at least, am a gone fox ; beware of the medical dogs, for they will scent you by the morning light. If they find you here, you are gone goslings.

Those non-professional bipeds who have watched the sagacity of our genus, and observed our hatred to each other, and our attachment to the public geese and chickens, must have observed the sneers of the miserable snobs who have nothing but their wealth to give them importance. There is our friendly and amusing little forest associate, the coon, who may fairly be called the representative of that excellent body, the clergy. I have heard

with indignation the insulting remark, as he goes hum-
bly along the forest, sagaciously smelling the earth for
his food, which some vile sinners have compared to a
cunning ability to discover and flatter the secret foibles
of his rich parishioners, "There goes that little black
devil, smelling for his fodder ; it is to be hoped he will
find some." What an insulting remark for a Christian to
make on an individual exercising a beneficent gift of
nature! Many of you, my dear children, will be obliged
to get your living by this kind of earthly sagacity ; that
interesting and innocent quadruped, the Norway rat, is
by no means to be despised for his abilities in securing
his share of the comforts.

My object in enumerating these useful examples, is to
make you thankful to Heaven for every accomplishment.
Our senses are given us for self-preservation, and it behooves us to keep them sharpened by continued use ;
laziness is a vice I have always detested. You can see
for yourselves that Providence has been bountiful in giving me such ample accommodations for the olfactory
nerve, that I can scent the game afar off ; the length of
my legs and arms, too, enabled me to secure many a good
morsel, which others were obliged to content themselves
with viewing in the distance ; would to God they had
availed me in avoiding this infernal trap! But regrets
are useless ; I must hasten to give you my last advice.

You know, of course, that I, like all of you, have
been held in captivity before ; I mean during my collegiate life ; but those were silken chains, compared to these,
that have been forged by my plotting brethren. Had I
gone on quietly, like the modest coon and the sagacious
Norway rat, who always begins to gnaw in the dark, at
the bottom of the bin, I should have enjoyed great comfort. It is true, I have plenty of food, but I am nearly

toothless ; and my eyes fail me so that I find it hard to watch the machinations of the cunning old professional foxes of the hospitals and the colleges, who, like the scorpion, always sting in the dark.

There is a miserable creature, of the species medical wolf, who prowls about the forest, and publishes a journal called the *Scalpel*, in which he endeavors to make light of your attainments, and to cheapen your efforts for the public welfare. Notwithstanding my aversion to him and his abominable journal, because of his hostility to you, when I think of my fetters, I sometimes have looked upon it almost with affection and admiration at the sagacity of its editor, for he seems to understand the ropes by which those infernal old imps, the professors and hospital surgeons, have got so many of us poor devils into their toils. I hate these wretches, because they do not acknowledge the righteousness of the old adage, "Dog shouldn't eat dog." Alas! my dear children, they will one day, I fear, crack your own tender little bones. They are only waiting for you to get a little fatter. Meanwhile, they use you solely as decoy-ducks.

Last year, when they decoyed so many of you to their great trap, which they impudently call the "American Medical Association," and set it up at St. Louis by way of getting the good opinion of the Southern and Western brethren, they very well knew, the accursed imps, that it would not be in your power, in your hungry condition, to resist the hospitable provisions of your warm-hearted brethren, which I see you even yet remember with tears of gratitude ; and when that Gross-ly hypocritical old coon made such an outcry, because some of you warmed your hearts with a generous glass, and got slightly unsteady in your dear little legs, he only did it to get a white foot with the hypocrites. Let him look into his

big book, a mere surgical hash, and account to Dixon for
the ideas he has stolen from his and other folks' volumes,
and acknowledge his thin-blooded, beggarly stealings of
instruments and ideas. He ought to be dispatched on a
medical mission to Borriooboolagah. There used to be
honor even among thieves, but it seems to be no longer
so. But I must get on.

I was first caught, when young, in that old, rusty trap,
that used to be set for so many years in Barclay Street ;
it was managed by six old medical and surgical foxes,
and used to be a pretty well conducted affair. They seldom graduated a shoemaker or a waiter ; but when old
Hosack, and Mott, and Francis, Macneven, and Griscom
set up the other in Duane Street, they commenced running a muck against each other, and the country was
filled with half-fledged medical goslings. They used to
have some affection for me when I had my pin-feathers
only ; but as soon as I began to show my bill at the public feeding-ground, many a slap did I get from the old
rogues, sometimes before my patient, but oftener in the
dark. I stuck it out till I got nearly starved, and my
coat looked as though it had been between the jaws of a
hungry wolf, till one day, it all at once occurred to me
that I had been a great ass. I had all along had a notion that the "Code of Ethics," my benevolent seniors
had prepared for my guidance when they let me go out
of their trap, was a one-sided sort of affair. In it, I was
instructed to stick close in my hole, and only to look out
with great reverence when any of the old foxes passed
by ; meanwhile, they never looked in to see if I had anything to eat. I used to hear a most attractive screaming
in the neighboring poultry-yards every night, but was
obliged to content myself with licking my chaps till
morning, when the cunning old fellows had hied to their

holes ; then I would crawl out, and pick up a patient in
the shape of a servant-maid or an Irishman. These were
poor picking, however, for a cub who had been used to
good feeding, and I was nearly in despair.

One day, however, I was summoned to visit a rich old
turkey of a cit, who lived near my hole, in Bleecker
Street, and who was suffering with a "foie gras," the result of high feeding. I licked my chaps in anticipation
of a glorious fee ; and, after smoothing my old coat, and
making myself look as innocent as possible, I presented
myself at my neighbor's elegant mansion. I was forthwith walked up stairs to the old turkey's roost, when he
coolly informed me that he had only sent for me to give my
opinion, as one of the old foxes was his family physician,
and he had every confidence in him till day before yesterday, when he positively forbade his eating turtle soup!
As he had never forbidden him anything before, and
always bled and purged him every fortnight, for his
headache, with the best results, he naturally concluded
something was wrong, and the doctor was getting crazy
with some new-fangled notion or other. My new-fledged
hopes were dashed at once to the earth. Here was an
admirable chance for a capital bill ; bleeding and a prescription, xx. and xx. jalap and calomel every fortnight,
and the extra visits for all the uncomfortable gripings, et
cetera! What could I, what ought I to do, with such a fat
turkey before my very jaws, and the old goose of a professor having absolutely frightened him into a doubt of
his abilities? (and with what reason?) Was it in the
nature of a medical cub to resist? Yet the "Code of
Ethics" forbade me opening my jaws to nab my fat
friend. How wisely have they ordained it, (for themselves,) that we shall not open our lips to contradict any
of their absurdities, unless they are present. My hunger

made me desperate ; I determined to strike for freedom
and turtle soup. I not only told him his attendant was
mistaken, but that a strong natural want was instinctive
demand, and must be obeyed ; turtle soup, I continued,
was admirably adapted to his constitution, and he should
have it immediately. I felt his pulse, and passing my
fingers over the bend of the arm, I remarked that he had
been repeatedly bled, no doubt with excellent effect, but
in fearful proximity to the artery, drawing in my breath,
at the same time, convulsively, as I had observed my preceptor to do, when strongly interested in a rich patient
narrating his case, and disapproving of his predecessor's
prescriptions. My ruse took beautifully. The old cock
was so thoroughly frightened, that the very wattle
around his beak, though dyed with the best of oporto,
turned pale, and I thought he would have fallen from
his perch. I seized a bottle from which he had been
imbibing, and let him have half a tumbler, good ; while
he was in the swoon, I took as much myself, and, as soon
as he recovered, I smoothed him down beautifully. I
told him to tell the old fellow that attended him, he was
a fool, and would kill him outright if he deprived him of
his soup ; that he was nearly blind, and couldn't bleed
him with safety. Then I fired my twelve-inch mortar,
to clench him ; I told him that arterial varix (!) had been
the frequent consequence of such ignorant butchery. In
short, I spoke with such pathos and feeling, that, what
with that and the port, and the fear that he would not
send for me again, the tears came into my eyes, when I
shook hands with him as I was about to take leave. I
felt, in my very soul, I had done perfectly right. I always
believed my preceptors to be great rascals, and I never
could discover why a young fox shouldn't eat turkey as
well as an old one. I am sure I never could tell why a

poor devil of a patient should be deprived of two independent and separate opinions respecting his precious carcass, as well as two legal ones about the title of an estate ; indeed, I think he is much more likely to require them, as doctors are an accommodating set, and will give them pretty much what they seem to desire, and so they get confused when they come to think it over.

My patient assured me he would keep my visit a profound secret ; but I told him "I didn't care a farthing ; he might tell the old ass as soon as he pleased, and I would like to be there to hear him bray. It was natural I should feel distressed and indignant to see the life of so valuable and intellectual a citizen thus trifled with."

Thus early did I commence my bold and independent career. Had I continued to follow my better judgment, I might have reached a happy and an honorable old age, and been spared this degrading condition, and those tears of anguish which it racks my heart to see on your youthful cheeks.

But I am faint, and it is yet an hour before morning ; run, two of you, my dear children, to the Fifth Avenue or Union Park poultry-yards, and fetch me a chicken or a young gosling, and I will refresh my old stomach for the last time, and then continue my narrative of the manner in which the cunning old vermin got me into this infernal trap. Do not be rash, my dears ; one of you can watch, while the other waits at the door of the coop. The chickens and goslings stray out o' nights, and the old hens and ganders are not very sharp ; you needn't be afraid of the dogs, for they keep none but poodles in those fashionable places.

7

ABORTIONISM.

To know a subject thoroughly, perhaps, is not permitted unto erring, sinful mortals. To treat a subject thoroughly, perhaps, has not been granted unto man, except by inspiration. Then, he himself has been unconscious of the power which he possessed, and had to work his knowledge out, in detail, like another man, and leave abundance of positions to be wrought out by after generations. The subject which we treat may not be agreeable, but there are fields of observation and investigation, which we think we have explored, that others scarce have seen. We believe it our duty to do all we can to check the horrible evil.

We have defined *abortionism* to be, "the knowledge and the practice of expelling from the womb, the ovum, or the fœtus, ere it is matured." What an employment for a human being! The plunderer of a temple, or a church, is justly execrated for his *sacrilege*, the act of stealing sacred things! Was ever any temple, any church, more sacred than the secluded sanctuary, where an immortal being is preserved and nourished? The Paradise of God is sacred beyond any other spot of this all-hallowed universe, because it is the dwelling-place and throne of God! The womb of woman is the holy shrine, where God, in all his wisdom and his love, creates another image of himself, fitted to live with him, in his own Paradise, in blessedness and glory!

Who dares to enter that august and lofty pile, solemnly dedicated to the service of the High and Holy One, and ruthlessly destroy the symbols and the elements of worship? None but the burglar infidel—the atheist thief! Who dares invade the shrine of glory, where, in his resplendent blessedness, the Hierarch of the Universe of Being dwells—to plunder and destroy? The arch-fiend Satan, only, dared attempt the deed; and he, for the black act, was doomed to dwell in everlasting fire and chains of darkness! Who is it forces the sealed doors of the enshrined and dedicated sanctuary of the womb, and ravages and tears from thence the sacred image of Divinity? The fell abortionist—who in his character combines the sacrilegious burglar and arch-fiend of hell!

Can man, rejoicing in the vivid imageries of the beauties and delights of progeny, endowed with the creative power, and worshipping himself in the mysterious shrine where he was wonderously developed—can man, with fraud and force, enter the temple of creation, and with fiend-like savageness destroy the image of himself—tear down his throne, dilapidate and desecrate his temple, and overthrow his dynasty? Can man do this? Can he who has been dignified with the exalted power of emanating an immortal being, and depositing the trust in the rich temple of formation; will he leap off from the Creator's throne where all is light and joy, and plunge into the abyss of the destroyer, where all is darkness, degradation, and damnation? Yes, man, degraded, fallen, lost to all his glory—may do this! Can woman?

She is by nature a producer, former, educator of her race. She is instinct with the desire of offspring, which nothing else can satisfy. Her soul is silently, but ceaselessly on fire, with love of progeny. The perils that

attend on pregnancy and parturition sometimes occupy
her thoughts ; the joys of offspring, always.

> " Man's love is of man's life a part,
> 'Tis woman's sole existence."

Her form, her make, her organization, her thoughts
and feelings, are expressly constituted, all for offspring.
The eye is not more evidently formed for seeing, the
hand for holding, and the feet for walking, than is a woman formed for offspring.

Conceive the penalty inflicted on the eye, when subjected to the privation of all objects for its vision, while
basking in the blaze of unreflected light!   Consider what
unmitigated misery is the lot of those who find no occupation for their hands, especially if their developments
of combativeness and constructiveness be full!   What
can be more annoying than to be debarred the exercise
of walking, when the feet and legs, which are a large
part of our body, have no other use—no other pleasure!

One of the most refined and subtle tortures of our being, is that of taking from us every sort of occupation
and employment.   Nothing so certainly produces madness, as silence, solitude, and inactivity.   The organs
that were wont to exercise their functions, being now forbidden them, the blood that circulates within them
stimulates to action, and like the steam pent up within
an engine, must be employed and suffered to escape, or
the whole force will be expended on the organs and
machinery.

The instinct, the inwrought desire of woman, is for
offspring.   She is constructed outwardly for this very
purpose.   Her abdomen and hips are large for the reception and gestation of her offspring ; her lap is ample
for its couch and resting-place ; her bosom fitted for its

nouriture and fondling ; her limbs and person soft and flexible, to make a gentle, yielding, easily compressible nurse and playmate. Her hands are delicate, and exquisitely formed for gently handling tender beings. Her feet are small, her legs constructed to take tiny steps, so suitable and requisite for those who have the office of accompanying infant locomotion.

One thing is most remarkable, and yet it seems to have escaped the observation of philosophers and physiologists. The beauty of the woman, both in form and feature, seems to have no adequate use, unless it is a constant object of attention to her worshipping offspring. Then, the true use of woman's beauty is encircled with a glory, which its delight for man alone would never give. When we consider woman's beauty, like the star of Heaven, or flowers of earth, an object of unfailing, never wearying joy to children, our estimation of its worth, and its Divine Bestower's goodness, are raised beyond the highest and most pure conception of mere woman worship. Where beauty terminates as it originates, in goodness, 'tis divine.

The bosom, face, and hair of woman, are so much more soft and winning than they are in man, that children are instinctively induced to seek their comfort and enjoyment in their presence. The power to please is always grateful, and nothing can afford a human being, purer, richer, more refined, and satisfactory enjoyment, than the power of making children happy. Possession of a faculty or power, implies, of course, delight in exercise, and the existence of the objects requisite to its enjoyment. The highest faculty with which we are endowed, is that of being able to produce, or to create, the objects necessary to our happiness. Here we are on an elevation, like to that of God. Such is the privilege of woman. Most amply and indubitably stamped upon her, though we have but cursorily viewed her, in exterior endowments.

Interiorly, he would be a dolt in knowledge, and an infidel in science, who did not see that every development of her mysterious organization is for producing and sustaining offspring. What is the womb? A pear-shaped organ, with a cavity which opens to receive the embryotic seed of a new being, and then instinctively closes and seals itself up, in order that it may incorporate the germ with a miraculous ovum, and nourish and develop it into a fœtus. What are the ovaries or egg-beds, but two organs, which supply, and periodically send off, the ova or the eggs, which steadily and surely seek for impregnation? The satisfaction of the womb is in receiving and retaining. To lose, is just as miserable for the womb, as for the hand or head. It is as impossible for loss to be converted into gain, as for miscarriage to be turned to happiness for woman!

The blank unsatisfiedness of the barren womb has been proverbial in every age. From the days of Rachel, who exclaimed with exquisite pathetic longing, "Give me children or I die," to the time of Solomon, who, in his universal observation of mankind, has recorded his intense desire, which says, "Give, give," and never can be satisfied, the constant testimony of the Scriptures is to the happiness of offspring, and to the wretchedness of sterility and miscarriage. Nor is there any change in the preceding or succeeding parts of Scripture. There is but once a woe denounced on offspring, and a blessedness pronounced on barrenness, and that was by the Saviour, in his beautiful lament for doomed and desolated Judah and Jerusalem. Pity and love to miserable woman, reversed the blessing and the curse for once—but not reversed her nature. The sun is not more native to produce, than is the womb of woman.

The function of the womb, untended or perverted, is as annoying to a woman, as is a faculty of the mind, when left uncultivated. It cannot be completely dormant. It necessarily influences all the other faculties and functions of the woman. The faculties of observation and constructiveness, if not attended to, may be unnoticed and overlooked, because they are not normally in action ; yet will they manifest themselves irregularly, by the prying, meddling disposition of the person who possesses them in their abnormal state. The function of the womb affects the woman in the same manner. If it be rightly tended, whether in active or in passive state, the character is softened, elevated, and refined. If it be rudely treated, neglected, or perverted, it gives a roughness, coarseness, and ferocity to woman, almost unsexing her.

The largeness of the hips and abdomen in woman, imply a prearranged capacity for bearing children ; and the well-known pleasure which a woman feels, when conscious of her pregnancy, that it adds unto her interest and beauty, are large additions to our argument, that love of offspring is not only natural, but a strong necessity of her being.

Perhaps the strongest portion of the argument remains to be adduced. The function of the breasts. The beauty of these parts of woman's structure, we have already briefly treated—too briefly, even, for our purpose. Their function is a wonderous one, and if there were no other basis upon which to build our argument, this single function would be quite sufficient for our purpose. Give us the breasts, with their rich function of lactation, and we have all the previous functions and performances required for offspring, inevitably guaranteed by all the laws of nature and of Providence. Prominent and commanding must be the desire, the love of offspring. The love of life, the appetite for food, the keen enjoyment of the senses, cannot surpass the keenness of desire for, nor the strength of love to offspring.

But we ascend to higher laws than physical—the mental and the moral laws, the higher part of which we designate as spiritual. To every organization there is an adaptation of the mental and the spiritual nature. Perhaps the real mode of stating this position is, that to each human being, there is an adaptation of particular and peculiar organization, exactly suited to, and requisite for, the mental and the moral qualities of which it is the willing minister.

A woman has a mental taste and spiritual feeling for the value and delight of offspring. The only mode by which she can make known her thoughts and feelings is by her organs. They are compelled to manifest the deep intentions, and the deeper sympathies of her nature. If, therefore, it be granted that a woman has a mental and a spiritual nature, and that her organs are but the instruments of thought and feeling, there is no possible escape from the conclusion, that the desire of offspring is an integral and most essential part of her existence ; and that to reduce her to a vegetable nature merely, could not more palpably change and pervert her essence, than to reduce her to an offspring-hating creature.

We have already drawn a little on our second, and our higher source of matter for our essay, the sacred Scriptures—but we have not left the field of nature yet. The dramatist of man, the ever fertile and exhaustless Bard of Avon, is with us, a part of our universal nature. An axiom of his is, in our estimation, safe for our guidance to the truth, as is the river's course unto the sea—firm as a basis, for the building up the temple of Philosophy, as are the rocky defiles of the river's bed. The most profound Baconian induction has not, with us, more weight than the intuitions of the prince of philosophic poets.

A few quotations may be therefore made, confirmatory of our theory, with good, and certainly, agreeable effect. The character of Rosalind, in "As You Like It," is one of Shakspeare's highest feminine creations. She is a tall and graceful nervo-sanguine beauty, vivid in her imagination, abundant in the flashes of keen, caustic, but unwounding wit, sunny as summer in her exquisite affections, and every thought and feeling deeply dyed with womanhood; but beautifully, innocently, yet not ignorantly chaste and pure. The function of her womb diffuses over her a rich and fascinating mellow moral feeling, which charms and chains admiring and transported man, and lights up woman's fancy, brilliantly and elegantly, displaying it in all the glory of a tropical profusion.

After the wrestling scene, when Orlando had excited in her heart, for the first time, the elegant, subduing passion of pure love, she sighs her feelings forth to her well-trusted sympathizing cousin, Celia. Rosalind's father being now in banishment, Celia, with admirable woman's tact, asks if all this is for her father; and elicits the reply which we italicize in our quotation. We give that portion of the scene, where it occurs:

"CEL. Why, cousin; why, Rosalind; Cupid have mercy! Not a word?

Ros. Not one to throw at a dog.

CEL. No, thy words are too precious to be cast away upon curs, throw some of them at me; come, lame me with reasons.

7*

Ros. Then there were two cousins laid up; when the one should
be lamed with reasons, and the other mad without any.

Cel. But is all this for your father?

Ros. No, some of it *for my child's father!*"

Nothing could be more natural, more elegant, and exquisitely feminine. She traces love to its appropriate
and desired results, with one of those fine replies, which
woman only has the power to give. She speaks the
thought and feeling of her heart—love and fruition.

In the Merchant of Venice, where Bassanio has chosen
the right casket, and the majestical but exquisitely simple Portia dedicates herself and fortune to him, in
language which, for gentleness and tenderness of sentiment, and elegance of expression, has no parallel—
Gratiano and Nerissa confess their love, and the two
charmed pairs, betrothed, are now proceeding to their
marriage. The merry soul of Gratiano, in the presence
of the queenly Portia, and her accomplished maid, Nerissa, fired with the joys of expectation, speaks, what he
knows will touch the golden chord of feeling in the
bosom of them both. Beholding his fair charmer, he
exclaims, " *We'll play with them : the first boy, for a thousand ducats.*"

Perhaps there is no higher aspiration of a wife, than
that her first born may be a cherub boy. The feeling of
delight which thrills the soul of woman, when she con-
templates, with reasonable expectation, that she will
bring forth a beauteous image of the being whom she
loves, surpasses all the loftiest emotions of her love to
man. Creation is her glory—offspring is the perfection
of her function.

Although it would be easy to complete our paper
with citations from this noblest of the philosophic poets,
we must content ourselves with only one more well-

selected case, which shall be taken from the picture of that paragon of virtue and true beauty of the soul, as wife and mother, Catharine, queen of Henry the Eighth. In that majestical and marvelously moving pleading, which she makes before the king, presiding over the court, assembled for the purpose of divorcing her—a pleading which, for shape, and course, and argument, and pathetic power, a hundred cardinals and proctors might in vain essay to compass—she has this exquisitely apposite, most delicate, and charming passage :

> " Sir, call to mind,
> That I have been your *wife*, in this obedience ?
> Upward of twenty years, and *have been blest*
> *With many children by you.*"

The richness of this most felicitous passage may not be apparent to the mind of every one. It will repay us for our trouble of displaying it, and none will be more pleased to have it clearly shown, than those who now perceive it. She first appeals to his known, strong propensity for the married life, reminding him that, in the quality of wife, she had supplied his wants, obedient to his will, for twenty years. Had she staid here, he might have felt the pain of obligation, a feeling most inimical to her present cause. She wisely, beautifully, puts the sense of obligation on herself. " *I have been blest with many children by you.*"

The poet shows his master knowledge of the human mind, by this acute perception of the feelings of a pure, high-minded, virtuous wife ; lofty in honor, yet a saint in meekness and humility. Had the king only, been the court to which she had appealed, she would have gained her suit—for when she left, he straight pronounced her eulogy, as fondly as a lover, dwelling on her enchaining qualities as a wife. A commoner poet would have made

the queen bring in the king a debtor to her, for his children. A commoner woman than Queen Catharine would
inevitably have so done, and most assuredly have missed
her mark.

The best of poets and of moralists would all be found
to coincide with the delineations of true woman's character, as drawn by Shakspeare ; but as we are compelled,
by the restraint of space, to limit our citations of authority, we only venture on another, ere we come to sacred
writ. That one is Milton. Of all men, not included in
the Scripture category of "inspired," Milton appears the
loftiest, the purest, and the most sublime of mortals.
He was the most profound of scholars—a master of the
sciences of mind and morals—most thorough in his
knowledge of mankind—a mighty statesman—a most
comprehensive and acute philosopher—and one of the
most sage and grave of theologians. How does he draw
the character of woman?

In that divine relation, which he put into the mouth
of Eve, recounting to her consort, Adam, her waking up
to consciousnss of life and being, she tells him that she
heard a voice, which said :

> " But follow me,
> And I will lead thee where no shadow stays
> Thy coming, and thy soft embraces ; he
> Whose image thou art, *him thou shalt enjoy,*
> *Inseparably thine : to him thou shalt bear*
> *Multitudes like thyself,* and thence be
> Called mother of human race."

In this passage, the Deity gives her the promise of
enjoyment of her husband, and a multitude of offspring.
This promise, uttered in the ears of modern, fashionably
educated, and perverted woman, would sound more like
a curse.

Again, in that celestial adoration which the first pair offer ere they go to rest, they say :

> "Happy in our mutual help
> And *mutual love, the crown of all our bliss—*
> *For thou hast promised from us two,* a *race*
> To fill the earth."

The poet himself, in speaking on this subject, says :

> "Hail, *wedded love, mysterious law, true source*
> *Of human offspring!* * * * By *thee,*
> Founded in reason, loyal, just, and pure,
> *Relations dear, and all the charities,*
> *Of father, son, and brother, first were known,*
> *Perpetual fountain of domestic sweets."*

Once more dilating on this subject, he exclaims :

> "*Our Maker bids increase—who bids abstain ?"*

Thus have we laid our corner-stone, on which to build our temple to the woman's love of offspring, on the broad basis of the rock of nature. Anatomy and physiology, philosophy, and poetry, are all replete with proofs of this great truth. As long as woman is controlled by this most sacred law of her mysterious but delightful functions, she is safe, both morally and physically ; for she cannot stoop to improprieties and vice, as long as she regards the function of her womb inseparably linked with reproduction. The love of, the desire for offspring, is the preservative of woman's virtue, her golden shield of honor.

A woman thus endowed and dignified, can never stoop to the base lusts of harlotry or fornication. The *end* of commerce with the other sex refines and regulates it. As wife and mother, she is dignified and elevated in the scale of beings. As fornicatrix or as harlot, she is reduced to chattelage and thingdom ; an article of commerce or of pleasure, available for others' purposes of pastime or of mischief, but of no value to herself nor any one beyond. Reduced from the true dignity of spiritual beings, to a paltry toy amid the catalogue of things.

We shall sustain and close this portion of our subject with an appeal to the decision of the Scriptures. Those who regard these writings as divine—and to ourselves, this view of them is as self-evident as that the rays of light and heat come from the sun—those will of course be pleased with confirmations of mundane philosophy, drawn from the highest and unerring sources of divine instruction and command. Those who do not regard the Scriptures as divine, if they agree with us in our philosophy, will be no less delighted, when they find that what by others is regarded as divine, confirms the sound conclusions and instructions of their own acknowledged source of truth.

Before we close this portion of our essay, we would offer something in the shape of an apology for our unveiling such a subject, which, in a healthy, pure condition of society, would never be required. We have been often urged to use our pen upon this subject, by those whose judgment we esteemed ; but the inevitable risk of public censure, and the doubtfulness of doing much " to stay the plague," were obstacles apparently too great for us to overcome.

However, as we find in our investigations that this subject of *abortionism* gives " the form and pressure of the time "—enters, with subtle stealthiness, into the circle of refined and social life—tracks wilily its slimy way amid the guarded portals and duenna-watched seclusions of the seminaries of the young—distills its aspen poison in the feelings of domestic life—inoculates with its loathsome virus the maiden and the, youth, who are to be the future guardians of the race—seduces the physician from his post as sentinel of nature—and corrupts the judge upon the bench, sworn to administer law and justice ; we shall avail ourselves of the resources of the physical and moral fields of science, to convince the reader, that for a woman to become the victim of, or aider in the practice of abortion, is virtually an abdication of a throne of majesty and glory, for a temporary wallow in a stye of degradation and contempt.

ICHTHYO-JECORO-PLASTY—AN ASTONISHING DISCOVERY.

THE nineteenth century seems destined to eclipse in scientific discovery all that has gone before it. Scarcely, has one wonder had time to subside into reality, before another breaks upon the startled ear, and our eyes are dazzled and our brain made dizzy with its successor. We have been led to these reflections by the knowledge hitherto only imparted to a few, though suspected by many, from the great enterprise of a commercial drug house in this city, in supplying the market with a vast amount of an article of the greatest value to suffering humanity, and which it was supposed could not be obtained in sufficient quantity to supply the demand. We allude to cod-liver oil. A method has been discovered, whereby an article containing all the virtues of that derived from the liver of the real cod, can be furnished in any quantity. The enterprising and philanthropic gentlemen who have procured us this blessing, were incited to their humanitary efforts, by a knowledge of the great amount of the spurious article with which the market was inundated by unprincipled men, as soon as the value of the genuine oil became known.

Thoroughly convinced of its unspeakable value, and burning with a noble determination to check the heartless imposition, they immediately dispatched the most scientific member of their firm to the Banks of Newfoundland, where they were confident of procuring an ample supply, as that is known to be a natural resort of the fish. His mission was successful in filling the earlier orders, but the supply threatened to fail. His active mind soon suggested a remedy, which, thank Heaven, has been found successful. Reasoning from analogy on the wonderful triumph of plastic surgery, and vaccination, it was determined to ingraft, after the manner of the various plastic operations performed on the human body, the entire hepatic region of the healthy cod, upon the corresponding region of some larger fish, whereby the liver might be saturated with the virtues of the cod, so as to yield an abundant supply of oil, possessing the almost magic power of the Oleum Jecoris Aselli.

The theory, though extraordinary, was in accordance with known facts ; but the difficulty of attaining the realization of the project, with the great expense and inevitable ridicule attendant upon a failure, could only be overcome by the most disinterested philanthropy, indefatigable industry, and genius. This rare combination of qualities has been found in the gentleman whose modesty shrinks from the praise to which he is so justly entitled, and which he will undoubtedly receive from future generations ; thousands yet unborn will bless his name.

No difficulty was anticipated in taking the small black whale, (the physeter niger of naturalists,) nor any in performing, by the aid of the interrupted suture, the very simple operation. The only real and apparently insuperable obstacle was found in taking the whales without injury, and detaining them in a state of health, in an inclosure sufficiently moderate in extent to admit of their feeding and recapture, when the process of union and the impregnation of the liver were completed. This was finally accomplished in a manner beautifully simple and effective.

An estuary, or narrow bay, extending several acres into
the land, was securely staked off at its mouth, all but a
narrow opening ; this was furnished with double flood-
gates, similiar to the locks of a canal.   Through this the
small whales are driven with powerful seines by the fisher-
men, who are constantly on the watch.   They come in
considerable numbers to feed upon the herrings and other
small fish, that seek their food in immense shoals along
the shores of Newfoundland.   The same method is adopted in supplying the whales with these fish as food,
whenever required, and in drawing them upon the
beach of the bay itself, for the performance of the operation.

The largest specimens of cod are chosen for this purpose ; these are taken by the hook and line, on reefs in
the deeper water.   Frequently as many as a dozen
whales at a time have been undergoing this extraordinary
process within the inclosure.   The cod completely as-
similates with its huge foster parent, and both are found
in a state of perfect health at the end of a month, when
experience has proved the liver of the larger fish to be
highly impregnated with the virtues of the cod.   Chemical tests detect the iodine, bromine, and all the other essential salts, the oil being, moreover, of high specific
gravity.

Thus has science completely triumphed over this apparently insuperable obstacle, and another imperishable
leaf been added to the volume of humanity, and sound
inductive physiology.

It is to be hoped that all who require the remedy, will
now be impressed with the importance of obtaining the
"genuine article," from the gentlemen who are evidently
governed by such enlarged views of science, and a humanitary principle so noble.

GREAT PHILANTHROPIC ENTERPRISE.

A CELEBRATED tonsorial (shaving) firm in this city, whose feelings have been severely lacerated by the frequent impositions of their brethren, in selling a spurious article alleged to be the genuine *axungia ursi* or bear's grease, whereas it is known to be nothing but *axungia porcinæ* or hog's fat, fired with a noble determination to procure an article of the very best quality, have sent one of the most scientific members of their firm to California, with ample funds to secure aid in capturing that formidable monster, the *ursus horribilis* or grizzly bear, in any numbers that may be required to supply their numerous customers with genuine bear's oil.

Reasoning from the well-known doctrine of the immortal Hahnemann, "*similia similibus curantur*," they concluded that the fat of the *ursus horribilis* of naturalists, or the grizzly bear of our newly acquired auriferous territory, as a stimulus for the growth of hair, would prove of far greater value, as that animal is well known to be clothed with a formidable capillary growth, and that the glands which produce it, originate in the cuticle directly over the thickest layer of fat. Their efforts have been crowned with complete success ; as the frequent accounts of the terrific fights with that formidable monster, and the vigorous growth from even juvenile chins in Broadway, will satisfy the most incredulous.

The following modest card of this enterprising firm, it

is hoped will receive immediate attention by all the young gentlemen desirous of sporting their manly honors :—

"Being now in receipt of an ample supply of fresh bear's oil, from *our* Mr. Swizzle-em, in California, which is extracted under his own nose from the fat of the *ursus horribilis* or grizzly bear, we shall be happy to receive your orders.   *Our* signature is over the cork.

SHAVEALL, SWIZZLE-EM & Co."

"N.B.—We publish the following in order to expose a Boston firm, who allege that they have an agency in California, and have got up a bottle similiar in all respects to *ours*.   We warn the public to look for *our* signature over the cork.

"Personally appeared before me, M. Monargas, Judge of the Superior Court of San Francisco, George Swizzle-em, Esq., having lost his left leg and right hand, in an encounter with a grizzly bear, whilst endeavoring to take the same for the use of Shaveall, Swizzle-em & Co., of New York, to all of which he made oath, this 13th day of December, 1850.

"M. MONARGAS."

SCENES IN EARLY PRACTICE.

THE OLD EAST WING OF BELLEVUE; ITS TRANSFORMATION—SCENES IN THE CHOLERA OF 1832—POWER OF ART.

———————

"Fearest thou to die? Famine is in thy cheeks; need and oppression stareth in thy eyes; upon thy back hangs ragged misery."

THERE is a wide, an immeasurable distance between two classes of our profession; we mean those who take it up from the lofty point of its broadly philosophical and humanitary character, and those who view it solely as a physic-giving and money-getting trade. Neither tongues of angels, nor the memory of the lost and loved, can speak to the one, but even dead walls sometimes reveal to the other all the sympathies of the soul. A few months since I was requested to visit a lovely boy, the brother of a friend whose noble sentiments on the true mission of the artist have often instructed our readers, and from whom they may soon expect the ripened fruits of trans-Atlantic travel.[*]

I had enjoyed the social and elevating companionship of this delightful family, since a previous professional visit of some two years before the sad occasion which now summoned me, and as that visit resulted favorably, I found no reason, in our pleasing intercourse, for concealing the moving reminiscences which were awakened on entering the house. The apartment chiefly connected with them, was the one in which I related them to my

[*] John Matthews, author of "Letters from Europe." See *Scalpel*.

friends ; then it was one of the cholera wards of the women's side of the hospital ; now, its walls are hung round
with medallions, and busts and statuettes are distributed about in profusion, the production of my friend Mul-
ler, the sculptor, whose genial soul and expressive face
have been well matched by the companion of his future
life and studies, he has had the good fortune to secure in
the family of my friend.   It is a grand old room of spacious size, and has a large centre-table, which, though it
does not contain quite a cartman's load of timber, yet it
somehow seems to me to be a very graceful piece of furniture ; whether in consequence of its noble proportions
or its hospitable use, I will not stop to inquire ; yet I am
always delightfully impressed by its attractiveness ; the
spirits might try to tip it, but if it be in spiritual science
as in electricity, that like repels like, I am quite sure they
would fail, for there is always some of their kindred,
not exactly disembodied, but occupying glassy tenements,
gracefully grouped on its surface, and their more ethereal
brethren would be guilty of bad manners to overturn
their less elastic cousins.   Some people might think
these spirits, when disembodied by that spiral persuader
—you know, reader—might chance to "tip" the em-
bodied ones that surround the said table, but the ladies
were always present, and it would not be proper to be so
familiar in the use of such deceivers.

On entering the house, a modern front and new stair-
ways and divisions had so completely renovated the interior that it was utterly impossible to recognize the old
west wing of Bellevue Hospital.   When I used to visit it
during my student's life of eighteen-thirty, that institution was quite a large village ; it comprised the entire
poor-house establishment, and occupied several squares,
and was supposed at that time to be so far from the city,

as to be quite secure from the invasion of streets and dwelling-houses ; now, it is confined to a single square at the foot of Twenty-seventh street, and is used as a hospital for the poor. It was not long after the irruption of cholera in the year thirty-two, that the wards were filled with wretched patients from the city ; the sedans and the hearse were in constant use, and large piles of rough coffins awaited their occupants in the yards.

One day, before the appearance of the disease at the House of Refuge, of which I then had the medical supervision, I went over to see what success the physicians had in treating the disease. The great gateway was then at least the distance of a square from the hospital, and nearly on a line with the Second Avenue ; quite a long walk intervened, and before you reached the hospital there were numerous offices and workshops stretched and scattered about, with that unusually clean exterior, yet indefinable carelessness, that would seem to belong to every great establishment where individual ownership does not direct industrial effort. In all places where men are engaged by forced labor to preserve order, and no one owns the ground—where the humanities are not the spontaneous growth of the heart, and where Christ's command, " Help one another," is not the sole motive power, you will always observe the general features of a poor-house. Poor old women and blear-eyed men, puffy and dough-faced children with short bow legs, hunched-up shoulders, thick, bloodless lips, and vacant faces, and unspeculative eyes, wandered about, gazing on the ground, never upwards—there was no motive ; the eyes were scrofulous, and the sun was too bright ; their beginnings were unwholesome, and partook of the cellar. Insolent officials who, being preferred from their own ranks, felt their power, and kicked and cuffed them out of the path. Two lazy dogs very fat, (they belonged to the higher officers, and were not fed from the poor-house table,) several sleek cows to supply the super-intendent's family with milk; bright-eyed and well-fed fowls and fat swine, also belonging to that functionary. His spacious cottage and beautiful lawn ran down to the river, and there were two peacocks on the grass, typical of his high position. A smith's shop, a bakery, a coffin manufactory, and a dead-house, formed the agreeable diversities that more immediately lined the path leading to the old hospital, where we were now taking our lunch with the delightful family of my friend, and the slightly different getting up of the *ménage*. Christ's command, "Love one another," was fulfilled under more favorable auspices : family affection, education, refinement, and a good table, are capital helps to religion.

We must apologize to our fair readers for troubling their sweet dreams with this "horrid sketch," but like some other professional doses, it may possibly do them good ; indeed we think it far more likely to answer the end we propose than most of such doses for the body. Pray, therefore, darling, incline your lovely bust a little more to the left of your "fauteuil," and permit me to ele-vate that charming little foot a trifle higher on the cush-ion. I fear you will be distressed at what follows, but I must beg you to take the prescription ; it may benefit your heart a little. Indeed it assuredly would if you only would eat a little more solid food, take a few miles of wholesome exercise properly shod and clad, and give up parties, and balls, and the opera for a few months, and visit the poor occasionally. A lesson in the humanities may help your morals as well as a fashionable ser-mon by Dr. Cream Cheese.

On our way to the hospital, (I say *our* way, for the reader will be amazed to know the editor was actually accompanied by a young divinity student—and I think he could not have begun his studies with a better lesson) we were hailed by a professional brother who stuck his head out of the window of the dead-house, and politely requested us to enter. Poor fellow, he, like his subjects, has long since turned to dust, and here are we! Check-aproned and sleeved, he looked, were it not for his intellectual face and bloody hands, and scalpel, not unlike in his habiliments, his neighbor the baker! Several students were surrounding the table on which he was demonstrating from "a cadaver" the softening of the intestinal mucous membrane, the chief change visible to the pathologist, caused by that awful and mysterious disease which has formed so grand a decimator of humanity, and which (we believe it reader) comes with merciful intent to freshen the ensuing generations by destroying the worthless of the present one. Do not shudder, my love ; the cool page of science might bring you to the same conclusion ; perhaps not you, but Charlotte Brontè, or some such coarse creature ; you may as well at present take up Lalla Rookh, or the last new novel, as a refreshment. My friend was as cool in his pathological disquisitions, as we are wont to be in our philosphical conclusions about fashionable life and its infirmities. I thought he always spoke rather sneeringly of medical treatment, considering the future occupation of his students and his visitors ; but poor Morrill was a philosopher ; he viewed pathology as the means of discovering the true laws of healthful life, by studying those changes of structure which by more remote or more rapid action had succeeded in destroying the body ; he did not expect by exposing with his scalpel the ravages of syphilis, scrofula, drunkenness and starvation, that he could discover how

8

to eradicate them with physic! therefore he always sneered when he came to speak of medical treatment by dosing,
and was accordingly hated by the young aspirants, and
the old medical pawnbrokers in physic, phlebotomy, and
fees.

One fact on that occasion forcibly impressed me ; I
then suspected its true source, and have since proved it
by the stronger esthetic impulses of advancing years, and
it has now become part of my religion ; it is this : I can
not respect either the living or dead body of a filthy person ; I had not then, and I have still less at present,
either feeling or sympathy for a filthy man or woman.
I cannot sit by the side of a Jesuit priest with his sweating black gown, nor one of his Irish proselytes in a rail-
car ; I can feel no respect for them, living or dead ; nor
can I believe that any penance, even of good works, can
be entirely acceptable to God, if the person who performs
it be unclean.   The hands and feet of the subjects my
friend examined, deprived me of all respect for their remains.   I have always approached the bodies of the
cleanly dead with a certain degree of reverence ; they
seem to demand respect ; you feel that filthy or trifling
speech, when examining the poor vanquished body that
only precedes you a little while, is an insult to the Creator ; an unmanly liberty taken with the dead, which you
would not perhaps dare take with the living.   All the cholera subjects I saw were filthy, and they were handled accordingly ; there was not a man there but would have
behaved himself more respectfully in the presence of
more cleanly clay.

After an hour thus spent, we sought the hospital ; entering at one end of the ward, the beds were arranged on
either side to the number of fifty or sixty at least ; a
passage-way, not exceeding six feet, ran between the two

rows of ghastly patients in every stage of the horrid disease ; some were writhing, their limbs knotted by cramps ; these were apparently parboiled ; all the serum or fluid part of the blood had run out of the myriad vessels of the intestines, and there was no counteraction to the atmospheric pressure ; the solid parts of the blood were driven inward upon the great vessels and viscera ; the valves of the heart were clogged; the engine refused to go without its fuel. Three students were busy making oxygen gas to stimulate the poor lungs and heart, and make 'em go! Poh! as well might the foolish boys, if they had a steam-engine, supply the boiler with tar, when there was only a tithe of the necessary water in the top chamber.

There was just as much oxygen in the air then as there is now, and it answered the purpose of such of us as had organic strength enough to resist the lurking infection. God knows we were breathing it then in its highest intensity, as well as the poor paupers, and here we are yet ; but we had wine and beef, and plenty of good vegetables, and good dry beds, and large rooms, with pure air ; blood-poisoned and air-starved bodies, close rooms, filth, and poor food, caused the mortality. Neither oxygen nor cayenne, opium, ether, nor camphor and opium, nor brandy, would cure the dying. The serpent was wreathing his awful coils around them and playing fantastic pranks with their limbs. I actually saw the yet breathing body lying by the side of the dead! In yonder corner was a poor noisy wretch shouting out from her bed, as a dead body was occasionally carried out ; " Give the poor creetur corporation plank enough this time, for God's sake. I shall take considerable more when I go ; have a good long one ready for me, that's a good soul, won't ye doctor?" Poor creature! I inquired for her next day, and she had her request; early that morning, with twelve others, she went up "to the field."

I had visited the hospital for several days, when we had our first case at the House of Refuge; the morning of its occurrence I had seen several patients in the neighborhood. The Refuge stood at the intersection of Broadway and between the Fifth and Madison avenues, in the present park. As I returned to my charge that noon, the gate-keeper told me one of the boys had just been carried to the hospital with "the cramps." For six weeks I slept in a room with my door opening into the large hospital, where we always had a full complement of patients. Bating the night-watching and out-door toil, I never had better health. Our steward supplied us with the best of sixpenny beef fried in hog's fat, with fly-gravy and bread-pudding at discretion; and we had a beautiful vineyard, and plenty of roses. Robert C. Cornell, the friend of man and of the unfortunate, sent me a basket of capital Madeira; and my little bird was away on the banks of the glorious Hudson, in health and peace. My poor boys did pretty well too. I fed them up beyond cholera point—all but two, and them we put away just outside the wall after night-fall; the children skip the rope and trundle the hoop over them now in Madison Square; but it's no matter. They were poor little orphans, and were kindly treated by us all; their *matériel* was bad, doughy, scrofulous; they had no life-force. I didn't physic them to death; on the contrary, I gave them good beef-tea and brandy; but their feeble blood ran away; their hose was out of order, and wouldn't supply the great boiler, the heart; the poor limbs withered, and so they died away gently, as the delicate little flowers close before the fierce sun-heat withers them. No mothers wept over them; their playmates looked at their poor little blanched bodies, and thanked God it was not them. They played marbles the next day quite as well without them. But I often heard them speak kindly of poor little Dick and Joe.

It was about ten years after this that an awful fever broke out amongst the poor women who were obliged to go to Bellevue to be confined in this ward. This is a mysterious disease, in its nature ; like the cholera and all other infectious diseases, we know nothing whatever about its origin, and, until recently, very little about its treatment. It is highly infectious to all after parturition, and generally "goes through the house ;" none else but those who have been confined are susceptible. It is useless to particularize its characteristics. I went up to see the changes produced on the internal organs, and was delighted to see the close attention to philosophical and inductive study by the students and their friend, Dr. Alonzo Clark, the accomplished medical scholar and refined gentleman, now Professor of the Practice and Pathology in the State University Medical College. He was instructing his class, and gave me great hope that philosophical medicine would yet take its deserved rank in our colleges ; but the speculative disposition of our people, I fear, will prevent it for many years. Diplomas and physic must be sold. The mortality was great, and many orphans were left to the care of the city. I lost several fees which I could ill afford, but I could not conscientiously attend those about to be confined, for several weeks afterwards ; the disease is so contagious.

Some two years since, after twenty-five years' interval, I revisited, as I have said, the old ward of the Bellevue Hospital. The visit was only of friendship, for the child of my friend was under the kind care of an excellent and humane physician. By that mysterious, and as yet in-

explicable law, which allows vigor, and health, and manhood, sometimes to two or three of the first children,
sometimes to as many of the last, and insures early death
to the others, two of my friend's later children were
swept off consecutively. A sister had preceded the lovely
boy I was visiting, and both died of disease of the brain.
We had been amused and delighted with his prattle but
a few weeks before, and nothing serious was apprehended,
until one day, on going to school, he complained of
double vision ; other and rapid symptoms followed this
alarming one, and in a few weeks he died—with all that
medical and devoted parental love could do to keep him.
Again I visited the old east wing, and most forcibly did
the contrast impress me. The hand of genius was every-
where visible. Statuettes and alto relievos, Washington,
Clay, Webster, Calhoun, a figure of America, and offerings to love and domestic happiness in the shape of
the busts of a new-found father and mother, a brother and
wife, were hung round the walls, and rested on pedestals and brackets. They were all by the chisel of
the sculptor of the "Minstrel's Curse." The grand old
table was removed from the spot where we had been so
happy, and where the laugh went round so merrily ;
and there rested in its place the coffin of that dear child,
whose life was so interwoven with the hearts of the living. Sweet and placid were the noble and calm brow
and features undisturbed by a wrinkle, and pure as the
marble block to which the hand of his new brother has
now transferred them. A wreath lay on the coffin, fash-
ioned by the hand of a sister, and friends and neighbors
gathered round. In a short hour the prayer was said,
the old massive carriage was rolled out of the stable, and
the friends and parents went their sad way with their
second darling to the tomb. On a beautiful hill in

Greenwood, looking to the south, the brother has placed his offerings to both. The boy looks proudly upward from his pedestal; the little girl is tripping along with an air so life-like; but both are very cold. The metal gives no response to a mother's or a father's love; yet oh, how warmly the sleepers nestle in memory! How lovely is the art that can thus baffle old Time! we thought, as we gazed upon the exquisitely simple statue of the sweet child, with her little satchel, going to school: what are we all but children going to school? These have only been dismissed a little sooner, and gone home!

It is quite surprising what an immense number of people are continually engaged in watching their dignity. Don Quixote was occupied for a whole night in watching his armor on the top of the cistern in the innkeeper's yard ; nor do we think he had a much harder time of it than some of our fellow-citizens. We often think of his measured and solemn step as he paced to and fro, when we see the grotesque exhibitions so common in society. There is a great difference in the quality of this armor of dignity, and it is got up in such a variety of forms, that the curious observer can divert himself all day, and begin afresh next morning, sure of an endless succession of exhibiters. Extraordinary as the apparatus is, however, it is generally most skillfully adapted to the wearer ; and if we may judge of the worth of the contents by the care that is taken in their wrappings, they must be often of extraordinary value. After a time the observer may come, in some degree, also, to judge of the character of his specimen by his face and gait, as well as his armor. Should he observe a gentleman with a very precise step, as though he were treading on eggs and feared to break them, a suit of black, and a white neck-cloth, he will of course pass for a clergyman. Now, I take it, that this peculiar unwillingness of the legs to get over the ground, is expressive of the degree of clerical authority their owner has attained. If he be naturally of a pliable temperament, and his congregation consist chiefly of women, he will not gain strength rapidly, either in his head or his legs ; the character of his mental property will be chiefly in the rear of the brain. If he have a few gray heads in the vestry, he may find it prudent to walk with circumspection for some time longer ; perhaps his investments in the anterior region of the brain will increase, and after a while he may attain the port and dignity of a natural man. There will be very little difficulty, however, in recognizing the clerical gait and dress, and if he opens his mouth, you are sure of him ; his words are too valuable for any but the most solemn utterance. Once in a while the acute observer will find a medical cub put on the sheep's skin, and assume the white neck-cloth and clerical gait ; but it's of no use, the twinkle of his eye will betray him ; he looks foolish ; besides, the feeble and slow step looks like a heavy heart and no business. The undertaker, as he passes such a fellow, gives no evidence of respect, and when he speaks of him he smiles pitifully, saying, as plainly as his face can say, poor young man, he's of no use. We give our clerical friends the first place, as in duty bound ; they seem always to get it, whether deserving or not, and we don't care to dispute their claim. The *Tribune*, in a late article, entitled "Health for the People," thinks it would be peculiarly appropriate for them to expound the laws of life to the multitude. No doubt they would excel in dietetics ; as they are so manly, we would advise the addition of gymnasia and athletic exercises—"sparring" by the Rev. Doctor so and so. Cooking would come naturally. Physiology would be rather doubtful ; it as been thought by free thinkers slightly anti-clerical.

8*

Should the student, as he goes down Broadway, observe a stout gentleman, clad in the extreme of fashion, with a diamond cluster on his shirt bosom, a large seal-ring on his little finger, and a severely sculptured cornice to an eye like a red hot brad-awl, which takes you and your pocket at a glance, and a well-dyed moustache and imperial, standing like a caryatide on one side of the St. Nicholas Hotel, (he never picks his teeth now, that has become too vulgar,) he is a gentleman who used to keep elegant bachelor's rooms in Broadway. At present we don't know what he keeps ; but he is still there, and no doubt will resume his occupation with courage when the new law is a little older.   At any rate he is there yet ; we apprehend it will be some time before he goes away, or goes to work.   This gentleman takes great care of his dignity, and is most punctilious in exacting the minutest attention to etiquette.   His elegant hospitality at his recherché apartments was well known to our verdant civic and country fast-gentlemen.   Some of them doubtless recur to the delightful memories of champagne and game suppers, when pursuing their geological investigations at Sing-Sing or California.   They got considerable dignity on their introduction to the gambling rooms, and can now watch it retrospectively in Uncle Sam's College.   A shaved head and striped jacket furnish a pleasant contrast, and quietness aids their reminiscences.   The facilities enjoyed are by no means lost upon this class of our citizens, and they not unfrequently become adepts in their respective callings when they graduate.   Comparison with seniors greatly facilitates their improvement. They may progress so well as to become available candidates for municipal offices, such Aldermen, Street Inspectors, Captains of Police, etc.   Wall Street is the beneficent Alsatia always ready to receive the unfortunate children who have strayed from their doting mamma, to revise their studies in ethics and finance at the college at Sing Sing.

A class of our civic aristocracy may be seen demurely walking about the streets, dressed in a very quiet and subdued tone, and presenting to all appearance specimens of common well-bred people. They wear little or no ornament, chew no tobacco, will not step on your toes, will courteously give you a seat in the omnibus, neither pick their teeth, chew the tooth-pick, nor clean their nails in public ; they are a very good sort of stupid people. The observer may know them as the descendants of the old Knickerbockers or Huguenot families, or of the old Puritanic stock, traveled, or else transplanted early to New York. There is one peculiarity that usually marks them most repulsively and distinctly, and that is the horrible wooden-ness of their cadaverous faces. This, however, has a cause, nor should we feel it right that it should pass without apology. They were not born so, but probably were ushered into the world with as good faces as juveniles usually have, *i. e.*, they looked as much like puppies or monkeys as the young of the genuine quadrupeds. The face, dear readers, is a matter of necessity. In a country where almost every man born out of a large city thinks he has an undoubted right to inquire into your private business, spit tobacco, and clean his finger nails, and blow the dust into your face, talk politics and religion, and drink bad liquor, and put his knife in his mouth at table, these poor wooden people have no other defence than to be deaf, dumb, and blind.

LIFE SKETCHES OF EMINENT NEW YORK PHYSICIANS.

"Black spirits and white, blue spirits and grey,
Mingle—mingle—mingle, you that mingle may."

In our classification of the brethren in the last number, we are quite aware we were not as accurate as Cuvier, and have reason to believe we omitted several species fairly entitled to notice ; we assure our medical friends, it was from no unconsciousness of their merits, but from pure forgetfulness. In our present effort, we shall endeavor to supply the omission with descriptions of such individual specimens only, as are deserving of notice, having included the balance of the genera and species, in an article on the Medical Infusoria—for our next.

The Ursa Major (the late Dr. Francis) is entitled to our first attention, not only from the prominence of his position as the late President of the Academy of Medicine, but from that uniform kindness and excellence of heart that make him beloved wherever he is known. Should the doctor think we are taking an odd method of proving our esteem by exposing some of his innocent peculiarities, we can only assure him that he pays the forfeit of his irresistible drollery. Like the Laplander, who proves "by thumps upon your back how he esteems your merit," or the grizzly bear himself, who gives you perhaps a gentle hug, and then quits you for more enticing game, we are only following out our nature ; a laugh-

ing philosopher is our admiration, and we honestly believe
a chat with our bear, even at the risk of a hug, is worth
all the physic in his wallet. Let us attempt a sketch as
we first saw him in the very zenith of his reputation,
when old Rutgers College—our venerable Alma Mater in
Duane Street—was in full blast, making doctors by the
hundred, its guns manned with Mott, Bushe, Hosack,
Macnevin, the Ursa Major, and Griscom, and firing away
at the old battery in Barclay Street.

Five feet seven or eight inches ; figure well set and of
equal dimensions ; glorious forehead ; massive nose, denoting great generosity and intellectual vigor ; large grey
eyes, covered with gold spectacles ; powerful and sensual
mouth, showing a high degree of animal life, and a perfect ability to appreciate good cheer ; hair grizzled, and
radiating from the forehead, whence, and likewise from
some other peculiarities, the name, Ursa Major.

Scene first : Dr. Bushe and Dr. Francis alternately
officiating in examining the students. Thirty pupils
present—ourselves entering very late ; the professor
examining the class. On opening the door, and entering,
an awful look through the glasses—"Mr. D——, who
discovered the thoracic duct?" Answer, "Pecquet ;"
and, in a louder voice—"Who discovered the lacteals?"
(See our article on Purgatives.) Answer, "Asellius."
Professor (sotto voce, yet loud enough to be heard all over
the room :) "The devil ! Professor Porson the second!"
—no more questions to us at that time ; if there had
been, we should have been shorn of our honors ; for it so
happened we were just from an indolent loll over our
classical dictionary, where all the doings of the defunct
worthies were posted up. The questioning was continued
where it was left off on our entrance, with a southern
pupil, and we had leisure to make our observations on our

friend. It was soon evident that nature had given him a
temperament equal to his body, and Caliban himself might
have envied him that. Glancing his eye over his spectacles anon on this side and that, like a buffalo chafed by the
hunter, he seemed every moment ready to gore some
unfortunate wight who should fail to answer ; yet believe
us, reader, this peculiar manner covered a heart full of
the warmest and kindliest sympathy, and a head replete
with knowledge. Alas! none can know how much there
is to produce a repulsive manner, in a man whose thoughts
are occupied with far other things than the foolish questions of the ill-educated student, or nervous invalid. No
man was ever more attentive to his patient, none had a
readier word of sympathy, a kindlier jest, or a more side-
splitting anecdote, than the Ursa Major ; and none more
willingly relieved the pecuniary wants of a patient, and
that in a manner so full of the milk of human kindness
and gentleness, that the donor always managed to leave
the obligation on his side.

Our next interview was in the library ; the doctor was
indulging in his favorite beverage of green tea, and re-
galias, puffing and sipping away with infinite relish, and
we were immersed in the quaint writings of some antiquated old quid, when a thundering rap announced a visitor. Starting from his seat, the professor sprang into
the middle of the floor, and was soon clasped in the arms
of the Phenomenon!—that wonderful little gentleman had
just arrived from Paris, dressed in the latest extreme,
filled with all the knowledge of the French capital, and
puffing and blowing like a speckled frog. Then began
a scene we shall never forget. The professor, always
ready for sport, actually spinning round on his feet as
on a pivot, with the body of the Phenomenon grasped
tightly to his massive chest, and the legs of the little man

making a radius as they flew round, while the words, half
smothered, ever and anon found vent—"Oh! my dear
Doctor F——! mon cher Paris! Dupuytren! Lisfranc!
Boyer! Roux! Larrey! and all the glorious constellation of worthies! Dear Doctor F——, I will tell you
all, only give me time. You know nothing—you can
know nothing. They know everything. Old things are
done away, and all things are become new. Oh! mon
cher Paris!" Thus the little man continued raving, alternately extending his arms toward "mon cher Paris,"
and looking round upon the Ursa Major's elegant library
with infinite contempt, assuring him in the most amiable manner it was all trash, and advising him at once to
sell out, and go to Paris. It is impossible to convey the
expression of the doctor's countenance at this rhapsody!
It actually outdid himself, as we subsequently learned—
though that is saying a great deal, for the doctor is high
pressure even yet, and the scene we describe is thirty
years ago. He seemed to enjoy it hugely. After half
an hour's quizzing as he only could quiz, the professor
accompanied the Phenomenon to the front door, and returned to the library with an expression of countenance
exquisitely comical. He drew up in front of the glass,
and addressed his reflection with infinite gravity, and in
a stentorian voice, utterly regardless of our presence—
"Dr. F——, you poor, old, miserable devil! sell out your
traps, and all your musty old books; go to Paris—and
drink at the fountain of knowledge till your soul is slaked
with the divine influence. For shame, you poor miserable old wretch, to sit here, while the very effulgence of
science irradiates—mon cher Paris! (mimicking the Phenomenon)—and a stray comet has shot off from the
glorious constellation and alighted in this benighted hem-
isphere," etc. All who know the professor's gift, or have

seen him on his high horse, will appreciate the style in which he went over this rhapsody. Then turning to us with great seriousness, and looking over his spectacles, assured us we enjoyed in his office a fine opportunity to study the various temperaments, and advised us to neglect no opportunity of improving ourselves in that necessary professional accomplishment.

It was not long before we found out the many peculiarities of our kind preceptor, and learned to appreciate his excellent heart. We will relate some more of them at a future time. The Ursa Major has a keen perception of the ludicrous, and an exquisite ability to enjoy humor. Dean Swift never said better things than we have heard from his lips again and again ; he is indeed a fine example of the old school ; long may he enjoy the reputation for learning, wit, and benevolence he so well deserves, not forgetting his green tea and cigar.

But who *was* he with coat of formal cut and white or yellow vest, and neckcloth of exquisite tie, yellow breeches, and top-boots, oh ! so brilliant ! and hair and whiskers trimmed and brushed with the utmost nicety, descending the steps of his mansion precisely at nine o'clock, A. M., and planting his feet with mathematical precision, each in the appropriate spot, while his coachman insensibly acquired the same habits, and almost his master's walk ? Thus continued our careful preceptor, patiently going his daily rounds, and using his excellent common sense, in planning and performing a series of unequaled and splendid operations, until he had made himself from a plain country lad, the most distinguished surgeon by all odds in the country, and in the operative department of his profession, equal if not superior to any in the world. As a lecturer, Dr. M—— is useful, not brilliant. He indulges in much repetition ; but his expe-

rience is boundless, and he always speaks the truth—
which is more than can be said of some of his colleagues.
He has built up his own reputation by the exercise of his
one talent in the good old way, peculiar to the sect of
which he was a member.

Our description of the doctor's toilette does not apply
to its existing state ; on his return from Paris, his well-
preserved and athletic figure was arrayed in the habiliments of a gentleman, worn in a manner undistinguished
from others, save by an old habit of solicitude to preserve the unsullied purity and folds of his linen, and
those absurd appendages of that most unclassical garment, the coat tails. May our careful preceptor long
enjoy his well-earned laurels and his new clothes.

But who is he with the sepulchral countenance, and
bent figure, wrapped in his long-tailed coat, and striding
along the streets with eyes intently fixed on the pavement, and ideas concentrated on some new problem,
just started in his teeming brain, touching the "vital
forces ;" or else bestriding a beautiful horse, of omin-
ous blackness? He goes daintily along, apparently unconscious of the load of wit and philosophy he carries,
as was the immortal Rozinante of that mirror of chivalry
who bestrode her. Oh! but the doctor *is* a philosopher ;
he rarely deigns to alight upon the earth in his sublime
physiological flights : no ground tumbling for him ;
he prefers the lofty ; careering amid the clouds and dancing upon the sunbeams ; he believes not in the vile doctrine of solidism—not he ; the blood, in his opinion, is a
very wicked thing, to be got rid of as soon as possible ;
full of mysterious dangers and pernicious properties.
The doctor is also anti-carnivorous to a wonderful degree :
the smell of beef never disgraces his domicil ; its origin
is telluric, and agrees not with his meteoric and celestial

views. Upon an occasion of extreme exhaustion, after
a most gratifying indulgence in several severe bleedings,
to such an extent that he was forced so unwillingly to
the recumbent position that he actually lay upon the floor,
a brother professor, of opposite sentiments, urged upon
him the propriety of taking a little "*nowishment;*" the
learned gentleman, having barely strength enough to raise
his head like one of those unfortunate turtles we see on
their backs at the doors of the refectories, replied with
great indignation as he essayed again to remove the bandage and abstract a little more of the pernicious fluid, the
words rattling in his throat from pure exhaustion, "Professor Pattison, I would rather die a victim to science than
be saved by quackery." Calomel is, with the professor,
emphatically the bread of life, and with the aid of the lancet, sufficient in his view to starve all the undertakers in
the land, while arrow root is fit food for a giant. Yet
with all his peculiarities, the professor is a sincere and
excellent man ; and absolutely necessary to complete an
assortment of philosophers ; without his aid the medical
reader would not have enjoyed this excellent sketch.
Surely we have all a right to choose our own doctors and
—butchers.

Now clear the course ; take away all vile odors, outré
spectacles, whether of garment or physiognomy, and all
other unseemly exhibitions, while we sketch the admirable Crichton of elegant and polite medical literature ; A
slight figure, plainly and unostentatiously clad in black,
without an ornament, a highly nervous temperament ;
large dark eyes, over-shadowed by a classic and thoughtful brow, and a well-balanced brain, his other features of
most unsensual character, looking as though the physical
man was kept utterly in subservience to the intellectual.
An eclectic and dilettante philosopher is Professor

Dickson. With the most comprehensive views of medical science, and the greatest industry and practical experience, he is evidently painfully aware of its utter insufficiency as a means of averting the results of universal ignorance and the countless errors of life ; he shows it in every line he writes and word he utters. There is no living man who can better fill his station as Professor of Medicine, and no man who would make a better practitioner if all were intellectual, and no stupid man ever seriously sick. The professor, both as a scholar and a man of the most delicate perception of propriety, is fitter to practice medicine in the valley of Rasselas, or in heaven, than in New York.

Silence, there, ye irreverent crew. Who comes, with measured step and slow, "in customary suit of solemn black ?" Methinks he is about to open a protracted meeting, as he produces a well-used roll of manuscript, and commences a disquisition on miasms, so ancient that its origin is lost in the dark ages. Surely it must have been a labor of love to concoct it : the professor returns year after year to the darling object of his youthful affections. "Some men there are," says Bacon, "who upon getting a favorite idea in their brains it is produced upon all occasions, never ceasing to keep up a buzzing in their ears, and those of every one who will listen to it." It is curious to note the conduct of the students as the mysterious theory is unfolded : the sophomore, fresh from the lap-stone or the plough, strains his ears not to lose a word, and his pen catch the droppings of the philosopher, while the senior closes his book, readjusts his quid, or tests the temper of his knife upon the bench on which he sits ; he has "seen the elephant" before. The professor proceeds with solemn accent, weighing out his words with such deliberation that it is evident he feels their value, and the vast intellectual effort they cost him, and is determined that all who hear him shall acknowledge it ; like a funeral train the lecture proceeds. The professor becomes metaphysical ; he arrives at that stage where the unfortunate tyro can no longer follow him ; "where entity and quiddity, the ghosts of defunct bodies, fly." "Proto-koino miasma" — a solemn pause—"deuto-koino-miasma"—another— "ideo-koino-miasma"—or mist ; the unfortunate student shuts his book in despair, and is soon summoned, to his great relief, to the class-room of the dirty professor, him of the uncombed hair, well-dyed finger nails, and stevedore toilette. But of him hereafter ; he must be cooked by himself.

Whoever remembers the glorious eye and superbly intellectual face of George Macartney Bushe, late professor of anatomy in the former Rutgers Medical College, will not be surprised to know that we should often fancy the present possessor of his immortal part—a gray eagle ; he used playfully, yet eloquently to defend the doctrine of the sage who taught that the souls of men passed into the system of animals, analogous in their impulses to those who sought their bodies as a refuge, when their own dissolved in death. Standing, as is often our wont, on the lofty brow of the palisades that skirt the western part of our noble Hudson, just above the village of Fort Lee, we have often fancied we could see the flashing eye of our lamented friend and preceptor, reflected from that of the monarch bird, as we almost felt the breath of his dark cleaving wing, as he sailed below the cliff and o'er the rolling deep, eager to drink of the life's blood of his palpitating victim, in the river or the forest beneath. Apply not the latter part of our simile, professionally, dear reader, to our departed and gifted friend, for no man was ever more anxious to preserve the life of a patient, which his matchless skill often enabled him to do. True it is, that during the early part of his short and brilliant career in this city, he was so oppressed with care and poverty, that his naturally irascible temper often made him seem careless of others' woes and sufferings, when he was harassed by so many of his own ; but Bushe had a kind heart, as we had ample occasion to know, for we more than once saw him give his last dollar to a pauper on whom he had operated.

Few can tell the effect of griping poverty and gnawing care upon a glorious intellect, aware of its power and ability to help the vulgar creature, conscious of nothing but pain, or the deprivation of sensual pleasure, and the depth of a well-filled pocket ; few can tell the gall that rises from the very soul and often overflows the lips, when such a creature ventures to use the power his wealth unfortunately enables him to exercise, in assigning a position to a man whose shoe-strings it would be an honor for him to tie. And when compelled by disease and public acclamation to admit his worth, he need not be surprised if he often experience rudeness in place of that servility he has been accustomed to command from his intellectual and poverty-stricken peers.

Dr. Bushe came from Dublin to this city, to take the chair left vacant by that beloved man, the late John D. Godman, in 1829, with the prestige of the most enthusiastic letters from Charles Bell, Benjamin Brodie, and William Lawrence. We entered under his private instruction when partner with Professor John W. Francis. Three courses of lectures on anatomy in Rutgers College, and almost daily office lectures on surgery, for three years, with the immense number of operations on persons attracted by the fame of the operator, gave us ample

opportunity to estimate his great eloquence and unmatched skill ; yet with all these advantages, for five
years he could scarce look forward to anything but starvation. It was not till a very inconsiderable operation
performed on a popular man, that he became at all
known, or sought for among the paying circles.

He then however rose very rapidly in public esteem,
and died about twenty years since, like our own beloved
Godman, of consumption, at the early age of forty-three,
in the full tide of successful practice. As we followed
the body to its quiet resting-place on the side hill west of
Jersey City, we thought of that flashing eagle eye now
closed forever, and remembering his quaint, playful, yet
eloquent defence of the doctrine of Metempsychosis, the
eye insensibly wandered northwards, "to the shattered
point of that shivered peak," where we have since so often
fancied we saw him reflected from the "bird that never
sleeps." Alas! how vain ; the earth is but the ashes of
the dead ; and although the material parts of the body
mingle indiscriminately from every division of the animal
kingdom, every aspiration of the soul proves our distinctive immortality. That all-powerful fiat, that will not
allow the mingling of the different genera, is no more
imperative in its action, than the fact that man's ultimate
attraction is proportioned to his immortal destiny. The
same beautiful law that leads the glorious reindeer to
love the simple moss and icy fastnesses of his native
region, and the massive elephant the varied and luxuriant herbage of the torrid zone, compels us to believe
that man, however he may sever for a time, in pursuit of
wealth, the attachments to his native land, seeks to be
re-united with those he has loved on earth before his eye
closes in death ; therefore his soul can surely only dwell
in consciousness, with his own kindred species hereafter.

Dr. Bushe did not cultivate the attractions of professional and social life; he saw too plainly the empty
pretensions of a large portion of the profession, to tolerate the patronizing air which the brethren love to assume
toward those who cannot exist in an atmosphere fit for
their feeble and selfish souls. His manner was often rude
to those he justly believed had no right to prefer a claim
to equality; but no man could more readily appreciate
industry and real worth; witness his long-continued
attachment to the lamented Roe. His dying moments
were disturbed by the frequent intrusion of an impertinent creature whose passport to immortality we have
made out in this number.

This singular association, he would often break up in
the most ludicrous and abrupt manner; and when his
desire to study the psychological peculiarities of his in-
significant annoyer allowed his cautious re-approach, we
invariably thought of that inimitable print of the dozing
mastiff and the cur—called "Dignity and Impudence."

NOTE.—The reader will observe that we have permitted all these sketches
to remain as they were written during the lives of their subjects. All but Professors Payne and Dickson are now dead.

AN ARTIST'S REVERIE.—NO. II.

"Spirits are not finely touched, but to fine issues."

MIDNIGHT—voiceless and ghostly midnight—steals up, and still the artist lingers with his trance-like dream ; but the utter serenity of his face passes away, as well as the death-like repose of posture. Now he shivers, and his flesh creeps to and fro, as the comings and recedings of the tired shore wave ; and now he turns paler and paler, and his features sharpen, by the race-imaginative and the cold-growing air, as the fire dies out, all save a few knot-wound and aged coals.

Hark to the cry of the rising storm, as the winds whistle and whine and shriek, while they canter up from the regions of the northwest ; see the tall chimneys, how they see-saw, and have their caps knocked off, and their pipe-puffs blown back into the mouth ; and listen to the breeze as it moans like the moan of the dog, prophetic of death. Large tears fall from the over-laden clouds, and tumble through miles of space upon the copper-plated roof, with a patter and a clatter like the distant tramp of mailed cavalry ; the unbroken-mouthed artillery of heaven talks with a tongue intensely loud, startling, fear-giving, and very awful, and then it stops to listen to its own magical echo ; and the blindingly brilliant lightning leaps and leaps, at intervals, through the pitchy night, splitting, as if in mere sport, rocks and temples and the human structure atwain. Yet this grand storm song, *sung by the Almighty*, comes but whisperingly to our visionary's ear, and simply elicits the low sigh, the shiver, and the slight shift of bodily position, fascinated as he is by things infinitely more grand, dire, transfixing and sublime—he sees a brother murdering a brother, and the perpetration of the first *unnatural* crime. * * *

THE DEATH OF ABEL.—"*With God is terrible majesty.*"— The earth appears sterile, stony, and unshrubbed—the sky leadeny, lurid, and near by—ungainly rocks burst up and scatter—and the ground here and there yawns, and shapes the frightful precipice and black abysm. On a declivity lies the corpse of the gentle and affectionate shepherd, Abel, with a handsomely formed and youthful head dangling from a pillow of rough stone—the hair-locks matted and extremely astray—the eyes lidded close, and fastened up by long, silky, and golden threads—the figure so carelessly flung, and the waxy, ivorial flesh sur-face sprinkled, and occasionally blotted out, by the yet freshly shed and brilliantly-crimson blood. And afar off, in the gray and misty light, stands a figure of gigantic size—gigantic chiefly by the illusion of the atmosphere, and the contraction of the cloudy earth dome. That fig-ure is Cain, the murderer of his youthful, gentle and guileless brother. Mark how he crouches and cowers, while pallor on pallor creeps over his system, and his forehead becomes beaded and torn up by a coronal of agony. See how he tries to persuade himself he simply dreams, and thus ventures to re-gaze, first at his brother's corpse, and then sheer up into the heavenly face of God. And now he re-raves and groans, oh, so heart-rendingly! and tears out handful after handful of his magnificent hair-locks, and his eye-globes seem so wildly dashing against their bony cells, or palsied by

9

terrific action and gushed-up-blood—blood that seems
the more out of place by its contrast with the corpse-like
pallor of the encasing cheeks.   And now he seems froz-
enly still, in a stooping attitude, with the hands clutching
at the thighs, and the finger nails deeply buried in the
thigh flesh, while the big tears burst from the soul's
fountain, and run in streams over the racked face, and
pour, and trickle, and drop upon the knees, feet, and
common earth, like a deluge of sin.   And thus Cain
stood, and wept and wept for hours, and strove frantic-
ally to open the gates of Hope, and when he found his
awful task fruitless, he met Despair, that thorn without
its rose, that crime without its Christ!   Then the fountains of the river soul dried up, and with his hands
across the lid-closed eyes, Cain flung himself prostrate to
the earth, face adown, thus striving to somewhat lessen
the horrors of the encircling scene ; but, alas for him!
as the quieting of one sense only quickens some other,
so this eye-closing only made the heart to rush madly
and more madly in its beat, and the brain to wonderfully see, by its own fire-light.   One instant he was
clasped by the love-flung arms of his boy brother, and
reposing in a most delicious partnership of happiness
and joy extreme ; while in the next he was a creature,
hopeless, self-loathing, colossally criminal, and utterly
abhorred and abandoned by heaven and earth!

Then he cursed himself, and his Maker, and his mysterious fate, and his visage loomed up grimly—desperation
strode over it ; the complexion became swart and brazen,
and the locks of hair rose proudly and erect, and, Medusa
like, seemed all alive with restless coils on coils of serpents, breathing flames ; and the brows gathered up
about the eye-cornices in stern, massy and richly mod-
eled folds ; the nose shrunk back toward the cheeks ;

the mouth assumed the firm and downward set, and the eyes seemed cavernous, tearless, fire-gleaming, and savage in expression, while the nostrils rose and fell in high action, and with their breath-play in perfect harmony with that of the magnificent and spacious chest ; and Cain now stood erect and daringly, his system being again well strung, as remorse had almost died away. And then again, even at that late hour, his memory redrew the picture of his strange career, and he gasped out entreaty after entreaty to the Almighty to take the erring wanderer back to a state of purity ; and then he listened and listened, but in vain, for a response—his sin-wail found no mate, no sympathetic echo.

A death-like stillness pervaded all things—not a tongue ventured to cross the path of the Genius of Evil, not even the faint twit of the swallow, or the murmur of the reed. But there did arise, in the gloomy voice-hush, phantoms—tall, shadowy, giant phantoms, that stalked by in the shape of Want, Drunkenness, Theft, Prostitution and Suicide, and many a group of Hell's grand inquisitors.

Then these aerial actors vanished, and the fratricide setting his teeth in strong lock, and spurring himself forward, bade a long farewell, if not an eternal one, to all his treasures ; so he raised up Abel's corpse with tender touch—oh, so tenderly !—and closely clasped it in the arms of a most wonderful love ; and he played with the luxuriant and silky tresses, smoothing and resmoothing them, and arranging them in various ways ; and then he kissed and rekissed the icy, senseless, purple lips, and placid brow. And he wandered wildly about, to and fro, and in a circle, still hugging and caressing his load of lost and unlost affection, pride, pleasure and peace, blended with a terrific guilt and dread. When, lo ! the cloudy ceiling of the earth opened, a blinding light sprung through, and the Lord God wrote on the criminal's brow, in letters of never-dying fire, the name of SATAN. "The heavens were stretched out like a curtain. They that did feed delicately are desolate in the streets. They that were brought up in scarlet, embrace dunghills. Hands shall be feeble, and all knees weak as water."

And now, wafted from Satan's embrace, and borne in the arms of a group of heaven's angels, may be seen the ascending corpse of the youthful shepherd ; while Satan, stark alone, feels quite refreshed and sleepless, and the surrounding air rings and rings with his sardonic laughter. Why, reader, starvation sometimes laughs, and so does overthrown reason, and the suicide when about to jump from the death-inflicting precipice, and the Indian when he dashes out the brain of the infant enemy! Why, judges laugh sardonically as they pocket their bribes, and consign the god-like spirits of Truth and Justice to the dungeon. Millions of your own species cower before the frown of those gigantic monsters, Church and State, while they only laugh sardonically at that of the Builder, Owner and Sovereign of the whole Universe!

A VISION OF THE DAMNED.

WHAT BECOMES OF THE DOCTORS AND APOTHECARIES WHEN THEY DIE?

It is curious what visions come to us when the mind is disturbed by anxiety, and we wander in the regions of dream-land. A few weeks since, having occasion to spend the night in attendance on a fair patient, we re-tired to an adjoining room in a beautiful villa near the city ; whether it was a very late dinner, or anxiety for our patient, an occasional groan from whose chamber reached our ears, we know not, but sleep played bo-peep with us that night, and left some intervals of semi-con-sciousness, filled with odd vagaries not very comforting as it regards the future. I dreamed that I had found my way at midnight into a fashionable drug-store in Broad-way, in search of a little morphine to quiet my patient's nerves ; the apothecary, on learning the simplicity and cheapness of my purchase, received me with no special amiability—indeed, I am obliged to confess, I am no favorite with that class of my fellow-citizens, whom I have heard on fitting occasions make no secret of their benevolence in consigning me to a climate considerably warmer than my physiological necessities require. He made no reply to my apology for disturbing him, but served me in silence, and retired doggedly to his cham-ber in the back-room. No sooner did the door close behind him, leaving me, as my dream ran, still in the shop, than I was witness to a scene I shall never forget. A terrible commotion commenced in all the bottles, as was visible from the agitation of their contents; the stoppers bobbed up and down, "salt mouths and species" rattled, the covers of gallipots danced, smothered cries came forth from every drawer, and deep groans issued from the cellar. Whilst I stood in horror and amazement, wondering what all this could mean, I was startled by a distinctly articulate cry, "Let me go! let me go! I will tear out his heart and pulverize his bones, if I can get at him—the infernal fiend, with his long nose and hickory face; let me go! let me go!" Another and another yelled out, and all their vengeance was directed at me, as was now evident enough, because various allusions were made to the *Scalpel* and its editor, all coupled with the hardest kind of expletives. I now clearly saw the faces of the speakers, and recognized many of them, as each one popped up from his especial bottle or gallipot, as defunct apothecaries—some of them very eminent ones, and formerly well known hereabouts; most of them brandishing in their bony hands a pestle or a sharp spatula. Why they couldn't get out of their respective bottles was not apparent, until a dialogue of extraordinary energy occurred between a very eminent apothecary, we used to trot out years ago in our pages, and his jailer, whose writhing and serpentine form I now plainly saw at the bottom of a large bottle of alcohol, with his snaky coils wound round the poor apothecary's legs; the conclusion was not very comforting to my future prospects: "Let him alone; it will be his turn by and by, and he'll be put into a bottle of aqua ammonia." This consoled me a little, however, for I really thought it would not be so very uncongenial as his majesty's imp imagined. I was getting weary of the scene of strife and discord, when it

lulled for a moment, and I had a chance to hear what was
going on in the cellar. The groans had assumed the
character of articulate speech, and to my great horror I
heard enough to convince me that the speakers were surgeons and doctors, evidently in no very comfortable
condition. I thought I could recognize the voices of
some old stagers I used to see when a student, going it
round the city in their carriages, with their sponges,
catlings, and scalpels. I was rather annoyed at this discovery of the disposition of my defunct brethren, for I
never believed the real devil would be so foolish as to
accommodate them in his dominions, and used to comfort
myself with the idea that they were let go scot free hereafter. Notwithstanding this unpleasant discovery, I was
amused at the grotesque appearance of a miserable old
creature, who sat with his legs crossed, smoking a long
German pipe and drinking lager bier in a corner of the
shop. He wore a superbly-flowered silk gown, shorts
and knee-buckles, with great diamond buckles in his
shoes, a smoking cap and long gold tassel. Notwithstanding all this apparent comfort and display, he kept
changing his position and rubbing his glutæi muscles,
and continually exclaimed ; "O mein Gott! mein Gott!
das is nicht goot, nicht goot!" On looking more closely,
I perceived that he sat on a lump of borax! some of
which he had evidently been pulverizing, for several fragments lay about, and he had a mortar and pestle on a
block near him. The thought instantly struck me ; it
was old Hahnemann, and this was his punishment for
selling borax as a newly discovered cure-all to his dupes
in Germany. A heap of guineas lay near him, which I
could not account for ; whilst I was speculating on their
use, the veritable old devil, with horns, hoofs and all,
came up from the cellar through a trap-door, and

approaching the old man, saluted him with apparent civility ; he replied with a grunt, and cast a look of horror at a cup which the devil took out of his pocket and poured into it some liquid brimstone ; then, taking a heaping spoonful of the borax from the mortar, he stirred them together with his finger, and presented it to the old quack, with a look of mock sympathy ; with a horrible grimace he gulped it down ; the devil then took up a guinea and put it in his pocket—this was the price the old man used to charge for his nostrum when on earth, and judging from the look of anguish he cast on it, as it disappeared in the devil's vest-pocket, it was the climax of his punishment.   The devil apologized for the lateness of the hour, assuring him that the morning dose should not be forgotten ; he had been engaged till quite late, in the cellar, making arrangements to accommodate a celebrated surgeon, who had just arrived from earth, and who on examination proved to be guilty of administering great quantities of medicine, and receiving a per centage from the apothecary.   He had placed him in a carboy of dilute sulphuric acid, and allowed occasional breathing time, when he was to be regaled with a sniff of assafœtida as a refresher, till he got used to it.   This class, the devil remarked, used to give him great trouble till the publication of the *Scalpel*, since which they have considerably diminished, only an occasional old stager now arriving.   It was now getting late, and as the devil had not perceived me, in consequence of my keeping shady behind the door during his interview with old Hahnemann, I took advantage of his departure into the back-room to confer with the apothecary, to slip out into the street.

I felt the delightful breeze, laden with the perfume of the honeysuckles which draped my windows, and awoke ;

stealing on tip-toe to the bedside of my lovely patient, I found her asleep, thanks to that beneficent gift of heaven, morphine. The exhausting pains were stilled, and a smile, sweet as if dropped by an angel's wing, told that she dreamed of her first-born.

9*

TOBACCO—ITS INFLUENCE ON THE BODY AND MIND.

The influence of Tobacco on the bodily and mental condition of American young men has long furnished an ample theme for the moralist and physiologist ; but for reasons not very creditable to his heart or his head, the practical physician and surgeon has for the most part held his peace. It would have been much more creditable to the "American Medical Association," if, instead of their silly discussions on medical ethics, and other wordy absurdities, and their quarrels about cutting out jaw-bones, they had given our young men a correct idea of the actual power of this giant enemy to destroy their manly character, and debase and stupefy their minds and bodies. As we are not trammelled by the fear of the frowns of our dear brethren, nor the loss of " patronage," we propose to give our readers the results of our observation of its power over the organism, during thirty-five years of practical observation on the young men of this city.

No man likes to hear his follies held up to public view. We therefore expect for this service a full measure of abuse. We received an ample return of that kind for the article on Lager-bier, for which we are duly thankful ; a contemporary says we "would rather be in a minority than a majority"—truth to say, we plead guilty ; for most of our profession are accustomed to speak so charily of the vices of their "patients," in consequence of their profound reverence for their pockets, that we have imbibed a great disgust for them : we take comfort from the conviction that we shall be soundly abused by a large class of our tobacco-smitten fellow-citizens, and approved by at least a *decent* majority.

Let us attempt to give tobacco its actual position as an agent amongst the catalogue of articles we take our into much-abused mouths. It is neither food nor drink—that's clear ; lager-bier, bad as it is, is in one sense food, because it supplies material for feeding the lungs. Without its use, the body would demand that its victims should eat more, or else grow thin by the absorption of their fat and muscle to supply material for combustion ; for the lungs are like a stove—they must be supplied with fuel, or the fire will go out.

Tobacco is a great demander of drink, because it constantly robs the body of its fluids by expectoration. Lager-bier supplies fluid at least, although it is deposited about the system in form very much like a beer-barrel, and gives its votaries a great deal of trouble to puff it away, and rid themselves of it by other unseemly and inopportune processes.

What, then, is tobacco ? Why, simply a narcotic—that is, (see the dictionary,) "a stupefier—a deadener of nervous and muscular energy!" If any man disputes this, and asserts that he finds himself more capable of intellectual or muscular effort when he has a quid in his mouth, we congratulate him on his improved astuteness ; we may betray our own want of the precious intellectual quickener, but we will venture the question : How much did it sharpen your logic-chopper when you took the first quid? And how majestically did you stand on your legs when you first felt its full effect?

Every one must remember the first effect of tobacco. *Nausea, vertigo, vomiting, and relaxation of the entire muscular system*, are its invariable effects ; and if continued, *relaxation of all the sphincter or closing muscles of the hollow viscera, bowels, bladder, and stomach.* This result is sometimes sought for by the surgeon, and produced by injecting an infusion of tobacco into the bowels, in cases of obstinate constipation, or for relaxing the grip of the openings in the abdomen, when the bowel slips through them in those who have rupture. We have seen the consequences in our own practice so awful from a very weak injection, which we administered to avoid the necessity of operating by the knife, that we resolved never to use it again.

Now, the reader will please to remember that all the symptoms he first experiences from tobacco, are the invariable results upon a *natural or healthy condition of the body ;* and if he succeed, by perseverance in its use, in overcoming the immediate consequences, it is only because the alarmed and abused nerves have summoned the forces of youthful vigor to bear the invasion as long as possible before they capitulate. Breath, food, and drink are the means of resistance, and the besotted youth soon discovers that the quantity of the latter must be increased, and its quality strengthened, if he would resist the invader and continue to perform his ordinary duties without showing plainly his incapacity to stand upon his legs. Thus it is that tobacco, either used by smoking or chewing, *is the direct introduction to drunkenness.*

Our remarks apply in a much more forcible manner to smoking than to chewing. Some people are so silly as to suppose, because they do not spit whilst smoking, that no harm can ensue ; but they should remember that the oil of tobacco, which contains the deadly NICOTINE, (equally deadly and almost as rapid in its action as strychnine,) is volatilized, and circulates with the smoke through the delicate lining membrane of the mouth at each whiff of the cigar, and is absorbed by the extensive continuation of this membrane that lines the nostrils, and acts upon the whole body. The smoke of tobacco is indeed much more rapid in its stupefying effect, as every professed smoker knows ; it is usually called "soothing" by its votaries ; but this is, of course, only the first stage of stupefaction ; it acts precisely as opium or other narcotics do. Moreover, the reader will observe that the older physicians used to throw the *smoke* of tobacco into the intestines, when they sought its terribly relaxing effects on the body in rupture or constipation of the bowels, or for reducing dislocation. *Nicotine* was the awful agent chosen by Bocarmé for poisoning his brother-in-law a few years since in Belgium, *because it killed and left no sign* whereby to convict him. At each whiff of smoke, it is known that a good portion of a large drop of the oil of tobacco circulates through the mouth ; we have often seen it blown out of the mouth and condensed on the thumb-nail, by men who had the ability to contract the lips to an opening sufficiently small for that purpose. Five drops of the oil of tobacco will kill a large dog. The throat often becomes excessively dry and irritable in smokers, and there is a morbid thirst produced that greatly debilitates digestion, by diluting too much the fluids of the stomach—robbed, also, of its healthful saliva by the spitting.

But there are other and far more mortifying and disastrous effects following the use of cigars. There is a law of the system, which, in a great number of cases, ensures similar morbid results to similar structures of the

human body. The lining membrane of the urethra is
very similar in its structure to that of the mouth. Here
the use of tobacco is followed by the most distressing
consequences ; it is impossible to particularize these in
this place. They are almost invariable in delicate persons, from even moderate smoking. The morbid and
absurd fastidiousness of too many readers would pervert
the object of the most refined and delicate teacher ;
many of our readers have very absurd ideas of propriety.
We can only say in this place that the morbid irritability
on the mucous lining of the urethra, and the fearful prostration of the lower parts of the body and extremities,
produced by the action of tobacco on the spinal nerves,
have often induced the doubt whether its use, and some
other revolting vices, were not the actual origin of so
much unhappiness in married life. If we have used a
moderate share of intellect and very extensive observation aright, we can find no cause of sufficient power except tobacco, capable of producing the wrecks of manhood that often come under our professional notice.
The dull leaden eye, the trembling hand, and insecure
and unmanly step, the vacillating purpose and incapacity
to reason correctly on the most simple subjects, are too
often seen connected with the aroma of the deadly
weed, as the victim unfolds in trembling accents his tale
of blighted prospects and chilled affections.

So far are we from doubting its power over the moral
and physical welfare of the race, that we have not a
doubt that it has infinitely more to do with the physical
imperfection and early death of the children of its votaries, than its great associate, drunkenness itself. The
deficiency of virile power in many instances of long continued smokers is very marked. Every surgeon of
experience must have observed it. The local surgical

and medical treatment most effective in these cases, proves conclusively that it is to the debilitating and exhausting influence of tobacco that these sad consequences are due. How, indeed, could it be that an agent of such universality of action on the nervous and muscular systems—one that at first invariably produces vertigo and blindness, and throws its victim prostrate on the earth in temporary death, should not reach its climax in the role of its peculiar power, in that mysterious system where nature has chosen to evolve redundant life? What is the period for this grand demonstration of Almighty power? What evidence does the Creator impress upon the countenance of its possession?

One would think that a man's—more especially a young man's—natural instincts would awaken him to the discovery that some horrid vampire was fanning him from mental sleep to physical death; he has before him every day the bright eye, the elastic step, and the lithe limbs of his companions; he sees, but seems not to understand, the quickly averted eye, the expressive and scornful face of insulted woman, as she refuses to take his offered but defiled seat in the omnibus or rail-car; he permits her to open the window and expose her health to the chill air, to get a little air untainted with the loathsome aroma of his foul breath; he is refused employment at many gentlemanly occupations by most sagacious men, and yet he persists in debasing himself; he must have his "narcotic," his "stupefier." A very good proof of its influence on the delicacy of a man's perception may be found in the frequent appeal to his opponents : "Look at me, it has never hurt me." This appeal is often made by men who, from the associate habit of beer or brandy-drinking, have become actually puffy with soft fat, and their breaths redolent of that indescribably filthy and disgusting exhalation from liquor and tobacco ; drenching the floor in a circle, and defiling your clothes with their constant expectoration, apparently unconscious of their filthiness, and their liability to a biting or insulting reply.

Both smoking and chewing also produce marked alterations in the most expressive features of the face. The lips are closed by a circular muscle, which completely surrounds them and forms their pulpy fullness. Now every muscle of the body is developed in precise ratio with its use, as most young men know—they endeavor to develop and increase their muscle in the gymnasium. In spitting, and holding the cigar in the mouth, this muscle is in constant use ; hence the coarse appearance and irregular development of the lips, when compared with the rest of the features, in chewers and smokers. The eye loses its natural fire, and becomes dull and lurid ; it is unspeculative and unappreciative ; it answers not before the word ; its owner gazes vacantly, and often repels conversation by his stupidity.

The foulness of the breath in most chewers and smokers proves positively that the oil of tobacco, with all its deadly powers, is carried into the blood and pervades the whole system ; it could not be continually thrown out from the lungs if it did not thus reach the air-cells and windpipe ; it is thrown out there with the poisonous carbonic acid. Some persons absorb the poison more freely than others. We have seen paralysis of both the upper and lower extremities in men scarce past middle age. A person who is saturated with tobacco, or tobacco-poisoned, acquires a sodden or dirty yellow hue ; two whiffs of his breath will scent a large room ; you may nose him before he takes his seat. Of this he is entirely unconscious ; he will give you the full force of his lungs, and for the most part such people have a great desire to approach and annoy you. We have been follow round a large office-table by them, backing continally to escape the nuisance, till we had made a revolution or two before our motive was perceived.

In eating, the tobacco-chewer must lose all delicate appreciation of flavor ; we have observed, indeed, that he is very easily satisfied by the filthy Irish cookery, and greasy and cold meat and vegetables of the hotel or boarding-houses ; he seasons his food very highly, because of his obtuse taste ; many of these unfortunates drink raw brandy for the same reason.

Finally, and worse than all, he ceases to appreciate the chaste salute from the rosy lip of love, and if the mistress of his blunted affections should permit him to approach her cheek, it can only be with pent-up breath, and averted eye directed toward his pocket—the only attraction a beautiful woman can possibly have for a tobacco-chewer. If there be a vice more prostrating to the body and mind, and more crucifying to all the sympathies of man's spiritual nature, we have yet to be convinced of it.

HUMANITARY SKETCHES FROM THE HIGH-WAYS.

THE RATTLE-SNAKE ANATOMIST—THE LAST FEE—RELIGIOUS PREJUDICE—DEAR SUE, DO I RESEMBLE YOU?

THE very limited sphere of observation of character which most of our brethren seem inclined to think belongs to their profession, has always appeared to us to give a large proportion of them the appearance of very stupid people. The awful gravity and exceedingly learned appearance of some of them, is well calculated to impress a large class of men ; but somehow it always excites our risibles to listen to their impressive demonstrations of their medical skill, in their measured sentences. The laughing devil, however, prevails but a short time ; for it soon begins to bore a man and annoy his nerves, when they attempt to display their intellectual wares to an old surgical wolf. Occasionally they venture into the editorial den, and we are lost in curious speculation on their moral and physical peculiarities ; the city brethren are mostly stereotypes of the irmedical exemplars ; some affect the style of the great Butcher surgeon ; some (but they are few, and the attempt is difficult, for he is a lively little fellow and has a keen eye) try to outswagger the Phenomenon ; and occasionally one actually deports himself in a simple and unaffected manner, like a gentleman. Now and then a natural genius comes in from the far-off country, and then we often enjoy a touch of unsophisticated nature. Lately we had a specimen, which proves the

THE RATTLE-SNAKE ANATOMIST.

truth of the idea advanced by some physiologists, that man approximates in action and gradually in formation to the animals with whose habits he is most familiar.

Weary with a pretty exhausting day's work, I had thrown myself upon that altar for the sacrifice of all manly ambition, a doctor's office couch, and for a moment the senses were oblivious of the world, and dreams of babbling brooks, the wings of flying birds, and meadows and forest shades, flecked and illumined by flowers, had usurped the place of the querulous and discontented invalid. Between sleep and waking, or when with such enchanting visions as I love to believe, floating between heaven and earth, my lids occasionally disclosing the beauties of an office and its fascinating accessories, a long individual of uncouth anatomy, and clad in awkward habiliments, colored with butternut dye, stole softly down the steps and knocked stealthily at the door. On bidding him enter, I was convinced I had a specimen of humanity of no ordinary kind before me. Personally he was unique ; six feet of bones, sinews, and nerves, apparently destitute of blood, with legs and arms out of all propor- tion in their great length, surmounted by a small head, covered with an old shaggy slouched hat, which, being removed, let fall a few locks of hair like the end of a weather-beaten and frayed hempen rope ; beneath and between these scattered locks gleamed intensely two sunken gray eyes, surmounted with sparse eye-brows of similar color and texture to the hair. The figure glided up to my couch and hissed out : "Are you Doctor Dixon?" "Yes." "The author of such a book?" (I am sorry I have forgotten the title.) "No." To this my visitor replied he was sure I was mistaken, and to my renewed asseveration that I was not, he began to hiss out several sentences, between each one demanding, "Don't

you know that—and that—and that?" emphasizing each
one till his last emphatic that, and the near approach of
his long arms and gray eyes, made him look like a
maniac. Accustomed to see some odd specimens, I succeeded in preserving both my coolness and my veracity ;
I stoutly denied the authorship of the work imputed to
me, and of which, from the passages quoted, I should not
have been ashamed, and finally got my visitor so far
calmed as to inquire what he had in a little flat box, of
some eighteen inches square and not over two in depth,
which he kept clutched in one hand, and which, from its
being tightly screwed together, I imagined must contain
something of extraordinary consequence, if not great
value. Possibly a collection of diamonds discovered in
the West, which, after California gold, seemed only wanting to destroy our republic, and reduce us to French
trifling and vassalage, under some magnificent liar and
thief like Louis Napoleon. I instantly became convinced
that the precious box contained a considerable portion of
the soul of its possessor. Taking a small screw-driver
from his pocket, he informed me, with impressive empha-
sis, that he was sure I would appreciate the scientific
labors of his life ; he was on his way to Europe to exhibit
the extraordinary result of his anatomical labors in comparative anatomy. A physician in the northwestern
part of the State, he had for many years devoted his
attention to comparative anatomy, and at length having
completed " his collection," he was on his way to exhibit
the result of his labors in Europe. As he used the term,
"his collection," in its widest sense, I felt at a loss to
conceive what possible relation the contents of a box
eighteen inches square and two deep, could possibly bear
to the science that occupied the life of a Hunter or a
Cuvier ; I fancied he had some simple and interesting

specimen to make me ashamed of my ignorance of so
enlightening a science—my own investigations having
been chiefly occupied by the human specimen. The
screw-driver at length revealed the darling pets of my
visitor, and caused me again to examine the owner's
anatomy, to find some new evidence of the doctrine of
Metempsychosis. I had heard him hiss, and no sooner
did I see the contents of the box, than I stepped off a
pace or so, expecting to hear the horrible rattle ; the
spirit of a rattle-snake ought surely to dwell in that long,
bloodless body. Arranged in circles, and neatly secured
on a sheet of white paper, were the skeleton heads of a
number of snakes! Standing off a pace or two, and
holding the precious little box at arm's length, he seemed
to enjoy his anticipated triumph. "That," said he, in-
dicating with his skinny finger, "is the Rattle-snake ;
that is the Copper-head ; that is the Pilot-snake ; that is
the Messessauga ;" and so on, enumerating a dozen of
the horrible reptiles, till he came to the Adder and Gar-
ter-snake ; then, placing the box on the table, he took
out a long style and pointed to sundry small bony projections, which he pronounced exostoses, and anchyloses,
—though these learned terms, in my humble opinion
conveyed nothing more than the irregular bony unions of
certain fractures, inflicted, according to scriptural command, by that Satanic exuberance of maternal fruitful-
ness—a country boy of larger or smaller growth.

My visitor had now seated himself, and allowed me to
examine stealthily his cranial developments. I soon saw
by the absence of the higher reflective faculties, and
causality and comparison, that his idea of comparative
anatomy began and ended with snakes, and his notions of
pathology were circumscribed by bone ; exostoses and
anchyloses, suitably varied, would for him quadrate the

circle ; in short, I could not but think that in a former
state of existence, he had often had his head broken by a
stone, and had learned how to squirm his way through
the rocks, and hiss defiance in the form of some one of
his favorite reptile specimens.		In practice, he had evi-
dently got no higher than mercury and quinine ; he
informed me with great sorrow that he formerly gave
seven or eight ounces yearly, but last year he used but
two.		He had saved enough money to carry him home,
and was then on his way to Germany with "his collec-
tion in comparative anatomy."		Doubtless his specimens
were far less destructive when in full activity amongst
their native rocks, considering their opportunities for
practice, than their unsophisticated collector would have
been with his medical artillery and ammunition, had he
lived in a more populous region ; very sure are we that
his ideas of comparative anatomy and pathology were
quite as enlarged as many of his city brethren.		We feel
rather shy about presenting this specimen ; "like seeks
like" often, we know, and it may furnish a doubt to some
of our professional Academic friends why our eccentric
visitor should have sought us out in so very special a
manner to exhibit his *snakes'* heads.		One thing consoles
us, however ; the king of the American tribe always
springs his rattle before he bites ; but the black snake is
a coward and gives no notice ; he either bites without
warning, or turns tail and runs away like a medical
slanderer.

Alas! how many beautiful flowers spring up in our
hearts under the genial influence of a pure humanitary
emotion and the recollection of our earliest loves, and are
withered and crushed under the fierce sun of prosperity
and the hard necessity of money.		Oh, that "society"
would allow some other criterion of merit than success

and money! then methinks many a manly spirit would be allowed to rekindle for a few hours, in some little nook, where the brook ripples, and the birds and crickets chirp, the fire that once glowed so warmly in the heart, when we resolved to be—MEN as well as doctors. The world demands too much of the honest surgeon, when it requires every hour of his time to secure the means of a mere appearance ; without which, in its helplessness of perception, it cannot see merit. These reflections spring unbidden by personal impulses to the pen. They are from the spirit-hoard of the past, and are always awakened when we pass a little nook in an old country churchyard, near a certain town we used to frequent during our peripatetic forays in cataract and cross-eye hunting. There, marked by a simple stone, rest the remains of a professional brother of no common character. Twenty years ago I met him professionally, by his own request, to operate on a case of cataract which his modesty and conscientiousness would not allow him to attempt ; he then gave me a portion of his early history. The son of a poor clergyman in one of the Eastern States, he was so unfortunate in his medical studies, as to imbibe a passion for physiological medicine ; he early saw the absurdity of expecting from pills and potions, what could only follow an observance of the laws of life. As this idea had taken hold of his mind, as a philosophical and honest man, it speedily showed its results in his practice. The community in which he resided, like that of nearly all our American towns, was extremely ignorant in all matters of natural science, and prejudiced against every innovation on their usual course of life, and especially so toward every one who attacked their sensualities, and was outside the pale of the established religion of the place, which was the old school of Presbyterians.

Added to his philosophical bias, my unfortunate friend, and a lovely wife he had brought with him from his native town, were Unitarians. As there was no church of that denomination in the town, the young couple cheerfully joined their neighbors to the extent of their limited means in the support of the clergyman, and aided in all the religious enterprises of the place ; they regularly attended the services of the church, but it was observed that they took no part in the weekly prayer-meetings. After several decided expressions of surprise by the clergyman, my friend could not consistently withhold his opinion ; which every Unitarian will know was not in favor of such exciting demonstrations of religious desires as are usually given by the zealous in these assemblages. These opinions were given with that mildness and perfectly unrestrained freedom, that every well-bred clergyman ought to expect from an equally well-bred and well-educated physician ; but they were decidedly distasteful. They parted amicably in appearance, and my friend continued his usual daily routine, but he speedily discovered the consequence of his candor. He was a great favorite with the ladies, from that gentle yet earnest manner that every woman instinctively admires, and he had built largely on this and his acknowledged familiarity with their peculiar diseases, as a sure foundation for future success, in earning at least a competence.

Practice began to fall off ; one by one his patients discovered that the doctor gave very little medicine—indeed, they often got well without any, and yet the yearly bills were sent in ; soon it was noticed that my friend rarely had a case of serious disease. Somehow Dr. ———, who had but lately come into the village, and purchased the handsomest house in town, had succeeded in raising several of his patients after fearful attacks. The apothecary—who had left my immediate neighborhood in the city, because he had killed a child by substituting strychnine instead of morphine, in a compound ordered by a physician—spread the report that "Dr. ——— wrote the most elegant recipes he had ever read," and evinced a "splendid knowledge of his profession." My poor friend always brought his own simple medicines; indeed, I know that he looked with horror upon most recipes of varied and powerful ingredients, such as apothecaries dearly love to sell. His means were limited, and his modest chaise was not as ornamental as his professional brother's superb bays. Matters went on thus for a year, when Dr. ——— joined the church, and my friend having declined to favor his professional brother's views in the administration of large doses of medicine to several former patients who had left him, but nevertheless insisted in calling him in consultation in some cases of severe disease that had been already over-medicated, was reduced to a practice not sufficient to support him. He sold his horse and chaise, and his wife established a small school; but this soon failed because of the Unitarianism ; he was outside the pale of the fashionable religion of the village.

About this time, his health beginning to fail, he resolved to eke out his meagre living by preparing some beautiful native birds for ornithologists and parlor ornaments ; this was soon discovered, and although the occupation gave that pliancy and practice to the fingers, which was evidently available in surgical and obstetrical business, it was pronounced " decidedly unprofessional," and sneered at by the two poor and ignorant village doctors, who took their cue from their rich brother, now his acknowledged enemy. He knew his health was too feeble to commence in a new place, and felt that he could not

10

avoid similar offences elsewhere. A cough had set in ; he was evidently smitten by that great leveller, consumption. At this period, a young and lovely woman, who had married a merchant, and had been a former patient of my friend, but had been compelled by her mother to call in Dr. ———, was taken in labor. The doctor was far from being a skillful obstetric practitioner ; indeed, as the result proved, he was quite unacquainted with that indispensable part of the science, the presentations. A very active labor of several hours failed to accomplish the delivery, and when Dr. ——— could no longer avoid the necessity, he yielded to the importunity of the husband, and acceded to the proposal of a consultation ; the patient herself insisted on seeing my friend, who was now confined to his bed ; but Dr. ——— had refused to meet him. In this emergency, nothing was left for the attending physician but to retire, and for the husband to bring my friend from his dying-bed. He obeyed the summons, although in so exhausted a state as to doubt his ability to render any aid, should physical energy be essential to its accomplishment. Indeed, his friend told me that when he discovered a mal-presentation, and that version was still possible during the long intervals of exhaustion between the pains, he felt that he should fail if he attempted it unaided by a stimulant. Calling for a glass of wine, and sustained by a will that had only yielded to hereditary disease, he speedily effected the delivery of a living child. He had been in the house less than an hour, when the patient slept her first sleep in two days, with a lovely and strong infant by her side. Dr. ———, before he so disgracefully resigned his patient, had urged the necessity of the most horrible of all the resources of the obstetrician to save the life of the mother only! the result admitted of no cavil ; it was pure science and skill *versus* ignorance and actual lack of the common rudiments of obstetrics. My poor friend could not leave the house of his patient for days ; indeed, they would not have allowed it at all, had his pride permitted him to remain. His kind wife spent her time between the bedside of her husband and the young mother ; and when they left for their own solitary home, my friend carried with him his last fee ; but two months afterward he was put in the village church-yard. Dr. ——— was at the funeral ; he could now meet him without fear of his science or his honesty ; and the poor old clergyman pathetically regretted the loss of so useful a man, and "hoped" that "God, in his infinite mercy, had taken him to a better world." We love to believe that some day we will all meet where neither religious prejudice, nor poverty, nor medical selfishness will separate us.

It is a beautiful thing to go out on the highway and behold the moving throng, and feel that we are brethren of a common family ; we may condemn the vices of a man : we may shrink from an entire class of the human family, as companions, but when the helpless cry of infancy or the trembling limbs of age demand our aid and sympathy, we are made to feel that each one of us is but one atom in the great ocean of humanity, hastening to that shore where the surging billows never cease as they carry us onward to our eternal destiny. Twice during our lives each one of us must inevitably require the aid of our fellows—at our birth and our death.

It is a dreadful thing, and one that the physician is often called upon to see, "when youth itself survives young love and joy," and the biting taunt and the sharp reply are given and sent between husband and wife, even the father and mother of children. What can be more shocking to a man who has seen a couple not yet past

middle life, through some of those awful scenes we are
called upon to witness, and then, from some trifling cause,
to hear them convince us that they are cultivating a bed
of thorns for that period when they will be left alone by
the world to sustain the weight of years by their own
companionship. Love is a beautiful thing in youth, for
it shows its origin in pure emotion, but it is always full
of fear for its continuance ; in middle life it is glorious,
for it causes us to have faith in God and man ; but in
old age it is hallowed, for it makes us remember its origin ; tried by affliction, it must have originated in purity,
for it has withstood all outside attractions, and hallowed
by time, in company with its first and last companion, it
approaches its heavenly source : " God is love."

Many years ago, when pursuing our thankless task of
visiting the sick in the highways and by-ways of the city,
we used to meet an aged couple walking arm in arm
down one of our main streets, and always engaged in
cheerful conversation ; this was the more remarkable, for
they were evidently very old, and though scrupulously
clean, very poor. The man was over eighty, and the
woman at least seventy, and he was completely blind,
the corneal or pellucid part of both eyes having become
opaque from violent inflammation ; one of them pro-
truded, being what surgeons call, in their nomenclature,
staphylomatous. Notwithstanding this, the old man was
actually handsome ; his other features were noble and
placid ; he was evidently a gentleman and a Christian ;
that face could not deceive. His companion resembled
him in so remarkable a degree, excepting the poor eyes,
(hers were large and blue, and very expressive ; she
evidently saw well, wearing no glasses,) as to induce me
to conclude they were sister and brother. Their evident
devotion to each other struck a sympathetic chord that

compelled me involuntarily, after several months' notice of them every morning, to raise my hat and bid them good morning ; this being kindly returned, in due time begot a passing remark about the weather ; finally, my curiosity could wait no longer, and with an apology for the freedom, I begged him to tell to me whether their close resemblance in features indicated the relationship of sister and brother. I shall never forget the reply, and I hope no young couple who may find the demon of domestic life darken their early love, will fail to remember it. Casting his sightless orbs upon his companion, whilst every other feature showed the soul that welled up in his breast, he replied : "Why, my dear sir, she is my wife ; we have lived together nearly fifty years, but I have not seen her for thirty." Then, musing a moment—for I was sorry I had asked the question and was silent—he continued : "Well, I have heard it so often, it must be so ; yet how strange it is, for when I first knew her, she was a beautiful young creature, and her eyes were very bright ; "Dear Sue, can it be—do I resemble you?"

Several years after, when I had long removed from that part of the city, I was requested to see a poor old woman, ill with cholera, whose husband had died that morning. In the northern suburb of the city, in a little frame house, I found the dead body of my old blind friend, decently laid out by the hands of kind neighbors ; he had expired that morning. In the front room (they had but two) lay his dear old companion, already nearly pulseless ; she knew me instantly, and smiled when I took her hand. On inquiry, she said she had no pain, but felt very weak ; she had taken her bed only that very morning ; there was actually no symptom of cholera, nor indeed any other disease ; the shock of her husband's death was too much for her, and she was about to die from pure exhaustion. I gave some wine and ammonia, which the kind friends had provided, and looked round the neat room. On a clean little pine table, spread with a snowy cloth, lay a Bible, a pair of old silver spectacles, and several pairs of shoes, some unbound ; they told the story ; poverty and love, industry and faith in God. She read my thoughts : "You said we looked alike," she whispered, "and he often spoke of it. I could never understand it, unless it was because I thought of him so much ; he was very patient, doctor ; although he suffered dreadfully, he only seemed to murmur because he couldn't see me ; but he will soon see me now—soon, very soon—don't you think so, doctor?" I told her I thought she would die, but I could not say how soon ; we would keep the body as long as possible. "Thank you, doctor," she replied, "you know what I want ; don't separate us." I assured her it should be as she wished. I called again the same day ; she was dead ; they brought the dead body to her bedside, and she held the hand in hers till all was still. I have not a doubt he has seen her ; such love could only originate and end in heaven.

SMALL POX.

INOCULATION—VACCINATION—WHAT ARE THEY ?—IS VACCINATION A PREVENTIVE OR NOT?

The most unfortunate of all human folly is vanity ; we can prove it, for look you : a suggestion is made, or an experiment : Now, it is highly probable at the very out-set, that the suggestor has had his mind for some time more or less occupied with the subject, and even if it be the more immediate result of a happy combination of thought, still it is the result of the workings of *another* mind than our own, and consequently it presents a sub-ject in *another* light : here at once we gain an advantage, viz., that of comparison ; if we had no other than our own ideas to work upon, the results of thought could nei-ther be so varied nor so valuable. All truth must come from small beginnings. Nothing ever was, or ever will be absolutely new ; we say ever was, or will be, and we care not to stop and defend the assertion : every thinking man will understand us.

Suppose our beloved and philosophical friends, the Doctors of Theology, had killed Galileo for his heresy. Suppose they and their enlightened brethren, the Doc-tors of Medicine, had killed Dr. Maitland and Lady Mon-tague in England, and Cotton Mather, and Dr. Boyl-ston in Boston, and ignorant mechanicians killed Fulton in New York ; suppose they had—and there were plen-ty of them who would have done it with a will—would that have killed philosophy or inoculation, or stopped steamboats? Not a bit of it; they would have gone on the faster. One man can't do everything, even if he be a lawyer, a physician, or a clergyman, or a college-bred fool. Inoculation *has* made a considerable noise in the world, and still occupies some attention. Notwithstanding the doubts some fifty years ago, most enlightened people used to get their children inoculated ; and therein we think love and fear elicited a little modesty on their parts, for which every physician at least should have been thankful—we don't mean for the modesty only, nor yet for the $1 or $5, dear reader ; a little for that (when they got it), but more for the mere pride of the thing— it was something actually done for humanity, and a tolerably heavy gun for them to point at the fools who loved to say they were all quacks. Suppose, now, the dear and enlightened people had gone on after Jenner discovered vaccination, saying the same of that they originally said of inoculation : "It's a humbug ;" "it's a crazy man's hobby ;" "it's flying in the face of Providence," etc., etc. Why, then they would have been all the while keeping alive the small pox by inoculating it in the systems of those they wished to protect. All those who were not so fortunate as to possess presumptuous and crazy parents to get them inoculated, would have taken the small pox in its virulent form from those who were inoculated. Now, we have brought you, dear reader, to the very point we wished—that of attention ; for we very well know that nine out of ten of ye don't know the difference between inoculation and vaccination ; pray, therefore, dear madam, don't curl that pretty lip and make your honest physician ashamed *for you*, when you forbid him to re-vaccinate your child, for you know nothing about it. He only wants to prove whether it was effectual.

But, first of all, what is small pox? Let us be modest, and simply say we don't know. It is a disease that came from India, a long time ago—Heaven only knows how long. Much learning has been exhausted on the subject to no purpose, other than to show we obtained the disease, like the cholera, from the East, where it had, in all probability, existed from time immemorial. The disease preceded the remedy many hundred years, and swept off an immense number of the human family. The proportion of deaths was very formidable, depending much upon ventilation and the amount of medication. Whether we shall ever know in what the essence of the disease consists, is doubtful ; but it is very certain that its greatest sympton—viz., the eruption—shows conclusively that the grand effort of nature is to expel the poison from the body by means of the skin. Under the system of modern or philosophical treatment, (giving no medicine,) the mortality of the disease has greatly decreased : of this hereafter.

Inoculation was the first great discovery toward preventing its ravages. The daughter of Lady Montague was inoculated in 1717 by Maitland, surgeon to the embassy then at Pera, and subsequently her infant daughter in London, in 1821, they being the first Europeans ever inoculated. Old Cotton Mather redeemed his witchhanging memory, by co-operating with Dr. Boylston in introducing the practice into New England. *Inoculation* consisted simply in taking the lymph from a vesicle of the small pox, from a person who had taken it in the natural way, and inserting it by a needle or lancet, under the skin of another person or infant who had never had it. It was observed that when communicated in this way, the disease produced but little fever, and very few vesicles or eruptions, and that the deaths were not more than *one in five hundred ; and that all these persons* were after-

10*

wards safe from taking the disease. This, then, is inoculation ; it is now forbidden by law, because it was discovered some fifty years afterwards, by Jenner, that *vaccination*, so called from *vacca*, a cow, (physicians chiefly use the Latin nomenclature because it is not subject to change,) had the power to protect the system from small pox, as completely as inoculation. Now, as inoculating kept up the small pox by distributing centres of infection wherever a person was inoculated, whence it might be taken by such as had not been thus protected, and pass through its natural and violent form, it became judicious to forbid it by law, and to substitute vaccination in its place. As Jenner made his first experiment in England, in 1796, and it was fourteen years more before it became general in America, all of the present generation, who are over sixty years old, were inoculated with small pox virus, and not vaccinated.

This, then, is the difference. Dr. Jenner observed that the fingers of such milkmaids as had milked cows that had a peculiar eruption on the udder, or teats, were affected in a similar manner, and that these persons, though not inoculated, *did not take small pox.*

This novel and extraordinary truth was soon made matter of universal experiment, and proved to the satisfaction of every one who took sufficient pains to investigate it. It is now also well known that small pox matter itself will, if introduced into the cow's teat, produce the same sore, or as it is now universally called, the vaccine pustule ; this has been done by Dr. Carpenter, of Lancaster, Pennsylvania, and others. They are, therefore, known to be essentially one disease. There is no doubt that the cows were inoculated with small pox virus from the fingers of the milkers who had taken the disease from others, in the natural way. The matter, as it is erroneous-

ly called, (for it is not matter, but an almost colorless and
pellucid lymph,) must be taken from the child after a first
vaccination on the sixth, seventh, or eighth day, according to the perfection of the little pearly circle that contains it ; this encircles the original and now dark red or
brown point, where the puncture or slight scarification
was made, and the virus inserted by the vaccinator.
Outside of this, there is a beautiful blush of inflammation,
fading into the surrounding skin. On the tenth day all
these points are better characterized, but it is then too
late to take the lymph. This is usually done by piercing
the pearl colored circle with a needle in a number of
places, and then rolling over the little round dots of lymph
that exude, a quarter of an inch of the barrel of a quill
previously scraped so as to take off the gloss and enable
you to see the virus on it. This end of the quill is slightly moistened when wanted for use, and rubbed over the
spot scratched with the lancet ; in doing this, much care
should be used not to draw more than a single drop of
blood, and even less if possible ; the vaccinator should
just abrade the skin, otherwise the virus will be too long
in drying and get rubbed off. The stupidity of most
nurses is so great, that unless you absolutely insist upon
tying up the sleeve of the infant, and sit by and see that
it is kept off the puncture for five or ten minutes, till it is
absolutely dry, you will have your labor for your pains—
it will be rubbed off three times out of five, and bring you
trouble and distrust. You will always be told, "your
matter was not good."

There is another misfortune attending vaccination,
which gives the young physician great trouble and anxiety ; often actually ruining his prospects, when he is as
guiltless of all harm in the matter as the babe itself.
This is the excessive inflammation of the arm, from the

frequent feebleness and constitutional irritability of the child, or else from bad nursing allowing the vesicle to be frequently broken ; this not only deranges the succession of changes it should present to the eye of the physician, so that he may judge of its genuineness, but it causes great distress to the infant. This of course, is called by gossips (and we are sorry to say, occasionally by wicked and designing physicians, jealous of their chosen brother) the result of "poison matter." We can conceive of such a thing, but we never saw a case traceable to this source. There is but one kind of matter that would with any certainty produce its like ; and we can scarcely conceive the possibility of such being chosen, unless by a madman. The "poison" is generally, as we have had to say on many occasions, when the case had either happened to ourselves, or when in later years it had been referred to us for an opinion, to be found in the head of an ignorant nurse, a frightened mother, or a designing and jealous brother physician's tongue. These cases always subside under a slight poultice : but in a few weeks the child should be vaccinated again for greater certainty ; for it may be that the virus has been all thrown off in the suppuration, or not enough absorbed to protect the constitution. There are many careful and experienced men, who now believe that a number of punctures should be made in several places, expressly to produce more of the virus in the arm, and thereby insure greater immunity from small pox. We are by no means sure this is not sound practice, although we have ourselves chosen rather to vaccinate again after a few weeks, in order to test the first trial, than to make so many sores at one time. Of course, if the first have been successful, the second does not produce a vesicle, or "take," as it is familiarly called. This brings us to the point of re-vaccination. How long does it protect? how long before it runs out? are questions frequently asked. And it is astounding to say, some are so bold as to condemn it altogether. There is no doubt whatever, that vaccination in time loses its protective power in a great number of instances. There are some even yet, who make this the occasion of especial self-laudation, alleging their own great experience in distinguishing the "genuine vesicle." These are either ignorant and conceited men, or designing ones. The most perfect vesicle may be followed by the milder form of small pox or varioloid. We have repeatedly seen it, and so has every other man who will consent to use his eyes, unblinded by prejudice. Even virulent and confluent small pox has itself twice attacked the same person! Let us then vaccinate our patients every six or seven years at least ; we will then do our duty. If there be any so mean as to insinuate we do it for gain, the remedy is easy ; let us do it for nothing : 'twill not be the only fee we shall lose from that sort of people.

AN ARTIST'S REVERIE—NO. III.

Spirits are not finely touched, but to fine issues."

YEARS have stolen by, since, at Milan, I heard the music of Paganini—the strange, unearthly-looking Paganini—those ravishing, delicious tones ; those lords over the unbroken smile of delight, the stoppage or free flow of the breath, or the impulsive gush of the heart's sigh and tear. Yet here they all are, as fresh, as vivid as ever—the twitter, the softly-blent tones, the thunder's roll, the drum's tattoo, and the sharp, startling, lightning-like crash—here they all *memorically* abide in perfect harmony with the child's dimpled glee, the dash of the waterfall, the murmuring of the brook, the moanings and shrieks of the wind, the howlings of the tempest, and the sad wail for the dead. (How easily such music masters the human will!—*as easily as the syren glance and touch.*)

And thus, thro' time and space, on chimes the Spanish bell—and mountaineers take song, and hark, to *the answering hills* . . and *Pasta* sings, and sings, and trills like the musical monarch of the forest . . and then, *the hundred singers* clasp their voices, and the mighty organ moans and swells and quavers, and sinks away to the merest flutter . . and *the single voice of a woman reigns* . . and the hundred voices chaunt and chaunt and move so swiftly . . and *all* the voices roll like

thunder ; and walls and dome and fretted roof reverber-
ate ; and marble saints and priests and Saviour seem to
join . . and then, (and as the mirror of one's memory turns in the noblest theatre of art,)—within the
moment's span, what multitudes of proud creations drop
the veil ! . . from ancient gems by Aulus, to the
gigantic ivory-and-golden Jupiter of Elis—the urn,
the tomb, the signet ring—the marble dream of Eve,
by Ctesiphon—and naked, laughing, sleepy, amorous
nymphs, by Titian !

A vast diversity—the starving child and the stone angel
—the rotting heart and the silver casket—jewels ! tho' on
dead finger.

Figures boxing ; figures vaulting ; figures dying ;—*the
reverse torch and the merry lyre !* the sibyl and the seraph ;
sweet Flora and Nell Gwynne ! And, as the air *sings*
thro' the fleetness of the comer's foot, we have *Apollo*—all
clothed in light and grace and lordliness and dazzling
beauty ! with the drapery still rustling, the feet scarcely
pressing the ground, and "the breath of the power of
God" quite *dancing* thro' the nostrils ! Truly, *the king
is held in the galleries of thy hair !* thy locks are *jutting
from their fillet as a jewelry of stars !* and in thy *shadow*
sit we with supreme delight ! Next, *Raphael*, with the
lovely form of *Fornarina* and *Mary* at the Cross ! And
Michael Angelo, with " *Moses*," that grand statue ! and
" *Night and Morning*," too—and, as with the music of *the
noise of chariots on the mountain tops*, the giant brain un-
locks its chiefest chamber, its *Last Judgment !*

"Askalon shall see it in fear ; and Ekron, for her expectation shall be ashamed—they wait for light, but
behold obscurity ! The stars know not the astrologers !
The golden bowl is broken !

There is *silence* in heaven—legions stand up for judgment—the voice from the Great White Throne *thundereth* —and *the abominable branch is cast out!* The Moon and Sun are as blots—Earth *wildly* takes her way—and mountain fires and molten lakes give but such *lurid* light! Grandeur and blackness ; majesty and madness reign ! *Peerless the scene*—the bold philosophy ; the proud conception—*sterling* the knowledge of the play of human trunks and joints and reinless passions! *Rich is the Sistine Chapel !* Down drop the myriads damn'd ! headlong and sidelong and grasping at air ! A heavy hail ! a rude jostle ! a monstrous tangle ! The false-balance ; the false shrift ; the face in flame ; the horrent hair ! *Caligula and sisters !* Down drop the myriads damn'd, and *frightful* apparitions ! Satyrs are there, and asps and royal mountebanks. * * *

Next, *Edom* comes. *Edom*, the solitary ! How is she become as a widow ? why do her nobles dwell but in the dust, and the cormorant and bittern lodge in the upper lintels ?—their voice alone sings from the windows ; and choicest vestibules are lairs for wolves and lions and their whelps ! *Edom*—the wonderful, the beautiful, the city hewn from solid rock ! niches and porticoes and statues all : how *very* desolate. . . *Edom*—man's pride, heaven's jealousy ! City—so people-stript by God ! what drew dead Edom from its mighty loadstone ? where went divinities and genii ; stray jasper and cornelian ? The socket's here—but *not the winged eye*—the serpent's cast-off coat is here—but *not* the *serpent ringed*—*fled* are those symbols so *eternal*, so *all-seeing !* *Dear Edom*—where's thy seed-time and thy harvest ? thy love-talks at the well ; thy graceful, flying horsemen ; and hosts on hosts of glittering, darting javelins ; and oval shields ?—all, *all*, are *hissed* away ! Thine excellency—dukes and daughters—flaming chariots and prancing steeds—all, *all*, asunder! *Edom*—proud tomb—when will thy human dust be resurrect? * * *

Next, *tens of thousands* of sarcophagi—and pyramids and sphinx—and temples all magnificent—and cities labyrinthine—and lo! the *costly, curious corpse and coffin of Cleopatra.* . . . Off with the lid! Unwind the bandage linen! . . . Ah! here's the face—the ghastly, tinselled face—of the once beautiful and voluptuous woman, *to build whose sepulchre an army toiled!* . . . and next, *the Memnons*—forms gigantic ; forms uncouth!—*monsters are in the stocks,* and *speechless!* Where now's the *charming voice* of old, so *sacred,* so *oracular?* Where are the million spirits with their *vocal magnet?* . . . And Cuyps, Vandyks, and strange old heads in strange old dress, (Arab and Greek and Parthian,) and strange old shields and jars and funeral urns, and clustering beards and sandalled feet and stately frills, and rings from fingers *long since* turned *by ashes into ashes,* at Pompeii—and strange old shapes, (in trance, in church, in iron shirts and papal caps,) who ever *clasp their hands in prayer, and keep a watch of angels by the pillow!* (as Frideswide's Saint, and Lord de Vere.) . . . Figures wrestling ; figures racing ; figures flying—like *fair Helen* —like *Icarus*—like *Scevola* with the flame! . . . *Vast the diversity!* The scrap of landscape, and the complex battle of the soul—the Etna and the Acteon. But—beyond all other brainal power, (in flourish since the days of Pericles,) looms that of the builder of *the Grand Cupola ;* the sculptor of *the Moses ;* the painter of *the Last Judgment!*—a power so immense in its strength ; and so *alone* in its sublimity, originality, bold and correct anatomical displays and wonderful grandeur of grouping! One of those mental giants that *refresh the Earth, once in two thousand years!* * * *

And now the busy brain of the artist wanders off from the old art-cradle of Europe to the western world and beholds in his glory that grand creation of God, the wild horse of the prairie! see how he flies (without wings) over the velvety, flower-enamelled and dew-spangled carpet of pure nature. What a beautiful, noble and gracefully-moving creature it is! with its proudly-arched neck; copious, silky, and wind-tost mane and tail; spacious and waltzing chest; compact shoulders and flanks; and limbs all so tapering, sinewy, and exquisitely cut at the knees, fetlocks and feet—and see the smallness and shape of the head, matching as they do with the heads on the Parthenonic frieze (by Phidias,) with the temples wide apart and indicative of an intellect equal to the chiming-in with other portions of the proud Athenian temple—and the nose, how slender it is, and tapering toward the tiny mouth; and the ears, so thin, agile, sensitive and leafy; and the cheeks, so angular, and made up of nothing save bone and cuticle, and a tracery of veins that runs about as gracefully as the winding streamlet!

Now, amidst the soft music of leaves and tumbling waters, and the cry and wing-flap of small and great birds, my wild horse halts in his dance of extreme joy, and merely crops the enspangled grass and flowret; and then breathes forth many a pleasure thrilled neigh, which floats over the scene, and dies off echoingly into the vast spirit-hoard or memory of creation's music! Now, with up-pricked ears and full opened and clear-balled eyes, the noble animal gazes and gazes around and snorts like the sharp and sudden ruffle and snap of the wind-met pennon! And now, he paws the earth, shakes his crest, kneels, sits, rolls over and over, and even *boxes at the blue heavens*—either *in prayer*, or else *in imitation of the poses and actions of the acrobat.*

Then he rises quite erectly, and sheets on sheets of heavy mist leap from his quivering nostrils ; and next he displays his open mouth, all adorned with palisades of ivory, and scarlet-velvet dome and floor, and a richly crimson-colored, writhing and throne-like tongue Then off he bounds over sward and bush and low-trailed trellis of vine, and elegant flowers in myriads . . . and canters and trots, and rears and plunges, and prances from side to side, and caprioles and curvets in many a way ; and then he again darts thro' the murmuring air like the arrow or eagle in full sweep! . . . Now he returns, and the ground rings with a hail-like patter . . how rapidly the limbs cleave the air and dash away the distance! He's near—with shaking neck and dancing nostrils and heaving chest, and clouds of smoke, and coat so wet and sable, and rich with masses and spots and sprinklings of a brilliant and restless foam! . . . Tired of sport, he suddenly stops, and again crops the emerald grass and delicious flowrets, and even bites off a magnolia or so just for the sake of variety—and now he looks searchingly over the twilight sky and earth ; seeks his mate and couch ; and kneels and falls asleep—sometimes to dream and neigh to himself, and play the horse somnambule !

*   *   *   *   *   *

And the moon shone and shone on the artist's figure, and displayed the face all worn and corpse-like, save when the scowl and grinding of the teeth signed of life, and misery, and desperation. What so racks the human spirit ? What but the perishing nature of shape and color—the oak and the rose-tree ; the superior mind and the closest love ! * * *

Notice the youth, as he springs (into the arms of death) from the tall column—and the next, as he cheer-

fully riddles his heart with the swift-winged ball—and
the mother, who breaks up life in the womb!

*　　*　　*　　*　　*　　*

But who is it *now* that shifts creation's glass *eccentrically*—curdles the blood of the helpless babe ; takes from
the fond mother her only child ; strikes down with lightning the man of meridian health and strength, and mental and physical majesty and beauty ; buries whole cities
after cities with flood, with lava, and the earthquake ;
and drives on the hurricane to rip-up and wither and
shiver the thousand-rooted and giant tree ? Who but
the Lord God !

On sweeps the spectral image train—the headless rider
and the city people-stript—the howl, the hiss, the curse,
the intensly piercing scream, and peals on peals of blas-
phemy . . . *and a host of shape and color was changed
for ashes !*

Up draws the Decollator—and Faliero falls—and Mas-
aniello—and St. John—and the pure and brilliant spirit
of Roland receives its immortal wings!

This is MARY STUART—that child of beauty and misfortune—now past the noon of life, yet still retaining a
rare loveliness of person and nobility of mien. The face
is scarcely out of its wonted oval, and but for a flash or so
of scorn, as unruffled as the sleeping lake ; the neck arises
from its throne of superb mould, with a grace and majesty
that dim away the swan's ; the nose is Grecian, bent,
almost perceptlessly, toward the aquiline ; the mouth
seems Beatrice de Cenci's—so beautiful's the form, so
lofty the expression ; the lips of costliest scarlet, so play
on strings of pearl.

But the great black eyes have spent their lustre, and
the weary lids drop o'er the windows of the soul, as the
aged Day yearns for the step of the youthful Night ;

whilst the silky lashes droop, like the flowers at twilight, and pencil away on their marble sills full many an angel's wing! But where are the roses of the wall beneath? Twined round the torn-off crown? Stolen by sister queen? Drowned in Lochlevin's lake? Or do they deck the Mercy Seat—their vase, dear Katharine Seaton's heart?

The sable-velvet gown falls in with the ravishing round-ness of the bosom and waist, after the manner of the purest ancient statue, and tells, all feignlessly, of grace beneath—of Nature's unchecked breath, *free as the eagle's wing! Nature like Ariadne's! Nature to charm Praxi-teles!*

The Oriental waist-shawl catches up the gown, and " throws " (as artists say) the loop-like folds ; but in bold and brilliant masses fall the foldings of the border ; and, at the wearer's slightest step, they start their thousand lights and lines and shadows and reflections ; and leap and glance, take voice, and lock and interlock, and stack their arms!

The neck ruff's very richly wrought ; and the necklace (of massive pearl and gold) suspends a heavy crucifix, (in ebony and ivory,) *lit up with diamonds!* (the figure of the Saviour, quite a miracle of Art!)

The profile lines *race closely with Apelles!* . . . But the fascinating creature scowls at the touch of the executioner, and quietly-undresses her own neck for the axe-blow ; and, as soon as the ruff and necklace are gifted away, the silky hair, escaping its fillet, breathes freely, and, in clusters, and with many a wild, wild tress, sports with the magnificent turns and undulations of the snow-white throat and shoulders!

*   *   *   *   *   *

She bids farewell to friends and servitors, amidst sobs,

and claspings, and re-claspings, and lip-touch after lip-touch, and *close imitations of death*—herself alone support-ing the tearless eye, the philosophic word, the untremu-lous nerve, and a radiance of countenance as fretless as the heavens *beyond* the clouds!

A rainbow on the face! a desert in the heart! a brain, a crowd of lightnings, thunderings, and awful voices. A thousand jangling harps! Music! *but clothed in mourn-ning*—the lute! *but out of season.*

A *fretless radiance* of countenance! whilst love and hate and pride and jealousy and victory *lie like Tityus on the rock*—and ghosts like these start up—the laughing child-like years and sunny clime—the floors of hell-stain-ed blood—the icy, calculating virgin-queen—and Beauty's Church, so thronged with *real* worshipers—and voices from the heavens themselves, (such cool and measured voices!) saying: "As a drop of water into the sea, so are a thousand years to the days of eternity! When a bird flyeth thro' the air, there remains no token of her pathway: 'tis as dust blown away with the passing wind! If ye desire thrones and sceptres; *honor Wisdom;* and reign *forever!*" . . . . And the closing voice fell upon the listener's heart as its Door of DANTE!

Yes; "thine Almighty word leapt down from heaven out of the royal throne, *as a fierce man of war into the midst of a land of destruction!*"

The officers of the crown closely watch their watches—the sufferer has yet a moment or so to live; looks pierc-ingly at the heavens, and is alone with her *all seeing, all powerful* parent. . . . But she's *prostrate;* the dark and silvery hair's thrust out the axe road—the neck's quite fit-ted to the block. Lo! she listens . . . locks her teeth; and then re-listens; whilst the blade gets poised;

and swung aloft ; and then swept down . . yes ; *thrice* swept down!

Off rolls the royal head—to be grasped up by the hair and *anathematized*, whilst the waxy eyes and ashy lips still quiver and strive to return to life . . the limbs give frightful jerks, and beat about ; and the trunk takes a leaden-sounding writhe, as its blood spirts and wells up, and tumbles, and gets shed like tears . . . lesser convulsions follow, and the slightest tremors and flutterings, until *all is still*—save the sheet wrapping, coffining off, embalmment, lying in bloody state, magnificent entombment, and record on the page of story. But stay—till I lift that hand, so pale, so statuesque, such tapering fingers—and lay from off the face these clotted locks—and peer about the pinched-in nostrils, faded lips, and eyes barred down, till Time shall be no more ! . . And let me cry unto the mountains and the rocks, "Fall on us ! but hurt not the earth, neither the sea nor the trees."

SCENES FROM CITY PRACTICE.

A TRIAL FOR CHILD-MURDER—THE VALUE OF EVIDENCE—CRIMINAL LAW HELP-
LESS WITHOUT PHYSIOLOGICAL EVIDENCE.

THE great question after all, is to determine to what
extent man is accountable for his actions. Casuists have
been hammering away at it—moralists have written—
philanthropists have sacrificed their lives—judges have
been gowned and wigged—codes of laws, in endless profusion, have been made—prisons and dungeons have
been built—scaffolds elevated—but Christ has told us,
"Unto whomsoever much is given, of him much will be required;" and both our hearts and our heads tell us, that
there is a wide ocean between the responsibility of men.
It is useless to discuss the question of punishment; our
object is to open a few pages of medical experience in the
matter of jury trials, and the value of evidence, and let
the reader form what conclusion he pleases; it matters
not to us a pin's point, whether his delicate nerves are
shocked, or his heart bleeds. We had painfully to gather
our own experience, and although its product has not
proved worthy of a Solomon or a Howard, we belong to the
common herd of humanity, and must of necessity leave our
own lights and shadows for a few fleeting moments on
its surface, ere we are swept onward to the great ocean
of eternity, and are no longer able to efface our errors.

We would not willingly leave a spot of perfect blackness—"none are all evil"—and if there be found in these

sketches anything unredeemed by humanitary motives, we would rather it were placed to the account of temporary insanity, however needful it may be in one not over-stocked with the commodity, to preserve what brains he may have in tolerable working order.

Well satisfied, then, as we are, that wide differences exist in the power to appreciate evil, we have always felt the responsibility of our position, when called into court to testify in cases of child-murder. The awful character of such a crime against nature, such a desecration of that holy and subduing passion, a mother's love for her helpless child, has always made us look with curious wonder upon the face of her who is charged with such a crime. The sight of the little creature, so mysteriously elaborated from her very heart's blood, after she has heard its first cry, and felt its breath against her cheek—sweeter by far than that of an angel's wing—one would think should protect its life, like the sword of Heaven over the gate of Paradise. And so it would, were it not for the awful consequences of uncontrolled passion and biting poverty. Many a mother, too, whose heart's blood is frozen by fashion, and who anticipates her child's birth by destruction, is quite as guilty as she who, having listened to some serpent of our own sex, seeks to remove the evidence of her folly by destroying her living offspring. How, then, can those officers of the law, whose business it is to seek out the poor trembling wretch, with her life-blood thinned by starvation and imprisonment, and a gallows before her eyes—how can they demand of her, with equal justice, the same estimate of the value of that sacred life she has assisted to produce? No, no ; depend upon it, the law may find it necessary to mete out but one punishment, but a humane jury will not be driven by its iron spur. We remember with great

11

pleasure the humanity of the late Judge Edwards, and
Nathaniel Blunt, the District Attorney, and her counsel,
A. A. Phillips, in conducting the case of an unfortunate
woman accused of child-murder. We felt bound to attend to the requisition of these gentlemen, as medical
counsel, and they aided collectively in giving us a higher estimate of legal character, than what we have been
wont to feel when witnessing the frequent efforts of another District Attorney to hunt some trembling wretch
to the foot of the gallows. Let it be a lesson to those
ambitious of such legal triumphs.

> " Mercy to him that shows it is the rule,
> And righteous limitation of its act,
> By which Heaven moves in pardoning guilty man ;
> And he that shows none, being ripe in years,
> And conscious of the outrage he commits,
> Shall seek it, and not find it, in his turn."

One day, some ten years since, I received a note from
the gentlemen above named, requesting, in terms of
pleasing though unmerited compliment, what aid and
counsel I could give in the second trial of a wretched and
friendless outcast from Germany, who was accused of
causing the death of her newly-born child either by neg-
lecting to give it the immediate attention it required, or
by willfully throwing it, while yet alive, into the privy.

Accustomed as I have ever been to respond to such
calls, I did not feel willing to refuse, although I knew
there were many young men quite as competent, and
with more leisure than myself, who could fulfill all the
requirements of the case, without any loss not amply
repaid by the interest and publicity arising from a trial
for murder, in which their talents were judged of sufficient value to be summoned by the State. The reader
will please to remember, that in a city like this, where

official corruption is so common that it is almost a disgrace to belong to the municipal government, and where the vilest quack, and mere nostrum-seller, is sure of the aid of the press to any extent his money will afford, and almost certain if he call in its vigorous and philanthropic assistance to a sufficient extent, of fame and fortune, the most brilliant medical intellect, and the warmest heart, may pine and die in obscurity. He sees the places of coroners, health-officers, and street-inspectors, usurped by the keepers of brothels and bar-rooms, who peculate the public funds, whilst the murderer goes free, and pestilent poisons fill the highways and riot in the almshouses. Gladly, then, will the young practitioner avail himself of every opportunity to make a fickle and ignorant public aware, through the columns of a venal press, of the fact of his existence and attainments, in an overlooked, and, for the most part, poorly qualified, profession.

I repaired to the court-room, and listened to the opening of the case, and the evidence for the State. It appeared from the indictment, that Margaret Morrell, an unmarried German woman, the mother of an idiot boy of some ten years, who was present in the court-room, and playing listlessly with some bits of paper at her feet, had been the occupant of a miserable garret beneath the eaves of an old dilapidated house in Canal Street; that one day in January, at seven o'clock in the morning, two laboring men residing in the same house, crossing the yard, observed spots of blood on the newly-fallen snow, and were attracted thereby to the privy, whence they heard cries issuing, so loud as to resemble those of "a cat upon the house-top;" on looking down, they perceived the infant. An alarm was given, and the body being raised, was found with its face disfigured by rats, and, it seems, quite dead. It was proved that the unfortunate woman had been locked in her room for the afternoon and night preceding the morning when the child's body was found; but that she had been heard coming down stairs at four o'clock, and seen with a pail going to the privy. On the top of a stove, a large mass of coagulated blood was found; and on the wall, blood had *evidently spirted out from a cut artery*, showing the full action of the heart. The child was proved to have respired freely, because the lungs floated in water, which they do not do when undecayed, and from a child born dead. The umbilical cord, by which it receives the mother's blood during its intra-uterine life, had evidently been cut with a knife or scissors, but had not been tied.

The usual evidences were presented, on examination, of the birth of a child. On this evidence the state rested the case; and it seemed likely that but a short time would seal the poor creature's fate, and a few weeks more close her wretched pilgrimage on the gallows.

During the rendering of this evidence, I often looked at her with curious wonder. There she sat, with her pale face and mild blue eye, clothed in rags, her poor idiot child playing about her feet, and ever and anon looking up into her face with unmeaning gaze, and pulling her ragged gown; neither hope, love, nor fear were there; all seemed weary, worn, and desolate. What mattered it to her what all these busy and anxious-looking people were about? The judge was neither gowned nor wigged, but his mild and handsome face was very manly, and often rested pleasantly and encouragingly upon the prisoner. Alack for her, the jury had once remained all night in deliberation on her case, and could not agree; it was too evident that the poor creature's life was in great jeopardy. Once or twice I saw the sad wan face hidden in the folds of the tattered shawl, and thought she trembled ; perhaps a pang shot through the poor heart at the thought of the babe that might have been nestling over it ; perhaps she thought of the fate of her poor boy when the law should have cut off her life ; but in a moment the bloodless face and heavy eyelids were again exposed in unmeaning vacuity. Why was I excited for her ? I could not, of course, feel that interest I should have done, had I been satisfied of her innocence ; and yet I could not believe her as guilty, even though I had been certain she committed the crime, as any other woman accused of a similar one, I had even seen—she was so utterly wretched and desolate. What had she to give it ? The starved and watery blood must have been very scant, and flowed feebly to the withered breasts beneath that tattered shawl. Alas! there was no place for the poor beggar-child ; but all are alike in death ; its handful of dust would make beautiful flowers for a bridal wreath ; or, perchance, to deck the tomb of some child of wealth, better worth a mother's love. Yet, wretched as she was, one helpless child looked to her for aid ; its light of reason feeble, it is true, but who knows how closely it may have wound itself around her heart? Who can tell what pleasant memories of the Father-land the poor boy brought up in dreams on her pallet of straw? I felt that I had a sacred duty to perform. The testimony of the highly accomplished medical gentleman who was now examined, and who had been called by the State Attorney, showed clearly to the jury that the child had been born alive and respired vigorously ; the lungs, when taken from the body, crepitated under the knife, as physiologists say when they crackle from the air that escapes from them when cut, and they floated in water both when whole and when cut in pieces, thus proving that they had been filled with air. My heart sank ; it was awful for the poor creature ; death stared her in the face. The District Attorney now asked the doctor whether blood could have flowed to the amount found on the stove, and whether it would have spirted forth from the divided arteries of the cord against the wall, if the heart had not acted vigorously at birth? He answered unhesitatingly, No : it was too true. As yet I saw no hope from any question I might suggest, when a lucky thought occurred to me. Those who have read the articles on the structure and functions of the heart before birth, will remember that it is so arranged till the moment of birth, that there are virtually but two of its cavities in action, the two that are appointed for filling the lungs not being used for that purpose till after birth, but both aiding the other two to circulate the blood through the infant's body ; for this purpose there is a valve between the two upper chambers of the heart. At the moment of birth, the blood rushes into and distends the infant's lungs, and closes this valve. Sometimes, and in no mean proportion of cases, this valve fails to remain closed, and thus the lungs, which at the moment of birth received a full supply of blood, soon feel the diminished quantity ; the child, which at the moment of birth cried and breathed vigorously, soon suffers seriously from want of breath, because when the lungs do not receive their proper quantum of blood, the arteries and veins which convey it through them, become distended and congested as we say, thus keeping out the air. The physician, fortunately, had not examined the heart at all! Here was a great point. At my suggestion he was asked the proportion of cases in which it was not fully closed for several days. The Doctor admitted it to be of frequent occurrence, but could not answer definitely ; the proportion is one in five.

I now suggested to the poor woman's counsel to ask him whether the profuse bleeding of the cord would not greatly aid in paralyzing respiration. Of course, it was admitted to be so.   Here was a fresh hope.   Who could say that she knew the child would bleed to death, if she did not tie the cord ; and how could we know but this valve remained open, and with the aid of the bleeding cord, effectually cut off the supply of blood to the lungs, deprived the muscles that raised the ribs of their power to act, and thus rendered suffocation sure!   I felt great hope ; and her counsel smiled complacently, as he opened the defence.   I looked at the kind Judge, and District Attorney, (alas! both are dust now,) and they seemed pleased ; the jury, also, were evidently relieved.   I will not follow Mr. Phillips through the examination of the witnesses.   I did what I could to explain the functions of the heart to the jury ; the closing address to them expresses the whole of. the convincing testimony, which, because it was not properly called forth on the first trial, had nearly sent this poor creature to the gallows or State Prison.   Let it serve to show legal and medical men the sacredness of their duties.   The counsel spoke with great feeling of her industrious and inoffensive character, drew attention to her lone and friendless condition, commented upon the testimony wherever it appeared lame or contradictory, and so adroitly used the medical evidence as to convince them, that if the child had really been alive at the moment, that it died within a few minutes after birth ; and that her lone and friendless condition, her bodily weakness and evident ignorance, would amply account for the neglect of those attentions which would have preserved its life.   Another fact will utterly destroy the value of the contradictory testimony of the two well-meaning but ignorant Frenchmen, who had evidently forgotten on the second trial what they said on the first, viz., "That they were attracted to the place by cries so loud, that they mistook them for those of a cat on the house-top." "You will also remember, gentlemen of the jury, that one of those men swore positively that the face of the infant was downward, and the other one that it was upward; and that he saw its mouth move with great distinctness, as it cried. This, you will remember, gentlemen, was at seven o'clock in the morning; but it has been proved that it was four o'clock when the poor creature went to the privy with the pail, and that she immediately returned to her room, and was not again seen till found locked in by the officers, shivering and starving in her wretched garret, with her idiot boy. Now, gentlemen, I have shown you by the weather-register of the New York Hospital on that morning the thermometer was at zero. I ask you whether an infant already deprived of half its blood, with that great engine of its life-power, the heart, fluttering for want of its distending fluid, its face disfigured by rapacious vermin—I ask you whether that child, with its natural temperature of nearly a hundred degrees, could have remained in an open sink, scarcely covered by a half destroyed shanty, from four o'clock till seven, of a bitter cold January morning, and then have uttered a cry as loud as that of 'a cat upon the house-top?' I think I can safely anticipate your verdict. I will assure you, we do not doubt that the child was born alive; kind nature had inclosed it with the protecting arms of her wonderful love; within that poor shivering body, it derived 'security from the wintry blast;' but, alas! man, less kind than a beneficent Creator, though he had made provision for the beggar-child, had not surrounded the alms-house with much attractiveness, nor did its position render it very accessible to the poor mother, who could not even speak her need intelligibly to those who control it; the law, it is true, with sagacity, demands provision of clothing to be made by her who knows a living child will soon require it. Yet the poor creature may have designed to seek from the hand of charity such aid as it should require, had it lived. You see, gentlemen, by her own and her poor boy's clothing, she is not very proud; a resting-place, a few rags, and a morsel of food, is all that such as she can expect. I trust, then, that you will give due weight to her poverty, when contemplating this point, which, I doubt not, you will hear urged by the two gentlemen to whose courtesy I have been already so much indebted, and whose humanity is too intimately mingled with their knowledge of the law, to permit the least fear on my part that the case will not be righteously presented for your final verdict; for, gentlemen, you will please to remember, I have no exceptions to offer, and I hope you will not again disagree. Your verdict must be final; a life of toil, and her rags and crust of bread—a gallows, or at least a living grave, awaits and must follow your verdict. Her poor idiot boy may miss the face he has been so long accustomed to look to as a solace in his childish grief, but no one else will; her dust will mingle in the beggar's grave with that of her poor infant, and soon all will be forgotten—all but that small silent voice which will come to you when none is near but your own hearts, and breathe into your ears, 'For unto whomsoever much is given, of him much will be required.' " I looked at the jury with trembling hope; several of them were in tears; poor Blunt, who had given a very fair charge, (God bless

11*

his kind heart his memory is very pleasant to me,) required his pocket handkerchief very suddenly; Judge Edwards gave a very dignified, just and feeling charge; the jury were absent but a few minutes, and returned with a verdict of not guilty. My heart was glad.

BEAR-BAITING IN THE STAR-CHAMBER.

LIFE SKETCHES OF THE NEW YORK PHYSICIANS.

"Why do your dogs bark so ? Be there bears in the town?"
"I think there are, sir ; I heard them talked of."
"I love the sport well."
"You are afraid, if you see the bear are loose, are you not?"

MERRY WIVES OF WINDSOR.

WHEN the court of Rome concocted the "Expurgatori-
um," with the view of preserving the strength and purity of
their holy influence over the people, and giving the Devil
the benefit of such seditious heretical intellectual efforts
as popular indignation and ferment brought to the surface of the public caldron, they were the unconscious
progenitors of an institution that had its origin some
few hundred years later, and at one period of its existence was illumined by the presence of Justice Shallow,
Esq., "Cust-alorum," and if we may believe Cousin Slender, "a gentleman born ;" who wrote himself "*Armigero*
in any bill, warrant, quittance, or obligation, *Armigero*."
This worthy gentleman, whose high privilege it was to
show the "dozen white luces in his coat," (pray heaven,
dear reader, for the honor of the Academy, don't alter
the orthography of the emblem, as did Sir Hugh) although
—we breathe it softly, we are not quite sure, from the
seedy appearance of some of the members, but they are
quite able to match the proud badge in its more familiar
orthography, and to say with him, "it is a familiar beast

to man, and signifies love "—this worthy gentleman, was quite as conscious of the dignity of the court before whom he recounted his wrongs, and sought redress from the incursions of the fat knight, as we are of the amazing effrontery of our occasional display of some of the pastimes of the " Armigeros " of the New York Academy of Medicine ; but they are so diverting, that for the soul of us we can't help it ; and so, with our most profound regards, dearly beloved brethren, hold up your heads, for we are going to prescribe for you.

This illustrious body of Savans, originated from the ruins of the Medical Society of the City of New York ; an institution embalmed in the memory of every venerable Esculapian who had an eye for the fancy.   The brethren were jogging on in the good old way, with their lancets, Dover's powders, jalap and calomel XX and XX, always ready, and relating their " wonderful cases " over their whisky-toddy, when that precious old charlatan, Hahnemann, whom we greatly affection for his genius and profound knowledge of human nature, loomed up from the mists of Germany, and threatened to obscure the coruscations of that galaxy of science—that Koh-i-noor of medical learning, that monthly irradiated the chambers of the old Marine Court !   But when the cunning peasant, Priessnitz, threatened to drown even the remnants of the rays that illumined their temple, and the shadows of the departed worth of a Mitchell, a Pascalis, and an Osborn, yet haunted the classic shades of the Pewter Mug and the Shakspeare, their "*esprit de corps*" was excited to a degree that was supposed incompatible with their former *vis inertia*, and they resolved to make a grand effort to save the ship.   About this time (we well remember the melancholy day,) we were summoned by the usual annual bull, (a medical circular,) threatening the direst

pains and penalties for failing to enroll ourselves with
the illustrious body of the brethren, and assured that our
non-compliance would forthwith be followed by a suit at
law, and the certainty of being mulcted in so unheard-of
a sum, that we were fain to make our first visit to the
menagerie to see the Simia in full and grand council.
Never shall we forget the scene that burst upon our
astonished vision. Had we actually beheld the horned
beast of the Apocalypse, we could not have been more
thunderstruck! We felt inclined to exclaim with the
poet—"Obstupui! steteruntque comæ, et vox faucibus
hæsit," that is to say, in more elegant English, I was
dumbfounded; my hair stood up like the bristles of a
fighting-pig, and the devil a word could I get out. An
immense specimen of the brotherhood from the far West,
(a recent importation to the menagerie, and a perfect
ursus horribilis) had seized upon a miserable cub of local
origin, and holding him about midway by the most adhe-
sive portion of his inexpressibles, face adown, was vigorously applying his other paw to that most sensitive part
of his anatomy—the gluteal region. When he had well
nigh whipped the life out of the wretched little cub, he
tossed him over the railing at the very feet of the President, and looked round with the greatest self-complacency, licking his chaps and rubbing his huge paws, as if for
some more. The poor little creature, like Slender, had
caught him by the chain, but foregad, he found him no
Sackerson. All was as silent as death till the terrible
animal had departed, which he soon did, according to
the usual custom of the creature, on observing no more
assailants. A hat was handed round to defray the expense of a hack, and the unfortunate little devil of a doctor was sent home to his affectionate wife in a very
pitiable condition. The meeting dissolved in despair,

and we saved our ten dollars.   It was the last assemblage
of the venerable Medical Society of the City and County
of New York.   The brethren, as they slowly wended
down the avenue, may have impressively uttered the exclamation, "Ichabod, Ichabod, the glory of my house is
departed."

As soon as the members had recovered from the awful
shock of so terrible an exhibition, in view of the impossibility of regulating the diversion by a proportional selection of combatants, and the prospective arrival of more
such formidable animals from the far West, and really,
secretly fearing the necessity of summoning the coroner,
but what was still more important, considering the low
state of the treasury and the high price of oysters and
whisky, with the absolute derision by the outsiders of
their legal threats for not joining and paying the fee, they
put their heads together in solemn caucus, and concocted
the New York Academy of Medicine!

It was well understood by the projectors of this glorious affair, that the real object was to regulate the diversion of medical bear-baiting, and to put down Homœopathy, Hydropathy and any other roguery than such as
was legitimately hatched at home and in the regular
way ; besides keeping a wet blanket ready for any aspiring cub that might show his claws, or open his mouth
in public, to utter any heterodoxy either against the
lancet, Dover's powders, XX and XX, or in any way to
dim the glory of Old Fogiedom.   It was fondly hoped
that the imposing appellation, and the white neckcloths
and gold-headed canes of the venerables, would keep the
cubs in leading-strings at least.   Alas, for the mutability
of humanity!   Our venerable grandfather, old Adam,
and his descendant the Devil, soon showed they had
not forgotten their beloved medical children.   Many and

infinitely diverting are the tricks they have stoked up the
brethren to commit. A general hug has often been threatened, but has not yet come off. The scene we gave in
our last was the nearest approach to it, but the badger
showed no fight, and was soon earthed. At a late meeting, an old bruin whose claws and teeth were somewhat
dull from long use, made a demonstration towards a hug
of the president of one of the colleges, who had been a
prominent actor in giving that diploma to the Aconitine
Professor. The president, however, showed the white
feather and turned tail; whereupon old bruin made at
him again, but was soon muzzled and compelled to draw
in his claws, and stop growling and showing his teeth.
This old gentleman is evidently rejuvenating and preparing for combat, and we may soon expect sport in the regular old way.

But these general descriptions are unsatisfactory; the
members will expect individual attention; we are quite
aware of their delicate taste in literature, and feel as
usual benevolently disposed.

The speculative pedestrian whose early morning walk
led him through Hudson Street, some thirty years since,
may have observed a dilapidated gig, that, for aught its
appearance indicated to the contrary, might have been
used by Wouter Van Twiller, or Ichabod Crane, at the
least; how it got there, or whom it belonged to, were
two questions that did not admit of the same facilities of
solution. The usual brass plate, with Dr. ———— in large
letters, directly opposite the vehicle, might have made
the latter sufficiently clear; but the absence of the con-
comitant quadruped, forbade the solution of the former.
It was one morning our good fortune to be the observer
of a scene not so easily forgotten by a lover of fun, that
made the whole matter perfectly clear. The machine

was ready for motion ; the " thills " and an antediluvian
collar and breeching, encircled the skeleton and ligamen-
tous mechanism of an animal that a hasty observer might
have been at a loss to classify ; but for our humble self,
being at that moment engaged in the study of comparative anatomy, and having enjoyed the opportunity of a
few post-mortems of more highly organized specimens of
the quadruped, with our friend Grice of veterinary notoriety, we were at no loss to pronounce it a horse ; or at
least that it once, under happier auspices, had been a
tolerable specimen of the genus. The horse-market,
where such samples of the quadruped are generally obtained, not ordinarily supplying better specimens of the
commodity.

It was in the month of December, and the absence of
any visible structure in which the animal may be supposed to have been accommodated, left the beholder in
doubt whether his remaining powers, after the previous
day's toil, had not been expended in going the length of
the hall and descending the three steps of his master's
residence, after a night's lodging in the back yard.
However this matter may yet be determined by the curious equi-medico-archæological inquirer, it is very certain
that owing to the weakness from long use of the rope-
gearing that suspended the ponderous thills to the sad-
dle, and thus brought the feeble muscular power of the
wretched animal to resist the earthward tendency of
the enormous vehicle—the rope on one side gave way,
the corresponding thill fell to the fetlock of the quadruped, and the opposite one being elevated against the
unusually upraised neck, the poor creature was caught
like the fingers of a thoughtless boy between the widely
dissevered limbs of a pop-gun, and the glacial condition
of the pavement, peculiar to the season, favoring the

catastrophe, the equine anatomy was carried off its legs, and thrown sidewise and helpless upon the pavement, the thills holding him in their embrace like a clothes-pin. What was to be done? Here was a predicament. The owner—God help us, beloved!—we have described the horse before his master ; let us remedy the error as far as possible, and offer our humble apology to the academician. Dr. ―――― came o'er the sea from Auld Reekie, some forty years since, where he had followed the occupation of a plaa-sterer ; finding the ground comparatively unoccupee-d, he bethocht him of the glories of the Scottish capital and its medical univa-arseety, where he had possibly once held a horse for Dr. Munro, and concluded to try his hand at phee-seek ; it answered vara weel, and in a few years he found himself in full practeece. He throve apace, and became a landlord of sundry small tenements, which he let at 50 cents to $1 per week. What with house-renting and medicine-mongering, he has become rich and an academician ; we have seen him in the highest place amongst the Illustrissimi, at their annual oration ! Some of the more domestic articles of his favorite therapeia are of a very extraordinary character—articles that would have blenched even the cheek of poor Tony far sooner than his crow, had they been thoughtlessly communicated to his understanding after being received into his stomach.

To resume : Our pseudo Esculapian stood by the side of his prostrate quadruped, wrapped in an antiquated cloak of faded tartan, now tugging at the thills, and anon encouraging the quadruped to exert his powers and assume the vertical posture. "Gee-up—up wi ye—ye will na ; will ye na? Bide a wee, ye auld deevil, and a-l see til ye." Then taking out an old jack-knife, he applied its point by way of a quickener to the intercostals of the hapless steed. Alas! 'twas no go ; twice he fell prostrate over the fallen animal, and would have utterly failed in the resurrection, had it not been for the aid of a friendly chimney-sweep, who offered his services ; they were effective, and after the rope-gearing was re-adjusted, he was rewarded with a " Thank ye, my gude lad. Gin ye e'er get seek, ye hae only to ask for the auld docther, and a-l come till ye directly ; or an ye want a tooth pulhd a-l do it for naething ; yer a gude lad and a kind."

The indescribable-looking Esculapian now climbed into his old vehicle, inflicted a few blows upon the sides of the miserable animal with a domestic gad, and the wretched quadruped, by a sad effort, called up his remaining powers of vitality, and the entire concern jogged, creaking and rattling over the frozen pavement, up the street. If we dared to communicate the nature of his domestic materia medica, as told in a moment of con-fidence to a gentleman of our acquaintance, we would show that, by comparison, the Hydrophobin of our ho-mœopathic brethren, and their tincture of Pediculi and Millipedes, are delicious morsels. In truth he carries out the idea to its completest extent, of the circular operations of nature ; the *e*-gesta and the *in*-gesta, occu-pying the reciprocal position of the regulator and the regulated. This is bad for the druggists to be sure, but à-la-Liebig, and decidedly economical. So far as we can learn by occasional assurances of the vulgar, such pre-scriptions are by no means unacceptable or unreliable to their understandings or their palates.

Like a picture whose lights and shades are so harmo-niously combined as to produce a full appreciation of its excellence, we sometimes meet, even in the ranks of our heterogeneous profession, an individual whose tout en-semble inspires us with instant confidence and esteem.

Such persons are broadly contrasted with the mass of their brethren, who often look as though "they bought their coats in Italy, their hose in France, their hats in Germany," and their behavior in Communipaw.

Dr. V——e is a descendant of a French family of great excellence, who sought this country from democratic political predilections, which were largely shared by the subject of this sketch. He was for many years the intimate friend and assistant of Dr. Mott, in all those great operations which lent such lustre to his name. Although his professional life commenced long anterior to our own, his appearance is so youthful, and his toilet so unexceptionably elegant, that no one not acquainted with his history could ever dream of his age and experience.

Such is his extraordinary modesty and good breeding, that we have heard the most dictatorial opinions advanced in his presence by persons totally unacquainted with the merits of the question, elicit not even a reply from him, when we knew that he himself could have contradicted the assertion from personal knowledge of the matter.

Indeed this trait of character has been a great hindrance to that popularity to which, if real knowledge and worth were appreciated, he would have presented claims in advance of a large majority of his brethren. We are delighted to perceive the doctor at a mature age, giving the benefit of his large experience to a select circle of intellectual friends who know how to appreciate learning and modesty. We rely upon his amiability to show a little of the other side of the moral picture. The Doctor is very lazy. Well do we remember his elegant figure, encased in a suit of black, buttoned up to the throat, the handkerchief thrust into the breast, (and if peculiarly recherché, probably the gift of some attached patient,) one end slightly visible, his brilliant eye and curling locks like so many living and jetty snakes, sauntering lazily into the operating chamber, ten or fifteen minutes after the appointed hour ; and then the peculiarly calm and expressively Quakerish stereotyped remark of his friend, "We must give the Doctor a little time, he needs it," all the while anxious to let him, as well as the patient, feel the point of the *Scalpel*, for the annoyance. With this drawback, there is not a more profoundly educated surgeon and physician, or a more honorable man, in the entire corps.

> Spirit of beauty, who dost sit at eve
> With the lone watcher on the silent hill,
> And weavest from the valleys of the stars
> Wild stories like the sighing of the rill ;
> Who bringest visions to the dreamer's heart—
> Shapes of the vanished—low sweet murmurings
> Of long hushed voices—Prophetess of art,
> Beneath whose wing thy favored votary sees
> Glimpses of fairy forms and spirit eyes "—

why wakest thou the memory of former years? Why openest thou the cells whose crystal drops no sterner passion can unlock? What whispers to my soul the unseen presence of him on whom "fond memory loves to dwell?" Yes, dear Godman,* thou indeed canst bring the "light of other days" around me. No circumscribed views of thy glorious calling bound thy soul to earth, even when that frail body yet lingered amongst us. Those eloquent lips, on whose trembling notes I have so often hung with the sad thought they were so soon to close forever ; those glorious and soulful eyes, whose boundless view was cast o'er all surrounding heaven ; those delicate hands that interrogated the structure, now

---

* Professor of Anatomy and Natural History in Rutgers Medical College, and author of several volumes on Natural History.

of the little shrew mouse, and now of the fierce and
lordly eagle, and drew from them lessons of love and virtue ; where art thou ? And she, the partner of thy
young love, and thy touching struggles with poverty and
life, whilst building a monument that will last as long as
science and virtue shall be revered ; hast thou whispered
to her that thy spirit is near ? She closed those glorious
windows of the soul with her own fond lips, as the light
of earth passed from thee ; the last throb of that noble
heart faded under her hand, and she best knew thy fit-
ness for a higher sphere. I believe that thou, who so
eloquently explained in the vestibule the works of thy
great Teacher here, hast been found worthy to enjoy the
glory of the inner temple.

SCENES IN CITY PRACTICE.

DIFFERENT WAYS OF PREPARATION FOR DEATH—THE MISER'S—THE OLD MUSIC
TEACHER'S—CHEATING THE UNDERTAKER—THE PHILOSOPHICAL GAMBLER.

"There *is* an art to find the mind's construction in the face."

A CURIOUS, a wonderful thing is the human face, with
its ever-varied construction, its constant play of muscles,
and its infinite variety of expression. Few people ever
think of it as we do : the criminal advocate becomes in a
measure skilled in looking through it into the heart, but
he usually meets with those who have long been trained
in vice, and has comparative facilities in reading its worst
language : he does not acquire the nice perception of
character often attained by the physician, who is perpetually obliged to look upon it when agitated by emotions
not likely to be influenced in their action by considerations of caution. If he succeed in winning his patient's
confidence, there are few things he will not hear during
some moment of agony or confidence ; hence his intercourse is of so sacred a character, that even the law
acknowledges his right to conceal communications it may
demand from others under grievous penalties. Many a
family would be broken up, if the physician did not
respect the sacredness of his trust. Nor would I enter
ruthlessly the sanctuary where private griefs repose.
Had I ever, even in a moment of thoughtlessness, betrayed
a professional secret, I should never dare to put my pen
to these sketches. Yet I do not conceive it incumbent

upon me to conceal the vices of humanity, when they illustrate some extraordinary phase of character. It is the purpose of these sketches to give the world some idea of the human rights of our profession. It has been too long conceded by them, that we are in duty bound to submit to their caprices and insults, and to hold our peace whenever we feel called on to speak of their ingratitude. I never yet heard the praises of a medical man, who was characterized by a manly firmness and self-respect in his intercourse with his patients. No matter what sacrifices of time or money, or what disgusting duties we may be called on to perform, we have only to refuse acceding to some unreasonable demand of a querulous invalid, or to submit to some impertinence of a meddlesome visitor who wishes to gain the good-will of our patient, and we are at once denounced as a hard-hearted demon ; but when we are obliged to urge the payment of a bill, (be it remembered a thing we should never be expected to do by a gentleman—I mean if our attentions have been received in friendship and confidence,) we straightway become the subject of the meanest kind of slander and abuse, more especially if the services have been required by the vices of the patient. This is so universal as to be acknowledged the most sickening draught the general practitioner is called on to swallow ; and he is obliged often to drain the nauseous cup to its very dregs, when he has waited upon his thankless patient with his very heart in his hand.

We give the following sketch with no pleasure, but simply because we think it belongs to a complete picture of human nature in one of its phases. It is certainly a marked example of its kind, but it serves to show the degradation to which the man descends whose soul is devoted to money. I have observed devotion to that god, often combined with just such piety and assurance of eternal happiness.

I was requested some years since to visit an aged man at one of our most fashionable hotels. He had been for some weeks under the care of a medical man, whose extreme amiability and devotion to his patient (a very nervous man) had induced its usual consequence with such people, viz., a contempt and distrust of his opinion. In this however he was entirely unjust, for a more amiable man than his physician I never knew, and his opinion was quite correct ; he had pronounced the disease a cancer of the lower bowel, and of course incurable. I approached the patient with that amenity I have always felt that my personal appearance requires me to exercise with peculiar care, on my first approach to a patient— for candid friends have assured me I resemble more a pirate or executioner than a surgeon ; my manner evidently pleased him, and left me at liberty closely to scan a set of features such as I had never before seen. He was about sixty years of age, with a head of a wretchedly unintellectual cast, nearly covered with sparsely distributed hair of snowy whiteness ; enormous bushy eyebrows overhanging cavernous eyes of gray, and throwing out as it seemed a single ray of light, as from a diamond point ; a nose compressed to flatness, and acuminated almost to a level with the thin and bloodless lips, and chin to match it, if reversed ; the whole face denoting a lifetime of devotion to care and money, and overspread with the corpse-like hue of cancer. I sat down by his bedside, and soon satisfied myself that a few weeks would give him an opportunity to test the value of his course of life as a preparation for a future state of existence. The reader will observe, I neither knew nor had ever heard of him ; but such faces never lie, and I was at once satisfied I knew the measure of his soul as well as his body. I told him frankly that he must not expect a cure, and that he would in a very short time be unable to reach his home in the interior of the State, where he told me he wished to draw his last breath. He named a fortnight as the earliest period at which he could conveniently depart, and requested me to cause a covered couch to be constructed, on which he might be conveyed to the steamboat; a canal going from the city of . . . . to his princely residence.

During a subsequent visit, I chanced to make a quotation from one of Lamartine's beautiful hymns; he clasped his hands, and raising his eyes heavenward, desired me to continue it. I did so, and he would never allow me to leave him without repeating some poetry of a religious character, which fortunately my youthful stores enabled me to do. I soon found that my patient was a most devoted routine, or rhythmical Christian; he took religious poetry by way of an anodyne, to efface memories of former misspent time. On one occasion he congratulated himself very warmly, with clasped hands and upraised eyes, upon the attention God had granted to his prayers. He had prayed for wealth, and it was given him to overflowing abundance; he had built a palace superior to any in the State; a son and daughter had been granted to his supplications; he was satisfied; he asked no more of Heaven, and was ready to die. His dignified and patient wife, who was nearly worn out in attendance on him, was never spoken of to me as the object of his solicitude; he had no nurse, and her duties were arduous and most repulsive. This had arrested my attention, and I received a short reply to my suggestion of a male nurse as a relief for her. Oh, how the old man shows himself in sickness! If he love a wife, how

12

gentle and thoughtful he becomes ; how solicitous for
her health ; and how he will conceal the severest suffering, for that dear object on whose fond breast he has so
often pillowed an aching head.   There is no trial like
sickness, of love or Christianity.

I soon found my patient a very exacting one.   He
demanded of me two daily visits, and the most repulsive
duties from his wife.   I begged her often to induce him
to get a nurse, for her own sake as well as his ; but she
assured me he would permit no person to come near him
but her ; he had repeatedly spoken of his great expenses
at the hotel ; but as he had assured me of his great
wealth, I saw clearly his miserly habits were at the bottom of his repugnance.   At the end of three weeks'
attendance he became very much prostrated ; and feeling,
as I supposed, his condition, he begged me to order his
couch to be prepared, as he designed to go in a few days,
having sent for his son for the purpose of escorting
him.

It was accordingly finished, and I directed the mechanic to leave it at the hotel and present the bill to me,
as I did not wish him annoyed with it until his departure, when he would probably ask me for it.   He had it
brought to his bedside and inspected it narrowly ; it gave
great satisfaction, and was removed to an adjoining room·
Some few days after the son arrived.   I continued my
visits, and as nothing was said of his departure, and he
was growing alarmingly weak, and his wife was almost
exhausted with constant watching, I ventured to suggest
his removal.   He had never used a sharp word to me
before, but on this occasion replied, with some petulance,
he would not be ready to go in some days ; and desired
me not to recur to the subject again.   I apologized, and
assured him I had only done it because he had desired

me to do so, and I thought he was awaiting my advice of the proper moment.

That night the son (a clergyman) waited on me and requested the bill for the couch. I handed it to him as it was made out by the mechanic in his own hand ; he looked at it and remarked, convulsively drawing in his breath, that it was very costly (I think it was some thirty dollars, including a very well made mattress and pillow, as he was to occupy it for two days, and also be carried on it a few miles.) I declined accepting the money, and sent him to the mechanic to make his own terms. In the morning I called as usual, and spent an hour with him, and alluded to my afternoon visit, as the son had told me he would not go till next week. I found the patient in his usual religious frame of mind, thanking God for all his mercies ; he requested me to read a psalm for him ; I did so, and took my leave. In the evening I called at the usual hour ; the old man had departed! I learned that he died two weeks after his arrival. Relating the circumstance to a distinguished lawyer some months afterward, he smiled, and assured me my patient's peculiarities were well known to him and every one who ever had business relations with him ; that his whole life had been devoted to money, and that my idea of abandoning my bill would probably give great satisfaction to his heir, who was a chip of the same block. On reflection I was quite ashamed of my foolish pride and weakness. Human nature is a varied page, and we cannot shame a rogue into honesty and manhood. I inclosed the bill to the heir, and no notice was taken of it ; three or four letters followed with like results ; finally a lawyer's letter brought me a check for the amount.

One day, some few years since, I was summoned by my friend, Dr. C——, to visit an old man of some seventy years, who was afflicted with a carbuncle. That disease, when of any magnitude at so late a period of life, is frequently fatal, and I supposed my friend, with his usual care for the feelings of the poor, would introduce me into some wretched garret or damp cellar kitchen, merely for charity's sweet sake, to give my learned imprimatur to the dismissal of some wretched being from a condition of squalid misery. I was singularly and agreeably disappointed. It is true, we ascended three pair of stairs in a house occupied by several families, and we were received at the door of his apartment by the patient himself. He apologized for being alone, as he was usually attended by a niece, and begged us to enter with such dignity and simplicity of manner, that I was quite charmed with the old gentleman. On expressing the hope that he was not seriously afflicted and would soon recover, he replied, as pleasantly as though contemplating a journey, that he could not anticipate a much longer delay of the final summons, and was quite prepared to meet it; he had lived a long time and was of little use, as his faculties were becoming obtuse; he was a music teacher, and had taught the piano up to the period of his attack; an old but well saved piano stood in one corner, and some other musical instruments in the other; a little sheet-iron stove, a few chairs, and an old bedstead, spread with snowy sheets, completed the furniture; several water-color pictures hung from the walls; and the question arose in my mind, of what little domestic heaven, broken up by death, are these the sad remains? for I saw that this room comprised his entire *ménage*. Surely woman has taught you how to love with that bland voice, thought I, as the poor old man, with evident reluctance at its repulsiveness, allowed us to examine his grievous affection; it was awful in extent, and on learning that he strictly declined all stimuli, I mentally gave him up to die, and declined the usual resort to incisions for the liberation of the mortified tissues. I thought it was of no use to give him pain, as death was sure. On leaving him with no addition to the local treatment, which was all conducted personally by my excellent friend, I was obliged to escape from the expression of his painful solicitude for his repulsiveness, as he expressed it, and his acknowledgment of my kindness. I inquired of my friend his history ; it was a very short one. He had taught for forty years, honored and beloved by all, always poor, and respected for his amiable and simple character, with a wife as excellent as himself ; she was a delicate creature, and faded away from earth, leaving him childless. The piano and the pictures were hers, and were treasured in the little hired room where we found him ; his niece and he lived there, with the aid of their poor neighbors in preparing their simple meals ; he longed to die and join his dear wife, as his niece was well provided for by her relatives. I paid him several visits, and was surprised to see the tenacity of life. His disease became so extensive that neither of us anticipated his recovery ; but he finally disappointed us completely, for my friend informed me, some weeks after my last visit, that he had ordered the old gentleman to breathe the country air for a few weeks, as he needed no attention which his niece could not render him. On the occasion of his last visit, the old gentleman, with a smile, compelled his acceptance of thirty dollars in gold, assuring him that he did not require it now, as he had laid it aside for the undertaker ! Surely the quality of men's souls differ as well as their bodies. The rich are often poorer with their millions than the righteous poor with their pence and misery.

Thus easily can men prepare themselves for the great
passage. Some require prayer ; some the thoughts of
their wealth evidently soothe ; some are beckoned away
by the loved and lost, and some step out by the aid of
poison and philosophy. Listen to a cool example of the
latter. I was summoned by an ex-alderman to see Monsieur R—— at his bachelor's rooms in Broadway. He
had been found in a state of stupor, lying on the floor,
and it was supposed, from an open pill-box lying near
him, that he had taken some narcotic poison. He was a
very elegant and accomplished man, of some thirty years
of age, who had fled from France for some political or
other offence, and had been ranging among the saloons
of the Potiphars, worshipped by the mothers and courted
by the daughters, as though he had been a scion of nobility or a royal boot-black. I had seen him in high
feather in the parlors at the receptions of Madame ————,
and recognized the man of fashion without a ray of principle ; he would have passed for a *debauchee*, were it not
for his quiet elegance and his superb figure. I found
him lying on a couch, wrapped in an elegant *robe de
chambre*, and breathing heavily. On raising the eyelids,
the pupils were found dilated till the iris was a mere
thread. I sent home for a strong galvanic battery, and
applied powerful shocks between the nape of the neck
and the heels alternately, while he was held up by two
men ; before long I aroused him enough to compel him
to move his limbs—one man carrying the battery on a
tray, two holding him up, and I applying the conductors
alternately to either limb and the upper part of the spine.
Before long I got him to swallow a small cup of strong
coffee ; this was continued every few minutes till he had
drank several cups ; it is one of the best stimuli, and supposed to be specifically counteracting to many of the

vegetable narcotics.*   After a few hours, during all of
which time we kept him walking up and down the room,
he seemed to recognize his position, and made several attempts to converse in English and French.   I left him in
charge of a student, and went to get some rest, as it was
near morning.   On my return to his room, I found him
very much prostrated but quite sensible.   On asking him
what he had taken, I found he had been a graduate of
medicine in Paris, and had written a recipe for thirty
grains of belladonna in pills, and he assured me he had
swallowed the whole !. "Why did you do it ?" said I.
" Why, my dear Doctare," replied he, "I had lost all my
money at play, and the necessity for living had ceased !"

* Caffein is now known to be the remedy. It has since saved a patient in the
same hotel from death by opium: a scruple of caffein thrown up the bowel
aroused him, and he recovered, after the seeming of death.

A DISCOURSE TO THE BRETHREN ON MORALS.

BY AN OLD SURGICAL FOX.

DEARLY BELOVED BRETHTEN :—In addressing you on this occasion, although I use the ordinary endearing appellation of the clergy, I by no means do it in a sarcastic manner ; although I have been accustomed to use a rather different formula in my discourses to you, I sincerely trust you will endeavor to rid yourself of all unkind feelings toward me. In my ordinary hortatory efforts, it is true I have often been obliged to speak of your vices, and occasionally to administer the rod, in order to impress my admonitions upon your memories ; yet at present I speak with hearty sympathy, for I observe many of ye are very lean, and look distressingly hungry.

There was once a very wise man who used to say, "Spare the rod and you'll spoil the child." I don't like to quote him professionally, because there is, I believe, a little doubt on the subject of his matrimonial morals ; he was supposed to be slightly tinctured with Mormonism, and, as a body, the faculty, I am sure, have no such predilection ; besides, he must have been exceedingly wealthy, or he would never have been able to build so fine a house, or to have amassed so many shekels of gold and silver ; of these habits, with few exceptions, I think it will be conceded, we are also free. Whether the latter part of his apothegm would apply to you collectively is also rather doubtful, as most of you, I take it, however you may require correction, have advanced beyond the years of childhood. It is true some of you, who have had the good fortune to get into the hospital crib, are still of rather small dimensions at both extremities, and will be obliged by your venerable associates to wear the habiliments of the nursery for some years ; yet I think I may with propriety consider you a promising body of youthful ganders, and fairly entitled to a warning from the old fox who is perfectly content to remain outside the goose-pen, and pick up his living from such rats and mice, and other small game, as have escaped the machinations of the faculty in other parts of the •Union, and now and then a gosling or a turkey from among the innocent denizens of the great civic forest, where you all go nosing along for your fodder.

Some of my readers may remember my pathetic narrative of their successful experiment in getting me inside of the hospital trap, and they will probably be surprised to find how I escaped their clutches. They will remember the morning was rapidly approaching when I had closed my last words (as I supposed) of counsel to the faithful cubs who were bewailing my fate outside. It was nearly an hour after I had refreshed my fainting stomach with the young gosling they so affectionately brought me from one of the poultry-yards in Union Square, and I sat stolidly awaiting my medical captors, when I began to feel a strange sensation of returning vitality tingling through my poor old bones and muscles. It was so infernal cold in the trap, and I had been kept so distressingly hungry for some years, as I was obliged to live on such small and contemptible game as I could catch in the outskirts of the city, in the shape of Irish laborers, etc. etc., that my courage began to fail. The

12*

trap was called "The Medical and Surgical Association" of that venerable institution, the New York Hospital. It had been set up by a few of the goslings who had been hatched in that old coop, doubtless with the intention of using the stupid medical cubs they might catch, as decoys for civic game in the way of surgical consultations, when they should become regular ganders in the great surgical goose-pen. I was excessively amused to study their peculiar natures, and to see how they were pecked and thumped by the reigning gander of the month. This they bore with exemplary patience for fear of being kicked out of the coop. One of them (the Irish Homunculus) had a passion for mimicking his gander that was truly diverting. He used to affect great feebleness in his pins, and pretended that he could hardly hiss audibly, because his gander was perfectly indifferent to all emotions, and always looked as though he was about to be blown away. He could not hiss you loud enough to be heard across the ward; the Homunculus was hatched from an Irish egg, and was sturdy enough in his juvenility, though the absence of blood was plainly visible in his communications with his brethren; but of them more anon.

When my captors came into the hospital and found me in the trap, one of them proposed my immediate execution without benefit of a hearing. This was to be effected by passing the manly resolution offered by Gander P——t, of allowing a majority of one to expel a member "without informing him of the reason for his expulsion." After this resolution had been for some time debated, and was about to pass in full conclave, I got a little sick at my stomach when contemplating my dignified captors, and it occurred to me that as I had now got my nose pretty well under the door, I could with a little

effort throw it up and be off. With a slight push I
cleared the trap, and told my honorable brethren to go
to the devil ; giving them a wholesome view of my claws,
I turned tail and made my tracks for home. Whether
they entered the manly resolution on the minutes I never
troubled myself to inquire ; probably they did, as it
seemed to meet with great favor, and their plans being
now discovered, they might possibly require it for future
use in expelling a stray wolf or fox who might get into
their trap.

I went to my old lair, feeling rather cheap at the character of my company, and for a long while imagining I
smelled of their propinquity ; but this was probably only
a morbid fancy, and in a few years I got quite clear of
the notion.

I now addressed myself seriously to business, and
found my faculties wonderfully improved by self-reliance ;
and not being hampered by those old ganders, I was so
successful in nabbing the game, that I waxed quite
fat, and my old coat became so sleek, that I could not
fail to see the looks of surprise the brethren cast toward
my hole as they rode by. Such a strange contradiction is
a medical fox when he has plenty to eat, that in a little
while I waxed so lazy and good-natured toward my old
enemies, the ganders, that I even took pity on them, and
returned their nods as they footed it past me, for I had
now found it necessary to mount a nag ; he was, to be
sure, a very vicious animal, but I was resolved to keep
him by way of counteracting my good-natured indolence.

One day, as I lay resting myself, like Robinson Crusoe,
in my cave, I felt so thankful for all the blessings I
enjoyed, and thought so much of the mysterious workings of Providence in getting me out of their trap, and
on the miserable conduct of my brethren toward each

other, and their lean and seedy appearance, that I resolved to do all I could, as soon as my indolence would allow me, to teach them how to better their condition. This idea got such a hold on my mind, that whenever I would hear of their cruel treatment to each other in the way of lies and slander, I used to busy myself in trying to devise methods for correcting them. I thought if I could catch one of them and bring him to my den, I would endeavor to feed him up a little and instruct him, and then send him abroad as a sort of missionary, to convert his brethren from their cannibalism. I was so fortunate as to catch one from the identical old coop, and I tried heartily, by every means in my power, to gain his good will. He seemed to take very kindly to me for some months, and I assisted him in several difficult obstetrical cases, letting him talk large before the patient, and listening with great apparent deference, and then doing the work and letting him pocket the fees. After a little while the old ganders bought him up with a small salary in the hospital, and he came to me no more. I tried several others who were more or less under the influence of the ganders, but they were too timid, and had as yet no distinct ideas of individuality ; they were only in their pin-feathers.

Notwithstanding my failures in all my attempts to civilize the old anthropophagi, I continued to please myself with the hope that I should soon catch a young savage that had escaped with his life from his brethren. Should I be so fortunate as to come across such a one, I was quite sure he would be tractable enough, because he would be pretty well starved and subdued when they had done with him. I used to dream of the pleasure I would have in instructing him how to behave like a human creature, and to forbear slandering and traducing his

medical brethren. I had stuck the sides of my cave all
over with anatomical diagrams and surgical plates, by
way of stool-pigeons to catch patients ; here I had hung
up a pair of forceps, there an awful-looking amputating-
knife and a torturing set of pulleys for reducing disloca-
tions. I slept on a fracture bed that my little House of
Refuge boys had made me when I used to lecture to
them, and give 'em brandy and beef, instead of salts, and
calomel and jalap. I had a chair with a swing desk to
it, on which I used to dissect, and draw, and drink tea,
and eat oysters, etc. etc. In short, my ménage was very
curious to behold. All these I would teach him the
use of, and bequeath him when I should die.

I was disappointed, however, in all my benevolent intentions ; I never could catch a man Friday from the
hospital. I had a number of medical parrots of the mean-
er sort ; a less fortunate kind, who had never got inside
the hospital crib, and were entirely ignored by the surgical ganders. I· discovered them in my surgical visits
about the island ; for I used often to be summoned to
help them out of their scrapes with their miserable Irish
obstetrical and other cases. I used every method that my
ingenuity suggested to tame them, for they had been
taught how to peck and scratch by their hospital exemplars during their pupilage, but I could never succeed in
taming one : they would come to me as soon as I sent
them the fee, and they had slept partially away the disturbance of their gall-bladders by the summons which
brought me to help them in their troubles, and after a
while I had even taught some of them to call me by name,
and now and then to eat my pancakes, and even to drink
tea ; but I never could make them eat raw oysters. If I
could have done that, I dare say I might in time have
tamed some of them so as to divert me in my solitary

hours ; but whenever I tried the experiment, they made terrible faces and left me in a fright, and never returned to my cave ; and yet I was continually prompted by some evil spirit to try them with this peculiar sort of food. I had got a notion in my head, that they would become completely enervated and cachectic by their miserable diet without the wholesome phosphorus I know the delicious bivalves contained ; and I never could endure an animal, either human or brute, that was half dead and half alive, like those poor medical hospital cubs.

. One day I was thoroughly astonished by receiving a visit from one of the oldest surgical ganders of the hospital. He came in great state to my cave in his carriage, and rolled himself into the door like a great cheese. He was a man of thick proportions, like a butcher's, with considerable formality of manner, and a curt utterance, clipping off his words as though fearful of being too condescending to an inferior, or possibly of being mistaken for a gentleman. He was clad in black, most professionally. I requested him to be seated, in my usual polite manner, but he waved his refusal most magnificently, and seemed most beneficently inclined to put me at perfect ease in his presence. Of course, I was duly impressed by his condescension, for I had even then a spice of fun in me, and determined to give him string.

He soon informed me that the object of his visit was to see my instruments for the operation of strabismus or squinting, " one of those little matters to which he had as yet paid no attention," and having a case of " a very wealthy gentleman," (for such is the way the old gander always talks,) he wished to " do it up with all the modern improvements." This was delivered with a very condescending smile, in the most recherché style of a Fulton Market butcher ; of course I bowed profoundly to the gratifying and delicate compliment. I offered him the loan of my little case, and explained to him the method of using the implements without, and with, an assistant ; for I had been obliged generally to assist myself in my lonely peripatetic tours in the country. He received my instructions with most magnificent impressiveness, pocketed the case, and rolled himself into his carriage. I soon dismissed the matter from my thoughts, and after my evening Irish visits and my oysters, turned into my fracture bed and went to sleep.

Next morning I was in the midst of my aromatic circle of Irish office patients, when I was surprised to receive a message from the old gander, requesting me to come round to his office. I was amazed at the condescension you may be sure, but I began to smell fun ; accordingly I donned my long blue, and did myself the honor to go round, for he lived on the same square with me. The first face I saw on entering, was that of a gentleman on whose eye I had refused to operate the day before, because the external rectus muscle (the one that allows the eye to turn inwards and upwards, when the opposite one masters it and produces that deformity)was so completely withered and paralyzed that it would evidently have been of no use to divide the internal muscle, as we do in this operation, because the external one could not pull the eye-ball central, even if it were done never so thoroughly. I had grieved to lose the case, for I was awfully poor, and I knew he was wealthy and would have given me a large fee ; but as I could not have cured him, I should only have lost reputation either as a surgeon or an honest man—certainly one, and probably both. Indeed, had I been foolish enough to have attempted it, even at the patient's urgent request, I could not consistently have taken the fee. I therefore dismissed the case

with many thanks, and a letter of explanation to the
kind friend who had spoken so highly of my skill, as to
produce a terrible disappointment to the gentleman at
my refusal to operate. But the desire of being "eyes
right" was so strong in a rich bachelor contemplating matrimony, that he found his way into the office of
the celebrated old hospital gander; here he received
every encouragement, and was no doubt duly informed
of my conceit and ignorance of the principle of the operation; next morning was appointed for its performance.
The fact that it was the very morning after I had received the condescending call of the old gander for the
use of my instruments, made the matter clear enough
even to my obtuse perception, as soon as I saw the patient and his squint eye. I, of course, returned the sal-
utations of both the gentlemen, and was informed that
the object of the summons with which I had been honored, was to get me to hold the patient's head! I avowed
my sense of the honor as gracefully as I knew how, and
the gander began to prepare the instruments. But my
friend with the squint eye was not quite ready; he had
slept upon the matter; and my adverse opinion, aided
by his fears and the gander's assurances, (he was to pay
a good fee, too,) had expanded the importance of my
opinion considerably, and he bluntly asked me my
present views of the probable success of the operation.
The gander began to swell; he made himself a head
taller, and looked at his watch. I replied that I had no
new opinion to offer on the case; I had come to assist at
the operation, and would willingly do so, when both
were ready; the case had now passed from my hands.
But all this wouldn't suit Country by a long shot; he
was determined to have a talk. The gander saw he must
now use strategy, or lose the case; accordingly he did

me the distinguished honor to take me into his private consulting room, blandly assuring the patient he should have the benefit of our mutual opinion, when we should come out. He was now quite courteous. I informed him in a very modest way of my views of the rationale of the operation, and the certainty in my mind of its unsuccessful result, should the muscle be divided. My magnificent friend assured me I was entirely mistaken, notwithstanding he knew that all the efforts of the patient could not budge the eye-ball a hair's breadth outward. I bowed, and assured him I was willing to assist him, but could not change my opinion. He was evidently full and ready to explode ; but he saw there was no use to argue the matter. We walked out, and he was obliged to state the conclusion to the patient, whereupon he refused the operation, and took his departure. As he went out of the door, I caught one glance at the gander's head, and thought he looked like a magnificent head cheese, made entirely of blood and muscle ; and no wonder : fifty dollars, thought I, just gone out of that very door : he looked as much excited as the proprietor of old Vauxhall did, when, upon occasion of a visit to that delightful establishment, I saw two Bowery gentlemen escaping over the fence without paying the shot, and the proprietor, with as high action as Richard III. when he offered his kingdom for a horse, summoned the waiters, and cried out, "There goes two teas and a brandy and water !" My magnificent surgical friend paid me for it with a hearty good will : I will relate how, hereafter.

THE EARLY TREATMENT OF CHILDREN—AIR AND BATHS.

So very discursive, as our readers know, has been the mode adopted in all our popular works, in presenting this subject to the view of parents, that a vast amount of really excellent advice and judicious caution has been lost to many, for want of the necessary connection of the immediate subject of instruction with its legitimate antecedent. There are many persons, the constitution of whose minds actually requires the greatest regularity in the presentation of a subject, or else the best directions the writer can offer entirely lose their influence. The reader must begin at the beginning, or he cannot get on with any advantage to himself or entertain any respect for his instructor. With a perfect conviction of this difficulty, let us endeavor, in the commencement of our fifth volume, to make ourselves perfectly understood. Firstly, then, we differ largely from our countrymen in their ideas of the superiority of the female character of our countrywomen over that of the women of all other nations ; we do most honestly and faithfully believe that the American women are under-educated and over-flattered by our sex (as a general thing) throughout the country. The very miserable ideas on physical education that prevail amongst them throughout the land, tend to the propagation of those bodily ailments, and that early development of the nervous system, that too often gives the young American girl a premature appearance of age, and embitters the whole of her subsequent existence. Whilst man is subjected to the wholesome vicissitudes of mental and bodily exertion and change, woman, from her earliest years, is often made the subject of overweening anxiety by a mother, who derives her only guide in the physical training of her child from the absurd fashion of the day. She is utterly unacquainted with a single principle that governs its animal existence. She realizes no more the necessity of air and exercise—[*i. e.* as a principle from which she cannot depart in its training, without the inevitable result]—we say she realizes it no more as the everlasting law of nature, or the word of God, than she does the law of gravitation itself! She knows not even the actual meaning of the appearance of its teeth? Does she not feed it boiled crackers, and sugar and water? Does she not smile when you tell her such conduct is monstrous ; that the elements of her child's nutrition, nearest its natural food, are found only in the milk of animals? Does she know even the natural temperature of its body? Why, then,. shall we flatter her vanity, and conceal our true feelings at her ignorance, when her very best efforts to do her duty by that offspring for whose preservation she would often willingly lay down her very life, are almost certain to result in its death? We have already handled this subject at length in the article on the Early Decay of American Women. Our present object is to go a little more into detail on the subject of air, and exercise, and bathing, because we feel that the difficulty lies principally in the absurd idea that our climate is not fit for exercise. When that is defective, breathing becomes less necessary, and digestion, and the assimilation of food, must suffer in a direct ratio; bathing is totally misunderstood.

The very first want of its animal existence, when the child appears in the world, is air; we have placed it in the motto on our cover before all the other wants of nature. Not a minute can elapse when its connection with the mother is severed, before suffocation will occur, if the air do not rush into the mouth and lungs. It is the first spasmodic expiration that produces the convulsive cry with which the child greets us the moment it enters the world! it requires air even before it feels the cold of the external world! before it recognizes the want of food! It is then apparent that the apparatus with which it appropriates this great motive life power, should be entirely unshackled by dress. Now there is not one mother in this great city, unless amongst those ladies who have lately been professionally educated, that can give a description of the structure, or even the actual situation of the lungs! There is not one in a thousand who realizes the enormity of the errors so often committed in the application of a bandage around the chest; if there were, no nurse, at least none that we have ever yet seen, would be allowed to offer a word of counsel on the subject, much less to apply it. It is extremely doubtful if any pressure whatever should be permitted, even from the usual abdominal bandage, unless the infant have some palpable structural defect in the walls of the abdomen. Any pressure over that region of the body must, by preventing the free descent of the diaphragm (which is the principal or great breathing muscle dividing the chest containing the lungs, from the belly,) any pressure, we assert, even on the abdominal region, must diminish respiration.

The temperature, too, of the body of the child, although

it is nearly one hundred degrees, and requires clothing enough to keep it as high as that, is by no means a criterion for that of the chamber in which it is kept; the body is a heat-producing machine : if the temperature of the chamber exceed sixty-five or seventy degrees, the lungs cannot have their required stimulus of cool air, and there will be slow and insufficient breathing, even if the chest and abdomen be not crippled with a bandage. This matter of temperature must be regulated by the wants of the child and not the mother; if she requires more warmth, let it be supplied by clothing. If indigestible food be given, such as pap made of boiled bread, flour, farina, or any of the humbug catch-pennies of the shops, with the certificates of medical ignorami attesting their value, the intestines will be filled with flatus from its decomposition, and this also will obstruct breathing, as well as produce pain. Look for one moment at the universal custom of covering a child's face with a handkerchief? Try it yourself, and judge of the inevitable suffering from the want of fresh air.

We have known the most delicate infants, so delicate as to make it apparent to the meanest medical intellect that they required all the heat their bloodvessels could produce, and the warmest clothing to retain it—we have known them to be kept screaming for fifteen minutes at a time in a cold-bath, with the view of strengthening them! Others, again, with cheeks like roses, and skins like boiled lobsters, par-boiled in water, the temperature of which had been tried by a gin-drinking nurse's hand! No nursery should be considered furnished without a thermometer; a bath becomes a directly exhausting agent, if over ninety-seven to one hundred degrees, by its relaxing power; if under sixty-five, which is the common summer temperature, and the child be delicate, and produce little heat, of course it robs it of what it does produce too rapidly, and insures also debility. From three to five minutes is long enough for the longest bath ; a quarter of a minute, or even ten seconds, is enough for the tonic effect of a cool bath of sixty-five degrees, on a delicate child, and then the body should be instantly dried and comfortably clothed. The nurse who cannot do all this in ten minutes, ought to be discharged. Unless perfect comfort, as evinced by cheerfulness or sleep, follow the use of the bath, it is always to be considered injurious.

We believe that the insane use of prolonged baths, as is so frequently observed in this city, is one of the greatest evils of the day, and has more to do with the rheumatism and chronic diarrhœa, than people imagine. Our countrymen are great sensualists, and in their eating and drinking often carry things to excess. A bath is a necessary thing ; it is not, as we call it, a luxury ; luxuries, as such, are always injurious. We know a gentleman who reads his newspaper, and smokes his cigar, in a warm bath ; of course he is a fool, though a good-natured and agreeable man ; the bath is often prolonged for half an hour. One day he nearly fell asleep ; fortunately he left the warm water running, to see how high he could bear the temperature! the overrunning of the water probably saved his life ; it might have proved a very easy way to step out of his mortal body. Always remember, that the temperature of the blood is from ninety-seven to one hundred degrees, and that a bath above that temperature, and prolonged over five minutes, becomes progressively debilitating ; it is tonic and strengthening to the system in proportion as the temperature is lowered, and the shock sudden. A plunge bath in cold water between July and September, is a great tonic to those who can bear it ;

the skin should always feel a glow in five minutes after
drying, or at most ten, or it is hurtful. Young ladies
make a most insane use of the cold bath ; on one occasion we were summoned to attend one, who actually
fainted in the salt water bath ; she had made a bet of
gloves with another how long they could stay in ; such
was the stubborness of her will, that she remained in the
water more than an hour and a half before she sank to
the bottom ; her companion proved stronger, and gave
the alarm, but was too weak to assist in raising her ; she
recovered with difficulty, although immersed less than
a minute.

Hip baths are tonic or soothing, as prolonged, or used
warm or cold ; in consequence of the general debility of
our city women, warm ones are rarely admissible ; this
bath, indeed, is so powerful that it is almost invariably
misapplied. We shall take up the subject separately,
when treating of the family of uterine diseases that requires its use.

The idea is entertained by many thinking persons, that
an infant should not be clothed in the customary formal manner, with skirts, petticoats, etc. There cannot be
a question of the soundness of such views. Nature requires no such paraphernalia ; the most rapid and healthful growth is attainable under the simplest attire con-
sistent with the preservation of animal heat.

All the articles in the *Scalpel*, on the organic elements
of the body, and on the structure of the heart and lungs,
are necessarily connected with this subject ; but they are
too extensive for this volume.

NATURE AS A PHYSICIAN.

THE NATURAL POWER OF THE BODY TO CURE DISEASE, VS. THE IMPERTINENCE
OF DRUG-GIVING.

"I HONOR the glorious name of medicine ; its promises so full of hope to mankind ; but for that which is called the 'art of prescribing' I have no respect whatever."—MONTAIGNE.

THE prejudices of mankind are sacred, and he who wages war with them must bring to the encounter an inflexible spirit, and patience not easily exhausted. The man who holds to a proposition because supported by reason, is in some cases aware that the premises are not well laid, or that he may have erred in his deductions ; but he who holds by prejudice has no such misgivings. Premises and deductions are, with him, of no account ; fact is supplanted by fancy, and assertion is equivalent to proof. Authority with this class of men is omnipotent—precedent their polar star ; the most comfortable faith supports them, and their zeal knows no faint-heartedness. Argument they condemn of course, and their purpose in action is well expressed by the slang phrase, "go it blind." Heaven forbid that I should be so mad as to engage in a tilt with such antagonists on any subject ; least of all on that of pill-giving. Invested with the dignity of academic sheep-skin, they are as secure in the admiration of their votaries, as the Pope of his vassals.

"The three learned professions," says that shrewd thinker, the Professor at the Breakfast-table, "have but recently emerged from a state of quasi-barbarism." This remark is amusingly sustained by the fact that few intelligent members of either of the three can be met with, who will not readily admit the substance of the truth of it, as applied to the other two, while maintaining the almost perfect maturity of his own. We may say of all of them, that they bear the mud of prejudice upon them as does the recently hatched partridge its shell, and so thick and tenacious is this foul incrustation, that the difficulty of penetrating it amounts in many cases to an impossibility. This is especially the case in our profession, when it is the subject of inquiry into the capability of the unaided animal system to resist disease or repair its damages. On this question we have no stores of experience to draw upon in our investigation, for since time began, as far as history is concerned, we can find no disease or injury of the human frame, that has not been "met," "treated," "cured," or bedevilled by some Obi-woman, medicine-man, or "sad and learned doctor." Greasing the spear-point was once a cherished remedy for the wound it had inflicted.

As far as we can penetrate the arcana of diseases, there are two chief divisions of the catalogue ; those which, from the first, are characterized by a malignant type, the prognosis of which is a fatal termination, and those which, after a longer or shorter duration, usually result in a partial or complete restoration to health. The latter comprise by far the larger number of diseases, and it is to them that we would at present direct attention. Now the question is, how far such ought to be left to the recuperative efforts of nature, or to such efforts protected and sustained by such philosophic adjustment of the circumstances surrounding the patient, as will give them the best opportunity to act without being in any manner

13

affected by the agents of the materia medica. To illustrate, we will take the word Fever, with the ideas it
commonly represents. There is thirst. Without entering into a pathological inquiry of the cause or nature of
morbid thirst, we follow the indication by administering
water. There is an exalted sensibility of the organs of
sight and hearing, with pain in the head. We will obey
the indication here by removing the respective external
causes of annoyance. There is a sensation of heat. We
will, if possible, obtain a cool atmosphere. There is muscular weakness. We will relieve the voluntary muscles
of the necessity of action, by placing the body in the
horizontal position. In this manner we will adjust those
circumstances which are visibly and positively under
our control, in the best possible manner to allow the
enfeebled, depressed powers of the system to regain their
healthy state. Can we do more? "Yes," cries the un-
plumed gosling, fresh from the professional hatching-
nest. "Yes," exclaims senile stupidity. "Fever is my
specialty," says the one, gravely conning his list of
"*febrifuges.*" "I have been in practice forty years, and
have *cured* hundreds of cases," exultingly boasts the
other. I admire aspiring youth, I venerate age; but I
cannot permit the crude flippancy of the one, nor the
mill-horse stupidity of the other, to blind me to the conviction that the God-established powers of life can be in
no respect made more efficient by such impertinent
interference.

If all human reasoning were as loose and illogical as
that which has been used in the service of experience to
prove the efficacy of medicine, we should be at this day
in extreme ignorance of many of the arts and sciences,
which are the boast of the nineteenth century. As it
regards astronomy, the earth would be still standing on

a turtle or something of the kind, and the sun going around it, ready to "stand still" or move backward to accommodate the wonder-recording historian of the feats of miracle-workers. The tea-kettle might have sent its steam from its nozzle till this time, but no steamship would have brought New York and Liverpool within ten days of each other ; and there would be but slight expectation of a submarine telegraph next year. By this loose logic, sequency of events is taken as proof of causation, and is thus made the foundation of medical experience. Nothing can be more illusory. To make such evidence conclusive, it should be corroborated by a closely cross-examined and uncontradicted mass of it. Is there any such proof of the ultimate value of any drug that was ever forced or coaxed into that truth-loving and almost reasoning organ, the human stomach? Any one at all conversant with the subject knows that it is directly the reverse of this. Who has not at times, in professional coteries, witnessed the expression of polite and placid incredulity with which some zealous believer in his own skill is listened to while he relates the success of a particular, and as he conceives, a new remedy. Each listener has his favorite, intolerant of rivalry, and when these various fondlings are compared, they are often found to agree but in one particular, that is, the odor of the drug-shop. It is true that some are inert articles ; but again, some are the most virulent poisons. A Minié rifle in the hands of a skillful marksman, who is neither an enemy, an insane, or a careless man, is an instrument that we look at with a quiet feeling of safety, for at the same time that we know that its owner will hit whatever he aims at, we know that he will not point his gun at us. Could the same thing be said of any drug on the list of the materia medica, or of any drug-prescriber in Christendom? Not by any one, I dare engage, who knows the susceptibility of the human system—the complex and inappreciable sympathies which influence it —the baneful properties of the drug, and the positive ignorance of the prescriber of what will be its effect in any given instance of disease.

In the diseases we are considering, ultimate recovery by the natural process is the rule, death the exception. On the contrary, the uninformed patient considers death the natural termination of all morbid conditions that are not *cured* in time. The meddling doctor takes advantage of this prejudice—exhibits his remedy "in time"— the patient recovers, grateful for the "cure," and the doctor notes it as another proof of the efficacy of medicine in general, and of his unerring skill in particular. Now, considering the discrepancy of opinions noticed above, the fair presumption is, that the so-called remedy had no effect whatever, beneficial or otherwise, but was probably enveloped and lost in the effete mass within the intestines and safely conducted out of the system ; or its baneful properties were overcome by the recuperative forces of nature, to which the evil of the disease and the poison of the medicine were equally indifferent ; or perhaps in a certain way the drug was beneficial, by making an impression which aroused certain sympathies, of the existence of which, as connected with the specific prescription, the prescriber was ignorant, or utterly unable to appreciate ; in fine, the result of the movement was *accidental health*, instead of *accidental death*. This view is strongly corroborated by the fact, that we seldom, if ever, meet with two medical Solomons, whether connected with schools, or standing alone as individual sages, who pursue or teach the same kind of treatment in any given disease ; yet both boast their "cures," each insisting on the exclusive merit of his method, backed by his patient's affidavit. Those who remember the treatment of the cholera of 1832, an example of mark among many, will appreciate the truth of this as far as we could ascertain by conversation with different individuals. After the subsidence of the epidemic, no physician during its continuance lost more or less than *six* patients ; as it regards the treatment, while some relied on unlimited quantities of brandy and opium, others saved *innumerable* cases by the use of ice, bleeding, and tartar emetic!

The treatment of the Typhoid Pneumonia, that first appeared as an epidemic in 1812, isolated cases of which have been occurring ever since, and of which, we presume, President Harrison died, is highly corroborative of the views expressed above. One party treated it by bleeding and purging, and the other with brandy and other stimulants. Some recovered under, and in spite of, each method, thus "heaping up" the proofs of the correctness of each. Who shall gainsay such evidence? Certainly no one in any individual case—but we take our stand on the firm ground of sound reason, so often extolled and so seldom followed, and assert that the sequence of the recovery to the prescription affords no conclusive proof of the necessary dependence of the result on the treatment, nor would it, were a thousand instances of the same kind adduced in corroboration. Yet it is by such evidence that the practice of drug-prescribing is supported. This being our view of the case, we would gladly doff our cap and make our lowest obeisance to Homœopathy for the great truth it has helped to teach us, of the utter uselessness of medicine in most cases, were it not that while it has successfully sought the truth it has lost all title to gratitude, and rendered the truth useless, by shrouding it in falsehood. The assertion that the division or attenuation of any thing in nature will increase its specific power, whatever that may be, is so grossly false, that we do not believe that any other age of the world than our own, past or future, ever did or ever will listen to such absurd nonsense. It is pitiful to see Philosophy stoop from her high eminence to cater to Superstition and Prejudice for the sake of the contemptible fruits of fraud. In this way the great good that we might have received has been rendered worse than of no avail, by the falsehood it has taught, that recovery from disease depends upon the most persistent drug-taking. The lie is made to knock the truth over. Better ignorance a thousand times, than knowledge prostituted to such vile purposes.

It is strange that the healing powers of nature, so universally relied on in the practice of modern surgery, should have taught so little to the medical practitioner. He has before him the history of the ignorance of the ancient surgeons, contrasted with the demonstration of the existence of the sufficing efficacy of the life-forces in the modern practice, and yet derives no useful lesson from the example. He sees in a broken bone or a sword-cut, nature instantly set to work, by vital and certain processes, to repair the injury, and this she effects without the impertinent interference of external means, provided a fair field be allowed for her operations. But in the department we are considering, where the morbid and the counteracting influences are exerted, as it were, behind a screen, the physician seems to make his blindness an excuse for boldness, and thrusts his weapon in the dark, necessarily uncertain where the blow will fall, whether on enemy or friend, or the depth of the wound it will inflict. The idea of ascertaining and being gov-

erned by fixed rules in the administration of medicine, if
the object is the ultimate benefit of the individual patient,
is, from the nature of things, impossible. Disease is not
matter, and it cannot be lined and squared and made to
obey those fixed rules to which we, with certainty, subject material substances. That in certain cases we can
procure certain effects, is unquestionable—but when we
reflect that we may arrest an apparently morbid symptom, without knowing but it may be a link in a chain of
salutary movements, which, to be beneficial, should not
be disturbed, our self-complacency may be, perhaps, a
little troubled. That such is the case in some diseases
we know. I will adduce Measles as one example. Now
here is a disease made up of different phenomena linked
together, and following each other with as much regularity as is exhibited in the planetary or other well-
ascertained movements in nature, and invariably resulting in health, that is, when there is no impertinent
interference, designed or accidental. Yet I have noticed
that when this disease is prevailing in some of our large
cities, the weekly bills of mortality frequently show the
number of deaths ranging as high as three and four per
cent. of the whole number.

More or less of the evil attending drug-interference
attaches to men of the best minds in the profession ; and
while saying this, we proudly challenge the world to produce from any other class, an equal number of men of the
same high order of intelligence, of culture, and of moral
excellence. Never yielding to the weariness of labor,
their charity is exhaustless and—silent. No voice rever-
berates through the arches of cathedral roofs in praise of
their benevolence, no trumpet-blasts from the market-
place proclaim their good deeds, but noiselessly they
"pursue the even tenor of their way," binding up

wounds and solacing misery. If the strictures we have
made have any just application to such men, with what
unmitigated reprobation should we visit the ignorant
and unprincipled, who for speculative and sinister ends
have stolen into the sacred corps, and, disguised under
its time-honored mantle, have gone forth to the *slaughter*,
till, loaded with ill-gotten gains—"the price of blood "—
they are at once enrolled among the Plutocracy—take
unquestioned possession of the seats of honor, and from
thence dictate to the world their articles of faith, and
codes of ethics.   For such, the prejudice of the people in
favor of the mysterious efficacy of drugs is an unfailing
resource.   They can not overdraw their credit.   The
tendency of mankind to worship mystery and believe in
miracle is an enigma hard to solve.   Men naturally love
truth, they like not to be told falsehoods ; but surround
a lie with mystery, and they surrender their judgment,
their suspicion, and their doubts at once.   Allege in support of any absurdity a supernatural agency, and their
common sense is lulled to sleep, and this in face of the
fact that in all the works of God there is neither mystery
nor miracle.

There is, undoubtedly, much in nature that is not
understood by man, but this is clearly owing to his not
having travelled far enough on the free and open road of
knowledge that lies before him—the road of never-vary-
ing fact, where the unfailing effect always follows the
sufficient cause ; the road which leads to the true knowledge of "Him with whom there is no variableness neither
shadow of turning," the road "through nature, up to
nature's God."

The following remarks from Montaigne, (*Essais*, liv. 2.
ch. 37,) though two hundred years old, are in some respects so pertinent to the subject in hand that I cannot

resist the temptation to quote them; for, though not over-looking the many splendid improvements of modern times, we must acknowledge that *man*, in many respects, remains very much as he was in the time of the old philosopher.

"But physicians have this advantage," (says Montaigne,) "according to the old apothegm, that the sun shines upon their success, while the earth hides their blunders; and besides this, they have a very advantageous fashion of serving themselves with all sorts of events; for that which fortune, that which nature, or some other strange cause, (of which the number is infinite,) produces in us of good and salutary, it is the privilege of the physician to attribute to himself. All the happy success of the patient who is under his rule he holds the credit of—the circumstances which cure me, and which have cured a thousand others who call no physician to their aid, they usurp the credit of in their subjects; and as to the evil accidents, they disavow them altogether, attributing the fault to the patient for reasons so vain and trifling, that they have no fear of failing always to find a sufficiently large number of them. 'He has lain with his arm uncovered'—'he has heard a strange noise'—'they have left his window open'—'his mind is troubled by anxiety.' Sometimes a word, a dream, a turn of the eye, seems sufficient excuse to discharge them from blame, or if they please they serve themselves with the worst aspect of affairs by means which can never fail them. So they comfort us, when the patient finds himself heated by their applications, with the assurance that it would be much worse without their remedies. He whom they have thrown into a quotidian chill, would have had, without their interference, a continued fever. They guard not against doing their work badly, since the evil the patient

13*

experiences redounds to their advantage. The combat of the drug with the disease is always at our expense, since the battle is fought within our borders, and the drug is an unreliable ally, by its nature inimical to our health. Let us leave things a little to themselves—the order which governs fleas and moles, governs also men when equally submissive. We may add to our ills by querulous impatience, but this brings us no relief. There is an imperious and unvarying order in nature, unaffected by the movements of our fear or dispair, which serve only to retard the relief which this order would bring. Disease has its course as well as health, and attempts to break one, by the aid of the other, often result only in the disorder of both. Let us follow *the plan of God*—it gently leads those who will follow, and drives those who will not, both their rage and their medicine together. Procure a purgative for your head : it will be better employed than for your stomach."

MEDICAL SHEEP-SHEARING.

"Great cry and little wool," as the Devil said when he sheared his hogs.

THE sheep-shearing of Nabal is said to have been attended by the Devil; and it is quite probable, that rural festival was the first incentive to the operation their shepherd was performing upon those interesting quadrupeds he is said to watch over so affectionately, when he gave utterance to the classical quotation with which we have embellished this production. There has been quite as terrific a squealing kept up since we have been shearing our flock. We are not exactly in league with his majesty, although we employ him occasionally, but our sincerest resolves to let the brethren slip for a number or so, are constantly opposed by some infernal imp of his, if not the veritable old shepherd himself, by inciting the brethren to commit such extravagant absurdities, and to cut up such diverting tricks in their Colleges and Academies, that we are constantly incited to invite him to the diversion. Indeed, we declare from the bottom of our diaphragm—nay, from our spleen itself, beloved reader—we cannot help it, they are so funny.

And yet it beseemeth us to have a care—albeit our organ of caution is not very large—lest we meet with the reward of that curiously disposed philosopher (slander-

ously called a madman) who, as the veracious historian
tells us, had an extraordinary penchant for the inflation
of dogs! We feel the more disposed to tell thee of the
doings of our predecessor, because it has been hinted
that our sketches are no great shakes, indeed, slightly
stupid, as some of our friends assert. Ah! beloved
brethren, did ye but know the diaphoretic effect one of
our shearings produces, on ourself as well as you, the
cudgeling of our poor brain, the sharpening of the
shears, and then, what is most to be deplored, the
meagreness of the clip, ye would think this medical
sheep-shearing no easy matter; and when we come to
blow up our curs, amidst all the squealing and yelping,
ye would pity us outright.

But to the philosopher : There was a madman in
Seville, who fell into one of the most ridiculous and extravagant conceits that ever madman did in the world.
He sharpened the point of a hollow cane, and catching a
dog in the street or elsewhere, he set his foot on one of
the cur's hind legs, and then lifting up the other, thrust
his cane into the bowels, and straightway, with much
labor, blew him up as round as a ball, and then giving
him a thump or two, let him go, saying to the by-
standers, who were always very many, "Well, gentlemen,
what think you ? Is it such an easy matter to blow up a
dog?" Now we are by no means satisfied of the insanity
of this inflator of dogs. Although our medical curs
don't require the operation, for they blow themselves up
tolerably well without the aid of a cane, we feel inclined
to repeat the experiment. Who knows but the philosopher was in search of some great therapeutic truth,
destined, had it only been discovered, to occupy a niche
in the temple of fame, and the brains of some of our
medical contemporaries. Have we not Hydropathy, Ho-

mœopathy, Neuropathy, etc., etc.? Why not Ventupathy? There's a hint for you, ye enterprising philanthropists. *Verbum sap*—we already feel our immortality—we shall go down the stream with Hahnemann, Priessnitz and Dr. Kirby.

The Homœopathic philosophers have scared up some capital fun for us; they have gone to considerable expense (to be paid prospectively when the new College shall be organized) in recalling that valorous gentleman from his eight years' rustication in a village up the River, whither he had gone to refresh himself after that awful midnight encounter with the four robbers some eight years since. We saw him a few days ago, and were delighted to perceive him in high feather, and evidently ready for a tilt with Allopathy or a whole host of robbers.

But let us introduce the Doctor formally—like old Jack Falstaff recounting his exploits to Prince Hal.

"I am a rogue if I were not at half-sword with a dozen of them, two hours together. I have 'scaped by a miracle; I am eight times thrust through the doublet; four, through the hose; my buckler cut through and through; my sword hack'd like a hand-saw, *ecce signum.* I never dealt better since I was a man; all would not do. A plague on all cowards? Let them speak; if they speak more or less than truth, they are villains and the sons of darkness."

Oh, but the Doctor's description next morning after the robbery, in one of the papers, was graphic! Somewhat of its solemn impressiveness comes over our spirit at midnight even yet. We quote some of the more dramatic passages: "I awoke with the consciousness of a living movement near my bed." . . "I saw the dim figure of a man through my half-closed eyelids as through a thick mist." . . "Instantly every sense became on the alert, and the eyes and ears strained to their utmost." "I could hear the blood as it rushed through the carotids near my ears." Our own blood runs cold to think of it : and then the astonishing dexterity with which the Doctor (in the dark!) threw the bedclothes over the rob- ber's head by means of his feet with all the precision of a South American lasso horse-hunter, the amazing pres- ence of mind with which he seized the sword-cane "so providentially standing at his chamber door," and the race down stairs, with the dreadful rencounter at the hall door where the awful wound was inflicted, the wrestling and death grip in the office, the doctor getting most skillfully "the under hold," and the warm life-blood of the victim pouring over "his gray hair," when one of the robbers already embraced by the doctor at the hall door, was accidentally stabbed by his brother robber in the dark, and exclaimed, "I am stabbed—" and the great clasp knife found next morning in that awful pool of blood ; and the night-gown "all stiff with gore" "so that it would stand alone!" Like Duncan, one feels inclined to ask—

> "What bloody man is that
> Who seemeth by his plight,"

As though he might

> "The multitudinous sea incarnadine,
> Making the green one red."

And that blessed rib which received the point of the dagger and saved the Doctor's heart, and elicited that eloquent finale. [See the account published!] What do we not owe that rib? more perhaps than that unfor- tunate one possessed by our great progenitor ; but a truce with nonsense. We are rejoiced to observe the "living movements" of the doctor show no tendency to decay, and trust that his excellent fancies have not been impaired by his long absence ; doubtless an encounter with the brilliant and piquant conversation of the Homœpathic brethren, will revive those delightful memories of former years, that lent such enchanting and romantic gracefulness to his conversation, and enable him to afford us further insight into an extraordinary department of medical psychologics, and another dish for the amusement of our readers.   *   *   *

It has often been said that "truth is stranger than fiction," and we think we are now going to settle in the affirmative that assertion for good, no matter what of proof may be added hereafter. The romantic and terrible encounter with the giants—no—with the robbers—(heaven help us, we are even yet in a state of nervous agitation at the bare description) which is only equalled by the doings of that glorious mirror of chivalry, whose deeds will never die : we say the Doctor's romantic encounter with the robbers, was actually fairly matched by a bona fide adventure of our friend Dr. F——s, of Second Avenue. The Doctor's modesty would have entirely concealed the whole affair, had it not been for the unavoidable publicity that it attained by the legal steps necessary for the commitment of his robbers, for they were no spirits conjured up by a fertile invention to attain notoriety (which the Doctor studiously avoids, being in the enjoyment of a position to which he is as much entitled by his science as the elegance of his manners,) but real flesh and blood robbers—and no less than three of them, all taken by the Doctor with the aid of his sons, two mere lads, *in flagrante delicto*, searching for his plate closet ; and all well and sufficiently bound, and marched at midnight by the Doctor to the station-house, sword and dagger in hand! The facts are simply these : The Doctor

was awakened by a "living movement" not "at his bedside," but below stairs. His senses being usually pretty
well on the alert, and his nerves well-strung—the Doctor
was educated at West Point—he stopped not for the
superfluous details of the toilet (which by the way he
was obliged to *commence* when he had bound the robbers
and left them in custody of his sons,) but went with all
his motors unobstructed by clothes to the top of the
basement stairs, where he could see the enterprising
gentlemen at work at a closet. Instantly returning up
stairs to the second story, where his sons slept, he
aroused them with cautious attention to avoid noise, and
armed them with sword and dagger, selected from a well
supplied armamentarium of ancient implements of war,
which he keeps as a museum for his children. With
great caution and no noise, he opened the front and rear
doors, and placed one of the boys outside at the area
gate where the robbers had entered, and another at the
back-door in the yard which they had opened, and then
went to the head of the basement stairs, and in a loud
voice summoned a surrender, at the same time proclaim-
ing his arrangements in the front and rear outlets, and
ordering his sons to shoot down instantly any one who
attempted to escape. The first who surrendered was a
powerful negro. The Doctor marshalled him to the back
piazza, and ordered the robber to lie on his face, which
he deemed it prudent to do, though armed with a billy ;
the son was stationed over him with a drawn sword, and
ordered to cut him down should he attempt to arise ; no
sooner had the Doctor turned to seek the others, who
afraid of the pistol in the hands of the young man at the
gate, remained passively awaiting their fate, than the
negro attempted to overpower his guard. Instantly returning, the Doctor settled him with a blow on the head ;

he then lay passive. By this time, however, one of the robbers attempted to escape by the area, but the youth drove him back by threatening to shoot him, at the same time levelling, pistol fashion, a Malay crease, the only weapon he had. The other also attempted to escape into the yard, but was driven back by the other youth. By this time the ladies of the family had alarmed the watch, who were with great difficulty persuaded to enter, and would not have done so, but for the Doctor's decisive assurance that there was no danger. One of the robbers feigned drunkenness, and had nearly succeeded in imposing upon the dogberries, but the Doctor speedily removed the impression by soundly cuffing his ears. The whole three were now thoroughly awe-stricken, and being well bound, they were dispatched to the police, and are now serving out their time in the State Prison.

There! beloved reader, have we not redeemed our promise; these were neither old Jack's men in buckram, nor Kendal green; and they were secured every one of them; we may say with old fat paunch, "you rogue, an' they were not bound, I am a Jew, an 'Ebrew Jew."

And now, mine excellent and faithful reader, having accompanied us thus far, through our sketches of our less romantic brethren, we must defend our claim as the historical Quixote in our attack on the medical wind-mills, and require thee to accompany us to the grand *dénouement* of the midnight rencounter with those robbers, which was so sublimely described in the papers of the day, by the ever memorable and chief actor on the awful occasion. We suffered the other sketch to intervene, dear reader, with the view of thy partial recovery from the effect of our introduction to the great tragedy. Now comes the grand finale by way of a coup de théâtre.

The day after the affair, there was an equal amount of

horror and amusement in the community, touching the
"awful robbery and attempted murder," as it was duly
announced by the penny-a-liners. Whilst some of the
more innocent and amiable of our citizens were pale with
terror, there were other hardy spirits, chiefly doctors,
who received the dreadful news with hearty peals of
laughter ; and some of the brethren not particularly distinguished for politeness, actually put their irreverent
fingers to the sides of their noses. The Doctor appeared
most gracefully and elegantly accoutered with a black
silk scarf to suspend a wounded arm ; "the biceps muscle," as he learnedly informed us, having been wounded
in the encounter. It was observed, however, that on the
slightest irregularity of movement in his magnificent
pair of bays, the ruling passion would assert its power,
and the Doctor, who is a great equestrian, would instantly grasp the whip with great vigor with the wounded
arm. The whole affair appeared next day but one, most
eloquently and graphically written out by the Doctor,
with a grand religious finale, quite a prayer. So great a
sensation was produced by it, that our enterprising
citizen, Mr. Mitchell, of the Olympic, announced its
appearance as a grand melo-drama. But those wretched
creatures, the doctors, persisted with their vile innuendoes and irreverent laughter ; soon, however, their laughter was turned to wonder, by a circumstance equally
unexpected and extraordinary. Four days after the robbery, the body of a man who had evidently died suddenly, and apparently from a stab in his neck directly
over the jugular and carotid, was found in a sack high
and dry on the shore, at Turtle Bay, East River! it was
brought to the Tombs for recognition and an inquest,
and it was confidently predicted that the robber from
whose neck came the torrent of blood that deluged the

Doctor, and " stiffened his gray hair and night-dress with gore," was found, and the accomplices would thereby be detected. Some of the more innocent members of the profession, and a great number of the ladies, were already satisfied, before the inquest, that the unfortunate man had met his death by the valiant arm of the Doctor. The knowing ones, however, were confident that Reynard had "doubled," and quietly and mirthfully awaited the *dénouement.* In a couple of days, no one appearing to claim the body, a coroner's inquest was held, and it was found that the wound in the neck not only did not penetrate the carotid or jugular, but from the absence of all those marks that prove inflammation, and the existence of *life* in the subject when the wound was inflicted, that it was actually made on the dead body ! there being no other cause of death visible externally, and this being totally inadequate to account for the death of even an infant, as a table-spoonful of blood could not have been lost by it, the Coroner was about to open the body to seek further light on the dark and mysterious transaction, when a young doctor attached to one of the dispensaries appeared, and immediately recognized the body as that of a patient who had died a week previous under his care, of inflammation of the lungs, and was buried in Potter's Field! To all this he made oath ; the barber also who shaved the man testified to the same, and a verdict was given accordingly. At this moment the Doctor appeared before the jury with that awful clasp-knife—but it was too late ; the verdict was given : Died from pneumonia, at No. —— Second Avenue, and conveyed from Potter's Field by some unknown person to Turtle Bay, East River !

The Doctor, disgusted with the reception of his tragedy, and the merriment produced by that accursed young doctor, sought the quiet influence of the country to calm his perturbed spirits. He now appears rejuvenated and refreshed, ready to fire his small homœopathic ammunition down the throats of his admirers, and his intellectual artillery at the devoted Allopaths.

There, bewildered and beloved reader! what think you of that? Are we not a great people? Who will say that our profession is destitute of romance? Alas! for you, Munchausen ; and as for you, bright mirror of ancient chivalry, hide your diminished head ; remain in the sable mountain and bewail your fate forever ; your glory has departed ; D—— now wears the helmet.

A BOY'S·THEOLOGICAL EXPERIENCES.

FAMILY ANTECEDENTS—PARENTAL AUTHORITY IN THE LAST GENERATION—COR-
POREAL PUNISHMENT AND ITS EFFECTS—READING HABITS—A "SERIOUS LIBRA-
RY"—TWO BOOKS AND THEIR CONTENTS—ETERNAL PUNISHMENT—FANCIES
ABOUT HELL—ILLUSTRATION OF THE IDEA OF ETERNITY—OVERPOWERING
DREAD OF BOTH, AND OF DEATH—IDEAS ABOUT DROWNING—IMAGINED LOCAL-
ITIES OF HELL—OF PEOPLE IN IT—THE DAY OF JUDGMENT.

WHAT I have undertaken to narrate is no fiction, no
story of complex or simple incident. If it possess interest, it will be because it is what its title indicates—a boy's
theological experiences—a statement of mental sufferings, I believe by no means uncommon in youth—youth
subject in early life to what are called serious impressions.

I was born of a religious family. I came of plain country stock, which based itself on the soil for at least three
generations, as far back as we have traditional knowledge of. My grandfather on the maternal side and my
father were the first of their respective families who
relinquished farming for a city life. Let me say a little,
preliminary of the latter.

He was of Puritan blood, which had localized itself in
one spot. Our family name is extant on many a tomb-
stone in —— churchyard, and I, in my boy-days, have
played with farm laborers on my uncle's estate, of my
own name and probable lineage. Left an orphan at an
early age, not, however, before his mother had unwisely
married again, my father had been put out to business

very early in life.   He was a weakly boy of nervous temperament ; he has told me that his step-father scarcely
expected him to survive.   His life, like those of many of
his generation, had passed monotonously enough in a
confined social atmosphere up to the time of his marriage, and, indeed, continued so for long afterwards.   An
apprentice in a country town, a steady attendant at
church and Sunday-school, at first in the capacity of
scholar and then of teacher, a clerk in a store, a thrifty
shopkeeper—he had five thousand dollars on coming of
age, by his father's will—a prosperous citizen generally,
and finally, who had retired from business at the early
age of thirty, on a modest competence ; these were his
successive experiences.   When married, he rented a decent house in the neighborhood, and brought my mother, who was city-bred, to live in it.

We are all more or less made up of our ancestors.   I
think my own individuality may be the better understood by knowledge of the stock I came of.   I had two
brothers, the second of whom died within a year of his
birth.   Ned, my elder, and I were brought up like most
boys in religious families.   Our mother loved us dearly.
Our father loved us too, for he, I believe, was of affectionate nature, though of nervous, irritable disposition.
But he had the old world notion of authority, and considered his children as much *subjects* as children, in which
I think he was wrong.   But parental rule in that generation had a heavy hand ; it was very commonly a rank
despotism tempered by maternal affection.

The elder-born of a family are generally subject to
stricter discipline than their luckier later-born brothers
and sisters ; time mollifies parents' tempers ; they learn
wisdom from past mistakes, and a milder, more judicious treatment often succeeds to one frequently produc-

tive of misconception, suffering, and mutiny. This is especially the case in religious families. It was so to some extent in ours.

My father beat us, not I think cruelly, though sometimes capriciously. I dare say we deserved it, yet as I remember we were rather afraid of him than possessed by any other feeling, the result was bad. Anything antagonistic to love and confidence between parent and child *must* be harmful. This fear and the estrangement attendant on it grew up rather in our boy-days than our childhood. *Then* I was his favorite. I recollect trotting about a certain quarry with him of sunny afternoons, and into the woods, and his cutting sticks for me. Often I have thought kindly of this, years afterwards, when I have been thousands of miles away, with the ocean between us.

He beat us, I repeat. At the age of thirty, returning home after a five years' absence in a distant quarter of the earth, I found the instrument of our not unfrequent chastisement—a leather strap—in a disused drawer. And—I am sorry to say it, but truth *is* truth—my heart swelled with anger at the sight of it. Hardest of all things to forget in this world is a sense of *past injustice*, of undeserved infliction on those who are weak and can not help themselves.

Let me get to my theological experiences ; I only speak of others as illustrative of my early training. I had always a taste for reading, preferring, indeed, poring over a book in-doors to healthier indulgence in boys' play in the open fields, which is hardly natural. My father considered reading, unless, " serious " books, only a synonym for idleness. " A pack of lies and nonsense," was his definition of all fictitious literature, however pure and harmless. The word " novel " has, even now, to my ears, a sound of indefinite wickedness, though I have read hundreds of them, and hope some day to write at least one; I had little chance of getting at other than "serious" literature. Our family book-case contained only evangelical magazines, Zion's Caskets, Whitefield, Wesley, Edwards's and Huntingdon's sermons, Bunyan's works, Fox's Martyrs, and the like. I read these in default of more appropriate intellectual nutriment. Not that I remember being especially encouraged to do so, though I believe it was looked upon as a good thing that a boy should take to such serious subjects. My father thought so, at least, and never inclining to cheerful views of existence, would have considered any sombre impressions I might derive from such sources as beneficial. For my dear mother, she was then like her children, too much under authority, and never thought of the mischief that might come of it.

Dear old Bunyan! may I be forgiven for ranking *you* with the others? Of course I loved the "Pilgrim's Progress," (indeed I learnt a poetical version of it by heart, on promise of possessing the book, by my mother,) and got no harm out of *that*. I cannot say the same, though, for the biography, "Grace abounding to the Chief of Sinners." Yet I wish there had been no worse books in our library. Two, I have cause to hold in especial detestation. These were entitled "The Arian's and Socinian's Monitor," and "Dialogues of Devils," both written by a Reverend Mr. McGowan. The first was the worst. How well I remember the accursed book! Oldish type, the ends of the top and bottom lines occasionally shorn off by the careless or unskilful binder—every way mean and common-looking; what a hell of mental torment did those pages open to me. *Hell*, that is the word. The book was all about hell. I will relate the

plot of it, which I remember as well as though I perused
it yesterday.

A teacher of the tenets of Arius and Socinus, the
"monitor" of the title, has died, and the narrator, his
disciple, wrapped in a state of spiritual self-complacency,
rambles into the recesses of a gloomy wood, the shades
of which grow darker as he proceeds. Presently he loses
his way, and directly the infernal pit yawns before him.
He sees it, I think, through an archway of ribbed rock,
and in a sea of raging flame, "the fire that dieth not,
neither is it quenched," he beholds the lost soul of his
late preceptor, damned forever. The spirit addresses
him at some length, the main bulk of the book consisting
of its observations. It closes with the appearance of
devils who drag it off to fresh torments.

There is nothing in this, ingenious, imaginative, or
inventive, nothing but vulgar horror, and trite, thread-
bare execution. All the worse for its simplicity in its
power of addressing a thoughtful boy's mind. Before I
tell how it did so, let me speak of the other book. That
may be dismissed briefly ; both are on the same plan.

In "Dialogues of Devils" the narrator again wanders
into the wood, and there, either in a deep ravine or pit,
while secreted within an archway, overhears the talk of
certain fiends. They appear (or, at least, were drawn in
an engraving forming a frontispiece to the volume) with
horns, hoofs, and the usual vulgar diabolic accessories.
They have Latinized names, as *Crudelis, Infidelis,* etc.
Their conversation is of their influence and power over
mankind, being sometimes of a grimly facetious character.

These books I read and pondered over, especially the
former, until their main subject, eternal punishment,
took exclusive possession of my mind. It seemed to me

14

as it has to many before and since—I need not say erro-
neously—that this one tenet, eternal damnation, was the
main doctrine of Christianity. At least it overshadowed
all others. I could think of little else as appertaining
to it.

To be damned in hell forever and ever! I began to
revolve the meaning of these tremendous words and
slowly to shape one. Hour after hour, day by day, and
night after night I thought of it, always starting from
the conviction that that was my destiny. How could I
dispute it? Had I been converted? had *I* received that
miraculous change of heart without experiencing which
all were under the just sentence of a wrathful God? I
knew well enough that my life, hitherto, had been simply
a boy's life, untroubled by any such questions, that I
didn't like going to church twice on Sundays, that I
thought learning a collect or psalm before I got any
fruit after dinner an infliction, that I regarded religion
in general as something disagreeable and repressive,
something that interfered with one's likings and pleasures. Secretly I wished my parents had not been religious. I knew families who were not so ; the boys were
jollier, went out to parties and had pocket-money.

All this I knew of myself and felt very wicked. If
ever boy were inherently subject to damnation, *I* was.
As remarked, I meditated on my presumed inevitable lot
continually.

A place full of fire, of dreadful inconceivable intensity
and fierceness, which never went out or slackened, peopled with horrible devils who tore and rent you with
fangs and hooked fire-forks, with monstrous serpents,
ten thousand thousand times bigger than the boa-con-
strictor in the magazine we took in ; this, in which my
body, so changed that it wouldn't burn up, was to suffer

more torment than I, *with continual trying*, could begin to think, was my boyish conception of Hell. This, in which I should burn, *always*; I had burnt my hand once with a red-hot poker and knew the pain of it. I had had a fever and lain in hot agony and weary wakefulness. I thought of these sufferings, endeavored to exaggerate them a hundred fold, summoned up all that I knew of pain, to aid me to form some idea of hell. I began to ponder on it in detail, especially attempting to realize some faint impression as to its eternal duration.

I had met an illustration in some book, sermon, or magazine, which seemed to attempt this pretty effectually. It will probably be recognized by religious people. Here it is :

Suppose the water in the ocean, or the sand upon the sea-shore, to be decreased by a single grain or drop every ten thousand years: when the whole bulk of sea and sand should be exhausted, that immeasurable length of time might represent, as it were, one second of eternity!

And this Eternity was to be passed *in Hell!*

I lay of nights lengthening out the dreadful idea, and thinking of the people *who were there* already. It seemed shocking that anybody should be able to go to sleep, to eat and drink, to laugh, to do daily business in the world when such awful, real suffering was going on every moment of our lives, and had been going on long before we were born, would keep on after the world was burnt up. Folks didn't think of it, of course, but how could they help thinking of it? Childhood is selfish, so I cannot say these reflections on the fate of others were prominent in my mind ; they occurred occasionally. Mostly I cared about myself. I began to be very much afraid of dying.

When I heard of loss of life by accident, I shuddered at the idea that it might have happened to me. We lived near a canal, a pretty winding canal, with grassy fields on one side of it, a tow-path on the other, and low-arched bridges which could be raised for the convenience of passing barges. How I dreaded that canal! How I remembered that under one of those bridges a boy had been drowned! How black and awful the shadows always looked at that spot, I remember, as though conscious of having closed over two piteously clutching hands, a ghastly face with a gurgling noise in its throat as it went down, and at last only a cold, naked human body. When I walked by the canal with my father I always shrank to the outer side.

Not that drowning or death was so terrible, but what came after it. I used to envy the animals immensely, their existence seemed so complete and satisfactory ; they were not to blame for anything they did ; they had no souls ; they died and there was an end of them. How happy! No fear of hell there. If I could only have been a dog, now, or even a pig. He was only killed and made into bacon, and what was a sharp knife to hell fire? *Always* burning!

At first I fancied hell must be in the centre of the earth, because of the volcanoes. It was an appalling thing to be walking over it, over the tormented souls of people I had perhaps known. I recollected an hostler, employed by a gentleman who lived next door to us, who had been discharged for some small theft, and had died subsequently of a fever. I liked the man : he once gave me a horse's bit, broken. But I thought him very wicked, for he swore and, I was told, got drunk. These traits, in conjection with the theft, made me conclude that he must have gone to hell. I wondered whether I should know him there ; I had heard that the damned hated and tormented one another, and fancied him flying at me with a dreadful cry, and more dreadful countenance.

Then I thought that the sun was hell. This idea came upon me suddenly of a summer's sunset, when the broad bright disk of the dying day-god looked like an orb of intolerably lurid, liquid flame. It appeared, too, so like what I fancied of the Creator, to put hell to a double use ; beneficial as well as terrible. I became quite sure of this identity, and for a long time never looked at the sun without thoughts of the agonies of which it was the seat. All of this went on simultaneously with my broodings on these agonies as my inevitable and unavoidable lot. For weeks and weeks I made no question of my damnation.

The texts in Scripture on the subject filled me with terror. I was very well acquainted with them, and particularly with the book of Revelations, which possessed peculiar fascinations for me. The tremendous fancies therein, culminating in the great Day of Judgment, when I should be bidden to depart forever into the lake of fire and brimstone, and my mother would be caught up into heaven—I never doubted *that*—were overpoweringly real to me. Perhaps the most dreadful fancy of all was that my mother would be so changed that she would think it right that I should be damned, and forget me. Once a thunderstorm at night produced such an overwhelming apprehension of the end of the world, that I sat up in bed in an agony, and, at my brother's request, prayed aloud. But he only shared my terrors temporarily.

I couldn't tell anybody about them. Once, I ventured on a few words to my mother, when she answered : "My dear, that's nothing to do with you ; Christ died for you, if you believe in him you needn't think of such things." But I could not take hold of the idea presented, I could only think of hell.

Before all this befell me, I had been fond of the Heathen Mythology ; we had a book of it. Somehow I longed to have been born in the times when that was the current religion. Jupiter, Neptune and the rest, seemed nothing like so terrible as the avenging God of the Bible : I was not afraid of them ; their doings were almost human. I even had a decided affection for Neptune, and recollect feeling hurt, when, years afterward, I found him in Homer, humiliated by Jupiter. Though I believed, yet I couldn't quite fancy that the pagans were all in hell, and at any rate it appeared they must have escaped the dread of it while living, and that, I thought no small gain. My boyish conceptions of paganism were of course erroneous and imperfect. It always presented itself as a pleasant creed to me, and I never could entirely realize its falsity. I have hardly done so to this day ; I seem to fancy that the gods and goddesses of the primeval world must have lived once, dying out or disappearing before the approach of a harder, more materialistic time, which *then* I regretted to have been born in. Secretly, too, I sympathized with the Philistines and hated the Jews.

Searching the Scriptures as I did, always with the one morbid object, it was impossible that I should not come upon the one crowning terror—*the Unpardonable Sin against the Holy Ghost.*

How dreadfully that idea took possession of me! We never know how much of hope lurks latent within our souls until precipitated into a deeper abyss of despair ; I, presupposing myself lost eternally, was yet in mortal dread of committing this sin. What was it ? how could it be committed ? With these thoughts came the inevitable sequel, the fascination presented by the precipice which you look from and involuntarily long to plunge down.

I, a boy of twelve, have gone about in agony with *certain words* in my mind—words which will probably rise now in the reader's—which, pronounced, would, I thought, have constituted the sin in question.   I have stuffed my handkerchief into my mouth to prevent my saying them, bit my tongue, struck my head violently with my fists, to divert the current of ideas from that one dreadful subject, through the medium of physical pain. Then I thought that as sin lay in intention, not in act, I *had* committed it, that these fancies were a proof of it, that it was no use crying or praying any longer, for I did both, fitfully and wretchedly.

I wondered, too, at what precise moment it had occurred, and what people would say if they knew, as I passed them in the street, that there was a boy who had committed the Unpardonable Sin.   I fancied them shrinking from me in horror.   It appeared to me that the same visible sign, some convulsion of nature, should have announced the fact to me.   How long the nights appeared and how I wanted to tell my brother, but refrained, thinking he would be afraid of me.   Words are but poor things at best to describe mental torture, but Tertullian himself, who longed to look on and see the enemies of his faith " burning and liquefying" in hell-fire, might have pitied me.   Shall I go on?   No; I have written enough on what has long ceased to be a painful subject to me.   Time and a naturally healthy nature enabled me to get the better of all such horrors as I have related, not, however, without occasional relapses.   I disentomb them now for the moral they teach.   What that is, the reader may judge for himself.

AN ARTIST'S REVERIE.—NO. IV.

"Spirits are not finely touched, but to fine issues."

It is now an hour or so *past* midnight—the storm has died completely away—clouds drive through the heavens—the stars step up—and streams of the silvery moonlight pour into the work-chamber.

How niches fret with silver touchings; and so do other forms on forms—touchings so tremulous ; so spectral—*half flying cloud, half moon !*

That satyr's head, that frowned five hundred years ago in Melrose church, now leers and jibbers. This—from a tomb at Canterbury—(helmed and with visor up,) seems livingly sedate and grim!

The fragments on the walls are shadowy and indistinct, and faintly move within their places—the countenances of angels shift from the smile to the frown : the death-face of Scott strives to lift the lids and stir the lips ; whilst the horse's head, from the Parthenonic frieze, is quite alive, and just about to prance!

The tremulous silvery light salutes the lion and the lamb—the monk, the clown, the saint, the concubine—and, on the Gorgon's brain-shell, keeps serpents after serpents in never-resting coil. Shades start o'er shades —a host of witchery!

And now, the artist, in his vision, and by the duality of bodily and mental torpor, and bodily and mental action, arose from his lounging posture, and, in the silvery moonlight, modelled away at the lady's bust ; and altho' until then, it had seemed as it should seem, yet now, he finds fault after fault, *the faults of the moon!* And he strove and strove to give the eyes more effulgence, and the lips more of a dancing delight! but, alas, the more he toiled, the more the lady grew like an image from ancient Mexico, or Thebes! Now he strives to refresh his sight—his judgment—his artistic strength—but quickly toils on and on, until, amidst frowns, regrets, and curses, he dashes the stubborn and offending image into ruin ; then buries his face within his hands, and seems himself a frozen model of Despair and Grief—as he sees, *by the brain's fire-light*, long, long lines of phantoms—of creations now dead and buried *forever and ever*, except in the land of dreams!

˙ See how the unearthly shapes flit by, and spring into their everlasting graves—mistress, and friend—statues, gems, and paintings—sympathetic touches from foreign climes and youthful days—friendly voices, friendly clasps, and friendly sympathies—and the air trembled with pleasant chats, and musical notes, and mimicry, and jests, and the jingling kiss of the wine-cups—and then passed countenances of goodness, countenances of the magnificent mind, countenances cherubic, and those of a brilliant beauty of shape and color, and a *radiance of spirit* infinitely excelling that of the sunsets most beloved by Claude Lorraine—and touches of the dance, by a lithe and sweet-faced woman, with large black eyes, and lashes that swept with a startling grace and witchery upon the marble face, *the raven's feather on a field of snow!* Now, in transparent drapery, she "leaps as a hart in the desert"—now floats with the rarest skill and *abandon*—sometimes scarcely stirring the air, and sometimes cutting it
14*

like lightning with the *staccato* music of her feet! Now, she rests, and sleeps, and brightly dreams—and starts, half rises, hesitates—and whilst the traces of joy and gladness still linger, and the upraised arm and pointed finger quicken the scarcely awakened brain, she falteringly exclaims : "'*Tis but a dream!*"

Here pass the early dead—poor Bonnington beneath the Bridge of Sighs! and such . . . . and then the visionary stole out upon the housetop, and boldly walked along the cornice troughs—for he knew not what he did, and the Lord God was his unerring guide—and whilst himself upon destruction's verge, he saw the awful, unique, mystic, and world-wide picture of the DELUGE! that dreadful tragedy when the Almighty drowned quadrillions of joyous things—man, tree, and flower—and changed the earth's romantic face *for a mere undivided, bayless, lakeless, sheet of water ;* on the bosom of which rode but a solitary vessel ; with a *strange* sort of captain, crew, and passengers! on a voyage so *strange*—and the delugic captain led his craft so *strangely*—not a compass! not a chart! and neither oar, nor sail, nor steam! with a mountain cap for *haven!* pilots? *a raven and a dove!* a quarter deck, but trod by strangers! flying strangers— *the pigeon and the eagle!* . . .

On moves the Ark, month after month, helmless and Zimmermannic! Its band of music ; *such* a band ; playing a requiem! *such* a requiem! . . . it frightens off the neighboring tenants of the deep ; what Babel sounds escape its huge bulk and float over the desert of waters, *as incense and as praise!* Hark! to the flute-like notes of a woman's voice, as it chants for the Almighty to set free the captive and let them once more see the glad earth.

O HUMAN VOICE, thou *broad* creation! thou *fall of cat-*

*aract and dew—moan of the ocean—gurgle of the rill—kiss
to the leper—perfume for the throne!* How it merrily
dances—laughingly leaps—tenderly pleads—skips and
weeps—echoes the hunter's horn and shepherd's pipe—
flutters as first and last breath of life and love—and chimes
in with the Christ-like music of the heart!

Oh Human Voice, thou magic mirror of the memory!
thou witch of Avon and of Calvary! Eternally thy
echoings flit from flower to flower : from Eden into Hell :
from infant to the Great White Throne! I hear voices
from the grave : voices from the rack and Catherine-
wheel : voices from grandest brain artillery! The gill
of death-dust whispers round my night couch, and comes
and goes with my heart's bride—and ancient battling
hosts will laugh and shriek at times—and maniacs speak
of brainal treachery! Ah! sweet Ophelia—silly thing,
with spears of straw for head-dress ; and fragile tree-
bough as thy favorite seat, *that* hung o'er the river's rap-
ids—how thy mad music flies from Avon's side to mine!
So like our crazy Jane's—the talking to one's self—long
stops of silence—rush of medley song—and gush of
dreamy joy—and brush through troops of youthful gaz-
ers and *eyelids big with tears divine.* Are not Compassion's cheeks just like sweet flowers still-ringing voice
of Wrong's Redeemer ? and now the brazen roar of the
lion for its proper lair and prey—the beggarly croak of
the frog for its poorest bed of slime—and the soft, piercing, liquid, and enchantingly delicious pipe of the nightingale, mourning its absence from the thickets, its spring
from bough to bough, and visits to fresh flowers to in-
inspire its song! The ark moves onward.

Music floats off the waters ; music for joy and grief ;
very merry ; very solemn! *Heaven deluges a world and
builds a grand museum!* vast is the artist's power; he wills,

and the giant statue steps from out the rock ; whilst beds
of clay spring into Babel towers ; Rome's mighty arches ;
and portraits (*endless* portraits) of the Homers, Solons,
Ciceros, and such. The Ark saves Shakspeare ; Shakspeare, Banquo's ghost! Some miser saves old Nineveh,
(as throned by Sardanapalus,) and we then save its mate,
in Layard, *curious* Layard!

Chaos ! *vast* chaos ! to the mortal brain and hand and
heart ; when will thy round of mystery withdraw its
veil—from floods and Chinese feet! and *artificial* flowers ; and *pasteboard* crowns ; and lofty spires with *lillipu-
tian* bodies—and *juggerly* done o'er the Saviour's cruci-
fixional wounds, and holy shirt, and mother's picture!
How proudly now looms Calvary the True ! Centurions
ride so *openly* to use the spear! and thieves *stand up*
like thieves! and but the *bodies* of the victims perish!
whilst *counterfeits* but *skulk* behind *the pillars of the
Church*, and strike the poor, benighted *minds of multitudes!* How oft, John Milton, I do sit with thee, (thou
noble student of Creation and Creation's Will,) and yet,
like thee, am *blind !*

Boundless doth seem the maze we tread—its tracts, its
symbols, and fantastic ceremonies! Its needless works,
ridiculous works, unrighteous and unhealthful works!
Fast fall the leaflets thro' the rottening trunk ! At every step
we meet impostors that insult our reasoning faculties by
the grave assurance that they are Christ's deputies to
bring us into the only *narrow* way that leads to and into
the Gates of Paradise, and up to the spotless and eternal
presence of the Kings of Kings !

Antiquated! antiquated! is the present throne of Man.
Caverns have been dug therein, exposing columns of
stone, found just like giant trees with vines bound round
them, and branches spreading to a *banyan* breadth! and

noble gothic arches, basket groinings and pendants, and flying buttresses, and charmingly carved capitals, done by the branch or trunk and the entwisting leaves. Hah! what *divinely* sculptured foliage. And these caverns were once guarded by monster sentinels, and owned by monster lords : for there yet stand therein, colossal shapes of serpents and wolves, birds, dragons, and fish, all strange to the present time ; and the impressions of lizards' coats, tree barks, and birds' beaks and talons, are still as sharp as the arisses of a finely wrought gem :

The Lord God, as well as Charlemagne, builds the palace *underground!* and often scoops the tomb of a wild Indian or his dog, *far* more magnificently than we for the Emperor—tombs of immense range, and with the never-fainting music of the water-drops tumbling in stormless lakes. What ceilings have these tombs—*these grandest mausoleums!* See the thousand flying arches! how varied ; how harmonious! and all incrusted with forests of stalactites and skillfully entwisted spiracles! What crypts and canopies ; and aisles and altars ; fonts and spandrils! What wreathed columnar work ; and stalks and dripstones ; and paneling so like the Persian ! *Eccentric* is the round of life. One lovely child dies out shark-broken and shark-eaten ; whilst another departs as gently as *the unravished flower,* and to be (as in kingly families, in oriental lands,) carefully laid away in a sarcophagus costing thousands, in a mausoleum costing millions ; the coffin, of fairest marble, being wreathed and overwreathed with flowers, that only breathe and dance and bloom *unnaturally !* Whilst the tressels, of ebony, are ablaze with their jeweled inlay : censers, of silver, are ever lit and swung ; and the great carved hatchments glow with the *pride of ancestry* for the mere accident of fathering the atom of dust within.

Why, reader, I've often seen human faces and hearts and consciences *turned into stone*—and borne about as trophies of Earth, and trophies of Heaven, and trophies of Hell! *the stony look, the stony laugh, the stony will, the stony faith, the stony gait—and epitaphs nothing* but *stone! stone tongues and stone lies—stone banners and stone warriors —and stone wives, children, saints, shields, swords, and lace —and a vast, vast sum of stony language—and stone images that laugh at Death, by proxy, and weep like paid weepers, and plumes that nod from the hearse top!*

There is a duality in all things—of the passions, thoughts, will, and action. So God creates what man destroys, and man creates what God destroys ; and the dualitic play is so vast, so complicate, that it is not wonderful that both parties often *falter* in the race of creation and of life, and run shock against the statue and the thousand-rooted tree ; burst the heart's bands ; and rock the brain into an artificial or death-like sleep! The sage needs this rocking as well as the infant : the heavens as well as the earth : the spirit as well as the body !

Man often shifts his glass eccentrically ; he builds up a family and social throne, simply to see them tarnish and crumble—the wife, the child, and friend, to bloom and wither, (physically, mentally, or morally,) and vanish away in their graves crowded with ugly phantoms! Man retails misery and joy ; God wholesales them. The best joys of man are ephemeral, and cost much close watching. There is no earthly love perfectly pure, save that of a mother for her child, *that most brilliant spot on the mortal brow!* Sexual love is selfish. Patriotism is selfish. Fashionable Christianity is monstrously selfish : and many a richly-habited priest is Satan in mask, and *the archest of all hypocrites!* Mortal bliss *too often* flourishes from out the blackest pools—the pools of folly,

crime, and treachery. Simplicity and Truth are too un-
spicy for the debauchee! When Ambition seeks victory,
Victory seems a heaven ; but Victory won, instantly fades
into nothing, *just like the finger-touched clouds!* By
itself, what is the columnar plynth ? but join it to its
shaft and cap, and then the trio from the noble harp *in
tune.*

Suddenly, yet slowly, the Almighty threw into ruin
the Earth's objects of Nature and Art, expanded by two
thousand years ; the blade of grass perishing with the
royal bride, the babe with grandsire! Mourn we may,
but the *aim* of the mighty and terrific *execution* buries
itself away in the Sealed Book. Picture after picture we
may paint—pictures of the plague ; and starving city,
with triumphal entry by the rosy conqueror—but the
Great Birth Giver of these grandest subjects? How he
veils himself away in the exquisite brightness of the divine glory! Wonder we may : as men make horses un-
limb men ; and Herods war with infants ; and Austria,
in her market-place, unclothes a noble woman, and lacer-
ates her inoffensive, heaven-stamped form! Yet wonder
more, when worlds get wrecked, and have to act as chief
Laocoön!

So the higher we fly the more we flare—whilst Vernet,
with philosophy, takes laurel after laurel, as soldier sa-
bers soldier—and Rubens, as he keeps afresh the ugly,
rankling spike-thrusts in the Saviour's feet! And so with
heads struck off fair women and brave men—the Neys—
and Lady Grays, those *wildest of Morning Glories, folding
their leaves at noon !*

Thus painter's pencil's fed ; and bowls of anguish
shift to cups of nectar ; and blackest soil yields bright-
est flowers! Delight, and Art, and Awe, and Terror, and
the grimmest Agony, all join like sisters! The skirm-

ishing of the clouds, and their mightiest shock and roar of artillery, and swift-winged, silver lightning strikes the temple and the infant; all join (like angels) with their God-thrown Signet Arch, and smallest blade of grass bending beneath its crystal diadem—an *Atlas shoulder-ing his Globe!*

The statuary's works are a part of the statuary; the chemist's the chemist: and God is just as inseparable from his own handiwork! *The lion is God, and God is the lion!* All works (heavenly and earthly) have their dross. *"There is no heaven without a cloud."* The grandest aim of Man is *the elevation of the standard of his race, physically and intellectually.* Court gladness, and shun grief. Never fret over the errors of the past, but regard them simply as the dross of life, and monitors of the future. *The grossest abusers of life are the voluntary penance doers.* Truth, charity and sincerity are divine characteristics; cleanliness and sobriety, cardinal vir-tues. Man (*individual*) is a trifling thread, yet inter-woven interminably throughout all creation's woof—an imperishable jewel in a perishable casket, *to be shifted and shifted as casket after casket perishes, yet eternally form-ing a ray in the glory of Heaven!* No mother's love, nor daring sympathy, nor wonderful abnegation of self can *die*—they are utterly imperishable, and *radiative thro' an infinity of space and time.* The casket perishes, *not* the jewel—and when such casket is unworthy of its contents, the separation is just and should be gladly met; and the merits of such mother's love and sympathy should be pleasurably relinquished from our own *narrow* protection unto that as broad, pure, brilliant and never fading *as is* Jehovah's! * * * *

THE CRUCIFIXION OF CHILDREN.

CRUCIFIXION OF CHILDREN BY THE ROUTINE SYSTEM OF EDUCATION—THE NATURAL CAPACITY CAN ONLY BE KNOWN BY THE STUDY OF THE TEMPERA- MENT—EVIL EFFECT OF CRUSHING THE WILL—THE SENTIMENT OF OMNIPO- TENCE—WILL MAKES THE MAN.

THE *reäctive life-force* is variously designated, whether in a spirit of recognition or condemnation, as *self-poise* and *self-will, combativeness* and *contrariness, firmness* and *obstinancy*, etc.

Personality may be accepted as a more integral defini- tion than the preceding terms, which only apply to some particular manifestation of it. Without much ratiocina- tion, sagacious managers instinctively appreciate and avail themselves of the laws inherent to passional forces. They often ensure the conduct which they desire by sug- gesting its opposite. They play a game of passional billiards, and calculate the composition of forces, respect- ing the will of another, as an elastic body on which the impact of their own will, if direct, can act only as an ex- ternal disturbing force to be repelled, on the principle that reäction is the echo of action, and the angle of reflection to the angle of incidence. Thus I have recalled smiles to the cheeks of my little favorite Emma when on a stormy day it also stormed within her sympathetic organism, for she and the elements were play-fellows.

But when, unheeding her mamma's remonstrance, I took her to the outside door, and opening, launched her forth into the flood descending, then she presently perceived that she was not quite a little duck, and came in surprised but calmed, and cured of inconvenient elemental sympathies for the rest of that day at least.

There is a radical falsity in all systems of education, whether intellectual or moral, based on the blind and forced obedience of child or pupil to the mandate of another will—relatively an external and disturbing force. The working of such system, in proportion as it really takes effect upon the life of its subject is, first, to paralyze the volitional principle, as in case of the phenomenon called psychologizing, biologizing or hypnotism, and to which the Jesuits have given an enormous extension in the discipline of their order, (see *Wandering Jew*, case of Hardy.)

In other cases, and indeed often combinedly with this passivity, we find an alternate evolution of hypocrisy, perfidy, mean selfishness or tyranny over inferiors in those thus educated, as a perverted and incomplete vital reäction from a long experience of constraint and fear.

Education in the despotic order, means the subjugation of individual wills and faculties in unquestioning submission to the established authority, which always pretends to be of divine origin. The aim of such education is to make of the people passive tools, a flock to be fleeced; burden-bearing animals in the service of a privileged aristocracy, clerical and secular. It is the celebrated *Vos non vobis* of Virgil.

> Ye birds, not for yourselves built nests;
> Ye oxen, not for yourselves plough furrows;
> Ye sheep, not for yourselves bear fleeces."

The Roman Catholic Church makes vital to the salvation of the souls of their proselytes, the "abnegation of judgment ;" she requires the blind acknowledgment of her creed. In her discipline it is of the first necessity to suppress free thought, to extinguish originality, to emasculate passion, to make machine men and women by the crushing and drilling of Routine. Routine is the keynote, the watch-word, the magic spell of slave-making and slave-ruling societies. The philosophical formula of this popular education, is the subordination of the *me* to the *not me;* of personality to authority, of reason to faith, of sentiment to interest, of volition to habit. Its mainspring is constraint, alike physical and moral, its *vis a tergo* is the lash, its last recourse punishment ; its sentiment is fear, its result passive obedience. No free gymnasia for such a people ; let its shoulders be rounded under the burdens of repugnant toil ; no free and daring evolution of the intellectual faculties ; let them passively receive the authority of the past ; paralyze them by inaction or stultify them with compulsory tasks ; let memory alone survive ; fill it with dead knowledge, with the musty trash of schoolmen, with solemn inanities that time has consecrated ; so that the useless man of learning may be a byword and a reproach among the people, and their ambition be deterred from ever arousing the lion that crouches on the threshold of eternal Truth. As to the spiritual passions, modern morality and religion will take care of them, and that so effectually that they shall be ashamed of their own names, and promiscously confounded with the morbid emotions, such as anger, envy, hatred, fear, lust, or cupidity, provoked by their compression or perversion.

Divine in their essence, they shall become infernal in their manifestation. No man shall dare to confess them, the very words passion and passional shall excite a hue and cry, and hypocrisy shall reign supreme under the ægis of morality. If it be true that possession is nine points of the law, then has despotic education an immense advantage over free and liberal education ; for the first exists, while the second is for us as yet a theoretic abstraction, preëxisting only in the aspirations and intuitions of the child, the lover, the mother, and the true philanthropist. While constraint is organized and sustained by the force of habit, of numbers, of clerical and secular interests ; attractional and instinctive development is but the happy accident of a sparse population in fine climates, or the privilege of the enlightened great, or the voice of Jesus in converse with the lily.

The constitution of our republic pretends to guarantee the right to life, liberty and the pursuit of happiness, to all who are not born chattel slaves.

But this pretension is fallacious, and so must remain until those who are intrusted with the education of our childhood regard it as their chief duty to discover the industrial vocations and aptitudes of young people, to provide them with attractive and useful occupations, to second with delicate zeal the development of each genius, and to remove those barriers, whether accidental or artificial, which may obstruct personal liberties. Still farther, it is necessary to enter the sphere of emotional or social life, to discover and appreciate those affinities of character and action which make the charm of social relations, and to promote them by every possible means. As yet, we are far from enjoying even the negative liberty of being let alone or left to our own resources. Besides our numerous population of chattel and wages slaves, the whole class of children and minors is liable to oppression, and is habitually oppressed by their parents, teachers, and elders. It is not meant as oppression, but as a necessary control. It is so to a certain extent. In the

absence of the proper material arrangements and social
stimuli, children cannot be allowed to dispose of their
own time, or to do what they please, because they would
not find the *motives* prompting them to do right, but on
the contrary, would pervert to mischief and destruction
the forces intended to serve in the useful evolution of
their faculties and passions. It remains so much the
more indisputably true, that the whole class of children
and minors are obstructed in the exercise of their liberties, that their personal spontaneity is outraged by physical and moral tyrannies, and that each step of their
emancipation, from the letting out of school at noon or
evening, to the final epoch of their majority, is anxiously
looked forward to, while the representatives of moral
authority are generally regarded by them with a certain
degree of odium.

Is it indeed a small thing to resign one's liberty among
the woods and streams, with all the fascinations of the
gun, the fishing-rod, the sail-boat, ball, kite, top, hurly,
and athletic games; our favorite occupations of farm-
work, the interesting cares of the barn-yard, of the flower-
garden, of the orchard; our observations on the natural
history of birds, squirrels, rabbits, and other wild creatures, our researches on the physical construction of
mills and mill-dams, our delight in the first handling of
tools in the work-shop, and all the manifold charms of
initiation into the physical sciences and useful arts, to
which Nature powerfully urges, as to the essential purpose and fruition of our restless and curious childhood?

Is it a small thing to compress the bounding spirit of
youth, to bury life under books at the epoch of its most
intense and exquisite susceptibilities for active enjoyment, in the liveliest play of those sympathies with Nature on which the incarnation of the soul here rests?

What a woeful fall from the elementary lessons of the sunbeam and the thunder-storm to stereotyped text-books and arbitrary methods invented by stupidity for the torture of mind, confounding all aptitudes under a common rule, and expecting the same tasks memorized in the same way by every child in the class! Is it a small concession to apply one's self, for six or eight hours, at an uncomfortable desk, with a hard seat, often too high, without a back, and perhaps as many more hours out of school, to abstract lessons, the subjects of which are foreign to our personal instincts, and which are too seldom made pleasing either by the manner in which they are taught, or by our love for those who teach them? and all because we are told that it is our duty, and that we shall be punished if we neglect them!

And it is in order to be thus crucified in their bodies and in their souls, that children are sent away from their homes and from all they love best, to be kept among strangers at a boarding-school. Yet this is but a slight and superficial view of the galling fetters with which we manacle childhood. Embittered by constraint, mad-dened and perverted in their instinctive life by this incessant tyranny, children complete among themselves, by quarrels and persecutions, the ruin of many a fair and hopeful spirit. At last the long-desired epoch of major-ity arrives, or at an earlier age the *privilege* is accorded of choosing our own course of life, of fighting on our own hook. Any one of the trades or professions, from the humblest mechanical art up to the highest branches of commerce and politics, demands of the youth a new apprenticeship, and now it becomes necessary for him to die to theoretical abstractions and transcendental morali-ties, in order to be born again into "the business world," into the world of facts.

How has the education of the schools prepared him for this initiation? Why, just at that period when his perceptive organs were most fresh, active, and impressible, when nature playfully led him from object to object, teaching him in three years a greater number of new facts than the hardened brain of the adult can acquire in thirty years, while he was thus in pure amusement laying the foundations of practical knowledge broad and firm, and appreciating the qualities of persons and things around him, this was the happy moment chosen by Education for locking him up in the school-room, as if the more effectually to prevent the exercise of his observing faculties; and there condemning the lower and first developed plane of perceptive organs overlying the orbits, to inaction; it calls on Analysis and Comparison, to master the subtle abstractions of grammar, and exhausts the memory by premature fatigue over tasks for which it has failed, nay, it has not even aimed to inspire the slightest interest. As a natural consequence, the bright original minds which cherish the sentiment of their independence, are disgusted, shirk their tasks, and turn towards frivolities and mischief, while the more passive and obedient, with those who have by organization an already almost morbid tendency to isolation and abstraction, are effectually vitiated by a system which cultivates Greek roots instead of elementary science, and scans Latin verses instead of making the child himself a poet in life and action. The superior plane of organs, which in the natural course of things comes into full vigor and activity only at a later period when the observer becomes the combiner and mechanist, having been deprived of that store of observations and practical expedients which its operations require, is necessarily turned aside from matter and practical realities, to ideas and verbal abstractions,

and thus it is clear why discoverers and great mechanists
are almost entirely men of the people, who have received
little school education, while we so seldom see the distinguished graduates of our colleges ever become distinguished in the sphere of practical life.

But were the acquisitions in real and useful knowledge
which are made in our schools as great and valuable as
they are actually trivial, in consideration of the time and
labor bestowed, still they would poorly compensate for
that original force which is paralyzed as soon as the
method of another mind is arbitrarily imposed upon our
own.   The unknown is greater and more important than
the known ; hence the genius for original discovery is
more important than a stereotyped familiarity with that
knowledge which is already common property.

Will, more than aught else, makes the *man ;* its potency
gives the measure of his manhood, and attests his affinity
to the order of spiritual powers.   What then is to be
said of a system whose primary maxim and effort is to
crush the will of its pupil, and to subject it implicitly
and unquestioningly to the will of the master?   What is
this but to cripple the evolution of the soul which asks
only to justify its divine paternity in each individual
child ?

Among the many ill effects of accustoming the mind to
surrender itself passively to the rules of an effete and
antiquated system of education, of crushing the present
under the burden of the past, and accustoming the soul
to look backward for its guidance, is that of intellectual
and moral cowardice.   Men educated in the schools dare
not reason for themselves, nor exert their powers of discovery in new spheres.   Yet the analytic faculty and that
of discovery are the most valuable of all.

Every attainment of the past ought to be made the

subject of a discipline to the faculty of discovery in those who learn it. Dr. Wells's researches on Dew, for instance, lend themselves admirably to such a discipline. Under the guidance of a judicious teacher, his experiments may be repeated, and the pupil's mind led along the whole train of discovery as far as science has yet reached, when it will be prepared, by a logical habit of thought and the confidence it has acquired in itself, to proceed and advance the conquests of science into unknown spheres. The laws of gravity, the sphericity of the earth, all the prominent phenomena of science may be easily re-discovered by a child, with a little skillful guidance from the teacher. An immense source of pleasure in education would thus be developed.

No features of a true education is more striking than its culture of the sentiment of Omnipotence! This Nature bestows in full measure on the young child, whose prophetic soul has no hesitation in claiming whatever attracts him, be it the moon, a butterfly, a dagger, or his father's nose; no apprehension of any limit to his possessions or to his authority over nature and society. His cries subdue father and mother and all the family to do his will, more effectually than any government has ever enforced its dictates upon the people.

This universality of desire, tending to integral exploration and conquest, distinguishes man from other animals more remarkably even than the fact that he is a featherless biped that uses tools and fire, drinks whisky and smokes tobacco.

The desires of animals are evidently limited to a small class of objects within the particular sphere of each. These attained, they are contented and make no progress or change. This seems to be true even of the bee and the ant, which show in their works, in some re-

15

spects, a hundred times more wisdom than man has yet done.

The sentiment of omnipotence needs to be gently modified by a culture which, from early childhood, shall artfully substitute the obedience of things for that of persons, and teach the means of obtaining this obedience by our sciences and arts. The intellect, working through natural laws, thus gradually realizes conquests quite as remarkable as those ascribed in the history of miracles to the simple command of the ancient prophets. The germinal instinct of power, thus developed by a practical education, ripens into self-reliant energy, and gives immense and magnificent results by the originality of thought and the intensity of will. But how shall we curb this will or direct it into its proper channel of action? The adaptations of a well-ordered nursery exclude from the notice of children whatever it would be dangerous or improper to trust them with, while they amply satisfy the sensuous and social wants by a special providence, up to the point at which the faculties of the child are sufficiently developed to become the successful ministers of his own will. Then amid the new, and to him gorgeous charms of the miniature work-shops and apparatus for arts and culture, his curiosity is awakened and he is amused by procedures which presently, in imitation of children a little older than himself, he employs to obtain what he seeks—here is the great safety-valve, the target against which he may shoot at will.

From the hour when a child *mechanizes*, the desired transition is effected. Then gradually, by a kind of second weaning, the personal obedience and aid of adults is withdrawn, and tools substituted, with instruction in their use. This throws him on his own resources, and leads him to extend the whole vehemence of that volition

with which he has hitherto controlled parents and
nurses, upon the matter on which he works, and in the
studies by which he learns to operate successfully.   Thus
from the first, the omnipotent child acts out from his soul,
and continues his incarnation by the extension of himself
into exterior forms.   Instead of this, the soul-murder of
our actual system begins by breaking his will—lever of
all future conquests.   It undermines self-reliance by
teaching the child how weak he is ; it dissipates all his
precious illusions ; it refuses him the satisfaction of
those desires which surrounding objects perpetually excite, and teaches him no means of obtaining them.   On
the contrary, it inculcates the moral precepts of self-
denial, such as, that little boys and girls must not have
everything they want.

After being refused the obedience due to infancy, by
parents and nurses, our unfortunate child grows up in
practical ignorance, and in privation of the miniature
work-shop, tools and examples of other children an age
more advanced, whose successes and privileges will be to
the little discoverer what the laurels of Miltiades were
to Themistocles of Athens, who could not sleep for emulation until he had equally distinguished himself.   Baf-
fled in the development of this industrial instinct, he is
at last prepared for that stupid system of abstractions
and text-book memorizing which is to fill his youth with
disgust, while withdrawing him from all chance of contact with his natural and practical teachers ; for the
first requisite of a teacher, is that he be the person spon-
taneously sought by the child.

In the absence of a general organization of social labor
and art with which true education is inseparably related,
the child's freedom of choice must be exercised within
comparatively narrow limits either as regard pursuits or

teachers ; but the parent who ignores a deep-seated disgust to a teacher, ignores a right implanted by nature, and one which must be respected, if we truly desire the child's health of soul. A teacher hated by a pupil is a perpetual provocation to deceit and falsehood.

Now what wonder after our Casperhauserizing of children, suppressing Nature's kindly work, and perverting the mind by false directions into the labyrinth of moral, philosophical, and theological futilities, without ultimation in any practical use, what wonder is it that our colleges turn out feeble and good-for-nothing creatures, or else rebels, prepared, by their disgust at our moral precepts, for a career of violence and fraud?

FASHIONABLE DRESS:

ITS INFLUENCE ON THE HEALTH AND DIGNITY OF WOMAN.

Our object, in reviewing the circulation, and construction of the heart and lungs in the lower tribes of animals, has been to show the continuity of the chain by which nature gradually reaches the perfection of a double and independent circulation for the appropriation of the great life-giving element ; and that where the Almighty guards with such jealous care, even in the lower ranks of creation, the process by which the great end is attained, man may well pause and wonder at his presumption in impeding its progress. How should we look upon the usages of society and the false taste of woman in trying to shut out by the murderous trickery of dress, the beneficence of Heaven, in supplying air to paint her lips with coral, and to add soul and expressiveness to her eyes, and softness to the hands, and fullness to the breasts with which she is to nourish the infant, so curiously and wonderfully supplied with her blood? What truth in physiology is better known, than that which assures us that the minute arteries that color the lips and add clearness to the skin, derive their life-force from the air? Fainting, which is a temporary partial suspension of the power of the heart and lungs, makes the hands and the countenance livid ; and if it continue too long, it passes into death. Partial filling of the lungs, which is all that is ever required or ever allowed by almost every pursuit of fashionable life, is only a degree of the same state that occurs in fainting. Only look at the position of a fashionably-dressed woman, sitting in her rocking-chair, embroidering ; see the approximation of her arms, and the bent neck and body. The chest containing the lungs has to sustain the whole weight of the head and arms ; they hang upon it almost like pieces of dead flesh ; the intestines are forced down upon the womb, and the great bloodvessels that supply the limbs are compressed. There is the beautiful spine, superbly arched by the Great Artist, with its exquisitely-arranged and graceful curves, to bring the centre of gravity between the feet, the very line of beauty, its unmatched and unequalled elastic substance between each bone to take off the shock of every step, the collar-bones to keep the arms apart and to allow the lungs full play, and to show the beauty of the breast and throat, with beautiful and grand muscles on the back to keep back the shoulders—the whole woman—" a dream of Eden when the world was young ;" and look, only look at the best results of Fashionable Society. Great Heaven ! Spirits of Guido and Raphael, do ye behold her ? Shades of Hunter and Bell, do not your bones rattle in your graves at the spectacle ? Such respiration ! with the lungs poisoned and irritated by the flocculi filling the atmosphere of the parlor, and the rank and stifling smell of a "magnificent" velvet carpet, filled with dust for the simple reason that it cannot be swept away ; the light of heaven shut out by blinds and curtains, will stifle three quarters of the natural demand for air, exercise and food ; it will congest the hands and eyelids, rob the colorless blood-vessels that nourish the window or pellucid cornea of the eye and give it its

sparkling lustre, and the skin its fairness, make the
finger-nails blue, take away the inclination and muscular
power to hold up the head and keep the shoulders back,
constipate the bowels, by robbing them of their secretions
and the constant motion imparted by a full supply of air
to their muscular coat, and make the whole woman a mere
half-vitalized machine, fit only to give the sickly replies
of mental inanity to the insulting twaddle she expects to
receive from the male fool that sits before her. This is
the actual condition of almost every fashionable woman
in this city, and it is brought about mainly by want of
exercise ; she is unable to take it from the construction
of her dress, and the slavish adherence to fashion ; indeed she does not dream of its necessity ; she feels the
wretched lethargy that presses with leaden weight upon
her soul ; she knows that the glad earth is full of music,
of love and happiness ; her smothered instincts tell her
she ought to share them, but a cold and monotonous
conventionalism threatens her with ostracism if she dare
allow a ray of nature to warm the generous impulse into
life. Great God! when I look upon the beautiful and
fair faces of my countrywomen, as they move before me
like so many automata, under the iron despotism of that
bloodless and sickly thing called fashion, my soul is sick
at the spectacle, and I am glad to escape into the forest
where I can see the wild bird hymning the praises of its
Creator, and listen to the unchecked murmur of the
winds, and the leaping of the dancing rivulet ; and when
I return to the duties of life, I look from my window
upon the little spot of verdure a city prison allows me,
and I hear the murmur of the bee, and see the little
humming-bird sipping the nectar from the honey-suckle,
my heart yet leaps with childish delight as the lovely little creature swings upon the branches ; I return to my

task, and feel that if I had the eloquence and benevolence
of Christ, I could spend my life in no better cause than
attempting her instruction in the laws of her being, and
showing her how beauty and truth, love and simplicity
are inseparably connected with the sublime science of
life.

LINES,

DEDICATED TO THE EDITOR.

Work!—while bright daylight on thy path is beaming—
        Work while 'tis day :
    Despair not thou, although thy task is seeming
        To last alway.
    Trust! when the dusky shadows o'er thee flying,
        Obscure the sun.
    Though Duty's task is ended but by dying,
        Let it be done!

Work!—while bright daylight on thy path is beaming,
        Though not for gold—
    Fame proves a phantom, and our idle dreaming
        Is a tale that's told ;
    But cherish ever with a grand emotion,
        A zest for strife !
    Our earthly birthright in this wild commotion,
        This threefold life.

Work!—while bright daylight on thy path is beaming,
        For night palls down.
    Work! while the lustre in thine eye is gleaming,
        To win the crown.
    Work with thy hand, and with thy many talents,
        Ay, with thy soul ;
    Thy threefold life weighed in eternal balance,
        Demands the whole.

HOTEL PRACTICE IN NEW YORK—AN INFER-
NAL ABUSE.

"He was a stranger and we took him in."

THE abuses of our profession demand the eye of Argus, and the arms of Briareus. If father Jupiter paid that old coon for guarding Io no better than our brethren pay us for watching over their characters, we don't wonder Apollo has given so large a number of them to the devil. It would seem that "respectable gentleman in black" (we think our brethren have selected a most appropriate color for their dress) has given them special counsel in getting up the system of practice at present pursued in the "Hotel Practice" of our city. The cookery and ventilation in these "magnificent establishments," together with the refined and fastidious palates of a large portion of the travelling public, afford uncommon facilities for practice upon their bodies and their pockets. The physician who has given a philosophical glance at the valiant trenchermen engaged at their suppers on board a North River steamboat, and then, after fortifying his stomach with a glass of brandy-and-water, and his nose with a piece of camphor, descended into that "inferno," the lower cabin at midnight, has had a practical idea of the facilities for "Hotel Practice." On board the boat, the patient spends but one night; at the hotel usually several; he is generally ready for practice by the third night, when the operation commences. Nine out of ten

15*

of the cases of sickness at these places are cholera mor-
bus, demanding no more than a purgative, with a little
laudanum, or tinct. hyosciamus, fresh air, and a little
light soup; but getting considerably more, as you shall
see. The modern discoveries in "Hotel Practice" may
be of service to our country readers; if editors will give
the hint, they will probably get no drinks gratis when
they come to the city.

A violent pull at the bell summons the porter, who is
requested to bring a doctor immediately; he may possibly be asked to bring a gentleman of character; 'tis all
one, however, he has received his cue from the bar-
keeper, between whom and the doctor there is "an arrangement." He assures the gentleman, in the midst of
his writhings and groans, that Dr. Snooks is one of the
first medical men in the city, whose skill has often been
tested in the house; the Esculapian is summoned, and
is soon at the bed-side. The sick man being in an admirable condition to acknowledge sympathy, receives it
in abundance, and at suitable intervals a few calomel
pills, and occasional reminders of the necessity of "doing
something" at a lower portion of his intestinal tract.
He is regaled at suitable intervals with a joke, a little
laudanum, and peppermint or camphor, with a few drops
from a wonderful little bottle, which the doctor takes
from his side pocket; he is learnedly informed that the
"primæ viæ must be cleared out." This is very satisfactory, and convinces him of the doctor's intelligence.
The window is judiciously closed, for fear of his "taking
cold." The doctor endures the poisoned atmosphere,
which has mainly produced the attack, by the aid of an
occasional escape and visit at the bar, or a drink from
his pocket pistol, and a walk in the hall. Toward morning, if nature be merciful, and the pills be retained,

relief follows. If the patient were now let alone, and could get a little fresh air, some clean and simple meat broth, and the attention of a mother, a wife, or a sister, he would be out next day ;—but this is no part of our philanthropist's plan ; it wouldn't pay house-rent and horse-keep, and servants' hire. He is therefore well dosed for three days, to overcome " the tendency to inflammation of the bowels ;" mustard plasters are liberally used, and he may thank heaven if he escapes leeching and blistering. When he evinces a disposition to bolt, and relates his former experience in a similar case, where he was not so fortunate as to meet with any one but his poor country doctor, (who, of course, knew nothing, and had only one old horse, and neither rent nor servants to pay,) he is frightened with tales of the "epidemic condition of the air in the production of dysentery, and several severe cases now under treatment," etc. etc., with the story of Mr. So-and-so, who "was doing very well till he insisted on going home, where he speedily died," etc. etc. Another week's treatment with tonics, is the consequence of this rascality, and a bill of $50 or $75, per centage to the bar-keeper off.

Those who come to the city with chronic diseases, desiring to submit to the treatment of some gentleman previously selected, generally escape this miserable rascality ; by no means, however, without hints and innuendoes of the superior skill of their favorite physician, who may, however, never in his life have seen or treated such a case as the one at hand. There is not a practical man in this city, of any character, who is not perfectly aware of the truth of this exposé, and we most earnestly hope this statement will be extensively copied. Our editorial friends could not better serve the cause of humanity. More of this anon.

MEDICAL EXPERIENCES.

BRANDY AND TOBACCO, COFFEE, OPIUM AND TEA—WHY HAS NATURE PRODUCED
THESE ARTICLES?—ARE THEIR INFLUENCES WHOLLY EVIL?—DO THEY SERVE
SOME PURPOSE IN NATURE?

MAN's history in connection with the narcotics and
stimulants is most singular and instructive. It is not
probable that the presence of these various articles in
the vegetable kingdom is an accident : we do not believe
that anything in nature comes by accident ; all God's
works have their cause, their object and end ; and that
tea, coffee, tobacco, alcohol and opium have their design,
is a fact so palpable that none will deny it ; for to deny
the operation of a benevolent cause in all the phenomena
of the universe, is to fling the works of creation into the
whirlpool of chance.

Tea is an article of universal consumption by whole
empires of men ; and in the currents of commerce it
floats to every part of the universe ; not a continent or
an island is without it, and it is consumed by hundreds
of millions of people daily. It acts upon our social qualities, and the female in particular is rendered social and
talkative by its use. It is the balm of all headaches,
pains, ills, and sorrows, and unless used in excess, none
are aware of any baneful effects from its use. It seems
not to disturb our animal nature, but is the reverse of
alcohol in its effects in this particular. The universal

instinct which causes its use in civilized life is not well understood.

Coffee is not as universally used as tea, and is more confined to southern climates. The Arab loves it ; its use is universal among the sons of the Desert. All civilized nations use it ; but the savage man does not incline to it as a beverage. Its effects are exhilarating and delightful, and it acts like tea on the social faculties, but never to any great extent disturbs the grosser passions of our race. In excess it weakens the nervous system by over stimulus, and induces a premature decay in the nervous powers. In the blood it acts as a chemical agent more potently than tea. It is more used in warm than in cold climates.

Tobacco has run a most remarkable career, having reduced to its sway two-thirds of the human race ; its effects are eagerly sought by the civilized and savage man, and its pestilent fumes scent the palace and the wigwam. The Russian, the German, the Hindoo and the savage both chew and smoke it. It sets up a constant chemical action in the blood, and weakens the nervous energies by excessive action. As the sexual organs constitute the final object of our creation, and they are only controlled by the spinal nerves, its depressing action in their region is peculiarly manifest. It blunts the passions and dulls the mental powers. No man ever wrote a good poem or speech under its influence.

Alcohol is the child of the Arab, and that strange people use less of it than any other people on the globe who can command it. There is not a savage man on the earth that has tasted but loves it : the American savage, the Negro, the Chinaman, the European, and the American. The dwellers around the Arctic circle love it above all other stimulants, and the Russian, the Circassian and

Tartar are equally fond of it. The German tribes prefer
it in the form of beer, and over the globe it is drank by
all people in whose veins runs the German blood. The
Frenchman and Spaniard prefer their wines and the
brandy made from distillation of the product of the
grape. Its use disturbs the animal passions more deeply than any other beverage, and it rapidly exhausts the
nervous energies. Governments have employed it in
armies and navies ; it has been carried all over the globe
to turn men into brutes and to make them water the
earth with tears. Some organizations are roused to
a high grade of mental enjoyment by its use. The
tongue of some is set in motion, and the dull talker
becomes animated and eloquent ; another gives loose to
mirth, songs and dancing ; but in the end it burns up
the nervous fibre, and the soul no longer has power to
make music on those willing chords ; their songs are
silent, and mirth loses its charms. The savage loves it
because it excites him to deeds of daring and blood. In
the highly organized man it quickens the mental current,
and brings to the surface all the power and vivacity of
the soul. I have known clergymen who always preached
under its influence : it lent wings to prayer, unlocked
the deep fountains of devotion, and called in rapid glance
before the mental vision, in bright array, all the garnered
blessings of the celestial world.

A curious fact in natural history shows the fiery Arab
of the Desert to have played a grand part in the great
drama of God in the earth. He gave to the world a religion which enjoined the worship of the sun and the
hosts of heaven ; it ruled the millions for centuries :
then he founded the Jewish ritual, and evolved a type
of religion that has remained unaltered for three thous-
and years. From this philosophy—exalted by the vis-

ions of the prophets—sprang Jesus, whose precepts have
gone over the earth, finding a response in the bosom of
the most enlightened nations. Then came the Mussul-
man, and with fire, and sword, and alcohol he ravaged
Europe and Asia. The Arab, the dweller in tents, the
"child of the Desert," has given religion to two-thirds of
the world, and furnished the whole with its liquor.

I cannot stop to reason on the results of alcohol among
men as a whole, but barely remark, that among the ruder
nations it weakens and exterminates them ; while among
the higher forms of the race, it goads his passions, sets
him in motion and on fire, and plays in its grand results
an important part in the progress of civilization.

Opium is to the Oriental what alcohol is to the European. It is used throughout Asia ; the Chinese, the
Hindoo, the Japanese, all regard it as a grand catholi-
con, and seek on all occasions to consume and enjoy it.
It impresses deeply the nervous system, and brings out
to the external perception the hidden mysteries of the
human organization. Bright visions float before the
awakened imagination, and dreams whose beauty surpasses the gorgeous scenes of the Elysium, enchant
and ruin the man who yields to its use. It becomes the
"unconscious minister of celestial pleasures," and gilds
its rainbow promise with elysian hopes.

Says De Quincey, "I had taken cold, and procured
some opium, and took the prescribed quantity. In less
than an hour, O heavens! what a revulsion! What an
upheaving from its lowest depths of the inner spirit!
What an apocalypse of the world within me! That my
pains had vanished was a mere trifle in my eyes ; these
negative effects were swallowed up in the immensity of
those positive effects which had opened before me in the
abyss of divine enjoyment thus suddenly revealed. Here

was the panacea for all human woes ; here was the secret
of happiness about which philosophers have speculated
for so many ages, at once discovered ; happiness could
now be bought for a penny and carried in the waistcoat
pocket ; portable ease might be had corked up in a pint
bottle ; and peace of mind could be sent down by the
gallon by the mail-coach."

About one-third of the human race eat opium, and its
deep and terrible effects on the brain, as well as those of
alcohol, bring into direct action certain portions of the
brain, whose activity and powers having been thus
brought into actual existence in the outer world, are
transmitted to posterity. The action of these powerful
stimuli on the nervous mass, evolves new forces, new life,
new thoughts, new faculties, which before were dormant
and unknown ; just as the acid acting on the zinc and
the copper evolves new forces from the metal which till
now were unsuspected. Alcohol acts on the base of the
brain, goading its powers into life, and those forces once
in action, re-act on the moral and intellectual regions of
brain. This view of the results of stimulants does not
preclude the fact, that vast evil may grow out of its use ;
but this philosophy of its effects is the only one that ex-
plains to me the instinct of all men for narcotics and
stimulants. All the forces of nature evolve in their
movements evil as well as good ; the force which rolls
the globe on its axis, may rend nature by an earthquake
and engulph a city. The good effects, if they could be
seen distinctly, even of these vile drinks, would doubtless outweigh the evil ; but as evil is the *outward* and
most glaring result, we are horrified, as we should be, at
the ruin that is wrought by intemperance. We can comprehend fully the evil resulting to a family by an utter
prostration of the parent by stimulants, but we cannot so

easily demonstrate the good effects resulting to individuals
or nations by a happy transmission of mental power by
the pen, to after ages, when such stimulus has reached
its highest point of allowable intensity.   This is a novel
theory, but it is the only one that " vindicates the ways
of God to man " in the permission of such articles as alcohol and opium.   It is more than possible that science
may yet regulate the action of these articles on the human organization, so as to elicit their highest possible
powers, as well as it has regulated the magnetic battery
so as to elicit a current of the highest possible intensity.

SHOTS FROM THE CAVE OF A RECLUSE,

AT THE MEDICAL ANTHROPOPHAGI.

"I had three large axes, and abundance of hatchets; but with much chopping and cutting knotty, hard wood, they were all full of notches, and dull, and though I had a grindstone, I could not turn it and grind my axe too."—ROBINSON CRUSOE.

GLORIOUS old Dan Defoe! whose father, praised be God, was a butcher of Cripplegate, and thereby entitled to our reverence as a practical philanthropist. Like old Dad Shakspeare, the wool carder, neither of ye belonged to a "learned profession," and therefore your children might justly claim the right of instructing their fellows in self-reliance and honesty, and renounce the glorious privilege of professional mendicancy. The inexpressible charm of the living pages of thy Crusoe enchained our youthful fancy, and gave thee the first warm offerings of a young and wayward heart; but the ripened judgment of manhood feels the spirit strengthened to breast the trials of life. Whilst we pore with increasing wonder over the rich treasures of thy magic page, the heart swells with gratitude, and we become reconciled to the mysterious providence of thy persecution—for that, like fire, but refines all it seems to consume. Who shall tell the influence of a Defoe or a Cervantes throughout future ages? What unborn intellects will not be sharpened by their wit—what self-reliance be born of their glorious suggestive power—what hearts be nourished by their virtue and wisdom?

But what, in truth, is there in Crusoe that has not its parallel in the position of every self-relying man? Write a medical quarterly if you would realize the straits of poor Crusoe! Cast your eye over the pages of the medical and miscellaneous press, and then if you are not convinced of the difficulty of winning your readers' attention, try to "turn your own grindstone and grind you axe too." Alas! dear reader, this is a tender point. We told you before, that we had a most feeling conviction of having built our canoe so large we couldn't get it to the water; and now we have "so long been cutting and chopping hard wood to build our fortifications against the medical savages, that our axe is all full of notches, and we can't well turn our own grindstone and grind it too," much less yours; and we have no special reason to suppose you do not require that operation, *i. e.* if we may judge of your capacity by the medical and other journals that seem to delight you so, and the abuses in society to which you so amiably submit. We have been so busy with the medical and surgical anthropophagi, that the few grains of rice and barley that came up, as it were, by the providence of God, at the side of our cave, are well-nigh famished, and we have scarce saved seed enough to try once again the productive powers of the arid soil. But let us be good-natured about our afflictions. Having got up our old grindstone so it will turn, let us try and grind our axe a little ; you may hold yours on at the same time, and we'll try and grind 'em both ; they'll bear it no doubt with benefit.

If you have an eye for the dignity of the Academy, and

its elegant and conservative ethics, we advise you by no means to ruffle your temper with this journal. Seat yourself on the side of a grassy bank in the cool of evening, and observe the graceful dignity with which a venerable gander will take the lead of his progeny, as he goes, with his mate directly behind him, down the side of the bank, into the muddy pool ; every gosling treads precisely in the footsteps of its predecessor, nor would one venture out of the path their sire has trod in for so many years. Excuse me, reader, if I compare you to the goslings, and the gander to some venerable professor who presides at the deliberations of our beloved brethren to whose ministrations you commit your precious bodies. But we have, as you will see, a small hump on the bridge of our nose ; this augurs a combative propensity ; it is the germ of the horn that reaches its highest perfection in the rhinoceros. We greatly affection that animal, for he at least knows how to stand his ground! he is hard to drive ; he should be the type of every reform journalist.

PERCENTAGE ON PRESCRIPTIONS.

Falstaff. When Mistress Bridget lost the handle of her fan,
   I took't it upon my honor thou hadst it not.
Pistol. Didst thou not share ? Hadst thou not fifteen pence ?
Falstaff. Reason, you rogue, reason ; think'st thou
   I'll endanger my soul gratis ?

IF Molière had known as much of the genius of the profession in this city as we do, he might have given a scene illustrative of the high sense of honesty cultivated by some of them, that would make an admirable addition to poor Argan's complaint. Some of our apothecaries, too, would make admirable yoke-fellows for Monsieur Fleurant, and Pistol. Whether they would condescend to the unprofessional employment of "conveying" (see Pistol's correction of Nym, Scene III., Act 1—Merry Wives of Windsor) the handle of a fan, is doubtful. The reader will form his own conclusions, and give us credit for exposing a monstrous abuse of confidence that prevails to a great extent in this city.

It is nothing less than a regular agreement between some physicians and their favorite apothecaries, whereby a certain portion of the price paid by the patient for every prescription, is given to the physician for his patronage ! In some instances this amounts to one half ! and in none we believe is it less than a third ! certain cabalistic signs being appended to the written prescription to show whether the patient will bear a high charge. What the result of this truly demoniacal arrangement must be, we suppose its bare mention will make apparent to the meanest intellect. For fear, however, any one should not understand us, we simply remark, that the more physic they take, the better for the doctor.

We have heard the innocence of the practice defended by some physicians, whose modesty or lack of ability prevented their collecting their fees, and their argument seemed quite satisfactory to their consciences. The thing is done in this ingenious and high-minded manner : Supposing these benevolent gentlemen desire to give the patient an ounce of salts, value sixpence ; this he would take upon the old plan at one draught, dissolved in half a tumbler of Croton water. Now they write it thus : always beginning with the sign of Jupiter, and generally ending in excellent hog Latin ; more especially if the apothecary cannot understand the language ; moreover, they write it in a miserable hand, because that looks learned—and abbreviate each word because their time is valuable.

$$R_{\!\!\!/}$$

> Sulph. Mag.................. ℥ i.
> Aq. Fol. Rosar............. ℥ viii.
> *Initials of Name.*

Now follow the abbreviated Latin directions :—"Cap. coch. mag. quæcun. hor."

This may be hog Latin or not, just as you please ; for by not finishing the words they avoid error. The meaning is conveyed to them by the text of the English book from which they copy it, or they would be reduced to the mortifying necessity of writing their own language.

But what does it all mean ? An ounce of Epsom Salts, and eight ounces of Rose Water : take a large spoonful every hour ;—that's all. But it costs half a dollar ; and if particularly marked, and composed of an additional half cent's worth of coloring matter, and essential oil to give it a higher flavor, (the whole only costing the apothecary seven cents,) why, then it may bring a dollar. The patient being told that it is a very particular and expensive preparation, and that the doctor always gets his medicine more carefully and reasonably prepared at Mr. So-and-so's—innocently swallows the lie, and a dose of medicine every hour, for sixteen hours ; he rarely gets off with less than eight.

This method is applied to an infinite variety of prescriptions ; and we have it on good authority, that a certain venerable gentleman, now deceased, received three thousand dollars a-year! His apothecary told us that he had prepared some hundreds of vials, containing a solution of six ounces of alkaline water, colored with cochineal, for which the doctor paid him two shillings each, and for which he charged each of the poor patients who were treated gratuitously, three dollars, returning the doctor two dollars and seventy-five cents on each bottle ! Ought not this unrighteous and cruel collusion to be exposed? Truly, this is giving a stone for bread, and a scorpion for a fish. Who dare deny that this is done extensively in this city? Reader, suspect the man who denies it, of similar villainy, for they all know it is done. But who are the physicians and who are the apothecaries? Examine their countenances, and their general deportment. These never lie. If you are not skillful in human nature, and suspect your physician, and a " very particular and favorite apothecary of his,"—go to some other than the one directed, of still higher standing for care and skill, and see how the physician receives your disobedience. Never mind his scolding ; you must obey his directions as it regards the administration of the medicine, or you ought not to employ him ; but you have a right to test his honesty in such a matter, particularly if he gives much physic. After you have detected him, it is your duty to report him. The man whom his apothecary betrayed to us was notorious in this city, and such infernal arrangements are still common.

But God forbid we should do harm to the sick ; we would leave no erroneous impressions upon the mind of our readers, with regard to the necessity of the hourly administration of remedies, or even every half, or quarter hour. This is often of such importance, that a failure to obey the directions of the physician in a disease such as pleurisy, or some other acute affection, might be the cause of its gaining such headway as to destroy life. To save the necessity of the lancet, or the reduction of the system by purgatives, in pleurisies and other inflammatory affections, physicians of the highest character for skill and honesty, often give medicines that require to be administered in this way ; therefore it behooves the patient to select a physician of probity and science, and to endeavor to win his confidence by respect and obedience. Such a man will show an interest entirely above all selfish considerations ; his patient will soon perceive, by his friendly and earnest instructions how to preserve health, that the highest gratification he can derive, will be to prevent the necessity of giving any medicine at all. There is nothing impossible in this ; nor do such men suffer in their reputation or pockets ; such men as John B. Beck, Moore Hoyt, Francis U. Johnston, were above such actions, and we will answer for a dozen more in this city. We hope to be the means of increasing the number ; they are not all past saving.

ADVICE

No one has as yet attempted, so far as we have read, the peculiarly disagreeable task of explaining the disadvantages under which people who require medical or surgical advice labor, when they seek it in this city. It is a thankless duty, but one which we are both able and willing to perform. If we have not earned a character for common honesty and plain speaking during thirty-five years' professional and sixteen of editorial life, this article will have no weight with the reader, and we had better have left it unwritten.

From the first two numbers, in January, 1849, we have endeavored to show in the articles, "Who shall Guard the Shepherds," the evil results of colleges, with their close boards of examiners and bought professorships, and diplomas purchased at $25 each. We have proved to the commonest kind of commercial dollar and cent common sense—and heaven knows that is common and mean enough—that anything like a fair examination of their candidates for diplomas, would result in the rejection of four-fifths of those who had paid for their tickets, either with money or promises, and were obliged to pay in good bankable funds for their diplomas. Now it would be simply silly to suppose that these professors would

16

give a conscientious examination, were it even certain that
they themselves were competent to do it : some of them
are, we know, and some are absolutely either below med-
iocrity in their acquirements, or so warped by prejudice
and obsolete theories, as to be utterly unfit to give a
philosophical examination directed to finding out a young
man's reasoning powers, and the probability of his making a safe and studious adviser.   But only look at the evils
of these *close* examining and diploma huxtering shops.
The commercial American is a snob, body and soul—
that is universally admitted.   He can buy a fine house,
a pair of horses, a pew in church, and a season box at
the opera!   He must have a fashionable physician, who
must be a professor, because that settles his *status* as
a physician or a surgeon with the simple public.   His
country friend looks up to him for advice, and dare not
do otherwise than he directs.   He may be a disciple of
homœopathy, allopathy or mesmerism at home, but if he be
so ill as to require more counsel and come to the city, he
must talk with his friends about his ailments ; and now
comes in the whole battery of conceit, pride of opinion
and self-love, to influence the poor distracted brain of
the invalid.   We may be supposed capable of a disinterested estimate of the comparative value of our city magnates.   We know men amongst them whose professional
opinions are perfectly reliable, to whom we never speak
from their social repulsiveness, and we know those who
are peculiarly agreeable, whose opinions are quite beneath contempt.   We know a man whose surgical experience is of the highest character, whose word is utterly
unreliable, when there is a possibility of losing the fee if
he speak the truth.   A man who, in advanced life, would
attempt, with trembling hand, to make an artificial pupil
in the human eye, if the offered fee were tempting enough,

and who denounces his pupils as pretenders. We know
men who will tell the person inquiring that Dr. So-and-
so is not a physician or surgeon, because he does not belong to the Medical Association or County Society, or
the Academy—and yet all those associations are mere
cliques, or trades unions, for securing business, or getting their names in some way before the public once or
twice a year. Catlin, the notorious aider and abettor of
the murderess, Cunningham, is now a member of the
New York Academy of Medicine! and the son of one of
our highest surgical magnates has been up before a
board of inquirers for stealing large quantities of hospital stores of the sick soldiers, and ought to have been
up for bribery in excusing those who expected to be
drafted for their country's service. The most elegant
scholar and refined gentleman we ever possessed, a professor in our oldest city college, the most acute intellect
and sagacious practical mind we ever knew, died in poverty and heart-broken from public and professional neglect. A man who will treat your disease allopathically,
homœopathically or astrologically, employing a "clairvoy-
ant" woman to examine his patients and say where their
disease is located, makes more money and is a more intellectual and agreeable man than any of his brethren in
this city! We are obliged to him personally for several
valuable surgical cases, and we know him to be a profound medical scholar, and are very far from believing
him to be an unsafe adviser. We present him as one
end of the moral scale of medical ethics : he certainly
meets a large portion of the public requirement. Our
own immediate opponents anathematize us as an adver-
tiser, and privately say anything they please about us,
all of which we presume by this time they know to be of
no kind of consequence. We despise the slandering pro-

pensity in all its forms, medical or clerical ; we honor labor, and believe that the debasing influence of politics and trade has seriously impaired our manhood, and produced our present political condition.

The question is, what are our country friends to do when they come here for advice. We honestly advise them to do that most difficult of all things, to shut their mouths and their ears. Choose your adviser, and address him as a gentleman ; do not try to cross-examine him as though he were a thief, and you another. You are quite incapable of understanding him without all your limited powers of attention. Don't try to be "smart ;" don't ask him if he "ever saw or heard of such a case before." If you do, he will think you a conceited, selfish fool. Don't ask him to trust you : if he investigate your case faithfully, remember he does it for the fee. If his opinion be worth having, it is worth paying for. He has always quite as many charity patients whom he knows as he can conveniently attend to. Never continue running to his house at daylight, because the poor man is probably asleep, and he will lose interest in your case if you persecute him and his family. When you have had his opinion, and he has answered your questions, go away : his office is not a saloon for entertainment. Never pick your teeth nor clean your nails when talking to him. If you smoke or chew, do neither in his office, if you wish him to consider you a decent man. Finally, if you come here to consult a mesmerist, an herb or Indian doctor, or an Academy doctor, do it with faith, and do it only ; don't distract your miserable brain with the opinions of others. If you are not a reading and thinking man, if you have no Encyclopædia at home, and must depend upon your own poor judgment or that of a doctor who has no head nor library, and if you believe that the man you are determined to consult can cure you, try him in Heaven's name ; swallow his physic, even if he pour eleven kinds into one tumbler ; he will not probably kill you on the spot, for that would be very foolish ; and these people are always, as Bacon says of the ant, " wise creatures for themselves." They want you to live as long as possible, so that you may take and pay for at least a hundred bottles, perhaps two, and then when death does come you will die happier, because you at least had your own way, and did not get kicked and cuffed into some one else's path who knew no more than yourself. You can do no more than use the brains God has given you, and we have generally noticed those who have the smallest stock, enjoy the uncontrolled use of them with the greatest zest.

THE LIFE FORCE.

"Air is the first and last want of our animal life ;
Our first sigh and last gasp attest its power."—SCALPEL.

MAN is born with a certain amount of life-force, or capacity to live ; this he inherits from one or both of his parents, or from their parents. It often shows itself in early youth or manhood to be of a higher or lower type than that of either parent, when infancy gives no hint of its future degree ; it will be found however that the bodily and mental condition of the mother during gestation, has much to do with the bodily condition and constitutional or life-force of the child she brings forth. The size and beauty of an infant at birth is a good criterion of its intra-uterine condition ; the organic law continues its control whilst the mother is nourishing it with her blood, but the moment it is born, an entirely new and precarious condition surrounds it ; all depends upon the humanity and intellect of its attendants ; its clothing, its food, its mental condition, every moment rests upon the intelligence of its mother ; on her alone depends its existence, and in a great degree its constitution or life-force.

The numerous articles on the organic laws of our

existence, on gestation, nursing and infantile diseases, scrofula and marriage, scattered throughout the twelve volumes of this journal, forbid us to amplify on those subjects in this article ; what we design at present is to show the absurdity of medical treatment in scrofulous diseases, and the necessity of more air, warmth, and food, for those laboring under a defect in the original constitution, or disease ingrafted on the young, by defective nutrition.

The impossibility of treating effectively tubercular or scrofulous affections of the bones, diseases of the hip and knee joints, abscesses and curvature of the spine, and delay in the establishment of the menstrual functions, without pure air and great increase in the quantity of food consumed, is now thoroughly understood by all intelligent people.

Medicine can never add material to the body. It cannot heal an ulcer in the lungs or spine ; it cannot effect the absorption of the tubercles which cause it ; it cannot straighten a curved spine or leg, or give blood to the feeble girl ; nor can the most perfect mechanism impart natural strength or tone to the muscles that support the spine or move the limb. Medicines are generally inert, and too often injurious ; they destroy appetite and digestion, which is the source of strength. Mechanical appliances are only useful adjuvants to take off the weight from the diseased part, and to aid the effect of a surgical operation, or what is far better, to prevent its necessity.

There is no true tonic but pure air ; there is no material of repair but blood. In all diseases originating in a low condition of the vital force, more air must be breathed, that more food may be consumed, or the red blood that makes and gives tone to the muscles that support the spine will not be supplied, the scrofulous tubercle will not be absorbed, nor will the ulcer heal.

All the food that we eat, however varied, whether animal or vegetable, is changed by the stomach and the first division of the intestine into one substance—ALBUMEN ; and yet albumen is the basis of scrofula and tubercular consumption, and the chief cause of spinal ulceration and ulceration of the joints.

A few hours after each meal, all the food consumed is found in the upper intestine, just below the stomach, in the form of a liquid milky substance called chyme ; it spreads over the surface of this intestine, which is covered by a vast number of open-mouthed little vessels called lacteals, because they appear as though filled with milk ; these all concentrate in one small vessel that goes up through the chest, behind the lungs, to the base and on the left side of the neck ; here this single vessel, no thicker than a crow-quill, and carrying every particle of food that we eat in the form of liquid albumen or white blood, now called chyle, as yet unmixed with air, enters directly into the angle formed by the great jugular vein of the left side of the neck, and the principal vein of the left arm ; these two veins unite, and the chyle, thus mingled with the great mass of red blood returning from the body, goes directly into the heart, whence at least two ounces of it is forced into the lungs at every beat of the right cavity of that great hollow muscle, and mingled with the life-giving oxygen. In health, when breathing regularly, the heart contracts and fills the lungs four times to each respiration.

Now the reader will observe that it is only when this blood, thus mingled—white or new blood—as yet containing no oxygen, and old impure purple blood, continually brought back from the body, where it has been performing all its wonderful functions of growth and repair—it is only when this mixed blood and chyle receives *all the air it requires*, that it can acquire and preserve its healthful red color. In consumptive persons, portions of unassimilated chyle or albumen—*i. e.*, albumen not properly mixed with air, are deposited in the tissues of the lungs, which are of course formed and nourished by blood, like all the rest of the body ; these portions of albumen are like small masses of cheese ; they have neither blood-vessels nor nerves, and will in time produce irritation and ulceration like a splinter in the flesh. These tubercular masses are often also deposited in the vertebra of the spinal column, sometimes in the glands of the neck, in the belly and brain, and in the ends of the long bones of the thigh, causing " King's Evil," consumption of the bowels, and tubercles on the membranes of the brain, and white swelling of the joints ; all these diseases are utterly incurable by medicine ; they produce either death or deformity, or loss of the limb.

Had the mixed blood received *all* the air it required, it would have continued the great round or circuit of the heart and blood-vessels, and been used to form all the healthy tissues in the lungs, neck, bones, brain and belly ; no tubercle would have been deposited in any of them. The reader will here please carefully to observe the remarkable fact, that this wonderful little vessel, the chyle-duct, enters at an angle formed by two veins which go directly *into* the heart—the heart is the great engine that supplies the lungs—and not into the angle of two arteries, which vessels carry the pure or aerated blood *out* from the heart to perform its great duties of reproduction and repair all over the body ; *the albumen must first go through the lungs.*

16*

Only see, reader, what a startling proof we derive of the cause of tubercular diseases from the domestic animals ; cows in confinement and fed upon poor and watery food, cats, dogs, confined pigeons, monkeys and parrots, often die of tubercular or scrofulous consumption of the lungs and bowels ; wild ones, when not maimed so as to prevent free exercise and food—never. There is no such thing as tubercle ever found in the bodies of wild birds that are used for food. Their temperature is from four to six degrees hotter than the human body (they fly rapidly and they eat enormously of stimulating grains and animal food,) and from ten to twenty above that of a feeble, pale girl ! We always say when speaking of such a one, " she is lymphatic ;" the lymph (chyle) or albumen, predominates ; she has cold hands and feet ; eats little, and breathes rapidly with only a portion of her lungs.

City life fosters scrofulous complaints ; in all classes of society, where large sleeping apartments, cheerful amusements and highly nutritious food can be constantly enjoyed, if scrofula be not born with the child and inherited either from parents or grand-parents, or if it be not developed by a vicious system of education, the children will be found to enjoy a good prospect for life. It is to the melancholy emulation of our middle and lower classes of the vices of city society, and the hot-bed forcing of the female mind in our small villages and country towns, to secure the imaginary luxuries derivable from wealthy city alliances, that one half the scrofulous affections are due.

Scrofula may be educated and lived down ; it is often done by the brother who is jostled and perhaps kicked about the world, whilst the sister dies—suffocated and starved by unhealthy blood at home. The precocious education of the passions by our vicious system of education, parental aspirations for premature marriages, the confined atmosphere of the chamber and schoolroom, late hours and badly compounded food taken at improper hours—witness that deadly institution, the mid-day lunch of cake and sweetmeats—insufficient clothing to protect the half blood nourished body—thin shoes—these are the causes of the terrible frequency of consumption and spinal complaints, in short of the " Early Decay of American Women."—SCALPEL.

There is too much free or unassimilated albumen ; the young girl does not breathe slowly, *deeply* enough—she breathes only with the top of her lungs—and here she is never sufficiently clothed. This is the place where congestion and tubercle almost always occur. Here, an atmospheric injury is inflicted, and tubercle is deposited. In the spine or knee, some mechanical injury—as a fall from inattention of a careless nurse, or from the shocking and dangerous swing, perhaps a blow from a playmate—causes congestion and slow ulceration, and we often trace the origin of the disease to a mechanical cause ; but always in such cases, the blood is starved of its healthful red particles that only can be produced by enough air and food to keep it moving and make all parts of the body alike strong.

There is a very fatal error in regard to exercise. It can never benefit when carried to the fatigue point in any young person. The laboring man endures it, but for the most part he dies in middle life and of congestive complaints ; the young girl or school-boy of healthy stock outgrows it ; but the feeble, and the precocious in brain and body, die of convulsions or tubercle, or dropsy of the head. No one can tell precisely when latent tubercle in the lungs or joints will ulcerate, or when the blood-vessels of the brain will give way, and convulsions and death in a chill will occur ; they will appear as soon as the blood is poor enough. Poor blood makes weak or porous blood-vessels.

The latter disease is as fatal as scrofula or tubercle ; for it is a constant attendant on defective nutrition of the blood-vessels of children's brains ; from want of healthful contractility in the tissues, the albuminous or white blood is allowed to percolate through their sides and oppress the brain, producing convulsions as in teething ; anything that excites the brain may by over action produce this result, whether irritation of the temper or a blow or fall. Mr. Beecher, in one of his exquisite sketches, has given an admirable idea of the effect on the disposition, of a blow from a brutal teacher on the head, conventionally called boxing the ears ; thousands of children have been thus killed. Who has not known fright to produce convulsions in a child ? We have seen a boy violently convulsed, and distinct squinting produced, under the lash of a brutal schoolmaster, and he ended his days in a mad-house. Most of our school discipline is debasing or murderous. The foul atmosphere of the school-room irritates the nerves of both teacher and scholar.

We may judge of the approach of tubercle in this way : The child or young girl is exhausted after the walk ; they say they are tired, and lie down perhaps on the floor ; then they say the hip, some part of the spine, or the knee "hurts them."

Flushing of the face, short breath and delayed menstruation, is evidence of starvation of red blood ; tubercle threatens.

A child, or young girl or boy thus affected, should have their entire course of life changed ; medicine can do no possible good. If you do not give more rest and less study, and place them under such circumstances that all the vital and organic forces can be raised, they will soon break somewhere.

Tubercles are not organized ; they have neither nerves nor blood-vessels ; they form no part of the *living* body ; as soon as the vital force of the young person sinks to a point low enough, they act precisely like a splinter in the flesh ; they produce ulceration of the lung or bone, and are thus coughed up by making their way into the wind-pipe, or ulcerating through the vertebra or the joints. In this struggle, fever and night sweats reduce the body and life is lost, or amputation or deformity ensues, and crippled nature shows what she might have done with the aid she demands. Air and food produce heat ; life is warm, death is cold. The seed germinates by sunlight, warmth, air and moisture ; then, if supplied with the necessary material elements, it selects its food,, lives and becomes a healthy plant ; it produces its fruit, pays its contingent to the earth in the fall of the leaf, and sleeps till the life-giving sun again asserts its power, and awakens the bud or the seed to its new round of life. Air is the first and last want of our bodies. Our first cry and last gasp attest its power. The lungs are the two fire-places of the system ; air is the fuel ; the fire smoulders in the air-tight stove till the valve is raised, when it bursts into flame ; air, food, sleep and the cheerful emotions, are the only restoratives to exhausted nerves and blood-vessels.

The reader's attention is directed in connection with this subject to the articles in past numbers of the *Scalpel* on Scrofula as the consequences of unphysiological marriages.

THE CAUSES OF THE WAR.

God is not a liar : liberty is the organic law. The blade of grass, the giant oak, the little shrew mouse, and the mighty elephant, are born free. The organic law of their existence demands the same air, and uses the same elements to produce the sap and the blood which form their bodies. " God made of one blood all the nations of the earth ;" the organic elements are identical ; the form and the color differ. Absolute freedom of respiration will alone insure the full action of the heart. Do you suppose, poor, foolish, thoughtless, cotton and sugar trading man of the North, that the Creator gave any consciousness of slavery to the child of the black man? or do you, ignorant Southern man, after you have put at naught that other organic law, that the black and white shall not mingle their blood, without deteriorating and weakening the bodies of the offspring, that your own child, when its feeble white mother's breast fails to supply it, because she is broken down by your dissipation your tobacco, your vile whisky and your licentiousness, and you put it to the breast of a yellow woman, do you suppose—poor fool!—that you can bend the organic law to your will? No ; your child imbibes a weaker organism with the milk of its mongrel foster-mother, and a licentious temperament both from you and her. When the passions are fostered, it is at the expense of the intellect ; the functional activity of the sexual organs is increased, and licentiousness is ingrafted on the child. Oh! how silly it sounds to hear a miserable tobacco and whisky-poisoned creature, with a yellow, sodden face, talk of slavery!—" God-ordained" slavery, the corner-stone of a government!—Oh, ignorant, stupid, licentious wretch!—or a Northern trading parasite say, "What shall we do with the niggers?" Poor miserable creature! what will you do with the Almighty? The South has had him on trial for eighty-five years ; they have found him guilty, and now they are trying to punish him! The debasing influence of trade has produced this war ; the Northern dough-face hypocrite has submitted to the autocratic temperament which is born of slavery, till it has culminated in an awful war ; all the vile conse-quences of trade, slavery and political villainy are seeth-ing in the mighty cauldron of rebellion. God grant that the scum and the filth may be cleared off, and human nature be purified. This war originated in the abuse of God and man. The South must be civilized, the North-ern trader and politician must be purified, and England's vile aristocracy must be humbled. The white man is de-based when he sells the incestuous product of his own blood for a harlot ; the slave-trader is accursed of God when he steals and sells the African ; and the world stinks with the hypocrisy of England, and weeps at her down-trodden millions. God must be justified ; Christ must be heeded ; Man must be elevated, or this country must be destroyed.

As the body, corrupted by the most loathsome disease, is purified by the earth, and when its elements are set free it arises in beautiful forms, so may this war purify the moral and social atmosphere, and make us a great, united and happy people.

THE CONSUMPTION-CURER.

LIKE a vulture, hovering over the battle-field, eager
to gorge upon the human prey ere the last sigh has escaped the expiring victim, this miserable creature continues his heartless robberies. The public papers have
announced him the possessor of two aliases, and we have
repeatedly been asked why our pages have been closed
against the exposition of his nefarious practices. Our
answer may be found in our last number ; the article on
the nature and prevention of consumption was the best
weapon we could use against the cold-blooded miscreant.
It brought down his wrath upon us, and showed that he
felt it where such creatures are most sensitive—in the
pocket. We urged upon some of our editorial friends
the propriety of giving the article a more extensive circulation, but his money has closed their hearts and
opened their columns. It is sad, but too true, that most
of our editors cannot afford to be independent ; the
wretched thirst for sickly romance and prurient and exciting paragraphs, makes these more desirable reading
than the most awful and important truths of the science
of life. Whilst the intellect is thus weakened, both the
body and mind are prepared for the operations of quackery. And the same agent that has filled the measure of
their mental requirements, conveys to the feeble perception, by its deceitful columns, the fancied cure for their
bodily infirmities. How far the daily press have earned

a place by the side of Judas, by lending their columns
for money to the impostor, and refusing to insert a remedy in the shape of popular instruction, let others decide.
We cannot but compare them to wolves, watching for
such share of the prey as the hovering vulture may leave
when he has satiated himself with the loathsome repast.
Meanwhile the soulless Jackal is still busy in receiving
his month's wages for his inhaling remedies—the price
of a coffin and a shroud.

PRINCE MURAT'S DEFENCE.

PRINCE MURAT, one of the Bonaparte family, lived near Bordentown, in New Jersey, and being in a false position amongst republicans, the lower class of his neighbors, when employed by him, took great pains to let him know that every one was equal in New Jersey, *i. e.*, that every one could do just as they pleased with him.

Murat was a very gentlemanly, good-natured man, of enormous size, some six feet two, and stout in proportion, and accustomed to severe exercise ; he would shoot all day in a monstrous pair of boots, going through morasses that would appall any sportsman but himself and Dr. Dewees, our accomplished contributor, who used often to shoot with him.

The Prince had employed a worthless fellow to groom his horses. One day he very civilly requested him, as was his constant custom, for he was very polite, to do something. The man flatly refused, and was so very insolent that Murat with his awful boot suddenly helped him to the middle of a barn-yard pool. As a matter of course, the fellow sued him for assault and battery, confidently anticipating a handsome sum of damages. The court room was filled with a very select audience, including many ladies ; for Murat was highly esteemed for his elegant manners and commanding person. It was understood that he was to plead his own case, and as he was extremely acute and quite learned, great sport was anticipated. The fellow too was provided with killing evidence, as was supposed, and Murat, it seemed, had little to hope for. On examination he was confident of having received as many as six violent kicks from Murat, and in short of having been grievously afflicted and misused. Murat demanded that he should show the precise spot where the bodily injury was inflicted; he endeavored to evade the demand, but the Prince insisted; he accordingly indicated the very lowest possible part of the spine, and again and again asserted that Murat kicked him six times. Here the defence rested, and the prosecuting attorney made a powerful appeal, filled with "the sacred rights of the meanest citizen," "monarchical oppression," "star-spangled banner," etc. etc., but not a word of the vulgar insolence nor dishonesty of the laborer, who always demands his full pay, whether a thief and a liar or as indolent as a sloth. Murat addressed the jury in the following conclusive style, which we cordially recommend to our doctors, lawyers, and jurymen, for its convincing use of anatomical knowledge and its humor.

Bowing profoundly to the bench and jury-box, which happened both to be filled with excellent common sense, he said : "My lord, de judge, and gentlemen of de jury, dere has been great efforts and much troubles to make everybody believe me a very bad man; but dat is no consequence. De man tells you I kick him six times! six times! so low down as posseeble. I very sorry of de necessity to make him show how low it vas, but I could not avoid it. Now, my lord, and gentlemen of the jury, you see dis part of de human skeleton, (taking from the enormous pocket of his hunting coat a very remarkable specimen of the human pelvis with the os coccygis complete and articulated with wires;) here are de bones ;

dese leetle bones vot you see here, (shaking them to the jury like the end of a rattlesnake's tail,) dese leetle bones are in de very place vere de tail of de animal shall grow ; dat is to say, if de man who sue me vere to be a veritaable jack—vot you call it—ah! jack-horse, and not only very much resemble dat animal, vy you see dese leetle bones, if dey vere long enough, would be his tail!" The court was convulsed with laughter, and the Prince being extremely acute, and knowing he had the best of it, drew his speech to an end by stretching out his enormous leg, armed with his shooting boot up to his knee, and clapping his hand on his massive thigh so that it resounded through the court-room, exclaimed, "My lord, and gentlemen, how absurd to say I could give him even von kick vid dat, and not break all to pieces his tail!" It was some time before the judge could gather enough dignity to sum up, when the fellow got six cents damages, and the Prince three cheers.

SYMPATHETIC NATURE OF DISEASE.

DISEASES OF THE RECTUM, BLADDER AND UTERUS—THEIR POWER TO SIMULATE
DISEASE IN OTHER PARTS OF THE BODY—CONCEALED ABSCESS OF THE RECTUM
—ITS SYMPTOM, ITCHING ; OFTEN PRODUCTIVE OF FISTULA.

THE SACRUM is that triangular bone on which rests the
spinal column of man. It is the central bone of three
that form the PELVIS or basin of the skeleton, that bony
chamber that contains the bladder, the seminal vesicles
and rectum or lower bowel in man ; and the former and
latter organs, with the uterus and its ovaria or egg-beds
in woman.

The sacrum is the key stone of the arch that supports
our intellectual, respiratory and digestive apparatus,
with the bony structures that contain and protect them,
and the powerful muscles that move the body on its three
pivots, the sacrum and thigh bones. The nerves that
give sensitiveness and power to the procreative organs,
and the two closing muscles of the bladder and rectum,
and send to the brain a knowledge of the wants and condition of these two great waste gates, that may be called
the janitors of the body, pass through holes in the anterior part of this bone to reach the organs they govern.

The re-productive and pelvic organs, indicate so
absolutely our power in carrying out all the great moral

and physical objects of our existence, that their healthful or diseased condition may be said emphatically to
measure our powers as men and women. So absolutely
do they control the expression of the face and the action
of the body, that the acute practical surgeon can generally judge the degree of their diseased condition, as the
unknown victim passes him in the street. This should
excite no surprise : if the Creator in His great plan
chose to make these organs the agents by which redundant life was to be evolved, to give almost that attribute
in which we come nearest Him—creative power—surely
the face and action of its possessor should indicate the
God-like boon. Our vicious system of society, with the
total destitution of physiological knowledge, has so fostered the premature exercise of the sexual functions, that
the attendant diseases have very seriously impaired the
physique and gait of great numbers of our people. One
has only to compare the bright and speculative mirthful
eye, the upraised head, the backward curve of the spinal
column, and the firm yet quick elastic step of a man or
woman in whom the pelvic organs are in health, with the
victim of personal abuse, Hæmorrhoids or Piles, Prolapsus of the Womb, or Rectum, Rupture, or Varicocele,
to see at a glance the difference. To this the surgeon
adds a practical observation of the facial muscles indicative of irritation and pain in some one of the pelvic
viscera, and the peculiarity of step from the irritable
spinal nerves, which supply motor messengers to the
muscles moving the lower limbs, and he can form very
generally a correct idea of the nature of the affection ;
we cannot take a single step without bringing the pressure of every muscle that steadies the body directly upon
the contents of the pelvis ; the brain takes cognizance of
the attendant pain and weariness, and the body expresses

it in its every action. The extensive prevalence of these diseases is very little understood ; four-fifths of all chronic affections originate in the exhaustion produced by some disease of the Pelvic organs.

No department of surgery more completely illustrates the folly of the American people in their insane devotion to business and sensuous indulgence, than that of the diseases of the Pelvic viscera. It is by infinite odds the most responsible and important branch of the science. The Rectum, the Urethra, the Bladder and its appendages, the Uterus and the Ovaria, not only allow the widest field for observation of the diseases of artificial life, but their re-action on the mind affords the most comprehensive insight into a series of nervous affections in other parts of the body, utterly unintelligible without a knowledge of the diseases of these organs. None indeed but a very ignorant person, or a designing and zealous pill-giver and opponent of popular instruction, will attempt to deny the importance of this department of our profession. But there is a great evil in the popular belief, that it constitutes a distinct branch, and can be pursued with no regard to other parts of the body ; when an educated man has had the opportunity of observing these diseases for many years in every variety that vice, folly, and hereditary misfortune produces, he almost unavoidably falls into the habit of classifying his patients the moment he first beholds them. He has gained a degree of quickness in the expression of the face and the general action of the body, as indicative of the existing disease, that makes him dogmatic in his mode of questioning his patients. This is unfortunate both for the patient and the surgeon. The former, knowing nothing of the structure and wonderful sympathies of the diseased parts with some other portion of his

body, cannot see the connection between the organ from
which he supposes all his troubles proceed, and some
local pelvic disease in which the surgeon knows the disease to originate. The patient may have nervous or
partial headache, be partially deaf, experience loss of
memory, have sudden fits of partial blindness, palpita-
tion of the heart, weariness in the loins, pain in the
thigh, or instep, etc., etc. When the surgeon, after a
few questions, insists on examining the rectum, urethra,
or uterus, the patient objects and is dissatisfied ; he does
not believe in any disease there ; he cannot comprehend
the meaning of a sympathetic affection directly consequent
on an unsuspected disease in a distant organ ; he will
often insist on a full detail of all his symptoms and feelings, with the domestic and quack remedies he has perhaps swallowed for years. The American man who seeks
advice, has either been isolated from the wholesome
mental stimulus of society and study, in some obscure
village or farm-house, or he has been subjected to such
a severe and health-crucifying pressure of business in
some small town or village, that he has neither mind
nor time to understand or listen to the warnings of nature, far less to those of a skillful conscientious surgeon ; he will either smile incredulously at the most
serious and earnest representations, and clamor for
pills and powders, or he will exhaust the patience of the
surgeon by foolish and irrelevant questions. Tell him,
when he insists on relating the numerous affections in
every part of his body, that every vital organ is actually
associated by myriads of nerves that excite sympathetic
action with the part first diseased (and the great "sympathetic system of nerves" is visible to the eye and is
constantly dissected in all its connections by the anatomist,) and he will smile at you for your pedantry. He has

come to you to buy a cure for his disease, as he would
buy a coat or a horse ; he is going to cross-examine you
as he would a suspected person, or what is equally painful and dispiriting to an earnest man, he will blindly
swallow every word you say to him, and submit to all
you require, and demand a cure in a fixed time, paying
no regard whatever to your exaction of obedience to the
organic laws of his existence. He expects to recover,
and to eat, drink, smoke, wear thin shoes and light
clothes, and commit every vice to which he has been
addicted, and to rely upon his surgeon for a cure in spite
of all his folly. It is solely with the view of instructing
such people that we prepare this article. Our first attempt must be to show the extensive sympathies of the
rectum.

Mr. Ashton, of London, in his carefully studied and
elegant volume on Rectal Diseases, remarks :—"But it
unfortunately happens that patients too often from a
mistaken delicacy fail to ask advice till the *constitution
has become seriously deranged*, or the local affection no
longer endurable ; or it may be that under preconceived
and erroneous notions as to the nature of the affection,
or from the prominence and severity of some one of the
sympathetic effects, the sufferers are induced to adopt a
variety of empyrical remedies, which fail to afford the
desired relief and restoration to health, and which are
often productive of the most pernicious results."

"Few classes of disease exemplify the necessity of a
wide and mature consideration more than those impli-
cating the rectum ; the same symptoms will often be
found existing under the opposite condition of cause and
effect. Thus in the female, many instances have occurred
of stricture of the rectum being supposed to exist, and a
long and useless treatment had recourse to, when ulti-

17

mately all the patient's sufferings were found to depend on a displaced uterus or some morbid enlargement or growth of that organ ; on the other hand, many females have been treated for leucorrhœa or uterine disease, whilst the real source of the symptoms has been in some affection of the rectum !"

We prefer citing the high authority of Mr. Ashton, rather than giving the result of our own experience, because our people prefer foreign authority.   He continues : " In the male also will be observed stricture of the urethra, diseases of the prostate gland and bladder, simulating those of the rectum ; and diseases of the alimentary canal, producing irritability and disturbance of the genito-urinary organs ; it is necessary therefore to bear in mind the remote sympathies induced in the cephalic, thoracic and abdominal viscera ; as evinced by *headache*, impaired vision, palpitations of the heart, pain and distress and sickness in the stomach, and deranged secretions from kidneys, as exhibited by the various urinary deposits."

If we had space, we might detail a vast number of cases illustrating all these contiguous and remote sympathies ; they have been under our daily notice for years. One omission of Mr. Ashton's we are sure is only an oversight, viz., the impaired hearing of most of these people ; that function is often impaired in a marked degree in rectal affections, especially in hæmorrhoids or piles ; not only does the discharge exhaust the body of blood, but the prolapsus of the bowel and stretching of its ligaments, exhaust the nerve-power by dragging on the nerves as they pass from the sacrum, and as our hearing of all our senses depends upon the most delicate organization of the nerves, so it will very often be found seriously impaired in persons who have diseases of the

pelvic viscera ; it is very often found in our own population, where tobacco and other vices have perhaps long
been preparing the way for it, by depressing the power
of the entire nervous system. All diseases that drain the
system of blood, matter, serum, or nerve-power, must in
time affect both sight and hearing and memory, and it
has often surprised us to find people of intelligence
unsuspicious of this great physiological truth. They
seem to isolate each part, and to forget that the human
body is only in health when all its parts act harmoniously ; we cannot be continually reminded of the existence of any part, unless something is going wrong in
that part. In high health, the body acts in such perfect
harmony in all its parts, that we do not realize that it is
made up of various organs. To show the reader the
importance of knowing the extent of local or near'sympathy, we extract from that acute observer and excellent
surgeon, Mr. Guthrie, of London. He says in his work
on the anatomy and diseases of the sexual organs, p. 146,
"The urethra is often sympathetically affected by disease
of the rectum, of so obscure a nature, that the patient is
scarcely conscious of any such complaint. The sympathy which exists with hæmorrhoids [piles] is generally
sufficiently marked, and whenever symptoms in the
urethra cannot be accounted for after an examination of
that part, the state of the rectum should be carefully
investigated. I have seen two very remarkable cases of
disease, attributed to the urethra, resulting from a small
fissure in the fold of the mucous membrane of the intestine, which remained for a very long time unrelieved by
all the means adopted for their cure, until at last the
fissures were discovered, and complete relief obtained by
division of the sphincter muscle and of the extremity of
the rectum corresponding to the fissure." We have very

often observed this origin of urethral irritability. In our own work on diseases of the sexual system, it is particularly noticed ; that work was published seventeen years since, and scarcely a week has elapsed without a renewed conviction of its truth. We do not find the severity of Mr. Guthrie's operation for fissure necessary, it is true, much milder means sufficing to cure ; but we are convinced, with him, that nothing but the fissure causes the disease of the urethra ; in piles, when long existing, the urethra and bladder are almost always affected, and we often refuse to treat the patient for supposed affection of these important organs, well knowing that all his troubles originate from piles.

Benjamin Brodie remarks, p. 310, in his Essays on Hæmorrhoids : "Internal piles often give the patient a great deal of inconvenience, besides which they are liable to irritate the neighboring parts, often producing the frequent desire to urinate, and at other times inducing spasm in the muscles that surround the membranous part of the urethra, so as to cause complete retention of urine." We have often been obliged to recommend laudanum injections for this condition of things, and it has been necessary to repeat them for days and weeks, the patient obtaining no permanent relief till the piles were cured. These cases are often a great annoyance to the surgeon, because the patient, notwithstanding the possibility of piles existing when they do not come down at stool, and he can neither see nor feel them, will not believe in their existence, insisting on the disease of the urethra only being attended to.

In diseases of the neck of the womb, the sympathy with the bowels is marked ; we scarcely ever find such a case without some morbid condition of the rectum ; either piles or fissure, to which women are particularly subject from constipation of the bowels, are often found associated ; the bladder scarcely ever escapes in a chronic case of piles, and we never think of treating their diseased condition separately ; the surgeon who understands these sympathies, will never be influenced by his patient's wishes to ignore one or the other.

If we have succeeded in conveying an idea of a sympathetic affection, we will feel better able to explain the actual disease that causes it. We will commence with an affection of the rectum that is in some degree an illustration of a continuous or near sympathy, with a disease originating higher up the bowel than the symptom for which the patient usually seeks advice, and which he invariably believes to be the original disease ; it is irritation or itching of the integument immediately surrounding the anus. Mr. Ashton, Dr. George Macartney Bushe, the plain and acute Quain, and Benjamin Brodie, all give special chapters on this exquisitely annoying disease, and all of them trace it chiefly to the friction of the parts excited by walking, or, in most instances, to the continuous irritation of the mucous membrane lining the entire bowels, produced by irritating articles of diet ; rarely do either of them speak of it, as produced by an ulcer immediately above the anus. Now the reader will remember we disclaimed any originality in these popular articles, nor do we intend to lay claim to it here, as all these authors admit it occasionally to originate as we here suppose. An experience of thirty years has however convinced us, that either internal piles, varicose veins, or actual ulceration of the delicate membrane that lines the bowels, is the cause of this affection ; in a great number of cases, after years of misery, the patients having exhausted the catalogue of popular ointments and scientific prescriptions of the books, we have found on a careful examination with the simple tubular speculum, either distinct patches of the mucous membrane of a deep red color, and of course highly congested, or actual superficial ulceration, sometimes reaching the muscular coat of the bowel. In a number of these cases, fistula has followed before the patient would consent to any examination ; the original affection having been pronounced and believed to be a superficial affection of the skin only.

When the red spot within the bowel has continued long enough in the congested or gorged state of its blood-vessels (and we can never judge how long it will require, as no two cases of disease are ever precisely alike)—ulceration in the delicate lining membrane of the bowel occurs, matter is formed and burrows beneath this membrane, both the ulceration and matter tending downwards from a law of nature ; the fæces work their way into the hole produced by the ulcer, and a small swelling, always called a boil by the patient, appears near the anus ; this is either for a long while stationary, the matter and fæces being pressed out again through the hole into the bowel by means of the weight of the body when sitting, or it is opened by the surgeon, developing to the patient's conviction its true nature by the discharge ; this, unlike an ordinary boil, is mingled with fæces and putrid matter long inclosed in the burrowing abscess, which forms a depending pouch, and thus prevents the issue of its greater portion backwards into the bowel. This is an incomplete fistula, when it is opened by the surgeon, or by ulceration it is a complete one. Of course it can only be cured by the knife or ligature ; but a slight application of caustic might, if applied early, have prevented its ulceration through the bowel.

WORMS IN PORK AND MUTTON.

THE existence of worms in the bodies of man and other
animals has been known from the earliest times : they
have been supposed to occupy the intestines and stomach only ; this is a great error ; they burrow in various
parts of the body ; they have been found in the lungs, in
the liver, in the kidneys, and in shut sacks ; they issue
from abscesses, and the muscles and livers of swine,
sheep, and rabbits are often penetrated by them ; they
breed and multiply to a great extent whilst feeding upon
the juices of the animal. We have found them in the
intestines of snakes ; the anaconda that died at Barnum's
had several inclosed in sacks in its body. The germ
must be eaten, or the progenitor must deposit its ova in
the rectum of the afflicted animal ; in hogs, cats, and
dogs, the sources whence they obtain their food admit of
a ready solution of the mode of entrance. Verminolo-
gists have, however, given us some remarkable facts with
regard to the origin of these parasites. Dr. Kuchen-
meister, of Germany, discovered that the ova of one
variety of worms, namely, the Cysticircus, which is found
in the muscles or red meat of sheep and hogs, and
which is no larger than a flea when of its full size, when
taken into the intestines of a man by eating mutton or
pork that contained these parasites, would produce a
tape-worm often fifty or even a hundred feet in length.

He ascertained this by feeding criminals, condemned to die, with diseased pork and mutton, and then examining their dead bodies. In every instance he found one or more tape-worms.

Another variety of worm found in muscles of hogs is called Trichina. It is transferred to the human body by eating the raw or even underdone flesh of the hog and also of the sheep.

In two villages in Germany more than three hundred persons have died from eating measly pork—as it is called when affected by the Trichina—and several cases have occurred in this city. We examined the sections of the muscles of those who died, by the microscope, and found them abounding with the worms. Thorough cooking of course will kill them. The Germans are peculiarly liable to it because they often eat raw pork. Cats and dogs have it often.

We call to mind an amusing illustration of popular ignorance, that occurred a few years since, in relation to parasitic animals, and the terrible *rôle* they play in the production of diseases, that will serve to show how difficult it is to make people think, even when the most startling and fascinating illustrations of the productive power of nature are presented to them. An enterprising man brought to this city a beautiful horse, with one of those wonderful creatures, a specimen of the filaria or thread-worm, in the aqueous humor of his eye. He proposed to exhibit the creature as an instructive curiosity. His first step was to obtain an indorsement of the veracity of his specimen from some one who was supposed to understand the phenomenon, and would publicly testify to its truthfulness. Accordingly he called, amongst others, upon us, and we were delighted at the rare opportunity of seeing what we only knew from books.

There was the worm writhing about, from the posterior to the antorior chamber of the eye, with wonderful rapidity and gracefulness, at least three inches in length, and white as snow, over the black ground of the pupil, like a piece of thread, as it name, "filaria," implies. We furnished the man with our humble opinion, which was duly published. The late Major Le Conte, certainly a very able authority, likewise gave him his certificate ; both were published in the papers ; and that was the end of his anticipated exhibition. Our opinions were received with a roar of laughter. We were duly called upon by some of our commercial friends and patients, and commiserated for our foolishness in being so "gammoned."

17*

"CURING" DISEASES—CAN IT BE DONE?

PUTTING medicine into the mouth to "cure" disease is an absurdity; you can "cure" a man or a pig only when dead. If you were to attempt to "cure either of them whilst living, nature would treat your salt as she generally treats your medicine; she would throw it from the stomach by vomiting or purging. She would treat it as you would a filthy fellow who intrudes into your parlor. You may perturb the functions of the body, but you cannot compel any one of them to do your bidding; they choose to work harmoniously and in their own way—not in yours and according to your theory. When Napoleon the Great said to his physician those memorable words—"Doctor, no physicking! We are a machine made to live. We are organized for that purpose; such is our nature. *Do not counteract the living principle.* Let it alone; leave it the liberty of defending itself; it will do better without you and your drugs"—he uttered a great truth. We have expressed it in different language in our motto on the cover. St. Paul also said: "And, whether one member suffer, all the members suffer with it; or one member be honored, all the members rejoice with it." What did he mean if not the sympathy of all the organs when diseased or deranged in their action, and the full rejoicing of all the members when in health?

Every note must be perfect. And when a foolish man,
with a theory of his own, attempts to "cure" disease by
medicine, he shows his stupidity, vanity, or dishonesty.
The sole business of a conscientious medical man is to
instruct his patients how to keep well, and how to regulate the natural agents—food, warmth, rest, and sleep—
so as to resist disease till the natural forces can overcome
it ; that is all—all else is experiment.

AN ALLEGORY:

ADDRESSED TO THE EDITOR.

A TALL old cedar, with branches wide,
Stood grandly, though lonely, by ocean's side
In the blast, and the hail, and the weird moonlight,
He hugged the sad shade with defiant might ;
Storms he loved, and the lightning's flash,
And thrilled with joy at the thunder's crash.
  Creak! creak! with a surge and a shriek,
   Full many a buffet, but never a moan ;
  With sinewy bend and savage freak
   He wrestles with spirits and holds his own!

A trim-cut tree, with smiling air,
Stood, yet scarce lived, in a garden fair ;
With its chosen companions nurtured with care,
Safe from the blasts of the wintry air ;
Yet oft imprisoned nature sighed
For the freedom in gardens trim denied.
  Mildly it smiled its life away ;
  One morn on the ground it quiet lay ;
  The gardener came, but he dropped no tear,
  For it had been hollow for many a year.

Thou tall old cedar, with branches wide,
Yet lonely standing by ocean's side,
Hath the blast not withered thy youthful fire?
Canst thou wrestle for aye with the Storm-king's ire?
"Ha! ha!" he cried, "though lonely. I'm free;
I'd rather be thus than yon trim-cut tree '
      Creak! creak! with a surge and a shriek,
        Full many a buffet, but never a moan;
      With sinewy bend and savage freak
        He wrestles with spirits and holds his own!

My tree is revealed by the lightning's flash—
He staggers and falls with resounding crash;
His grand old nature 'twas there I found,
And I wept as I gazed on his heart so sound;
And the storm-spirits sought the spot with tears—
There was strength to battle with untold years!
      Creak! creak! with a surge and a shriek,
        No force of the storm could extort a moan;
      But struck by the thunderbolt's devious freak,
        He has died as he lived—alone, alone!
                    JOHN MATTHEWS.

IRELAND, AMERICA AND FENIANISM.

IRELAND reminds us of a beautiful widow with a priestly vulture at each breast, and her arms stretched out towards America.

Fenianism reminds us of a man struggling to get possession of a razor to cut his mother's throat.

A REMARKABLE QUACK.

Poor Spolasco is dead, and his old white horse and magnificent silver carbuncled harness, and his gold spectacles, tremendous shirt-frills and ruffles, and re-markable white hat, no more excite the wonder of travelers and the smiles of our citizens. A man so crazy for notice as to rig himself up so fantastically, would hardly be content even in the other world without some notoriety, and as we have often been told that our journal was adapted to circulate in both spheres of the spiritual world, we hope the Baron will not object to the publica-tion of this enumeration of his titles.

MOVEMENTS OF DISTINGUISHED PERSONAGES.

Baron Spolasco, M. D.—Doctor of Medicine—Physi-cian — Surgeon — Apothecary — Man-midwife—Surgeon-accoucheur—Consulting Physician—Medical Practitioner —Specialist—Prescribing Physician—Operating Surgeon —Physiologist—Pathologist—Nosologist—Toxicologist—Therapeutist—Pharmaceutist—Oculist—Aurist and Den-tist —Allopathist —Homœopathist—Hydropathist—Elec-tropathist — Galvanopathist — Mesmerist—Electrician—Spiritualist Physician—Herbalist—Rootist—Red Pepper-ist — Fomentationist—Embrocationist—Wart-charmer—

Corn-cutter—Perfumer—Fumigator—Enchanter—Special Professor Extraordinary of Medicine, Surgery, and
Mid-wifery, in the Royal Baronial Spolasconial College
of Medicine, Surgery, Pharmacy, and Mid-wifery, Hair-
curling, Preserving, and Dyeing, and the kindred sciences
of Astrology, Rat-catching, Bug and Roach Exterminat-
ing—Knight-commander of the Faithful, etc., etc., etc.,
was moved from his baronial and collegiate halls in
Spring Street, one day last month, by order of the Ward
Court. His unique and valuable collection of canes,
crutches, and other progressive apparatus, with a comprehensive collection of old boots and shoes, and stuffed
monkeys, rattlesnakes, and dead babies, were summarily
ejected into the street in consequence of the non-payment
of certain demands of the nature of—rent.

MEDICAL CONTENTS

OF THE

S C A L P E L .

This volume " Backbone," is published as a fair specimen of the Scalpel. The entire work from the first to the forty-seventh number, neatly bound, lettered and indexed in Six books of 500 pages each, may be had of the Editor only, for $18, any single number 50 cts. The volumes cannot be furnished by Booksellers, as they cost all that is asked for them. It is intended as a great health library for the People: only a tithe of the contents is given. All orders must be addressed to Edward H. Dixon, Box 3,121, or at Dr. Dixons residence, 42 Fifth Ave. Single numbers at 1 Vesey street, Astor House.

C O N T E N T S .

No. 1. Abortionism in New York; its History and consequences. What do we know of Rheumatism? Can it be cured? What are the remedies, and how are they to be used? The proper Diet and Treatment for the Nursing Mother. Ether and Chloroform in Childbirth, are they safe? Tobacco: its Effect on Virility.

No. 2. What is the nature of Scrofula and Consumption? Can they be cured? By what method? Functions of the Skin Cold fatal to Infants. Abortionism—continued. Six cases of Childbirth under the influence of Chloroform. What are Piles? Can they be cured? By what means? Rascality of a celebrated oculist: Description of Cataract and disease of the Nerve of the Eye: how to distinguish them. Varicocele: What is it? Produced by sexual excess and self abuse.

No. 3. To what extent is Medicine entitled to confidence? Fistula, Fissure and Prolapsus of the Rectum: What are they? Ought they to be cured? How can it be done? Has the Imagination of the Mother any influence on her unborn Child? What is a Hernia or Rupture? Truss swindlers in New York.

No. 4. Purgative Medicine: Villainy of Pill Venders. Treatment of Pulmonary Diseases by Inhalation. Remarkable instance of the effects of the Mother's imagination upon her unborn Child. Abortionism, its anatomical and physiological consequences.—(Last Article.)

No. 5. Contagious and Infectious Diseases ; Examples ; is Cholera contagious? Life Sketches of eight New York Physicians ; the Editor, by himself; serious, humorous and satirical. The Effects of Tobacco on Virility ; the Causes of Stricture of the Urethra. Dysentery : What is it? How does it differ from Diarrhœa ?

No. 6. What are the Causes of Early Decay in American Women? Falling of the Womb, its causes, anatomy and cure. New method of Exploring the Fallopian Tubes to Detect the Cause of Barrenness. Pressure in Spermatorhœa, from self-abuse.

No. 7. Hysterics : continued from the article on the Early Decay of American Women. The Proper Method of Supporting the Prolapsed Womb.

No. 8. Hereditary Descent of Diseases ; Consequences of Intermarriages of Blood Relatives. Life Sketches of New York Physicians, Medical Philosophers, Litterateurs and Rascals.

No. 9. The Causes of Cancer of the Womb ; Difficulty in the Monthly Periods ; Description of those Diseases : Treatment of them. Pregnancy under Extraordinary Circumstances. Nervous Diseases ; What are they? Diseases Mimicked by Hysteria.

No. 10. The Shape, Proportion and Ornament of our Modern Apartments. Medical Fantoccini ; or, Life Sketches of New York Physicians. The Frequency, Symptoms and Progress of Cancer of the Womb. The Radical Cure of Rupture.

No. 11. The Construction, Ventilation and Warming of Sleeping Apartments. Lead Poisons : Our Cookery and Croton Water Pipes, Zinc, Walnut Leaves in Scrofula and Consumption :

No. 12. What is Cancer? Experiments in its Cure by the Application of Freezing Mixtures : with Illustrative Cases. Description and Origin of Worms and other Parasites that infest the Human Body.

No. 13. The necessity of a Varied and Nutritious Diet to the highest development of Moral, Intellectual and Physical Excellence : The Elements of our Bodies. The More Extraordinary Parasites of the Human Body—Hydatids : the Filaria, or Intermuscular Worm : the Guinea Worm : the Giant Strongle, or Kidney Worm : the Face Worm : the Liver Worm : Whence do these Creatures come? Physiological Use of the Beard ; its Electrifying Properties.

No. 14. Muscular and Constitutional Strength : its origin : Vegetable and Animal Diet : "Arise, Peter, Slay and Eat." The Toilette of the New York Ladies : The Actual Consequences of Damp Feet : Life is warm—Death is cold. The Causes and Evils of Celibacy.

No. 15. What are the Causes of the great Prevalence of Dropsy in the Head, and Convulsions in Children in New York—Their Symptoms and Treatment. The Education of our Children : The Child's embodiment of God : Beauty, Order, Justice and Truth. Dysmenorrhea, the Cause of Barrenness ; its Treatment.

No. 16. Hotel and Club-House Life in New York; their Pernicious Influence on Morals and Manners; the Art of Furnishing a House with Economy and Simple Elegance. Passional Excesses, Overheated and Unventilated Apartments, Tight Clothes and Bad Food, the Causes of Diarrhœa and Dropsy in the Head of Children. Pregnancy Extraordinary; or, Humor and Science; a Western Consultation; Laughable Result of a Medical Pow-wow. Cases of Disease of the Neck of the Uterus and their Treatment.

No. 17. Ergot of Rye as an Agent assisting Labor. Will it produce Abortion? Regular Aid to Quackery: Treatment of Cancer; alledged Remarkable Cure. Successful Case of Extraction of a Living Child by the Cæsarian Section, after the death of the mother:—Ovarian Tumors: what are they?

No. 18. Scarlet Fever: What are the causes of its dreadful Fatality? true method of reasoning the subject; Scarlet Fever, Rash, and Scarlatina, the same; how to distinguish it from Measels. The Preservation of the Eyes: Dangerous consequences of Pressure; evil results of opening the Eyes in Water.

No. 19. The Structure and Functions of the Nerves: What is paralysis? two varieties; Paralysis from Sexual Passion. What is Croup? Its Symptoms and Treatment.

No. 20. The Summer or Teething Diarrhœa of Children: Its Causes and Treatment; has medicine any control over it? the Physician should explain its Nature; the order in which the Teeth appear: Temperature, bad Air and Teething; its Treatment; what should the Child eat? how should it sleep? what Medicines are proper?

No. 21. What is the nature of the Nerve Power? Its action on our bodies under the various stimuli; its power over the Contraction of the Muscles; the Influence of Prolonged Inspiration in curing Diseases and giving strength to the body; how does it compare with other systems of Cure? What is Whooping Cough?

No. 22. The Structure and Functions of the Human Heart: The Heart of the Veins; the Circulation through the Lungs; the Heart of the Arteries; the Circulation through the Body. What is a Common Catarrh or Cold? What is Dyspepsia? How can It be cured? What influence have the passions over it? The True Method of curing Dyspepsia. How shall the People know when they are properly Vaccinated? What is Vaccination? What is Varioloid?

No. 23. The Motive Power of the Heart is Oxygen; rate of the Heart's Action in different positions; number of Pulsations at different periods of Life; interesting Experiments to prove the Heart the great Moter; fashionable Dinner Hours—their sad consequences; cold and warm Air; hot and cold Baths—their influence on the Body. Education, Physical, Social and Moral: Grecian Gymnasia; Influence of Exercise on Nobility of Character; Religious duty of cultivating the Faculties; the Soul is manifested through the Senses; Exercise prevents the Vicious Propensities; every Sense should be exercised agreeably; Legislative Power should cultivate the People.

Sketches of a Western Student's Life: The First Case; the Poisoner; a young Demon; sin is caused by contempt of God's Laws; the nature of the Soul depends upon the Organism; beautiful Scene; a Western Camp Meeting; sweet and painful Memories; a tremendously hot Sermon; the lost Soul; Nervous and Psychical results; philosophical explanation of a Revival; hard work to get a second one; mischief in the Camp; Zaccheus; Camp Meeting wolves; a midnight attack; true character of the Methodist Preacher.

No. 24. The Construction of the Heart before Birth: how the Fœtus receives its nourishment? Crippled condition of the Lungs in most Women; Invocation to study Nature and to teach it. Enlarged Veins and Ulcers of the Legs; their Causes; How are they produced? In what kind of People? Their Treatment; Method of Cure —by pressure. What are Epileptic Fits? How do they differ from Apoplexy? Description of them; Time of Life of their most frequent Occurrence; Symptoms of their approach; where do they originate? Circumstances that predispose to them; abuse in Early Life; difference between Hysterics and Epilepsy; what can we do to prevent them? Is there any law for the Contraction of Marriage, by which the human race may be improved?

No. 25. The Sore Mouth of Early Infancy, commonly called the Sprue, Thrush, etc.; what is its nature? how should it be treated? What Causes are sufficient to induce the Physician to advise the early Weaning of the Child? Personal appearance of a Good and a Bad Nurse; Causes that derange the Milk Secretion. What does a Physician mean when he calls a Child Scrofulous? Ulceration of the Lower Bowel often mistaken for Piles and other Diseases.

No. 26.—The Causes that tend to Depress Character in American Youth; The Laws of the Human Temperaments in relation to Marriage; How to choose a Wife; Reason why Similar Temperaments should never marry; why Washington, Bonaparte and Jackson were childless; Proper balance of Power in the Sexes; Why are Diseases Hereditary.

No. 27. How to Grind your own Axe; Cost of Living in New York; Cost of Food regulates Mortality; Infernal Results of Forestalling Food; Liquor Law versus Market Law. Influence of Vital Force on the Mind; the Base of the Brain determines the amount of Energy of Character and the Tenacity of Life; How to determine the probable Length of Life—bating casualties; Proofs that force of Character depends on the Base; Anterior Brain alone is unfit to govern; Proofs from History of this Truth; Proofs from Robbers and Pirates; the Clergy for the most part unfit to govern. A popular Explanation of the manner in which Cod-liver Oil cures Consumption; Also the use of Acids; Rational Medicine; Salt, Quinine, and some others—how to cure Fevers? What is the nature of Bilious and Low Fevers; Absurdity of Ancient Theories. Brandy, Tobacco, Tea and Coffee; Why were they created? Are they all evil? A sad Visit to a young Friend; the Devotion of a True Woman; What Ordeal will she not court? Faith and Love will save; Influence of Tobacco on the Unborn Child.

No. 28. The Time-serving Clergymen; How to prevent Bronchitis; A Reverend Jockey; Dyspeptic Bronchitis; What is it? A Clergyman's Experience in Medicine; A Pious Surgical Wolf; His Death, Burial and Eulogium. On the Protection of Society from Crime: Punishment; What are its results? Legitimate extent of. Physical Education: How does it compare with Medical Treatment in preventing and curing Diseases. The Consumption Curers: the SCALPEL and the Public Press; Duties of Editors. Astonishing Discovery: The Origin of Tape-worm, Extraordinary Experiments of the German Physiologists to determine the Value of Water, Alcohol, Tea and Coffee, as Food. Shocking Outrage by the Academy of Medicine on Medical Humanity; Awful Result of Injecting the Lungs with Nitrate of Silver; Death of the Victim at Bellevue; Duty of the District Attorney.

No. 29. What is the nature of Consumption; or, Tubercle in the Lungs? Inhalation and its Advocates: Will it cure the Disease? Will Electricity cure Disease? Will it remove Mercury and other Metals from the System?

No. 30. God the Chemist, and the Human System the Laboratory: Chemistry accounts for some Diseases; nature of Gout, Diabetes, Rheumatism and Gravel; their dependence on Imperfect Digestion. The Diet Question: What is the cause of the great frequency of Consumption and Chronic Diseases? the Remedy; What should be the Diet for Health?

No. 31. Influence of the Daily Press in the Propagation of Quackery; Can we effect Reform without its Aid? The great Consumption-curer. Some account of the Birth, Life, Experience, Death, and Resurrection of a "Medical Heretic:" a veritable Autobiography; the natural and acquired Process of learning how to Lie: the Lie Religious, the Lie Medical. Can Consumption be Cured? Extraordinary Cases to prove Nature's Intention.

No. 32. The Natural History of Crime; and the comparative value of Medical and Lay Evidence; A Lecture delivered at the request of several distinguished Members of the New York Bar, for the Relief of a young Barrister in ill-health, at Hope Chapel: by the Editor. Gothic Germany versus Celtic America; A few Queries to Dr. McElheran on the compliment paid us in asserting, we are not Anglo-Saxons, but Celts—Sarcastic. Tobacco; the German of it; by Heimzen of "the Pioneer," Translated—Humorous and Sarcastic.

No. 33. Pork and Potatoes: their Influence on the Bodies and Minds of our People; Wisdom of the Mosaic Law. Ventilation: its Necessity and Defects. Our Three Nationalities: Lugubrious Letter-writing, Physic-taking, and Dinner-bolting. Our Public Sewers in their Relation to Health; Who should Construct, and Direct them? Champagne: "The Best Brands" made in New York; Its Real Character; The "Peculiar Variety," prepared by a celebrated Medical Philanthropist for the "Splendid Palaces" of Mercer street. The Lager Bier Mania; Its Influence on the Mind and Body; Republished, by request, from the Quarto Number.

No. 34. The Criminal Condition of our City: its Causes. A Preventive and Detective Police; what should it be. Medical Hygene in Consumption. The Movement Cure: What is it? Is it "Orthodox?" Gymnastics, as practised in this City: are they rationally pursued? What do you mean? The Natural Use of Spirituous and other Drinks.

No. 35. The Natural Treatment of Consumption; Reason and Nature vs. Quackery and Superstition. Fever and Ague; how to live in Unhealthy Situations; how to prevent, and how to Cure it. Influence of badly constructed Wells in producing Fevers. What are Piles or Hemorrhoids; How to cure them.

No. 36. The Natural Treatment of Consumption; What is the Effect of Alcoholic Drinks on Consumptives? A Medical Consultation; What is it? its Elastic Character; Has a Man a right to buy an Independent Opinion with his Money? Structure and Functions of the Kidney; its Diseases. A Popular Article for all inclined to Gluttony and Drunkenness. Hooping-cough, Scarlet Fever, and Measles; ought they to be treated with Medicines? Impropriety of giving Purgatives. Letter of Advice to Consumptives by a Southern Physician; should they go South?

No. 37. Our Meat Markets; Diseased condition of the Cattle slaughtered; Villainy of Butchers; Evils of over-fattening Cattle; Apathy of our Citizens; the only Remedy. Special Diseases of the Kidney and Bladder; Bloody Urine; its Causes and Treatment; Stone in the Bladder; Suppression of Urine; Retention Urine; Irritable Bladder; Nocturnal Incontinence of Urine; Inflammation of the Kidney; Bright's, or Granular Disease of the Kidney; Immoderate flow of Urine; Diabetes; Inflammation of the Bladder; with their Symptoms and Treatment.

No. 38. The Martyrdom of the Innocents; Corruption and Villainy of our Civic Law-Givers; What kind of Sanitary Government does New York require. The Food and Exercise of Infants; What is the Natural Law? Cold and warm Baths Dangerous. Fever and Ague; What is it? how to prevent it.

No. 39. On the Natural Law of Marriage; what Temperaments should and should not Marry; Physiological Incompatibility between the Sexes in Relation to Progeny; Physiological Incest; Scrofulous Forms of Disease; Juvenile Mortality; Tobacco; Improper Marriages; American Precocity; the Vampires of America. Sun-Light and Shadow; Life and Death; Window Curtains and the Glory of God; Influence of Sun-Light on Animals; its Absence causes Consumption; Effect of Confinement in Convents; on Animals, Pigeons, etc. The Importance of an Independent Professional Opinion.

No. 40. A Wholesome Ride for the Japonica Philosophers on the Physiological Buffalo; What are the Temperaments? Importance of distinguishing them before contracting Marriage; The Life Line; Is it possible to tell, by measuring his Head, how long a Man will live?

Do Intellectual Pursuits add to Longevity? Incompatibility between the Sexes in relation to Progeny; Cases illustrating the subject. Bonner and the New York Ledger; His Position; Summing up of the Nature and Merits of his Magazine.

No. 41. The Popular Medical Race-course; A diverting article on family affairs, which the reader will probably understand better at the end than the beginning. The Hypocrisy of Gymnastics; Violent Exertion Hurtful to Youth. The Clergy and the Religious Press; Review of their Papers; The Clergyman in the Pulpit; Advantages and Disadvantages of his Position. The Lager Bier Question; Will that Delectable Beverage Intoxicate? Editor's Experience. What Moral Considerations should prompt the limitation of Family.

No. 42. The Construction of Sleeping Apartments in Country Houses; What Influence have they had in Reducing the Life-Power of our People? Suicide; Is there any Organic Law Favoring its Commission? A Remarkable Instance. What is Quinine, and what is its Use? Editor's Opinion. The Women of New York; What they are, and what they ought to be.

No. 43. A Slight Diversion for the Pauper Philanthropists: The Organic law; Pauperism in New York; What is to be done? Syphilization; Can Inoculation cure Syphilis?

No. 44. Practical Observations on the Use and Abuse of Tobacco: Its two Deadly Elements; Is Smoking or Chewing the most dangerous? Description of all the Diseases produced by each; Will a Cigar communicate Syphilis; Cancer produced by Smoking; also Disease of the Heart; Loss of Virility; Dyspepsia; Apoplexy; Paralysis; Mania; Amaurosis; Incontinence of Urine. The Cure of Consumption; Injection of Nitrate of Silver into the Lungs again.

No. 45. Our Old and Young Farmers and Villagers; What is the matter with them? Are they living Rationally? Proposition by the Editor. Sir Benjamin Brodie on Tobacco; Does it act on the Nerves? Editor's Opinion and Experience; Continued from last number; Does it produce Piles? Rearing Children Physiologically; Rules for Parents. Retention of the Placenta after Abortion; New Instrument for removing it, with Plate. What is Tic-Douloureux, or Neuralgia; Why so common in American Women; its cure. Constipation; Are Injections hurtful to the Bowels? Nature and Cure of Popliteal Aneurism without an Operation; Cure of a Student of Medicine by the Editor.

No. 46. Diseases of Defective Nutrition in the Young Girl; Can Medicine cure Scrofula, Consumption, or Diseases of the Joints? What should be done for them? Hygiene of Children? Exercise; What it can do? What does it do? Disease of the Rectum, Bladder and Uterus; Their power to simulate Disease in other parts of the Body; Concealed Abscess of the Rectum; Its Symptom, Itching; Often productive of Fistula, and impotence. Infant Mortality in New York; Will the present war improve the Race? How? A case of Lithotomy: The Stone extracted through the Rectum by a New and Simple Instrument invented by the Editor, with a Plate of the Instrument and Stone in position as it was withdrawn. Do Idiocy and Scrofula originate most frequently from the Marriage of Blood Relatives, or are they due to Incompatible Temperaments? Evils of Diploma Shops; Advice to Country people. Abuse of the great Organic Law of our Race, the Cause of the War. "A Lecture on Pathology and Treatment of Stricture of the Urethra, and its instant cure by the Wrethrotome, with three cases—one one of each variety of stricture: Causes, Symptoms, and Situation of Stricture; Treatment of Complete Obstruction; Stricture from Kicks and a Fall on a Board; Stricture from the Abuse of Caustic; A New Instrument for that Operation; Danger of Lallemand's Instrument; Treatment of Gonorrhea always Empirical; Directions to Patients; Gleet: What is it? How to treat it." Is it Proper that any Considerations should be allowed to Check the Increase of Family? Treatment of Stricture by Internal Incision—New Instrument for that Purpose; Rationale of its Application according to Mr. Syme; Editor's Views; Loss of Virility —an Unsuspected Cause; Circumcision—Was it a Religious or Hygienic Rite? Its Origin and great Antiquity; Editor's Views; What is Varicocele? Should it be Operated on? By what Method? Leucorrhea; Prolapsus Uteri and Hemorrhoids; their Influence in Producing Neuralgia, Starvation of the Blood, and Consumption; also, a Lecture on Irritable Urethra and Incontinence of Urine: What is Irritation? How produced? How does it produce Incontinence? Will Medicine Cure loss of Virility? What medicines are those which promise any relief? This lecture is one of the course delivered to his private surgical class by the Editor. Twenty-eight pages extra.

No. 47. Sixteen Years of Editorial and Thirty-four of Professional Life: Editor's Origin; Is the Scalpel the Production of a Vertebrate Animal? Delights of Early Practice in New York—its Æsthetics and Economics; The Tender Mercies of the Brethren; The Kappa Lambda Society; Patrick and his Wife the Tormentors in the Medical Purgatory. Our Sewers and Tenant-Houses—what Relation do the bear to the Cholera? Can the Present System of Draining this City effect the Object? The Poor Man: Where shall he Live? Who shall Build his House? How shall he Buy his Food? And who shall smother those Jackalls, the Grocer and Coal Dealers? How shall he get to his Daily Work? Editor's Plan.

Twenty-eight pages extra. Inclose fifty cents for any number to Box 3121, or No. 2 Vesey street, Astor House. The Editor will not supply single numbers to city applicants. He receives none but professional visits at his residence.

A VALUABLE HOUSEHOLD BOOK.

SCENES

IN THE

Practice of a N. Y. Surgeon.

BY EDWARD H. DIXON, M. D.,

EDITOR OF THE "SCALPEL."

Embellished with Eight Exquisite Engravings, from Original Designs, by Darley. Engraved by N. Orr. Elegantly bound in cloth, gilt.

PRICE $1 50.

This highly interesting work is the embodiment of much that is valuable in science and striking in incident. The facts and narratives here grouped together have been gleaned during a practice both varied and lengthy, and from the sources the most diverse both in means and matter. The canopied couch and the lowly pallet—pampered luxury and starved mendicity—have each contributed to illustrate some of those phases, the peculiarity of which has led many a reflecting mind to exclaim—"Verily, life is a mystery, and death the solution thereof!"

"Let us hope that, whatever truths useful to humanity may be found within these pages, will live for a little while after the hand that sketched them is resolved into its elements, and mingled with the atmosphere and the earth whence it originated."

The following is but a small portion of the Contents:

SCENES IN CITY PRACTICE.—The Cholera of '32—The Broadway Workwomen—The Young Mother—The Last Day's Work—Terry's Courtship.

THE NERVE POWER.—What is the Nature of the Nerve Power?—Its action on our Bodies, under the various Stimuli—Its Power over the Contraction of the Muscles—The Influence of Prolonged Inspiration in Curing Diseases and giving strength to the Body—How does it compare with other Systems of Cure?

ON HOOPING COUGH.—What is Hooping Cough?—Period of Occurrence—First Symptoms—Subtle Character of the Contagion—Period of Duration—Its usual attendants—Manner of Treatment—Has Medicine any power over it?

WILL MEDICINE CURE CONSUMPTION?—Origin of Consumption—The Stethoscope—Formation of Tubercles—Cough an early Symptom—Bronchitis.

SCENES IN SOUTHERN PRACTICE.—King Death in his Yellow Robe — The Proud Merchant—The Lovely Creole Wife.

ON CROUP.—What is Croup?—Its Symptoms and Treatment.

SCARLET FEVER.—What are the Causes of its Dreadful Fatality?—Has Medicine any control over it.

RECOLLECTIONS OF CITY PRACTICE.—Privation—Our Two Lodgers—A Faithful Sister—First Affection—An Unworthy Object — The Artless Victim — The Young Mother—The Wedding—Maternal Love—The Legacy—The Closing Scene.

IMPORTANCE OF TRUTH IN EDUCATION.—The Right of Discovery—Fairy Stories—Children Should behold Truth in their Parents.

SCENES IN A WESTERN PHYSICIAN'S LIFE.—What is Memory?—College Life in the Country—The Pious Student—The Orphan Betrayed — The Robin's Nest — Maternal Reflections—What is Love?—The Funeral Pile : what is its Philosophy?

FUNCTIONS OF THE SKIN.—Cold Fatal to Infants.

SCENES IN CITY PRACTICE.—1. Death's Quartette in the Garret—Delirium Tremens—2. Precariousness of Medical Life in New-York—A Professional Martyr—The Curse of an Irish Practice—Death of the Physician, his Widow and Child—Parental Love—Mercantile Affection—The Love of Money.

For extracts from the leading Journals of the United States and England, see the next page.

EXTRACTS

FROM THE

LEADING JOURNALS

OF THE

UNITED STATES AND ENGLAND.

"This fascinating volume glows with a warm and genial spirit of humanity. It is from the unmistakable pen of Dr. Dixon. It is distinguished for its striking intellectual ability, its tone of manly sympathy and touching pathos. Every line of its author is of value to the whole human race."—HORACE GREELEY.

"It is truly surprising, that a man engaged in a laborious and extensive practice should find time to make a volume so absorbing and wonderful in its power. It transfixes your attention from the first to the last page."—New York Times.

"Dr. Dixon, though a thorough and accomplished surgeon, has given us one of the most useful and powerfully written volumes of the day. It is unlike any other production in English literature, and in our opinion greatly surpasses the 'Diary of a London Surgeon.'"—New York Spectator.

"He amputates, prescribes and dissects with about equal skill. The scenes are drawn with a tenderness and fidelity to nature that reach the heart of the reader, as we are sure their delineation welled up from the glowing heart of the writer."—United States Journal, New York.

"This book gives us a perfect insight into American life in the practice of a professional man in a large city. It is written with the gracefulness of Irving and the simplicity of Goldsmith."—London Times.

"It is written with the power of a skilful dramatist, and yet has all the freshness of a young writer. Its wit is irresistible; its pathos and tenderness melting."—London Examiner.

"It is seldom that a man of Dr. Dixon's position and attainments, rises superior to that position and caste, and dares to speak such truths as are contained in this volume. Every woman in the land should read his words of life-giving wisdom."—Advocate, Green Bay, Wisconsin.

"It is the work of a gentleman and a scholar. It is printed and illustrated in a manner that becomes its author. We commend it to every mother and daughter in the land."—Mobile Daily Register.

"The author is one of the few men of genius in his profession, and though the most bold and imperious of men, has a heart full of tenderness and love for his race. His writings exceed in brilliancy and vitality anything we have ever read."—Hudson County Democrat, Hoboken, N. J.

"Dr. Dixon paints with his pen, you not only understand, but you can see what he writes. It is the most fascinating book we ever read."—Eagle, Memphis, Tenn.

"He describes with wonderful power, scenes that have transpired in his own practice, and throughout the book he carries captive the heart and the head."—Register, Yarmouth, Mass.

"It is beautifully printed, and is a most fascinating and faithful record of scenes that transpired in the practice of one of the most eminent surgeons of the United States."—Circular, Quebec, Canada.

"No novelist could excel the power of these sketches, and the physiological articles possess a charm with which dramatic sketches are usually invested."—Gospel Banner, Augusta, Me.

"Dr. Dixon has given us a book of unrivalled character. It has all the attractions of tragedy and comedy, and its didactic articles on health are unrivalled."—Marshall Statesman, Mich.

"It is especially a home book, and should be in the hands of every parent in the land."—Gazette, West Byron, N. Y.

☞ Copies of the above book mailed to all parts of the country, free of postage, on receipt of price, by

R. M. DE WITT, Publisher, 13 Frankfort St., N. Y.

www.ingramcontent.com/pod-product-compliance
Lightning Source LLC
Chambersburg PA
CBHW020239110726
47898CB00004B/1317